A
Garland Series

VICTORIAN
FICTION

NOVELS OF FAITH
AND DOUBT

*A collection of 121 novels
in 92 volumes, selected by
Professor Robert Lee Wolff,
Harvard University,
with a separate introductory volume
written by him
especially for this series.*

THE AUTOBIOGRAPHY
OF
CHRISTOPHER KIRKLAND

Eliza Lynn Linton

Three volumes in one

Garland Publishing, Inc., New York & London

1976

———

Bibliographical note:

this facsimile has been made from a copy in the
British Museum
(12620.p.12)

———

Library of Congress Cataloging in Publication Data

Linton, Elizabeth Lynn, 1822-1898.
    The autobiography of Christopher Kirkland.

    (Victorian fiction : Novels of faith and doubt ; 80)
    Reprint of the 1885 ed. published by R. Bentley,
London.
    I. Title. II. Series.
PZ3.L658Au3   [PR4889.L5]   823'.8   75-1532
ISBN 0-8240-1604-1

Printed in the United States of America

THE AUTOBIOGRAPHY

OF

CHRISTOPHER KIRKLAND.

BY

MRS. LYNN LINTON,

AUTHOR OF

'THE TRUE HISTORY OF JOSHUA DAVIDSON,' 'PATRICIA KEMBALL,'
'THE ATONEMENT OF LEAM DUNDAS,' 'UNDER WHICH
LORD?' ETC.

IN THREE VOLUMES.
VOL. I.

LONDON:

RICHARD BENTLEY AND SON,

Publishers in Ordinary to Her Majesty the Queen.

1885.

To

EDWARD BARRINGTON DE FONBLANQUE.

DEAR MR. DE FONBLANQUE—

In asking you to accept the dedication of this book, I do not wish to make it appear that you either share its opinions or sympathize with its aim. I merely wish to claim you as one who, like Christopher himself, loves honesty and practises sincerity, and who will therefore forgive even his defence of vivisection, to which you are so notoriously opposed. Neither do I seek to entangle your assent to that profound respect for man as the highest thing we know—that belief in his glorious future and infinite progress, by the law of moral evolution working from within—which is my hero's support and consolation. This optimistic belief is a matter of faith; and faith, the result of temperament, is out of the control of the individual. The Pessimists, who see only the hopelessness of man's misery and the limitation of his powers, count as many strong brains among them as the Optimists, who judge of the future by the past, and recognize no barriers which may not be overcome. Each school is as sincere as the other in its creed ; and as neither can prove its doctrines, neither has the right to scorn the other for its special gospel. Wherefore I trust that, differing in certain essentials though we do, you will none the less accept this dedication as an expression of my friendship and esteem.

E. LYNN LINTON.

PREFACE.

IT is impossible to write an absolutely candid autobiography. Our relations with others, and the artistic proportions of events, forbid that completeness which, to be perfect, should include every circumstance of the life. For just as plants and organisms are built up and developed by microscopic cells, so are our characters and minds formed by all the circumstances which surround us, how minute soever each may be in itself. At the best then, no more can be given than those salient points of thought and action which furnish an intelligible outline but do not include fractional details—which show the completed fabric but not the whole process of construction.

Within these limits every autobiography which is clear and symmetrical so far as it goes, has its value. As no human being is absolutely unparalleled, but each embodies in his degree the moral and intellectual characteristics of certain orderly types already established, it necessarily follows that no personal history can be without the interest which comes from sympathy and likeness. The ways by which some have arrived at certain landing-stages must needs be those by which others have gone or are going; and the experience of one serves another as warning or guidance, according to the secret bent of his nature and his dread or desire to be led to the right or turned to the left.

For this reason, I, a pilgrim rapidly nearing the great Mecca of the grave, write here as faithful an autobiography as I may or can. It will not be useless to show where a man who has ardently desired to know the Truth, and who has been neither afraid of his own conclusions nor ashamed to confess his convictions, finds himself at last. The Isis at whose feet he stands will hold in her hand, or a torch to light forward or a flaming sword to stay, the advancing steps of those who read, as they may sympathize with the process or be repelled by the result.

CHRISTOPHER KIRKLAND.

THE AUTOBIOGRAPHY

OF

CHRISTOPHER KIRKLAND.

CHAPTER I.

I WAS born before the age of railroads, steamboats, electric telegraphs, or the penny post; and when society in the remote country districts of England was very little changed from what it had been a hundred years before. In those days living was simple, locomotion both difficult and restricted, and absence from home a rare event, save for the grandees who were bound to be in London for their place in Parliament or for their attendance at Court. Women of the upper middle class kept their houses and looked after their children with more vigilance of personal superintendence than now ; and if there was less taste there was less finery, nor was extravagance made into an æsthetic virtue as it is in these present times. The religious revival had not begun for the nation at large ; for all that Wesley and Whitfield had done good work among the rough men of the West, and had transformed a large proportion of the Cornish miners and fishermen from brutalized savages and wreckers, among whom the King's writ did not run, into God-fearing and law-abiding citizens. Education was at its lowest possible ebb—though local grammar-schools in the North were plentiful, kept up by old-time grants and bequests from former founders and benefactresses ;

though Robert Raikes had established Sunday-schools here and there, where minds had begun to awaken to the need of saving souls; though Joseph Lancaster had got a fair trial for his system of teaching; and though even infant-schools, which we generally believe to be emphatically of modern establishment, languished feebly in certain populous places. Still, none of these waves of progress, as yet slow and sluggish, though gathering, as they went, the volume and power we know of, had stirred the stagnant shallows of remote country places at the time of which I write; and society, as found on the moors, in the dales, and in the villages among the mountains, was satisfied with the most elementary knowledge for the so-called educated classes and absolute ignorance for all the rest.

The Reform Bill, Catholic emancipation and the emancipation of slaves, the political rights of the Jews, free trade and a free

press, were all as yet the golden apples of
liberty and justice held in the closed hand
of Time.   The press-gang was a recognised
institution; felony was punishable by death
—and stealing sheep, as well as any article
the value of thirteen-pence halfpenny from
the dwelling-house, was felony.   Though
Howard's remonstrances had had some effect,
and Coldbath Fields prison had been built
in accordance with his views, our gaols
were in general a disgrace to civilization,
and our laws were still justly stigmatized as
' written in blood.'   Monday morning hang-
ings were part of the week's ordinary work;
and my father just remembered to have seen
thirteen men hanging in a row at Tyburn,
with never a murderer among them.   Besides slaves in Jamaica, we had climbing-
boys, who were substantially slaves, for our
chimneys at home; and apprentices were
still greatly needing the protection they did
not get till comparatively the other day.

Gipsies and vagrants were laid by the heels at the will of the authorities; and to be homeless was of itself a qualification for the stocks. Belief in the divine right of Kings; in the saintly martyrdom of Charles I.; in the criminality of Cromwell and the hypocrisy of Puritanism; in the good cause of Charles Edward; in the diabolical origin of the French Revolution, of which the echoes still reverberated through the awakening world; in the infinite iniquity of Bonaparte; in the capacity of any one Englishman to lick three 'mounseers' single-handed; as well as belief in the damnable instincts of the 'many-headed monster,' as the people proper were generally called—formed part of every true gentleman's creed. He who thought differently was either a traitor to his order or no true gentleman at all. Party spirit in the country ran as high as it ever ran in Florence or Verona, when Guelfs and Ghibellines slew peace and humanity between them;

and no man with a soul to be saved would have consorted in friendship with a wearer of the hostile colour. As well ask Juliet for Romeo, as ask of a Tory father his daughter in marriage for the son of a Whig, when the one sported blue and the other purple and orange, while brickbats were flying and bribery stalked about the contested town with never a mask to hide its face nor a cloak to conceal its hands.

Our family house was for many years in one of the most primitive of those untouched country districts of which I first spoke; and the recollections of the elders of my own generation carry us back to a wonderful state of things.

My father was a clergyman and the holder of two livings. The second, of which I shall speak farther on, was one of the most beautiful places in England, where the ordering of life was simple and homely, but not more than this. The other was a large, rambling, sparsely-populated parish, where the people were half-savages, and where the very elements of all that makes our modern civilization were wanting. Not a school of any kind was in the place, though there was one at the quaint old market-town some few miles away; but in return, for a village of about three hundred inhabitants, there were seventeen public-houses and jerry-shops; and the man who did not get drunk would have been the black swan which the white ones would soon have pecked to death. No one, however, tried the experiment of sobriety. There was no sense of public decency, no idea of civic order and as little private morality. The parish-constable would have thought twice before taking up a crony for any offence short of murder; and then he would have left the door of the lock-up ajar. Not a man would have held himself justified in marrying before the woman had proved her capacity for becoming a mother; and when the lovers were united according to the law of the land—just in time to legitimize the child—the customs and ceremonies of the day were almost as brutal as, and certainly more drunken than, those of the North American Indians or Tierra del Fuegians. Indeed, they were evident survivals of those primitive times when the bride was taken from her tribe by force and compelled to submit to violence, before dawning civilization made the whole matrimonial transaction a matter of sale and barter. But for the most part the young people slipped by night across the border to Gretna Green, preferring, as they said, the blacksmith's forge to the joiner's shop, and liking the mock romance of a pseudo-elopement which saved the parson's fees and the wedding-dinner, and thus 'gave folk less cause for clack.'

If the people were thus uncivilized, their

appointed pastors and masters in the off-districts were very little better. About eight miles from Braeghyll, my father's parish, was a God-forsaken moorland incumbency, the 'priest' of which was in no wise beyond his flock either in refinement or morality. As Braeghyll was the mother-parish, our village was naturally the local metropolis where the inhabitants of the surrounding hamlets found their pleasures and excitements. These were for the most part 'murry-neets'—dances in barns and public-houses, where the men got drunk, the women fuddled, and the marriage ceremony was discounted all round—and the Saturday-night fights, which came as regularly as the Sunday-morning shave. To these fights the priest of Moss Moor, of whom I have spoken, came more punctually than he went to his own little chapel the next day. He was a fine, stalwart fellow, who kept up his muscle by week-day working in the fields, like any hired herd or ploughman; and, 'stripped to buff,' as the phrase was, he took his turn like a man, did his fighting gallantly, then got drunk with the best; and so was trundled home to his stone cabin in the wilds, to sleep off his intoxication in time for his ragged duty to-morrow morning. My father's curate himself brought his unwedded wife to the parish and married her about three weeks before the child was born. No one thought the worse of them for their impatience; and, 'Nae, what!' they said with the broad charity of moral kinship, 'young folk will be young; and men and women are kittle cattle to shoe ahint!'

Accustomed to such ministers as these— men who were intellectually in advance of their flock only in so far as they could read and write, but whose example was a direct encouragement to both lawlessness and vice —the people of these wild districts would not brook interference nor admonition from such gentlemen as might be appointed to the mother-parishes. My father tried to bring about a better state of things when he first undertook the care of these shaggy souls at Braeghyll; but the men swore at him, and threatened to do him a mischief if he did not hold his noise, when he rebuked them for their intemperance or tried to stop their brutal excesses; and the women jeered him, for a Molly who put his nose where he had no concern, when he would have taught them a little modesty as maidens and decency as wives. Thus the heart was taken out of him; and, being naturally indolent, he soon dropped the reins which at first he had attempted to hold, and the parish went on as it would without let or hindrance from him. They were more respectful to my mother, who was sweet and gentle and very beautiful; and who was, moreover, assimilated to the every-

day experience of her sex by the rapid
' bairn-bearing ' which never left her without
a child in the cradle and another at her
breast.   But she had too much to do at
home to carry her energies abroad; and
district-visiting, mothers'-meetings, Bible-
classes, and all the other modern circumstances of parochial organization, were then
things unknown.   Besides, there were no
educated women to have 'worked the
parish,' even if there had been the thought
or the endeavour.   There was only one
gentleman's family besides our own ; and as
the squire's lady bore child for child with
the parson's, she was naturally as much tied
at home.

Things were no more satisfactory in the
church than they were in the parish.   Not
more than twenty people came to the
service, for the fullest attendance.   The
average was about fourteen.   On afternoons,
when folks were late, the old clerk would

ring the bell for a short three minutes, then shut the church door in a hurry—even if he saw some one coming in at the lych gate —glad to be quit of his irksome duty for that day.

'Nay, what, i' fegs, we bain't agoing to maunder through t' service for yon,' he said one day contemptuously to my father, when remonstrated with for shutting the church door right in the face of Nanny Porter.

According to old Josh, souls counted by the gross ; and the parson's own household did not count at all; and it was a wicked waste of force to spend the means of grace on a unit. So Nanny Porter had to go home again and leave her prayers unsaid ; and old Josh took the responsibility on his own soul, and swore a big oath that hers would be none the worse for the lapse.

This morally unsatisfactory living was pecuniarily valuable. The rector was Lord

of the Manor as well as rector ; and heriots
and fines on the death or displacement
of tenants, together with tithes in kind,
rent-charges and compensations, raised the
income to a good round sum when all was
told.   There was always bad blood at
tithing time, when the parson's tenth
' steuk ' was sure to be the largest of the
row ; the parson's tithe-pig the fattest of the
litter ; while the geese, ducks, fowls, etc.,
driven into the rectory back-yard for the
service of the church and in payment of
these despised and neglected functions, were
beyond compare the finest of their respective broods.

When I grew old enough to understand
how things were, I confess I felt both
ashamed and revolted when my father, as
he sometimes did, went about the fields
himself, and chose his own tenth ' steuks ' in
the face of the world of reapers and before
the eyes of the farmer.   They thought

nothing of it ; and as my father did his doubtful work naturally, cheerily and genially, he lost no honour, but on the contrary gained in personal favour as a 'good 'un of his kind,' though his kind was bad enough. It was only my own callow sense of personal dignity and democratic justice that suffered.

Our place used to overflow with produce at tithing-times. At Easter, eggs came in by the hundred, and at 'shearing-time' wool was by the cartload. Everything else was in like quantity. The tithers' supper made a supreme holiday for us young ones. They always had hodgepodge, plum-pudding, and a glass of punch to follow; and sometimes a cracked fiddle was put into requisition, when our maids used to dance with the men, threesome reels or foursome, and jigs where the women held their aprons ('brats' we called them) by the two corners, and flourished them, thumbs up-

ward, with clumsy coquetry as they jigged.
There was a grand quarrel between my father
and his parishioners when the Tithe Com-
mutation Act came in force ; and the seven
years' average, which had to be struck as the
basis for the consolidated income, differed
considerably in the estimate of the one who
was to be the recipient and the others who
were to be the paymasters.   Things quieted
down at last ; and when Mr. Blamire's
labours came to an end, the new system was
felt all round to be better than the old, as
giving less occasion for subterfuge here,
suspicion there, and heartburnings on both
sides alike.

CHAPTER II.

EDEN, the second living to which
my father had been presented,
just before I was born, was by
no means so rough and riotous a place
as Braeghyll. It was as drunken and
immoral, but it was less ferocious and
uncouth. There were more resident gentry
to keep civic order and restrain the law-
less impulses natural to strong-bodied
and uneducated men. There was too, a
tolerably fair High School under the management of twelve 'statesmen,' which
knocked the rudiments of knowledge and
some small sense of discipline into the un-

kempt heads of the boys and girls who attended or played truant at their parents' pleasure and their own will. There was a great deal of honest moral courage and sturdy personal independence among the people, mainly owing to the large number of these same 'statesmen,' or peasant proprietors, who owned no master and were no man's hire. Some of them had title-deeds dating from the time of Edward VI. and were both nominally and substantially the 'kings' of their respective dales :—I say were, for now they have almost disappeared as a class ; not all to the gain of the country. But, as I said, the drunkenness of the men and the lax virtue of the women kept about even step in each parish alike ; and though manners were less barbarous, morals were no purer at Eden than at Braeghyll.

In those days a South-going coach ran twice a week through Eden ; and the journey to London took three days and two nights. A letter from London cost thirteen-pence halfpenny ; and—as once happened to ourselves, when we were told the contents of a brother's letter as it was handed to us through the little window of the house in the square where the post office stood—if of likely interest to the public, it was quickly read by our sharp-tongued Mailsetter before delivery to those whom it concerned. As envelopes had not then been invented, and the folded sides of the sheet were always closely written over to get the whole worth of the postage, a little practice in peeping made the process of deciphering easy enough ; and the main threads of all the correspondence afloat were in the hands of our Mailsetter aforesaid. The franking system mitigated the severity of these postal expenses to the rich. It was only the poor who suffered without any mitigation. They had either to pay a formidable proportion of their week's slender earnings, or to go without hearing from the absent ones at all. For it was a legal offence, carrying large penalties, to make the carrier do duty as a postman and take, for twopence, what the Post-Office charged sixpence or eightpence to deliver at the next town, some ten or twelve miles away. People evaded the penalty by making the letter into a parcel and tying it round with string well sealed; but, if discovered, the evasion did not hold good, and the penalties were enforced as a warning to others.

All the carrying trade was done by these carriers, who were often men of shrewd wit and keen observation, and who brought a breath of larger life into the small places, as they passed through and told what they had seen and heard elsewhere. A great part of the commerce too, of the time, was in the hands of pedlers, who came at stated seasons to tempt the weak, profit by the savings of the thrifty, and supplement the poverty of the mouldy little shops where the shopkeeper was the tyrant and the customer was his slave. I remember to this day the kind of Arabian Nights' splendour of gems and jewellery, silks and shawls and 'farlies' of every description, which little Pedroni, the Swiss-Italian who wore huge rings in his swarthy ears, used to bring out of his cases with a certain mysterious reverence, as if each article was worth a king's ransom. What a good fight my eldest sister made for that green shawl with the kincob pattern!—and how I inwardly resolved to save up my money when I should be a man, and become the proud possessor of that monstrous silver watch, as big as a small warming-pan!

Beside our punctual pedlers with their packs, we had also our recognised gaberlunzies—our established tramps of either sex. These also came in their appointed seasons, and were hospitably entertained with a bed in the outhouse, a supper at the kitchen door, and sixpence or a shilling at parting in the morning. My father always added to his generosity a little homily, for the honour of the cloth and the tradition of good things. Also we had our village idiots, who could do nothing but sit in the sun and make mouths at those who passed ; and our half-witted men and women, who could scramble through a rough day's work of a purely mechanical kind, were as happy as kings and queens with sixpence for their 'darrack,' and who married, had children, and stuck peacocks' feathers in their ragged hats and bonnets. We had our poachers and suspected smugglers—generally the handsomest, strongest and swarthiest men of the district—who were looked on with profound respect by us boys, and a deadly animosity by the gentry —which to us seemed infinitely unjust. Why idealize and honour Will Watch if Black

Jack Musgrave was a scamp? And we had our scares, when the maids were hysterical and moony—scares which now meant burglars and now 'bogles,' and now again Burke and Hare, a report of whose sudden appearance in the Lime-pots ran like wild-fire among us, and made the women afraid to venture over the threshold, even so far as the stick-house, after dark.

Our church was a fine old Norman structure, choked with barbarisms. The frescoes had been whitewashed over by successive generations of churchwardens; so had the magnificent freestone pillars. The stained-glass windows had been taken away and plain squares, among which were interspersed a few bulls' eyes, had been put in their stead; the pews were the familiar old cattle-pens of every size and shape, wherein the congregation sat in all directions and went to sleep in the corners comfortably. The choir was composed of a few young men and women who practised among themselves as they liked and when they liked, and sometimes essayed elaborate anthems which resulted in vocal caricatures. The orchestra was a flageolet, on which the clerk, as the official leader and bandmaster, gave the key-note; and at the feet of the choir, in the dark at the west end, the High School boys and girls sat on benches which every now and then they tipped up or overturned, played marbles, had free fights, laughed aloud, and were dragged out by the hair, kicking and yelling, when their conduct was too obstreperous for even the lax reverence of the rest to bear. With all this we had a peal of bells which was the pride of the parish and acknowledged to be the best in the county; and our bell-ringers were renowned as past masters of their craft.

In my early youth, two families only among us kept a carriage or a footman;

and no one thought of hiring a car, as our tubs on wheels were called, for anything short of a day's excursion to the neighbouring lakes and waterfalls. When evening parties were on hand—we never or rarely gave dinners at Eden—the ladies tucked up their skirts and the men turned up their trousers, and walked gaily through the snow in winter and the dust in summer, lighted by lanthorns when there was no moon, and wearing wooden-soled clogs shod with iron when the roads were 'clarty.' Picnics on the lake, where each family contributed its quota, were the grand summer amusements of Eden; and walking expeditions up the more practicable mountains, all returning to the proposer's house for tea and supper and a dance or a round game in the evening, took the place of modern tennis-parties. Without question, things were merrier for us than our children have known how to make them for themselves.

There was less luxury and more simplicity; people were easily amused because not worn out by premature experience; and there was a greater sense of homeliness and friendliness than can be found anywhere now.

Perhaps some among us went a little too far in the way of simplicity and homeliness, as when the Roberts' girls—the daughters of the great literary light who shone at Eden—took down the soiled house-linen to mend in the drawing-room at Rydal Mount, where they were on a visit, to give Mrs. Hemans, who was also there on a visit, a practical lesson on the value of good house-wifery and no nonsense. Mrs. Hemans was somewhat superfine and lackadaisical; and these girls, the youngest of whom was famous for a certain quiet hardness which amounted to calm brutality, thought that to darn dirty linen before her eyes would be a useful counterpoise to her Rosa Matilda proclivities. The result was that the poetess fled from the room in dismay, and ever after cherished the most profound horror for the uncompromising Marthas who had so wounded her delicacy.

My father and that great literary light did not get on quite well together. I have never understood why. There had been no quarrel that I know of; the respective children were playfellows; and Dr. Roberts was as orthodox as my father himself, and notoriously a dutiful son of the Church. But they were not the friends one might have expected two cultured men would have been; and though Dr. Roberts came regularly to church, as any other decent body might, when the prayers were over he ostentatiously folded his arms, shut his eyes, and sat during the sermon in a state of frigid indifferentism, like one no more interested in the proceedings. He had done his duty to God and the Establishment by saying his prayers and following the service ; to the sermon, which was purely personal, he openly refused to give his attention.

At the other side of the vale, and not in our parish, was a very notable family—incomparably the most liberal and enlightened of all we had. Thoughtful and large-minded, they were remarkable, among other things, for the quiet dignity of their lives; their inflexible sense of public duty ; their orderly management as proprietors and masters ; their close friendships with the best thinkers and foremost men of the time ; and the determination with which they discountenanced all local gossip and petty scandal. The father, and his son after him, were men who make the unwritten but vital history of England, and furnish the solid material of English greatness. The other son, however, belongs to the written history of our time, and has left a name and done such work in literature as will never die out.

This family belonged, unfortunately for me, to the elder section of my generation; so that I was not able to profit by them in the forming period of my life, as I might have done had I been fifteen years or so older. It was only when I was a grown man that I came to know and recognise the moral greatness which was their inheritance. And then I was made. But to this day I have a curious feeling of loyalty and clan-ship towards the survivors of the house— especially towards one, the last of the elder generation, whose wonderful charm can be as little described as the perfume of a flower or the melody of a song. Indeed, she is very like a human flower or incorpo-rate melody—and of all emblems the Daisy and the Pearl suit her best.

Then there was a county magnate, whose house by the Bay where the water-lilies grew, was a kind of sentimental Paradise to my elder brothers. Three beautiful girls

made the charm of those woods and gardens;
and three of my elder brothers fell in love,
as was but natural; and the tears shed in
vain by these poor young erotic Tantaluses
were matters of family history for many
years after. Besides these, were retired
officers of both services, who had come to
Eden because the country was lovely and
living was cheap—with here a gentleman
living on his estate, and there an outsider
who only rented and did not possess, and
who never took quite the same place as the
autochthones by inheritance, or even the
naturalized by purchase. We were also in
those days tremendously exclusive; and
when the rich Leeds manufacturer bought
the estates of our historical attainted Lord,
he was considered decidedly below the salt,
and there were anxious consultations among
the impecunious well-born as to the propriety of visiting him and his. I have
lived to see all this nonsense knocked out of

the place; which maybe has been converted to the compensating worship of wealth somewhat over zealously.

Beyond these again, were the local oddities—the old maids with sharp tongues renowned for queer sayings; the well-endowed widows with large hearts — 'mothers in Israel,' as they were called when the days of cant came upon us; the Will Wimbles who played the flute were 'characters' and flighty, not to say more; the hunting parsons who rode to hounds whenever they could, and when they could not, did the best they could for themselves by riding into Eden, jack-booted and spurred, to meet the coach and talk horseflesh with Tom and Arnold; the scientific recluses who got a name of terror because of their anatomical studies, whereby they were supposed to be too friendly with the Evil One; the retired sea-captains, choleric and litigious; the Scotch doctors,

drunken and clever, who performed wonderful operations when half-seas over; the
men-servants and maid-servants who were
part of the family and called by the master's
name, as Birkett Tim and Crosthwaite
Molly; the maiden shopkeepers, who were
the humbler members of the society, greatly
respected and esteemed, with whom the
aristoi would sometimes take a cup of tea
and not hold themselves as condescending
unduly : — these were as individualized,
and some were as queer, as anything to be
found in Sterne or Smollett. But the
queerest of all were the incumbents of the
small chapelries - of - ease made off the
mother-parish—all of whom were St. Bees
men, while many were as drunken as our
old priest at Moss Moor, and none were men
of education and refinement. I remember
how, at a visitation dinner at the vicarage,
one of these outlying pastors stood up in his
place, and, asking the Bishop familiarly if

he would be served, carved the cabbages before him with his own knife and fork. He had already eaten generously with his knife. They all did in those days.

Our own way of living was simple in the extreme. Our servants wore short woollen petticoats; cotton bedgowns and blue-checked aprons; huge caps with flapping borders and flying strings; and thick-soled shoes, with which they wore out the carpets and made a hideous clatter on the bare boards. We had a gardener who had been a soldier, and who, in memory of his past glory, always wore a scarlet waistcoat on Sundays; and we had a hay-field, a farm-yard, and two cows—'Cushie' and 'Hornie' —which in the summer evenings we used to go with the cook to bring home from the field to the milking-byre. I think I could replace every dock and ragwort and plot of nettles and mayweed in that ragged bit of pasture-land, sloping down to the little

brook where the minnows were.   Our food
was oatmeal-porridge, night and morning.
For dinner we were allowed meat only twice
a week.   On the ' banyan days ' we had
large tureens full of milky messes of exquisite savour, or enormous paste puddings
—' roly-polys '—of fruit, jam, or undecorated
suet.   It was simple fare, but it made a
stalwart, vigorous set of boys and girls;
and out of the whole dozen, only two were
relatively undersized and only one was
delicate.   The rest averaged six feet for
the men and the full medium height for the
women.

My mother, who was of higher social
standing than my father—for he was a
simple vicar and she was then the Dean's
daughter—had married him against the
consent of her own people.   She died when
my eldest brother was fifteen years old
and when I, the youngest of the brood, was
five months.   Ten rapidly recurring steps

between these two limits filled the quiver to overflowing.

My grandfather, at first violently angry, at last—when he had been made a Bishop —proved his forgiveness of his daughter's disobedience and my father's presumption by giving him, in succession, the best two livings in his gift; as well as certain sinecures which the lax ecclesiastical conscience of those days made it possible for an otherwise honest man to hold. But this liberality, added to the original sin of the marriage, only served to alienate the rest of the family more completely from us. For, as all my uncles were in orders, and all my aunts had married clergymen, and plurality was then in force, and nepotism the first duty of a patron-parent, it was but natural that they should resent this apportionment of the big plums to the least desirable of the sons-in-law, rather than to the more commendable who had the better claim, or to the sons who had the most right.

This professional jealousy, backed by social disdain—for the family, as a family, was one of the proudest, most exclusive, and most worldly in England—and my father's total want of kindred on his own side, explain the isolation in which we lived, and why, after my grandfather's death, we knew none of that kindly super-intendence which the children of a dead sister so often receive from those still living. While my grandfather lived we were taken care of at the Castle; but after his death we were abandoned; and my father was left to bring us up as he would, unhelped and un-checked by the influence of his wife's kins-folk. He chose the rough and ready way of corporal punishment for all offences. He believed in Solomon and the rod, and put religious conviction as well as muscular energy into his stripes. It was a brutal system. But the times were brutal all through ; and my father was neither worse nor more enlightened than his generation. He sincerely believed that he was doing his imperative duty when he thrashed us in accordance with the inspired command; and that were the rod spared the child would be indeed spoilt. And when a passionate temper takes with it divine sanction, the punishment it inflicts is softened by no misgiving as to its wisdom or its humanity.

My stately grandfather himself set an example of almost incredible severity in his family. His sons never called him anything but ' Sir ' or ' My Lord ;' and he was never known to kiss one of his daughters, save by rare grace, or on supreme occasions of marriage or departure, coldly on the forehead. Sometimes however, he allowed them to kiss his hand. He gave his wife half-a-crown at a time for pocket-money;

and—like Mrs. Primrose, with the guinea she 'generously' let each of her daughters have 'to keep in their pockets'—she was exhorted not to break into it nor spend it. It always went in ' goodies' for the grand-children.   When the sons were beneficed clergymen and married men with children, they dared not have asked for a glass of wine at their father's table ; and he would have been a bold man who should have addressed my Lord without first being spoken to.

A dark and terrible family tradition was whispered from each to each, under the bond of absolute secrecy, how that once, when one of my aunts had reached the ripe age of eighteen, my Lord Bishop had whipped her bodily with his own august prelatic hands.   He was a tall and dignified-looking man ; famed for botany and scholar-ship, and held to be the handsomest Bishop on the bench ; but he was a queer successor of the Fishermen ; and I doubt if the Master would have recognised him as a wholly satisfactory representative. Yet it was told of him that once, in a rare fit of humility confessing some trivial weakness of character, he said to my father with admirable condescension to the frailty of a common humanity : ' After all, Mr. Kirkland, a Bishop is only a man !'

Naturally indolent and self-indulgent in his habits, but a man of the strictest temperance—never once in his whole life, in that drinking age, having exceeded the bounds of absolute sobriety ; fond of shining in society, where he knew how to make his mark, but almost impossible to drag out of his study for any form of social intercourse ; flattered by the notice of the great when it came to him, but neglecting all his opportunities and too proud to accept patronage even when offered ; a Tory in politics and a Democrat in action ; defying his diocesan and believing in his divine ordination ; contemptuous of the people as a political factor, but kind and familiar in personal intercourse with the poor ; clever, well read and somewhat vain of his knowledge, but void of ambition and indifferent to the name in literature which he might undoubtedly have won with a little industry; not liberal as a home-provider, but largely and unostentatiously generous in the parish ; fond like a woman of his children when infants, but unable to reconcile himself to the needs of their adolescence and refusing to recognise the rights of their maturity ; thinking it derogatory to his parental dignity to discuss any matter whatsoever rationally with his sons, and believing in the awful power of a father's curse, yet caressing in manner and playful in speech even when he was an old man and we were no longer young ; with a heart of gold and a temper of fire—my father was a man of strangely complex character, not to be dismissed in a couple of phrases.

With a nature tossed and traversed by passion, and a conscience that tortured him when his besetting sin had conquered his better resolve once more, as so often before, he was in some things like David; — for whose character he had the most intimate kind of personal sympathy. 'For I acknowledge my faults, and my sin is ever before me,' was the broken chord of his lament. But to us children, the echo of his loud midnight prayers, waking us from our sleep and breaking the solemn stillness of the night—the sound of his passionate weeping mingled in sobbing unison with the moaning of the wind in the trees, or striking up in sharp accord with the stinging of the hail against the windows—gave only an awful kind of mystery to his character, making the deeper shadows we knew too well all the more terrible by these lurid lights of tragic piety.

My poor dear father! The loss of my beautiful mother, and, a year after her death, that of the eldest girl, who seems to have been one of those sweet mother-sisters sometimes found as the eldest of the family, had tried him almost beyond his strength. His life henceforth was a mingled web of passion and tears—now irritated and now despairing—with ever that pathetic prostration at the foot of the Cross, where he sought to lay down his burden of sorrow and to take up instead resignation to the will of God—where he sought the peace he never found! He had lost the best out of his life, and he could not fill up the gap with what remained.

There was one thing I have never understood:—why my father, so well read and even learned in his own person, did not care to give his children the education proper to

their birth and his own standing. The
elders among us came off best, for the
mother had had her hand on them, and the
Bishop too, had had his say ; but the
younger ones were lamentably neglected.
I do not know why. We were not poor.
Certainly, we were a large tribe to provide
for and my father often made a 'poor mouth;'
but his income was good, the cost of living
was relatively small, and things might have
been better than they were. At the worst, my
father might have taught us himself. He
was a good classic and a sound historian ;
and though his mathematics did not go very
deep, they were better than our ignorance.
But he was both too impatient and too
indolent to be able to teach, and I doubt if
the experiment would have answered had he
tried it.

So time went on, and he allowed neither
a responsible tutor for us boys nor a capable
governess for the girls, nor would he send

us to school.   He engaged, as a very per-
functory kind of crammer for two of my
brothers, the son of a small hamlet hand-
weaver, a young St. Bees man whose parents
denied themselves almost necessaries that
they might give their son a good education
and see him in the ministry.   This young
man, who was both plain in person and
ungainly in manners, fell in love with my
eldest sister, and inspired her thereby with
a physical horror that became almost a constitutional antipathy, such as certain people
have for cats.   When she was quite an old
woman she used to say she should feel
if Mr. Donald came into a room at her back,
where she could not see him.   She would
feel him in a shudder down her spine and
goose-flesh over her skin.

When my father had engaged this young
man, he thought he had done all for his
boys that was demanded of him by duty
or need.   If ever the subject was broached

to him, he used to lose his temper, and always ended by saying that self-educated people got on the best. He forgot the pithy saying that a self-taught man has had a dunce for his master.

One of our family traditions, rounded off of course by repetition and the natural desire to make a good story, tells how that, after our mother's death, my grandfather sent for my father and urged him to do such and such things, whereby he might increase his income and provide for the fitting conduct of his family. To each proposal my father found insuperable objections. At last the Bishop, losing patience, said angrily :

'In the name of heaven, Mr. Kirkland, what do you mean to do for your children ?'

'Sit in the study, my Lord, smoke my pipe, and commit them to the care of Providence,' was my father's calm reply.

And he acted on his decision. He did emphatically commit us to the care of Providence; and he was satisfied with his trustee.

Practically, this meant the control of the younger by the elder. The eldest brother was the master of the boys, the eldest sister the mistress of the girls ; with intermediate gradations of relative supremacy according to seniority. Hence there reigned among us the most disastrous system of tyranny, exercised by these unfledged viceroys of Providence over their subordinates — a tyranny for which there was no redress, however great the wrong. It was of no use to appeal to my father. Had he sided with the complainant, things would have been worse in the end, and there would then have been revenge and retaliation to add to the original count. It was better to take things as they came, or to fight it out for one's self. And there was always some one still younger to whom it could be passed on ; which was so far a comfort! Our house, in those days, was like nothing so much as a farm-yard full of cockerels and pullets for ever spurring and pecking at one another. It was the trial of strength that always goes on among growing creatures—especially among young males; but it was bad to bear while it lasted. Add to this a still more disastrous system of favouritism, and the knowledge that no justice was to be expected, from my father downwards, if such a one were the plaintiff and such another the defendant—and the breaking up among ourselves into pairs of sworn friends and devoted allies—and this slight sketch of the moral rule that obtained during the early days of my childhood is complete.

CHAPTER III.

WE all suffered much from the want of intelligent supervision, but I, by the inherent defects of my character, as well as by my place as youngest, suffered most. Quick to resent and sensitive to kindness, rebellious and affectionate, wilful and soft-hearted, I was ever in tumult and turmoil, followed by disgrace, punishment and repentance. But I must say in self-exculpation, that, tiresome as I must have been, I was as much sinned against as sinning.

Easily provoked and daring in reprisals, but as the youngest the least formidable and the most defenceless, I was too good fun to be let alone. I was like the drunken helot told off to self-degradation for the moral benefit of the young Spartans; for I was teased and bullied till I became as furious as a small wild beast, and when by my violence I had put myself in the wrong, I was held up as an example to Edwin and Ellen to avoid, and flogged as the practical corollary. I do not suppose a week passed without one of these miserable outbreaks, with the rod and that dark closet under the stairs to follow.

These repeated floggings did me no good. Physically, they certainly hardened me to pain, but morally they roused in me that false and fatal courage which breeds the dare-devils of society and makes its criminals die game. But I was subdued at once when anyone, by rare chance and gleam of common-sense, remonstrated with me lovingly or talked to me rationally. I

well remember my ambition to prove myself worthy of his trust, which was like
sunlight in my tempestuous young life,
when my father, instead of accusing and
threatening me, relied on my promise to do
what was right and to my word when I
said I had not done what was wrong.   Nor
he, nor anyone who trusted to me, ever found
me even then a defaulter.   Like a faithful
dog, I would have stood to have been hacked
to pieces before I would have broken faith
or forfeited my childish honour.

These halcyon days of moral dignity
were painfully exceptional; and my father's
confidence in me was that gift of God
for which I longed more ardently than
for anything in my life before or since—
and how seldom granted !   I only remember two occasions—once when I was believed
about that broken drawing-room window,
of which I had not been the ball-playing
cause ; and once when I was allowed to pick

red currants for preserves, and my father trusted to my promise not to eat nor filch. As things were, I was always being guilty of some act of mischief, some flagrant disobedience to rules, or some outburst of temper which gave those in authority reason when they thrashed me, if they were in the wrong when they misunderstood me. So much I must say for my past turbulent self :—I never remember being flogged for an act of meanness nor for a lie ; and I do remember twice taking his punishment for Edwin and not betraying him. I never told tales of the others, and I was always ready to brave danger and its consequences if asked to do a service. Thus, though I was undeniably the black sheep of the flock, I was the one trusted to when a steadfast agent was wanted.

At this moment there comes before me a little scene which must have taken place when I was a very small boy.

I was sent to steal some sacred apples for some of them—I forget who they were now. As I shook the tree by means of a light garden-rake hitched up on the branches, it fell and cut open my head, covering my neck-frill with blood. But I gathered up the apples in my pinafore, and took them to my brothers or sisters hiding behind the wall on the little bank which to this day is golden with the 'shoes and stockings' I remember so well; and then I marched sturdily into the house, where Mary the nurse cut my hair, strapped up the wound, and put me to bed. The next day I was taken to my father and flogged. But I would not tell for whom I had stolen the apples, nor would I plead in mitigation of my punishment that I had had none myself.

Our then ' viceroy,' the second brother— the eldest being away at college—was a young fellow of eighteen, with a violent temper and a heavy hand. He was generous and affectionate at bottom, but he was irritable, jealous and tyrannical to an overwhelming degree. One day, a Punch-and-Judy show came on the lawn before the dining-room windows. We were all there, watching the raree-show. I suppose I was excited and in one of my impudent moods, for I persisted in calling my brother 'Dicksy,' a name he disliked and specially forbade the smaller fry to use.

'If you say that again I will thrash you,' he said to me angrily.

I looked up into his face. How clear the whole thing is before me! The squeaking and unintelligible Punch; the sunshine on the grass; the close throng, clustered like flies against the window; and my sense of my brother's towering bigness and formidable ferocity. But I was a daring young rascal, and always ready to brave the unknown.

' Dicksy !' I said defiantly.

Whereupon Richard was as good as his word, and then and there beat me severely.

The brother who stood next to Richard, with one sister between, was three years his junior. He was as tall, but naturally not then so strong ; as passionate in temper, but of a deeper nature and finer mental and moral quality altogether. These two were natural foes and rivals, and were always fighting—the one tyrannizing, the other rebelling. Before this day I do not remember this brother Godfrey. He is lost in the crowd of the elders, from whom we little chaps were separated as entirely as if they had been lions or we had been mice. After this day he became one of the enduring loves of my life. I distinctly remember how he turned upon Richard and fought him for his cruelty to such a little fellow as I was—not quite five years old, and still in frocks like a baby ; for I can yet see the weals on my shoulder made by Richard's vigorous fingers. After the scuffle Godfrey took me on his knee, and kissed me to comfort me. From that moment there woke up in me a kind of worship for this brother, just ten years my senior—a worship, which, old man as I am—still older as he is—I retain to this hour. We have lived apart all our lives. In over forty years I have seen him for two at a stretch. But when I realize the ideal of knightly honour and manly nobleness —of that kind of proud incorruptibility which knows no weakness for fear nor favour—I think of my brother Godfrey far beyond the seas; he who as a boy braved his elder brother for the sake of a little fellow who could not defend himself—as a man calmly faced an excited mob yelling for their blood, to place under the shadow of the British flag two trembling wretches who had only his courage between them and death.

The early life and adventures of this

brother are a romance in themselves. Had
he lived in mythic times he would have
been another Amadis, a second Wallace.
He is like some offshoot of heroic days,
rather than a man of a commercial generation ; and in him the grand old Roman
spirit survives and is re-embodied.

Godfrey was my lord, but Edwin was my
natural chum. Some eighteen months
younger, I was the stronger and bigger of
the two. He had always been a delicate
boy ; and the nursery tradition about him
was that when he was born he was the
exact length of a pound of butter, was put
into a quart-pot, and dressed in my eldest
sister's doll's clothes :—the ordinary baby-
clothes were too large, and her doll was a
big one for those days. I was his slave and
protector in one. He had none of the emotional intensity, none of the fierceness of
temper, the foolhardy courage, the inborn
defiance, neither had he the darkness of

mood nor the volcanic kind of love which characterized me. He was sweeter in temper; more sprightly as well as more peaceful in disposition; more amenable to authority; of a lighter, gentler, more manageable and more amiable nature altogether. He was the family favourite and the family plaything. Long after my sisters had left off taking me into their laps they would let Edwin sit on their knees for hours; and when my brothers would have kissed a hedgehog as soon as me, they kissed him as they kissed Julia and Rosamond and Ellen. He was never in mischief and never in the way. He cared only to play quiet games in the garden when it was fair, or to sit in the embrasure of the window when it was wet and we were forced to keep the house. In consideration of his delicacy he had been taught wool-work and netting; and his supreme pleasure was to sit on his 'copy' (a kind of stool), in a

' cupboardy house '—that is, in the midst of
a ring of chairs forming a defence-work
against intruders—while I told him stories
' out of my own head' or Ellen good-
naturedly read to him.

Besides this constitutional delicacy to
make those in authority tender in their
dealing with him, he was the most
beautiful of us all.   Godfrey was incomparably the handsomest of the grown
boys—did not his beauty once save his life ?
—but Edwin was the loveliest of the children.
He was like one of Sir Joshua's cherubs.
His head was covered with bright golden
curls, his skin was like a pale monthly rose,
and he had big soft blue eyes which no one
could resist.   Everyone loved and petted
him, as I have said.   Our father, who saw in
him the reproduction of our dead mother,
had even a more tender feeling for him than
for any of his other favourites ; my own
hero, Godfrey, loved him ten thousand

times more than he loved me; and Richard, our tyrannical 'kingling,' who spared no one else, spared Edwin. But no one sacrificed to him as I did, and no one loved him with such fanatical devotion. It was but natural, then, that he should lord it over me with that tremendous force which weakness ever has over loving strength; and that I, the born rebel but the passionate lover, should give to that weakness the submission which no authority could wring from me. Also it came into the appointed order of things that I should bore him by my devotion, and that he should pain me by his indifference. It was a preface to the life that had to come—the first of the many times when I should make shipwreck of my peace through love.

Yet had it not been for this devotion to Edwin, and the feeling that I was of use to him for all his coldness to me, my life would have been even more painful than it was.

I was so isolated in the family, so out of harmony with them all, and by my own faults of temperament such a little Ishmaelite and outcast, that as much despair as can exist with childhood overwhelmed and possessed me. Three years after his defence of me, when he was eighteen and I eight, Godfrey left home; and I lost the Great-Heart of my loyal love—the one I always felt was somehow my own special suzerain, if I were but a despised kind of Dugald creature to him. But even at the best, the difference between our ages prevented anything like friendship or companionship. He was my lord, but he was never my familiar.

I remember how, after he had left, and though I knew that he was out of England and countless miles away, I used to expect him to return suddenly and by miracle; and how sometimes I used to look for him about the place—in the cupboards and unused lofts. And I remember, too, a strange horror that used to seize me, of expecting to find a pool of blood in the place where I looked for him.

Perhaps this odd kind of horror was due to a terrible scene which had had a great effect on me. Our two brothers, Richard and Godfrey, were shooting in a field not far from the vicarage, and we were watching them from the windows. Suddenly there was a tremendous report, a large volume of smoke, a cry and the hurrying of men together; and then we saw a body carried on their shoulders, and brought up to the vicarage. It was Richard, the barrel of whose gun had burst. The stock had wounded him severely in the stomach, and covered him with blood. Godfrey was safe, but singed. Perhaps it was some obscure association of ideas which added this ghastly horror of expected blood to my grief for Godfrey's mysterious flight and my insane belief in his miraculous return—unable as I was, like all devotees, to accept the unalterable law when dealing with love.

In these outcast days I used to dream a strange dream—strange, considering my age —how that I was not one of them—not my father's child at all—but a foundling, some day to be reclaimed and taken home by his own who would love and understand him. I had a favourite hiding-place in the lime-trees at the foot of the garden, where I used to lose my time, my strength and mental health in this fantastic idea. Granting all the difficulties my family had to contend with in me, I do not think the desolation of a young child could go beyond the secret hope of one day finding himself an alien to his own—of some day being claimed by the unknown—strangers coming out of space sure to be more gentle and sympathetic than those others! But I always added, as a codicil to this testament

of despair, that if ever I did find these
unknown dear ones, Godfrey should still be
my king and Edwin my beloved, and that no
new tie should break these two golden links
of the old sad heavy chain. As another proof
of my childish desolation, if also of my
intemperate nature, I remember how once, in
a fit of mad passion for some slight put on
me by my eldest sister, whereat the others had
laughed and jeered me, I first fought them all
round, then rushed off to a large draw-well
we had in the coach-yard—we were not then
at Eden, but at my father's private house
in Kent—intending to throw myself down
and end for ever a life which was at the
moment intolerable and emphatically not
worth living. The heavy cover was over
the mouth, and I could not move it. While
I was trying the gardener came along ; and,
seeing that I had been crying, he good-
naturedly took me to the apple-loft, where he
filled my pockets with golden russets—which

consoled me grandly, and lifted me over that little stile of sorrow into a flowery field of content.   I was then ten years old.

If Edwin had died when he was a child, the spiritualists would have had a case.   He woke one night sobbing piteously, and woke me, sleeping with him, by his crying.   When I asked him what was the matter, he said that he had just seen ' poor mamma.'   He was on one side of a broad black river, and on the other, in a garden full of flowers, stood our mother draped in white with wings like an angel.   She held out her arms and called : ' Little Edwin, come to me!   Little Edwin, come !'   Then he woke, and cried because he had again lost the mother whom he, of all the children, most desired to have had and known.   For not even those who remembered her regretted her loss so much as did Edwin, who was not quite two years old when she died, and who did not remember her at all.   He had no illness after this, nor did he die. Thanks to the pure blood we have all inherited, notwithstanding his early delicacy he is alive and well to this day. But had he died then, this dream would have been accounted a supernatural vision, and he would have been held to have been called to death and paradise by his mother's spirit.

If all the failures in presentiments and warning dreams were recorded, I fancy they would considerably outweigh the co-incidences.

I had not Edwin's pathetic yearning for our mother. I found her substitute in Nurse Mary, whom I loved with over-whelming force, and got into trouble as the result. As, once when she had been away for a week's holiday and had returned at night, I was wakened up out of my sleep and taken to her bed. I was so glad to see her that I cried; and finally cried myself into what was, I suppose, a fit of hysterics;—

when they whipped me as a useful nervous counteraction.

This nurse was an undisciplined kind of woman, who now hugged us till she nearly squeezed us to death, and now beat us black and blue. But I suppose my own volcanic nature understood her violent one, for I could not live out of her sight, and she was good enough to me. I am afraid she drank, poor Mary! Things dark then are clear now; and those mysterious and sudden illnesses which she used to have pretty often were, I fancy, due to brandy rather than to disease. She left us when I was nine years old.

I was about eleven years of age when the first distinct stirrings of my mental life began to make themselves felt. Godfrey's adventures—for he had returned after two years' imprisonment in Russia—had something to do with the new light that began to dawn in my young brain. I had

always had a passion for books and pictures,
and I knew almost by heart those few that
we possessed. In contrast to the wealth of
modern days, it will not be uninteresting
to give the full catalogue of our special
library. Mrs. Sherwood's ' Little Henry
and his Bearer'; ' William and the Wood-
man '; ' Sandford and Merton'; ' Paul and
Virginia'; ' Evenings at Home'; ' The
Arabian Nights' Tales'; ' Tales of the
Castle'; ' Tales of the Genii'; ' Robinson
Crusoe'; ' Pilgrim's Progress'—where the
occasion was generally improved for my
benefit, as I was identified with Passion,
while Edwin was Patience; Miss Edge-
worth's ' Moral Tales'; and ' Elizabeth,
or the Exiles of Siberia,' formed our
whole stock of profane literature. For
Sunday-reading we had ' Mrs. Barbauld's
Hymns'; the ' Dairyman's Daughter';
' Fox's Book of Martyrs'; ' The History
of all Religions'; ' The Life of Christ'—

of which I remember only the pathetic pictures of the Agony in the Garden and the Crucifixion, where two little angels held up cups to catch the blood; and sometimes we were allowed to look at the coloured plates of the 'safe' volumes of the 'Encyclopædia Londinensis'—the battle-horse of the study library. When we grew older we had to read one of Sherlock's sermons—Sherlock was my father's favourite divine; or he read to us in the evening, before prayers, a chapter out of Doddridge's 'Family Expositor,' when all of us youngsters invariably fell asleep and were scolded for our irreligious drowsiness.

But, as I say, when I was about eleven years of age, almost suddenly I seemed to leap out of this narrow circle and to demand a larger mental area altogether. There woke up in me the most burning desire to Know. With all the intense physical enjoyment of life given me by my keen senses and strong animal nature—with all the delight I felt in putting out my strength and learning how to increase and sharpen my growing bodily powers—I had a dim consciousness that life meant more than mere pleasure; and that it was as important to know history and geography, and what the problems of Euclid proved, and what those unintelligible books in strange tongues said to those who could read them, as it was to know how to swarm up a smooth-boled tree, jump standing and leap running, and clamber like a goat over the crags and rocky places. All these things were necessary and delightful; but higher and beyond them all stood Knowledge.

By this time our family at home had decreased by death, marriage and absence, to five—less than half the original number; and things educational were worse for us, the youngest two boys, than they had been for the elders. Edwin's health was too frail for school-life; and as he could not go, neither could I. I was wanted at home to be his companion. It was in vain that I begged my father to send me to school. He would not; and I vexed him by my entreaties. Nor would he give us masters nor a tutor at home. He promised, but he never fulfilled his promise. All the instruction I ever received was of the pot-hook-and-hanger degree—the mere elements; the rest I did for myself. And so years passed on, and still Edwin and I were kept at home to do what we liked, provided we did not get into mischief and did not bother.

Part of that liking with me went into learning for myself what there was no one to teach me. I took up languages; beginning with French. Year after year I attacked one after the other, till I had got hold of a good many. But, as I learnt only to read and was not phenomenally laborious, I scamped the grammar and devoted myself to translation—that is, I neglected rules and learnt only words. This is the reason why, when I could read with ease and translate aloud rapidly while I read, French, Italian, German, Spanish, with a little Latin and less Greek, I could neither parse any of these languages correctly nor speak one fluently. I learnt without method, and I have never been able to disentangle my mind from the false order of the start.

This want of early training explains all my persistent intellectual deficiencies— my want of dialectical skill, my want of scientific accuracy, and how it is that I know nothing analytically, from the foundations upward, but only synthetically, concretely, as it stands. This must needs be, seeing that I have never built up any study brick by brick, nor chamber by chamber, but have only entered on the results of other men's work—inhabiting where they have created. Essentially self-educated as I am, that self-education began at an age when the elemental drudgery, which always seems useless to ignorance, is naturally shirked for the more interesting results. Learning, with me, was only a means to an end. For instance, I learnt French out of curiosity to read an old illustrated 'Telemachus' that we had, and thus to understand what the pictures meant ; Italian to know about Petrarch and Dante, whose conventional portraits in our encyclopædia had fascinated me ; German, for 'Faust' ; Latin, to understand those brown-leather folios in the study library; Spanish for 'Don Quixote'; and Greek in the vain hope of following Homer in the original— the awakening touch here having been given by Godfrey telling me about the 'far-darting Apollo' and the 'silver-ankled Thetis.'

And being by the nature of my intellect quick to understand, and by temperament impatient to possess — 'a temperament founded on ultimates,' as my friend Garth Wilkinson said of me in later times—I had not mastered the rudiments when I plunged into the middle term, and bounded on to the end. Thus, never subjected to that severe mental discipline which is but another form of moral control, I grew up in absolute mental unrestraint; and I have never been able to put myself into harness since.

This independence of thought is not presumption nor vanity, nor any of the hard things believers in authority say of the self-reliant. It is the result of antecedent conditions, for which a man is no more responsible than he is for the size of his skeleton. And he can change the one as little as the other. Those who are to be disciplined must be taught their drill and made to obey; and no one can be at once self-reliant and submissive.

This then, was how things stood in my early boyhood, after the stage of childhood proper was passed—say from between eleven to seventeen.   In my mental life, undirected and unhelped, save by opposition—which has always been a powerful stimulus to me —I strove to learn, to know, to possess. So far I was justified by my conscience and at peace with myself; and if I lost my time, took things by the wrong end, and amassed a world of rubbish which did me no good then nor since, I did not know my mistakes, and my ignorance was my bliss.

In my family I was still under the old cloud. I was snubbed by my father, whom I constantly worried and often angered ; roughly handled by my brothers, whose authority I defied when they came home for their vacations from college ; sent to Coventry by my sisters whom I revolted by my violence and affronted by my impertinence ; made his slave by Edwin, who did not really love me in those days ; but with all this I knew that I tried to do right, however poorly I succeeded, and that I would have died rather than I would have done what seemed to me mean or false, or cowardly or selfish. And ever and ever I longed with a hungry passion that ran into pain, for the love which my own turbulence of nature made it impossible for others to give me.

If our dear mother had lived, things would have been different. She would have understood each and would have done justly by all. Under her wise management there would have been none of that neglect in direction and harshness of punishment when things went wrong which had been the rule of our upbringing. And her gentle influence would have tamed the tempers and regulated the actions of all alike. All our troubles were due to her death ; and my poor father was as much to be pitied as were we.

I have dwelt so long on the early life of my childhood because it gives the clue to all the rest.   The boy is father to the man, and the first chord contains the key-note of the whole succeeding harmony.

CHAPTER IV.

AT seventeen my future profession was undetermined and
my real education had never
been begun. My father's constitutional
indolence had greatly increased of late
years, and nothing was so difficult to
him as to take a resolution, excepting to
act on it when taken. Hence, Edwin and I
were still hanging about at home, doing
nothing that should in any way equip us
for the life in which we had to take our
place and pull our pound with the rest.

Though we two were incomparably the
worst off for tuition, our elder brothers

themselves had been but slenderly furnished, all things considered. Therefore
they had failed to make for themselves
such positions as might have helped us
youngsters against the dead weight of my
father's inertia. It was as much as they
could do to fend for themselves and struggle
into comparatively good places. And some
of them, in revolt against their difficulties,
had flung up the attempt here at home, and
had cast their lines in the dark but brisker
waters of emigration and exile.

There never was a family with so much
power left to run so cruelly to waste for
want of timely cultivation as was ours! It
is no vanity to say that we were an excep-
tionally fine set all through, and that, had
we been properly trained, each one of us
would have made his mark. There was not
a dunce among us, nor a physical failure.
All my sisters were pretty; all my brothers
were well-grown and handsome; and Edwin,

who was the least robust in person, was the most beautiful in face and the most lovely in character. I have often lamented the waste of good material in our family, and the loss to the world that it has been. When I see the elaborate education given to boys and girls with brain-power of the most ordinary calibre, and note what careful training has made of them, and then remember the large amount of mental and physical vitality among ourselves, and what ordinary care might have made of us, I confess I feel heartsick—foolish as it is to look back, like Lot's wife, over the irrecoverable past. All the same, it was a misfortune ; and it has been a real loss.

It might have been so different! My father's office and position made him an influential person in society ; my mother's family kept us abreast with the county magnates, at least in theory, if, owing to my father's disinclination to society, scarcely in practice ; and we had friends who might have helped us if they would. There was, for one, the great Tory member whose historic name was like a battle-cry—he had power enough, if he would have used it for gratitude without being entreated. For my father would have cut off his right hand before he would have asked a favour of living man. When an election was on hand, and every vote was of consequence, Sir James used to come to our house, make much of his dear friend Mr. Kirkland, praise his Latinity and his poetry, admire the girls, kiss the children, and hint at substantial services for the boys. When he was returned he forgot all about his dear friend as cleanly as if he had never existed, and did not lift a finger to serve the sons of his faithful partisan, who were also the grandsons of his old master, the Bishop. His want of gratitude never touched my father's political fidelity ; for no man was

ever less a self-seeker than he. He did his
duty at a personal loss quite as stoutly as if
it brought him grist and grain ; though he
suffered from ingratitude, as any man of
sensibility would. But he never complained, even in the privacy of home. I
have never known anyone more entirely
free from all spite and bitterness than he.

By this time I had formed my theory of
the universe. What thoughtful boy of
seventeen has not ? I was firmly convinced
that I held the fee-simple of all great truths
in my hands, and that no views other than
those which seemed to me right were worth
consideration. All were the outcome of
either ignorance or falsehood — of either
blind superstition which could not see the
light, or wilful tyranny, conscious of its
iniquity but determined to hold on for the
oppression of truth. No question could
have two sides ; no opponent could be
an honest man ; no ultimate development

of my own theories could eventuate in evil.
Does not every individual, like concrete
society, go through this phase of bigotry
—tyrannous and unjust by its very intensity of conviction ?

I was comically proud of being an Englishman. I had no doubt that we were
God's modern chosen—His eldest sons and
peculiar favourites ; that the English Protestant Church was the very Delos of Truth
—the ark of the Christian covenant ; that
even Christian prayers said in a foreign
tongue were not heard with so much pleasure, nor answered with so much precision,
as ours—while prayers said to a Being who
did not exist—to Allah or Brahma, Vishnu
or Buddha, not to speak of the Madonna and
the saints—were neither heard nor answered
at all ; that we were the best gentlemen, the
bravest men, the most enlightened and most
virtuous people on the face of the earth;
and that every departure from our special

ways of living and thinking was a wandering into the desert with destruction at the far end. That is, I was bounded by my own circumstances, and could not travel beyond my experience.

Also, I was an ardent Republican and a devout Christian. Indeed, I was the one because the other; and, in spite of that injunction to pay tribute to Cæsar, on which my father so much insisted, I could not see a 'via media.' Nor could I understand the compromise between faith and practice, consistency and expediency, made by the believing world; nor yet how men, who would have roasted alive an infidel had the law permitted, could deliberately break all the commands given by the Saviour. That fine satirical problem of how to hold together, on the principles of the Sermon on the Mount, an empire founded on the breach of all the Ten Commandments, had not then been formulated. But the spirit of it was in my own young head, and the difficulty involved was one that puzzled me as it has many more than myself, and will continue to puzzle others for some time yet to come.

For my own part, full of youthful zeal and the logic of consistency, I determined to live the Christian life so far as it was possible ; helped thereto by the influence and example of the strong old heathen times. I, at least, in my own person would be faithful to the Lord and a man among men.

I began by renouncing all the pleasant softnesses and flattering vanities of my youth, and made myself a moral hybrid, half ascetic, half stoic. I accustomed myself to privations and held luxuries as deadly sins. Sensual by nature, I cut myself off from all sweets of which I was inordinately fond ; and because I was a heavy sleeper and fond of that warm enervating morning doze which made me always late for breakfast, for a whole year I lay on the floor and despised bed as an unrighteous effeminacy. Never cowardly to pain, I taught myself to bear mild torture without wincing—as, when I one day dug out a tooth with my knife as a good exercise of fortitude. Because I once saw myself in the glass with a strange and sudden consciousness of the beauty of my youth and personality, I turned that offending bit of blistered quicksilver to the wall, and for six months never saw my face again. During that time I had to undergo many things from my sisters because of the untidiness of my general appearance; for though I had become scrupulously clean by now, as part of the physical enjoyment of life—clean even to my long brown freckled hands, surely the test-piece of a boy !—I was but a sloven in the decorative part, and never knew the right side from the wrong, and scarcely the

back of things from the front. I gave
away all the ' treasures ' I had accumulated
since my childhood, in imitation of the
Apostles and according to Christ's injunc-
tions to the rich young man; and no one
but myself knew of that little altar which
I had built up in the waste-place behind
the shrubbery, where I used to carry the
first of such fruit as I specially liked, to
lay it thereon as my offering to God—to
wither in the sun or be devoured by insects
and birds. I set myself secret penance for
secret sins. I prayed often and fervently,
and sometimes seemed to be borne away
from the things of time and space and
carried into the very presence of God, as it
were in a trance—a still living Gerontius.
I realized my faith as positively as if it had
been a thing I could see and touch. My
confirmation was a consecration; and when
first I received the communion, I felt as if
I had tabernacled the Lord in my own

body, and that I was henceforth His, so that I could never sin again.

In these days of boyish fervour, had I fallen into the hands of a Roman Catholic I should have become a monk of some severe disciplinary order. My whole inner life was one of intense religious realization. God was far off, the paternal King and inexorable Judge of all, and His 'un-lidded eye' ever watched me with awful attention. This thought was sometimes so oppressive that I used to shrink and cower under the consciousness of being always looked at; when I would cover my face in my hands and say aloud:

'Oh! if I could but be sometimes alone—if I could but hide myself and be able to think as I liked and not be watched nor heard!'

And then I felt that I had spoken blasphemy and committed the unpardonable sin.

My consciousness of Christ was softer. He was my gracious Prince, to obey whom brought the joy of loyal serving. To disobey pained rather than angered Him, and caused Him that ' crucifixion afresh' in which I believed as firmly as I believed in Gethsemane and Golgotha. The angels were my invisible companions, of whom I was not afraid; and I felt the grim presence of the devil at my back and in the corners of the room, as one feels the presence of a murderer in the dark. In a word, I lived in the Christian's sanctified egotism—believing that all the forces of heaven and hell were mainly occupied with the salvation or destruction of my one poor miserable little soul; and that the most important thing between earth and sky was, whether a hot-blooded lad with more sincerity than judgment flew into a rage when he should have curbed his temper, or heroically checked his impulses of sensuality in the matter of jam - pudding and the fruit garden.

But during all this time of my faithful endeavours after a higher life I was just as intolerable to my family as before, and my passions were still my masters. My anger blazed out in the old fierce way at the smallest provocation; and when the blood mounted to my head, then I was again the helot self-degraded I had always been. Heaven was shut against me, and I was spiritually in the Hell I was predestined to eternally inhabit.

I was vehemently penitent when the fit was over, and resolved in my wild way of repentance to bear with Christian patience the next affront put on my sensitive pride. Alas! nature was too strong for me, and my progress in self-control was like nothing so much as the twirling of a squirrel in his cage. For all my efforts to deliver myself, I was up to my neck in the Slough; and my prayers brought

me no more spiritual grace, no more godly
fruitage, than so much water poured out on
sand.   The boiling blood I called on God to
calm boiled ever as madly as before ; and
with all my faith in the Divine presence
and power, I was conscious that I was not
answered.

What agony I went through!   What an
infinite sense of being fated to sin, fore-
doomed to perdition, possessed me, as I felt
that I was left to fight with my wild beasts
unhelped—to struggle to get free, that I
might take refuge in God, and to be hopelessly in the clutch of the devil!   It was as
if some monster held me bodily, while I was
striving to deliver myself that I might
rush into the outstretched, loving arms of
the Saviour opposite.   But that Saviour
waited for me to go to Him.   He did not
and would not help me.   Only those who
have gone through a like period of spiritual
endeavour and frustration can realize my

sufferings at this time, which, I remember, threw an awful kind of light on the myths setting forth the endless labour of Sisyphus and the fruitless work of the Danaïdes in hell.

Clergyman though he was, all this ebullient zeal and youthful extravagance of aspiration annoyed my father as if the translation of faith into practice had been an impiety, and not an effort after godliness. We will grant the clumsiness of the method —still, the effort was always there. Logical Christianity seemed to him a dream as fanatical as it was inconvenient. All that was necessary for our salvation was—to believe the Bible, obey our parents, say our prayers night and morning, go to church regularly, and keep ourselves free from forbidden sins. More than this was to fall on the other side and go over into presumption.

He venerated the saints and martyrs of

past times ; but he maintained that the past was not the present, and that the age of enthusiasm, like that of miracles, had died out. Had persecution been revived, he would have stood firm for his own part, and he would have exhorted others to a like fidelity. But as no more fires in Smithfield would be lighted, at least in our generation, and no one would now call out: ' Christianos ad leones!' he held spiritual assent more valuable than practical imitation, and quiet walking in the cleanly parts of the broad highway better than scaling eccentric heights and shouting ' Excelsior!' from the clouds.

It was useless for me to turn to him for guidance. He repulsed me with coldness, or testily chid me with arrogance, when I carried my difficulties between faith and practice to him. He accused me of presumption in thus questioning the lives of men older, better, wiser than myself—such a mere unformed lad as I was! And ever, with perfect justice and uncompromising logic, he pointed out the inconsistency of my aspirations after superior piety with my acted life of passion and misconduct. My conscience told me he was right when he thus flung me back with the argument 'ad rem.' What had I to do with good or godliness—I, the child of sin, whose very love was a tempest, whose quarrels were volcanic eruptions, whose repentance was a tropical storm, and whose virtues themselves were as unsettling and disturbing as were his faults ? If I could just scrape in by conformity, that was all I need hope for. To attempt more was as irrational as if a lame man who could not walk should try to leap.

The wave of religious revivalism, just beginning to break on the arid shores of ecclesiastical indifference, was to my father a sign of storm and shipwreck, not of healthy movement. He stood apart from both Evangelical enthusiasm and Tractarian authority with equal dislike for each. Through the former, moreover, he had received personal annoyance of a grave kind. During his five years' absence in Kent, his curate, one Mr. Black, had 'awakened' and 'converted' the parish of Eden to a high pitch of evangelical fervour. A schism in the place was the natural consequence. The Evangelicals said that my father had not been a faithful minister of the Word, and that the Gospel had never been preached to them before the advent of Mr. Black ; and the sleepy old souls, who disliked innovations, stood by their kind-hearted vicar who did so much quiet good in the place, though he did not 'pan out' on free will and prevenient grace, baptismal regeneration and faith before works. They scouted the new order as fantastic and extreme ; and thought evening parties, where prayers took the place of the former round games, and expounding recondite doctrines that of the old forfeits, not only monstrously dull but also unseemly.

Their sheet-anchor was Conservatism and keeping things as they were. What had done for their fathers was good enough for them, and ought to be good enough for their children. No improvements, however much they were needed, met with their support. They saw no good in the Sunday-schools, which had been built and were kept up by a rich adherent of the energetic curate; and the 'restoration' of the old church by the same generous hand was an offence to them. Munificence had a hard fight with chronic obstructiveness before it got leave to bestow; and every stone that was laid and every ornament that was added was subjected to hostile criticism and opposition.

Naturally my father was not so backward as this. He recognised the good and beauty of all these changes. The restored church was really magnificent; and the fine organ, with its organist and well-trained choir, was a decided advance on old Adam and his pitch-pipe. The Sunday-school teachers too, kept those unruly children in order; while the low pews, all looking one way, held the congregation together and prevented the sleepy-heads from snoring. But the finer surroundings demanded a more stately method; and in his heart my dear, indolent father, when he came back into residence, regretted the old familiar ways, and felt strange in all this new niceness, where he had to be for ever on parade and always alert and in order. If the glory of God could have been fitly set forth without so much ado, it would have been more pleasing to him. He thought it just a little in excess—as he thought my poor, purblind efforts very greatly in excess.

My father and I, not in harmony on reli-

gious matters, were at issue in politics—
High Tory, according to his age and training, as he was; Republican of the crudest
academic type as was I. We had many
a stormy scene; for I was such an impulsive
fool I could never hold my peace, and when
my mind teemed with thoughts that
knocked at the door of my lips, they had to
come forth, for good or ill.

'I would rather see the devil himself let
loose on the earth than the Radicals get the
upper hand in the country!' my father said
to me one day in a paroxysm of rage, when
I had rashly introduced the subject of the
first Chartist petition, just then presented
to Parliament.

'And I hold all kings and tyrants as
direct emissaries of the devil, and that " Vox
populi, vox Dei,"' was my defiant reply.

For which piece of impertinence my
father called me a puppy and incontinently
knocked me down.

In those days O'Connell was my political
idol ; and I seriously thought of running
away from home to offer myself to him as
the servant and soldier of liberty, good for
any work he might give me to do.   Had not
Godfrey, that best and noblest of us all,
gone to join the Poles in their rise against
Russia ? and was not the freedom of a
country beyond one's own small nationality?
Wherefore, for all my patriotism, I rather
inconsistently longed for the Irish to take
up arms, that I might imitate my brother's
splendid example and fight their tyrants—
ourselves—for their liberties. I thought
Byron's ' Irish Avatar ' the finest bit of
poetry the world had ever seen—run hard,
however, by Campbell's ' Song of the
Greeks ;' and I used to declaim these two
poems with a ferocious energy which made
my sister Ellen call me, in her quiet way,
' a perfect monster '—while Edwin added :
' You are just a maniac, Chris, and ought to
be put into a madhouse.'

If I found in O'Connell my Leonidas, my Brutus, my Tell—any one you like who shall best express the anax andrōn of history and liberty—Sheil was my Demosthenes ; and I used to devour his speeches as if they had been the text of a new Gospel. In the smaller men, of whom our own Liberal county member was the natural chief, I saw the modern representatives of the immortal Three Hundred. The French Revolution was the divine birthday of European liberty —I am not far from the same belief now ! Lafayette, thin and respectable mediocrity that he was, took, in my ardent imagination, heroic proportions and colossal merits ; and I undutifully rejoiced over the discomfiture of my country in the American War of Independence. I believed in Greece and abjured Turkey. I adored Poland and I hated Russia. Joan of Arc, the Maid of Saragossa and Charlotte Corday, were my feminine ideals ; but the old Judaic heroines,

7—2

such as Judith and Jael, were even then abhorrent, and I marvelled much how God could have found them worthy.

I envied the dead of all times and in all places who had known how to die for Liberty ; and I held the apotheosis of humanity to have been reached in Old Greece and Republican Rome. I burned as with fever when I read of old-time tyrannies, and shouted to the skies when they were avenged ;—for the past was as the present to me, and my vivid imagination bridged the gap with the living lines of sympathy. I raged dumbly, or broke out into stormy deprecation when my father, as he often did, read aloud the most pungent bits of the ' Anti-Jacobin ' and I held Canning as no better than Judas Iscariot. All of which means that I was as intolerant as the men whose intolerance I reviled—as arbitrary as the tyrants who had oppressed free thought and slaughtered independent action.

And I tried to indoctrinate Edwin with all this burning hatred of oppression, all this admiration for the assassins of tyrants, all this sympathy with revolt which filled me as with a divine afflatus. But when my proselytism was more noisy and aggressive than usual, he simply shook his fair curly head with his favourite little action of disdain, and told me that I was an ass for my pains—for we were a plain-spoken lot, and did not mince our terms among ourselves. And when I bothered him too much he lost his patience and got annoyed, telling me that I was the most un-endurable nuisance and the biggest idiot going, and that if I did not hold my tongue he would leave the room. Then I stormed at his civic and political indifferentism, which to me was a real crime ; and prob-ably tore out of doors to work off my anger and cherish my sense of isolation by long lonely rambles among the mountains, where

I felt like some exile banished for the sake
of liberty — friendless among men, but
supported by the immortal justice of his
cause.

It was towards the beginning of this
political phase in the 'Sturm und Drang'
period of my life that the Chartist riots
were on hand. With what vague dread and
sympathy combined they filled me ! I was
quite sure that their cause was holy and
that their demands were just ; but the
thought of danger, when brought home to
my own people, froze the blood in my veins
with horror. I might shout 'The Song of
the Greeks' to wind and sky for as long as
I liked, but I had no fancy for seeing the
beaks of our home ravens crimsoned with
the precious blood of friends and family !
Still, if there were to be a general revolution, I used to assure Edwin, I would protect them all. Of course I should join the
insurgents ; but, if the worst came to the

worst, my Brothers the Chartists for my sake would hold harmless all I loved. And they would place an armed guard at our gate, who would require the password from all who came near, and allow no one to enter with evil intent. And we would receive into the rectory all our best friends, and I would be their saviour. For myself, if the royalists won, I would not take my life at their hands at a gift.

I do not think my assurance had a very tranquillizing effect on my brother or my sisters, who somehow, with the illogicality of youth, made me responsible for their terror. How young it all was!

I shall never forget my strange emotion when, one day, we heard the guns over by Carlisle—we were then at Braeghyll, which was at the back of the mountains. We were walking on the high moor which runs into the plain where Carlisle stands. My father said it was the Chartists firing at and being fired on by the soldiers; and he looked grave and anxious, and did not abuse the poor fellows. His kind heart carried it over his political passions, and he was sorry for the men who would have to suffer. And how vividly I too realized the fact of war being within this measurable distance of our home; but oh! how my blood leapt for hope that the cause of Liberty would prevail! But I dared not speak. When my father was in such a mood as to-day, I was awed by loving reverence into silence.

About this time a party of about thirty men one day surged in at the rectory gates, and came up to the house, demanding bread and money. My father chanced to be from home this day; which was as well; for the men were at first inclined to be blustering and rude, and my father's quick temper ' flew ' at insolence as quickly as the seed-vessel of the balsam flies at the touch. He

would have been kind enough to them had
they been respectful; but he would have
braved all consequences had they been
brutal. The sight of my pretty sisters,
however, and of us two young boys,
soon soothed them into a pleasant
frame of mind; and when I went out
boldly among them, and fraternized with
them, joining with them in their general
abuse of all aristocrats and mill-owners,
and talking seditious nonsense with the
best, they grew quite friendly and confidential. One of them justified my former
boasts by assuring me, with an oath, that
when their day came we should have no
cause to be 'afeard.' The rectory should
be marked with white chalk, and not a hair
of our heads should be harmed.

'For thy sake, my brave lad!' said the
speaker, laying his hand on my shoulder
kindly.

So the adventure passed off without more

damage than that which came from a temporary domestic famine. For the men
generously refused to take any money from
such a young, irresponsible set as we were:
' Nay, we isn't rogues!' they said ; and after
their bread and cheese and beer, they left us
with a ringing shout, and ' God bless the
parson's childer!' flung back as their parting
words, when they passed through the gate.

Another time we got into an excited crowd
as we were driving back from Carlisle.
There had been a mass-meeting of the mill-
hands there, and they took my brother Godfrey for Feargus O'Connor. They swarmed
over the carriage in noisy and rather inconvenient enthusiasm, insisting on shaking
hands with us all ; till Godfrey grew angry
with their familiarity to our sisters, and,
knocking one drunken fellow down, drove
off at a smart pace. His ideas of fraternity
did not include grimy paws thrust into
Ellen's pretty hands; and half-drunken oper-

atives claiming us all as their 'mates' was
bringing the ideal down to the vulgar real
with a run—making of Bellerophon carrying
Theseus a cart-horse driven by a satyr.

CHAPTER V.

HOW bitter-sweet life was to me in this forming-time of my character! and how violent the contrast between my mental troubles and the keenness of my physical enjoyments! No one who drew in the sweet breath of flowers or stood against the storm-winds, glad in his youth and rejoicing in his strength, enjoyed the great gift of Life more than I. And no one suffered more. My recollection of all my young life is that of a tempest. I never knew rest, never compassed the outermost circle of serenity. I was always either violently elated or as vio-

lently miserable—always one with the gods
or down among the demons who people hell.
But, full of unrest and turmoil as was the
present, how resolved I was that the brilliancy
of the future should repay me with more
than compound interest! Once give me my
liberty, my majority, and my share of the
small fortune left us by our grandfather, and
let me go into the world for myself, and I
would be happy. I always said to myself:
' I will not be like other men, miserable and
discontented, because failures and weak-
kneed. When I am my own master I will
be happy, because I will conquer fate and
compel fortune; and I will then make friends
who will love and understand me.'

For I would be famous and do great
things. I would cover my name with glory,
and all those who had not believed in me
with confusion ; and my own should be
proud of me. I used to dream of the senior
wranglership at Cambridge and of the

leadership of the House of Commons. I would go to the bar and be Lord Chancellor, or remain a free lance and be Prime Minister. I would make a name; I would be great. Whatever I did I would succeed. And I felt as if I could not fail.

I also felt as if I could not die—as if there were no forces in nature which could destroy that strong vitality, that passionate outstretch and possession by which I knew how the gods of old were framed and fashioned. Belief in immortality is the correlative of strength and youth. It is only when we are old and tired that eternal rest seems possible and unbroken sleep desirable.

At one time I had been undecided whether I would be an artist or an author. I was intensely fond of painting, and ' Anch' io son pittore' was a phrase that had rung in my ears like the sound of a golden bell. It struck a chord which has vibrated ever since in the pride and joy I take in my profession, and I well remember, the first time I walked to the —— office with my first commanded leader in my pocket, I said to myself aloud: 'Anch' io son pittore! I also am one of the leaders of public opinion and the makers of modern thought.' But I was very short-sighted ; and when I thoroughly realized the disadvantages of this defect, I gave up the idea of being a second Raffaele and stuck to that of over-topping Gibbon or Scott instead.

Many things helped on this final decision. I had always had the power of 'telling stories out of my own head,' and I could imagine things so vividly, I was not always sure whether I had seen or only fancied that I had seen them. Fired by the thrilling adventures of my beloved Godfrey, who had returned from Russia and imprisonment when I was about ten years old, I had already begun a novel to be called ' Edith of Poland '—the idea of which had come into my mind during a dull sermon at our parish church of Shorne, when we were in Kent. And was not that a sign by which to steer? A book published by the Christian Knowledge Society, and I think called 'Difficulties of Genius,' had greatly influenced my mind. It had given stability to my hopes, and, as it were, a practicable backbone to my ambition, by the example of others who, as untaught as I, had yet by their own industry and resolve risen to be the shining lights of their generation. Thus directed and encouraged, after long wandering round the outer circle of possibilities, I finally gravitated to the centre, and chose the profession of literature as more within the range of my powers than any form of plastic or pictorial art. And as the most useful preparatory tools were languages, I had devoted myself to the study of tongues, with this graver end more or less consciously underlying the pure delight I felt in the

mere acquirement of words and the ability
to read what else would have been so many
sealed books.

It was about this time that a curious bit
of hallucination came to me. It was All
Halloween, and we of the North still believed in spells and charms. My sisters,
Edwin and I were melting lead, roasting
nuts and wasting eggs—whereby the white
drawn up by the heat of the hand through
water might determine our future—when I
was dared to that supreme trial :—to go upstairs into my bedroom, lock the door, and,
with the candle set on the dressing-table,
deliberately pare and eat an apple, looking at
myself in the glass all the while. I would
in those days have accepted any challenge
offered me—to go into a lion's den, if need
be:—this bit of fantastical bravery was easy
enough! Jauntily and defiantly I bounded
up the stairs, locked the door, pared and
began to eat my apple, with my eyes fixed

on the glass. And there, suddenly out of the semi-darkness—the eyes looking into mine—peered a face from over my shoulder; —a dark, mocking, sinister face which I could draw now as I saw it then—how many years ago! Broad in the low, flat brow, with dark hair waved above the arched eyebrows—the eyes deep-set, dark, and piercing—the nose long and pointed— the thin mouth curled into a sneer—the chin narrow, but the jaw wide—it was all so vivid that I turned sharply round, saying: ' Who is there?'

No one was there, of course ; and I spoke into a void more gruesome than that grim Presence would have been.

The vision did not return, and I ate my apple to the last pip steadily ; but when I went downstairs they all laughed and said I was as white as if I had seen a ghost ; and they were sure I had ; and what was it like ?

' The devil,' I said gruffly ; on which Ellen said mildly :

' Upon my word, Chris, you are more like a bear than a boy.'

Long after this I had in my ears the sound of rushing wings. They were so loud that I used to wake from my sleep with the noise as of large wings about my bed. And with these were mingled whisperings and voices ; but no intelligible words ever came to me ; though I made no doubt they were the same voices as those which haunted Christian when passing through the Valley of the Shadow. I was studying very hard at this time, and in the full swing of all my private penances and eccentric self-discipline ; and my nervous system was for the moment strained, despite my powerful constitution.

Our lives at Eden, whither we had finally returned, were not remarkable for variety. There was little incidental amusement for

us, and we had to make our own pleasures
in the best way we could. On the whole
we managed pretty well, and never knew
the want of artificial aids. Boating in
summer; skating in winter; riding; long
mountain rambles and more distant excursions; picnics in the daytime and 'tea-
parties' in the evening, helped to make our
young existence glad and to redeem the
monotony of the hours. And as time went
on, and the new influx of life and motion
through railroads and the penny post
stirred even our stagnant little stretch of
backwater, we became more like the rest of
the world. But we lost in individuality
what we gained in catholicity. No longer
great ladies, like the Duchess of St. Albans,
travelling post with multiplied precautions,
sent up a message, which was a command,
requesting my father to go down and spend
the evening with them at the hotel. This
was to do honour to the cloth, while avoid-

ing the tedium of a lonely three hours after dinner.

No longer distinguished strangers from afar, unendorsed, came among us as superior beings to whom the whole community was cap-in-hand. On the contrary, we were taken up by men of authentic name and acknowledged light and leading, and we became vastly more critical and less credulous than we had been. Knit up into closer communion with the larger world outside—for we had now daily coaches and a railway-station not more than twenty miles away—we were less the countrified 'hoodie-crows' we had been; and Eden became one of the favourite show-places of the kingdom, and as luxurious and polished as the rest.

The most important to us of the 'strangers,' as the summer visitors were generally called, were the reading-parties —the collegians—who came down for the

Long, sometimes to vagabondize and get
into mischief, and set the place in a flame
by reason of their rowdyism—*e.g.*, by those
hot 'coppers' flung to the rabble of small
boys in the street on Sunday, when the
decent folk were coming home from morning
church—and sometimes to read hard and
walk mightily, according to their traditional
intention. We used to get acquainted with
them through the tutors, who generally
managed to know my father ; and we found
them delightful variations to the main
theme of our existence. My sisters had
their love-affairs which began with roses
and ended with thorns ; and we boys had a
glimpse of other lines of thought which did
us infinite good. But the circumstances
which most influenced my own life at this
time were the creation of a new ecclesiastical district taken off the old parish
and the strange influence which certain
books and stories had over my thoughts.

The incumbent of this new district of
St. Mark's, Henry Grahame, was a man of
wide cultivation of mind and great sweetness of manner. He was essentially a
Coleridgean, able to reconcile Faith with
Reason by the higher way of the Understanding, just as now certain of the Broad
Church reconcile Genesis and Darwin by
the elastic theory of Development. He was
a 'made,' as opposed to an instinctive and
natural man; one who held art to be superior
to nature, and the intellect a greater thing
than emotion. Of the ancients, Plato—of
the moderns, Goethe and Coleridge—were his
'dii majores;' and the schools of Sappho and
Pindar, Schiller and Byron, he abhorred.
My first introduction to Coleridge was
through him, and he made me also read
Wordsworth and Carlyle. For himself, he
was eminently eclectic. What he could not
receive—as, for instance, following his friend
and teacher, Maurice, the doctrine of eternal

punishment and the personality of the devil
—he rejected as mistranslations of meaning
and the misdirection of mediæval ignorance.
Other doctrinal difficulties he accepted, as I
said, by that Understanding which Coleridge makes our spiritual Universal Expositor.

Satisfied as he was with his own interpretation, it was perhaps natural that he
should be intolerant to the mistakes of
others. He was serenely confident that he
knew. Those who differed from him were
therefore ignorant. And ignorance is not
a state that demands respect—pity, if you
will, and enlightenment, but not respect.
Thus, those whom he undertook to teach
were bound to be humble and obedient, as
their first step towards true knowledge.
They must accept without cavil such
dogmas as he offered them. He who
knew, and they who were dark and dense
—what else could be demanded but hu-

mility and obedience when he gave them
the living truth ?

Liberal as he was, in reference to the
ecclesiastical section to which he belonged,
Henry Grahame was like all other unscientific men who believe in spiritual enlightenment, void of proof. Personal conviction
stood with him for so much tangible and
ponderable reality ; and that mental state to
which he had attained was therefore the
absolute norm for others. He could not
tolerate divergence ; for all divergence
meant to him error, and error was Apollyon.
Humane, gentle, loving by temperament,
this consciousness of culture superior to the
mass, and of the secure possession of Truth,
made him intellectually both exclusive and
scornful. He was a moral Brahmin who
drew away his skirts from the Pariah. He
despised the common run of men and minds,
and looked on the majority as his inferiors,
thinking humanity but a poor job at the

best. To be sure, Christ had died for men of all degrees—the Gurths and Wambas as well as the Platos and Aristotles of the Christian world ; but Henry Grahame put aside the inferential respect which it would seem but consistent for Christians to have for the creatures who once produced their God ; and, standing on the heights of his own intellectual Pisgah, judged calmly, but condemned inexorably, all who were inferior to or different from himself. He reverenced only culture, and despised ignorance as much as he shrank from vice and ugliness.

His wife was a woman of like mind to himself ; but also, sweet and good as she was, with a little more artificial stillness of manner, and a little more conscious effort after grace. She had been born and bred a Unitarian, but had now come into the Church ; and the effects of her early training, in its chilly æstheticism and self-subdued purity, still clung to her. Both showed that

they felt themselves here, among us un-
awakened and unæsthetic creatures, like
Crishnas among the cowherds. They were
of another order of intelligence, another
school of thought altogether ; and their
sense of mental isolation was manifest.

They did not like my father, nor did he
like them. They found him arid, unenlightened, fossilized—a leafless stick in a
stagnant pool. He found them unsound,
fanciful, unreal—painted sparrows passing
for birds of price. There was very little
intercourse between them and him ; and
soon the new incumbency became as completely differentiated from the old parish, as
is the frog from the tadpole. Thoughts,
doctrines, modes and hours of conducting
the service, all were different ; and though
St. Mark's created no schism among us, it
made a complete division between the old
and the new. Meanwhile both Mr. and Mrs.
Grahame were very kind to us young

people ; and especially so to me, whose turbulent nature and now troubled thoughts they set themselves to calm and guide.

They also introduced us to some notable people. I remember once meeting Mr. Carus at their house, and how frankly shocked I was by the joyous, buoyant tone and manner with which he announced that he had just left the death-bed of his dearest friend.

' I was so glad to know that he was with Jesus ! It was one of the happiest days of my life to feel that he was safe in the arms of the Saviour !' he said, a smile of supreme satisfaction beaming over his face.

I was too instinctive to understand this queer pleasure, which seemed to me both false and strained; and I felt a disgust for the man I never got over.

Another notability met at the parsonage was Whewell. This was when my faith had begun to fall away at the base; and

I see still the satirical smile with which he accompanied this coda of a long speech setting forth the necessity of faith in the unprovable :

' " Sceptic and septic "—there is only the difference of one letter between them.'

Also I saw Carlyle, at the house of our dear local chieftain, spoken of before. I had then begun a classical romance—my most important book; for I am antedating in these fragmentary recollections; and Carlyle thundered in his deep bass against the foolishness of going back on the past and writing about trouserless heathens, when so much work was lying to be done in the present for honest Christians—and how young fellows who maundered about bull-god Apis, or Pericles and his Impropriety-Aspasia, had better be set to break stones by the road-side—which at least was useful for the mending of the highway we all had to travel on.

Another of my almost friends at this time was poor Hartley Coleridge. I say mine —for all that I was but a unit, a fraction, in the family sum—because he distinguished me from among the others with special attention, and talked to me more than to the rest. He had the habit of gathering piles of books under his arms, walking about the room while he declaimed on all things under heaven, or read aloud as he went. His reading was charming. He had the Coleridgean sweetness and rotundity of voice, and read with perfect grace—not too theatrically, and without affectation; in both of which snares his brother Derwent ran his feet and tripped—but with just enough artificiality to make it art, and lift it from commonplace into beauty.

Because of his besetting sin he could never be kept long on a visit anywhere; and his comings and goings were therefore always cometic and unsatisfactory. But I like to remember him and to picture him at his best, and as he always was whenever I saw him; for I loved him with a strange pride in his special notice of me and his evident affection for me, unformed, uncouth hobbledehoy as I was then. He and the Grahames were the first persons who distinguished me by their special attention, and who thus brought a certain sense of light and companionship into the dim and lonely chamber in which my soul had hitherto lived.

Now I must go back to the main thread of my story, and to the troubled perplexity of my thoughts.

CHAPTER VI.

I WILL give, so far as I can, the genesis of my first change in speculative thought.

Undirected in my studies and unhelped in my thoughts, I read where I listed and came to such conclusions as seemed good to me. In the superstitious and pre-scientific period of life, when marvels are accepted as of the established order of things, I was inclined to the mysterious and the weird at all four corners of my being. Thus, I believed in magic of a stately and learned kind; in alchemy and astrology; in the Rosicrucians and second-sight; in fortune-telling, magic crystals, and the Egyptian boy's power of seeing the past and future in a few drops of ink held in the hollow of the hand; in mesmerism, ghosts and spiritual visitations generally; but by some good luck of latent common-sense I did not believe in vulgar witchcraft, though I did in the Witch of Endor. But then, she was not vulgar; and she was in the Bible. The supernatural powers of such men as Cornelius Agrippa and Albertus Magnus I took to be undeniable. The charmed circle surrounded by smoke wherein the demons appeared to (I think) Benvenuto Cellini, was a fact; and I had no doubt but that Surrey did see Geraldine in the magic mirror. The Indian jugglers, of whom my eldest sister sent home such thrilling accounts, were evidently mighty magicians; and he who had the courage could, if he would, conjure up the devil even to this day. I remember how greedily I devoured, and half-ashamedly, half-defiantly, believed in the notes to Sir Walter Scott's works, telling of the wonders that had been. Gilpin Horner the goblin, crying : ' Tint, tint !' and Thomas of Ercildoune, who lived with the fairy queen and was sent for by her again when his time had come ; the ' Book of Might ' and its strange glamour ; the magic potency of that shadowy Virgilius whom I could never reconcile with the more solid humanity of the Virgil who wrote the ' Eclogues ;' the egg on which Naples is built ; the naked child running three times round the barrel ; the Mauthe Doog ; Sir Kenelm Digby's sympathetic ointment ; the Irish banshee and the Scottish seer—all were cherished faiths with me ; while the historical mysteries of the Vehmgericht and the secret worship of Bafomet seemed to put a backbone into the more purely imaginary qualities of the rest.

Other things of an unprovable nature also troubled my imagination. I was intensely fond of mythology, in which ˌI saw neither the sun nor the dawn, nor yet the ark, but simply the divine and the human.

How dear that little idyl of Philemon and Baucis was to me ! Its simplicity and realism made it almost Scriptural ; and though I did not dare to bracket it with the visit of those three divine beings to Abraham and Sara, still, I thought the one account as true as the other. No poem ever written equalled in my eyes the loveliness of that sweet picture where Endymion lies asleep on the heights of Mount Ida, and the virgin goddess leans over him lovingly ; and the majesty of Minerva was equalled only by the beauty of Apollo. Aurora and her dappled steeds surrounded by the Hours casting flowers as they fly ; rash Icarus and rasher Phaethon ; the deluge of Deucalion and the dragon's teeth which Cadmus sowed—they were all products of the border-land lying between romance and reality, and I was never quite sure of the line of division.

The stories also of the Greek maidens who met the Gods among the reeds, in the court of the temple, in the woods, gave me cause for much crude speculation. Like our own sacred mystery of how the Sons of God came down and loved the daughters of men, they woke up in me incessant wonder at the difference between those old times and the present day, and made me ask myself : ' Where are the Sons of God now ?' and with more faith than critical faculty : ' Why should not be again that which has already been ?' I remember when I first read Byron's ' Heaven and Earth,' how the characters of Anah and Aholibamah, and the superhuman yet manlike beauty of Samiasa and Azaziel struck me with living

force, and coloured my dreams for many
nights. But the story which impressed
me most was that wild and weird account
of Gilli-Doir-Magrevollich, the Black Child,
Son to the Bones, found in the notes to the
' Lady of the Lake.'

I cannot say why this strange unwholesome legend took such hold of me.
Perhaps because it was unwholesome. I
could not shake myself clear from it ; and I
had a haunting kind of prevision that more
hung on it than its own superstitious
fancy. I had just heard, too, of Joanna
Southcote ; and altogether my mind was,
as it were, fascinated by this subject of
virgin births — their possibility now as
their certainty in times past — and by
the whole range, indeed, of divine interposition in the works and ways of
man—whether it were in the assumption
of the human form or in the gift of
prophetic insight, or inversely in the

darker mysteries of magic and the power of conjuring up the devil. This was a different thing from belief in spiritual communion. It was what one may call the materialistic form of supernaturalism— belief in which belongs to all unscientific and uncultured minds, and the abandonment of which is the first step outward towards enlightenment.

One early summer's day, I was sitting where I had no business to be, under the hedge of the as yet unmown hayfield at the foot of the garden. I had taken with me to read in quietness, Ovid's 'Metamorphoses.' If my father had seen it in my hands he would have forbidden it to me ; which was why I went where I was not likely to be found even if looked for. I was digging away at the myth of Nisus and Scylla, and the purple lock wherein the old king's strength lay, when, for the first time, I was struck by the likeness of this story to that

of Samson and Delilah. Hitherto all the
Bible stories had been on a raised platform
apart, and there was no analogy with
them to be found elsewhere. I knew my
Ovid pretty well by now; and immediately, on the discovery of this point of
resemblance, there flashed across me also
the likeness between the story of Myrrha
and that of Lot's daughters—of Iphigenia
and Isaac for the one part, in the substitution of a doe for the one, of a ram for the
other; and of Iphigenia and Jephthah's
daughter for the other, where the human
element is alone retained. With this my
mind went off on the now familiar track of
the virgin births, when suddenly—in that
strangely rapid and vivid manner in which
such things come to me, as if it were really
the quick opening of a closed door and the
headlong rush into a newly-furnished and
brilliantly - lighted chamber—there shot
through my brain these words which

seemed to run along the page in a line of light : ' What difference is there between any of these stories and those like to them in the Bible ?—between the loves of the Sons of God for the daughters of men, and those of the gods of Greece for the girls of Athens and Sparta ?—between the women made mothers by mysterious influences, and those made mothers by divine favour ?— between the legends of old times and the stories of Sara, Hannah, Elizabeth,—and the Virgin Mary ?

When this last name came, a terrible faintness took hold of me. The perspiration streamed over my face like rain, and I trembled like a frightened horse. My heart, which for a few seconds had beaten like a hammer, now seemed to cease altogether. The light grew dim ; the earth was vapoury and unstable ; and, overpowered by an awful dread, I fell back among the long grass where I was sitting as if I had been struck

down by an unseen hand. But this physical
faintness soon passed, and my mind went
on following the line of thought I had begun,
as if I were talking aloud to some one at
hand.

'No one at the time knew anything about
the miraculous conception of Mary's child.
Joseph himself was only warned in a dream
not to doubt her, for that she was with child
by the Holy Ghost, as announced to her by
the Angel Gabriel. Does any one know
more now than was known then ? If this
Christian marvel is true, why not all the
rest ? Why should we say that Mary alone
spoke the truth and that every one else has
lied ? But spirits do not come to women ;
there were no such beings as those old
gods who were said to have come down
from Olympus to mingle in the affairs of
mortals ; that passage in Genesis about
the Sons of God is a mystery we cannot
fathom. And we know that there is such

a being as the Angel Gabriel—such a Divine person as the Holy Ghost. Do we know this ? Have we more certainty than had the old Greeks when they believed in the power of Jupiter and the divine manhood of Apollo, and in the celestial origin of those fatherless sons brought into the world by maiden mothers, who swore to their womanly innocence for the one part and their human exaltation by divine favour for the other ? Surely yes ! The Miraculous Incarnation has been affirmed by all the churches ; and the proofs are—the star which guided the Magi, and the song of the angels in the sky to the shepherds watching their flocks. But who can certify to these proofs ? Why did not others see that star as well as the Magi ?—and who knows whether the shepherds heard the song, or only imagined it?'

These thoughts clung to and left me no peace night nor day. Ever and ever the Mystery of the Incarnation became more and

more a subject of perplexity and doubt, and
of dread lest that doubt should broaden
into denial. Brought into line with these
legends of former times—contrasted with
the old classic myths and the stories in the
very Bible itself—it suddenly seemed to lose
its special character and to be merely one like
others. It was no longer exceptional and
divine—it had become historic and human.
Therefore, it fell within the range of criticism and might be judged of according to
its merits and the weight of evidence at its
back. What was that weight ? Outside
its own assertion—absolutely nil. No con-
temporaneous testimony vouched for the
story of the Virgin Birth—for the Annuncia-
tion of the Angel Gabriel—for the Star or
the Song ; and Mary herself alone knew the
truth of things. All therefore rested on
her word only. Sweet, beautiful and pure
as was her personality—Godlike as was that
Christ she bore—was that word of more

intrinsic value than that of the Greek girl who told how she had met the god in the reeds by the river side ?—or than that of the nameless mother of the Black Child, Son to the Bones, denying human knowledge and accusing the unseen ? Was it ? Had there been more miraculous births than one ?—or no miraculous birth at all, and the laws of nature interrupted for no one— for one no more than for another ?

While my mind was torn and tossed by these terrible questions, I was one night looking at the stars from my bedroom-window, wondering at the mystery and glory of creation and speculating on our relations with the universe—when again in that same sudden way these words came to me as distinctly as if I were reading them in a printed page:

' Has God in very truth ever become man ? We, the inhabitants of only one out of such countless millions of worlds—our world of a lower order of cosmic splendour than so many, and ourselves of conscious mental deficiency—why were we singled out for such a transcendent act of mercy? Why should God have cared so much for us, vile and troublesome as we have always been? Was it true? Has the great Incommunicable First Cause ever clothed Himself with flesh—born, living, suffering, dying as a mortal man, and all the time very God?'

Then, as vividly as if I had seen Him in the body and spoken with Him face to face, I saw Christ as a peasant translated to our own time. I realized the minutest circumstances of His humanity; when a loud voice, like the rushing wind, seemed to echo from earth to sky—to fill all space and to command all time, till I was conscious of nothing but these words: ' Man—not God ; man—not God!'

The voice was so loud, the words were so clear, I wondered the whole house did not

wake to listen. And how bright the stars
were! Each star grew to be like a sun
which changed the darkness of the night to
almost overpowering glory; and I seemed
to hear the weaving of the great web and to
understand the complexity, but the unity,
the universality, the rush and pressure and
stream of life—everywhere life, even as
here!

Why did they not all hear and see as I
did ? But no one moved. I turned to
look at Edwin. He was tranquilly asleep
in bed at the other end of the room—a
beautiful child rather than a youth of nineteen—innocent, troubled by spiritual doubts
no more than his favourite cat which was
curled up on the pillow beside him, and
desiring to learn no more of the great
mysteries than he had been taught in his
childhood. No! he saw and heard nothing.
The voice and the glory and the great
weaving of the web of life did not exist

for him. It was only I who heard and saw and knew.

But now, coming up from the study, over which our bedroom immediately was, my father's voice broke out in prayer; of which I heard these words: 'O Thou, who came into the world to save sinners, have mercy on me!'

Then all my exaltation passed, and I was once more alone in the dimness of the starry night—alone, in the dark, and ignorant.

I flung myself on my knees and asked pardon of Him whom I had crucified afresh by my doubts—longing only to die and to have done with all this ignorance—longing to die, that I might then Know and sin no more.

The light under the door betrayed me. My father, passing along the passage, saw it and came in—to find me in this state of spiritual anguish and contrition.

When he asked why I was not in bed? and what ailed me? I could not confess to him.   I knew of old how unsympathetic he was with this part of my life; and my wound was too sacred to lay bare to eyes which could not understand and would probably rasp it afresh.

My silence, which looked like sullenness, angered him.

'Why was I ever cursed with such a son!' he said vehemently.   'Look at your brother there—why cannot you be like him —a reasonable creature who gives no trouble to anyone?   Why are you so foolish, so irritating?   Not Job himself could have patience with you, Christopher!'

He went up to Edwin's bed, leaned over him and kissed him fondly; and my brother, roused by the light and the action, opened his eyes and smiled, putting up his hand to our father's face with the caressing gesture of a child.

I was too much moved to resent or defy, as I should have done in my ordinary mood. I only longed to receive the same love as that which was given to others—to be included—to be taken out of the solitude and banishment in which I lived.

'Kiss me, too!' I said, holding out my hands. 'Father, dear! kiss me too!'

'No,' he said coldly ; 'I cannot kiss you, for I neither believe in you nor respect you.'

So there it was again!—the old bitter contrast—Esau and Jacob; Ishmael and Isaac ; Cain and Abel ; and the poor goat, laden with sins, sent into the wilderness, while the sheep fed about the Master's feet and the lambs were carried in His bosom!

For all this I could not stop my thoughts. They came as of their own will, and I was forced to listen to them.

Bracketed with the more human difficulty

of the Divine Incarnation came one yet more
mysterious.   Christ, to whom we pray
under the name and form of, and as actuated
to pity by His experience as, a man—was
He always Jesus Christ—the Divine Man
from all eternity ?   Was then the Godhead always tripartite ?   The Jews were
taught the unity of the Divine Essence in
the one supreme Jehovah, and knew nothing
of this division.   When did it come about ?
—when Mary conceived ?   Did that which
had been from the beginning take a new
form at a moment of time ?—and was
heaven, in point of fact, acted on by earth,
and God determined by humanity ?   If not,
why then was Christ hidden so long behind
the overwhelming personality of the Father?
—His very name and being concealed until
He had taken the form of man ?   Was He
powerless till then ? and did God, the great
Spirit, need to become flesh before He
could save flesh ?   Was the Athanasian

Creed wrong, and were the Persons unequal?

Again, was the grace which lies in Christ Jesus, the crucified Saviour, dormant for all these countless generations? But why? Why should not the world have been redeemed before? There was no manifest historic reason why that special moment should have been chosen; and for the worth of the men saved—surely Plato and Aristotle, Socrates and Aristides, Buddha, Confucius, Marcus Aurelius—and how many more!—were as worthy of redemption from the eternal doom meted out to ignorance as those nameless lepers and minor disciples who had neither commanding intellect nor enduring influence!

I carried my troubles to Mr. Grahame, and he set himself to resolve them. He took the last first, but refused to admit that this was a subject which fell within the range of discussion.

10—2

'The reason for that moment When is hidden with Christ in God. Why, Wherefore, How, and the need which God in Christ has of the love of man, are of the mysteries whereof no man knoweth,' he said reverently 'It is a waste of time, and the encouragement of spiritual presumption, to speculate on them.'

'Would you have said that to a Greek wanting to know why Chronos devoured his own children ?' I asked.

'The cases are not parallel,' he answered.

'Parallel in so far that we are the children of God, and He let us be lost for all eternity because He delayed His salvation,' I answered. 'The only difference is that which lies between the active and the passive.'

'Things which are beyond reason are beyond dialectics,' he returned. 'We have to deal with completed facts, not with energizing causes nor yet with reasons why. The fact of the Miraculous Conception is all that concerns us.'

'How do we know that it is a fact?' I asked; and again went over my roll-call of analogies.

'To compare the Divine Child and His Mother to the absurd legends of a rude people in a rude age, when the most monstrous myths were accepted without examination, and the laws neither of nature nor of evidence were understood, or to the patent falsehoods of a few unfortunate girls!' said Mr. Grahame with gentle contempt. 'Have you so little sense of proportion—beauty—verisimilitude? But we need not go farther on this line. It pains and revolts me. So far then, I take it that the ground is clear. The Mystery of the Trinity is beyond our comprehension; the virgin mothers of men are myths; but the Incarnation of the Divine in Jesus of Nazareth stands four-square to all the winds of doctrine. It is the one Great Fact on which humanity can rely and by which it is saved.'

'Why this more than those others?' I asked. 'To assert is not to prove—is it?' I added hurriedly, a little frightened by my own audacity in standing up against one so infinitely my superior.

He was sweet and gentle and mild.

'By its own internal evidence,' he said. 'I disregard the external, about which you trouble yourself so much, and take my stand on the character and life of Christ alone ; and on the results of Christianity in history. We want nothing more to prove the divine origin of our faith. Such a being as Jesus of Nazareth must have been divine, seeing how far He was beyond humanity, both in His life and teaching. And the work which Christianity has done in the world could only have come through a God-given revelation. I ask you to look at nothing else but the life of our Lord, and the influence of Christianity on society.'

'Yet Buddha's life was pure and holy, and Mohammed redeemed the Arabs from gross idolatry to the spiritual worship of the One God,' I said.

'And Buddha and Mohammed were both divinely inspired and divinely led,' was his reply. 'Rivers are fed by many streams, and the river of righteousness with the rest. Buddha, Mohammed, Luther, Cromwell, Savonarola, Galileo, Newton—all the great men who have taught great truths of any kind, have had their portion of inspiration, the perfect fulness of which is found only in our Lord. The instruments of God are many—the melody from each is the same—and the Hand which masters all is the Only One. Study the character of Christ. Trace the influence of His teaching on the morality, the history, of mankind, and then you will realize for yourself the

Divinity which needs no circumstantial evidence to substantiate it.'

This argument did not satisfy me for long. At first I thought I had found in its deeper insight and wider outlines the resolution of all my difficulties and a sure harbour of glad refuge. But after a time I slipped back into my painful groove of doubt, and, with doubt, of despair.

There were certain things in the character and doings of Christ—beautiful as was the one, benign and loving as were the others —which seemed to me simply and purely human : as, His wholesale denunciations of the Pharisees and Sadducees; His cursing the fig-tree for its natural and normal barrenness ; His sending the devils into a herd of swine, so that the innocent brutes were all drowned, while the devils were presumably not damaged, being of the nature of immortal spirits ; and a few more of those elementary difficulties over which all inquirers stumble. And as for the effects of Christianity on society—divorced from civilization, surely these have been more disastrous than beneficent! Religious zeal has only added another and still more pungent ingredient to the fierce compound of the natural man, by adding fanaticism to cruelty. It has made of a peaceful paradise a reeking hell in South America; devastated the Low Countries; set Catholics to shoot down Huguenots, Episcopalians to massacre Covenanters, and all dominant sects to destroy all nascent ones; it has deluged the earth with blood wherever the Cross has been raised and the Beatitudes have been preached in the name of the Prince of Peace and the God of Love.

And then the popes and bishops, the cardinals and abbots, the Roderick Borgias and Balfours of Burley—men who have wallowed in sensuality or waded through blood—where was the Sign of the Lamb on them ? Were popes like Hildebrand and Innocent III. true Vicars of Christ ? Was Thomas à Becket or was Wolsey a fit successor to the sweet St. John or the humble-minded St. Andrew ? And was our own prelatic Church, with its worldly wealth, political influence and social dignity, the same Church as that which the Twelve Apostles planted when they went forth without scrip or purse to preach the poverty they practised ? ' Le grand sansculotte !' Was my grandfather, the Bishop, a Christian after the Archetype? Indeed, were any of us who lived daintily and fared sumptuously, while our brothers wept and starved, Christians such as Christ would own ?

I said all this in my headlong way, vehement in manner, crude in method. And to Mr. Grahame I must have seemed as unphilosophic as the chalk scrawl on a barn-door would have been inartistic to Etty or Maclise. I had no logical method ; no reserve force ;

no critical discrimination of values. I flung my bricks on the ground without order or constructive endeavour, unskilfully, rudely, where he pieced his mosaic bit by bit and line by line, till the pavement was smooth, compact and without a flaw.

Still, he was very kind to me, and let me talk myself out; sitting with his eyes half-closed, his white hands touching each other by the finger-tips, and a serene smile just lighting the curved corner of his bland mouth ; while I, heated, excited, my rough hair tossed and tumbled, my lank face crimson with emotion, stood before him pouring out my fiery thoughts like lava that scorches as it flows.

Yes, he was very kind. For a fastidious scholar as he was, to whom method was as valuable as matter ; for a philosopher who had overcome all dialectic difficulties and supplemented the darkness of Reason by the light of Understanding ; for a theoso-

phist, sure that he knew the mind of God,
and could map out, as it were a chart, the
whole plan and order of divine dealing with
man through Christ and the Church ; for
an intellectual master where I was but a
hodman, he was marvellously patient.   It
fills me with wonder now, when I remember
how long-suffering he was, as I can measure
the provocation I must have given him both
by my want of scholarly finish and by my
intractability.   For neither his eclecticism,
urging me to put aside as non-essential
all those points which troubled me, nor
Maurice's books which he lent me, removed
the doubts by which I was harassed.   And
the internal evidence on which he dwelt so
much was no more convincing than the
external.

And now another thought came to me.
Like the running loops of a chain, whereof
the first has broken, my doubts were multi-
plying and these unanswerable questions

were increasing. This was my new difficulty : If Christ were God—that is, Omniscient as well as Omnipotent—why did
He not teach things that could be tested
by man and proved by experiment, rather
than those which are assertions only ?
Why, for instance, instead of telling us
about Lazarus in heaven, leaning on Abraham's bosom and separated by a great gulf
from Dives in hell, did He not give us a
form of political government whereby men
might have been made happy, with equal
justice to all ? Why did He not tell us
that the earth is not the centre of our
system, and that our system itself is not
the all-important part of creation we have
imagined it to be ? Galileo would not then
have been subjected to the Inquisition, and
Giordano Bruno would not have been
burned. Why did He not tell us about
electricity and steam ; and reveal the law of
gravitation and that of optics and of

dynamics; and show us at least the way to the great chemical discoveries that have since been made? How many crimes would have been prevented, and how many falsehoods would never have been believed, if He had!

To say that man has to find these things out for himself, and that to reveal would be to destroy endeavour, seemed to me but a weak argument. For, at the best, only one man finds out, while all the world—after they have persecuted him and perhaps put him to death as a blasphemer—quietly accept his discovery without any endeavour at all. And was it worth while to leave the whole human race in ignorance, that Copernicus should centralize the sun or Newton formulate the law of gravitation, when Christ could have done both? Surely, in view of a Divine Teacher who might have told us in one moment of time what it has taken so many generations to learn, the argument for the necessity of search—which only means isolated teachers and delayed discoveries — is an excuse rather than an argument! And, on the plea of help to the race to be saved—is not intellectual truth as necessary for the right-mindedness of a man as the spiritual is for the salvation of his soul?

I said all this to Mr. Grahame—each question a doubt—but his answer was:

'All this is immaterial. Christ came to teach us only spiritual truth; His kingdom is not of this world.'

And I was to him as dense-witted as a buffalo, when I answered as before:

'But the spiritual life is not divorced from the intellectual. The crimes committed by superstition and ignorance—witness the crime of witchcraft—might have been prevented by a little timely enlightenment. Would not that have been more to our good than telling us about the turning of the moon into blood, and the falling of

the stars from the sky ? Yet the very
Apostles themselves believed in witchcraft,
and their words gave an impetus to the
terrible persecution which disgraced our
humanity and only proved our hideous
ignorance.'

I did not say this with irreverence.
It was simply because the present and
material good of man seemed to me more
important than something to happen in the
far-off, undated future. And also because I
was beginning to think that the Teacher
was not divinely omniscient, and knew no
more than His epoch.

One day the fragmentary benevolence of
the miracle of healing wrought on the blind
man suddenly struck me with a sense of incompleteness and partiality—and therefore
not as divine, but purely human. By my
reading I knew that ophthalmia is, and always
has been, one of the physical curses of the
East ; and: ' Surely,' I thought, ' it would

have been more like the act of an impartially
benevolent Deity, had Christ taught how this
evil might have been removed for all time,
rather than simply opening the eyes of this
one man. Why did He cure only that
one ? To set forth His power by a miracle,
and thus compel the halting faith of those
who would not receive Him ? Would not
a universal remedy have done that as well
as this one event only, besides benefiting
the whole human race ?'

Reminded that I, a young creature with
a finite intellect—and even what I had of
intelligence neither well-trained nor well-
developed—had no right to question the
modus operandi of Divinity, I could only
answer by my one cuckoo-note of evidence :

' This modus operandi has been manifested
to us by human media. We therefore have
the right to examine into the credentials of
these media—and part of these credentials

lies in the moral harmony of the account. If things are said of God which shock our own conceptions of justice and generosity, we are not blasphemous in refusing to believe that they are true.'

Reminded again that some of the greatest minds and acutest intellects have believed implicitly both the Old Testament and the New, I answered, as others have answered before me :

' What men have believed is no measure of external truth, however great the individual intellect. Plato and Socrates believed in the Gods of Olympus—would you support yourself on their authority?'

' In the confession of the Divine Life within man ?—Yes,' he said.

' No ; in the special manifestation,' I answered ; ' in the then mystery of the armed Minerva springing from the head of her father, Jove—in the unborn Bacchus carried about in the great God's thigh.'

'Your parallels, my dear boy, never run on all fours,' said Mr. Grahame mildly.

'Why not these manifestations of divine power as well as our own ?' I asked.

'The world has settled that long ago,' he answered.

'So perhaps, the world of the future will settle our questions,' I said. 'In their day the doubters of Jupiter and Bacchus and the whole hierarchy of Mount Olympus were held as infidels and treated as criminals.'

'And justly ; if they had no better faith to put in the place of the old!' he flashed out quickly.

'We must destroy before we can rebuild,' I said.

'Meanwhile the unhoused souls starve,' was his reply. 'Man must have a faith— that is incontestable ; and no man has a right to destroy before providing a sub- stitute. Your substitute for the Chris-

tianity you would uproot ?—the living affirmation in place of your death of negation ?'

' Monotheism,' I answered.

He did not answer for a moment.   Then
he said :

' But Unitarianism—which is our modern
Monotheism — confesses the divine life in
man.'

' Inspiration—not incorporate Godhead,'
I replied.

' We must judge by the Understanding,'
he said.   ' The Hidden Wisdom is felt, not
demonstrated.   You have it, or you have it
not.   You cannot argue about it as you
might argue about a philosophic theorem or
a painted picture.   It is a thing which the
Best have agreed to accept as final and
fixed.'

' No question can be called final, Mr.
Grahame, while there are dissidents and
doubters.   We do not deny that two and
two make four, nor do we question the laws

of gravitation. While two opinions exist on a subject it cannot be called proved—granting these two opinions to be held by men of the same calibre of intellect and the same degree of education.'

When I said this, Mr. Grahame, smiling softly, first shut his eyes, and then opening them full in my face, asked mildly, as if seriously demanding information :

'My dear boy, are you one of those men of intellect and education qualified to judge for yourself on these abstruse points, and to argue with me ?'

'No,' I said, 'not if I stood alone. But others think as I do. It is a question of schools, not individuals.'

'There have always been schools,' he answered, still smiling. 'One of these schools once believed in Simon Magus ; one gave glory to Cagliostro ; and one denied the Copernican theory.'

'That was the Church,' I said, yielding to the temptation.

'Of Rome ? Yes. That was the Church of Rome,' was his calm reply.

'But Rome is Christian,' I said.

'And Sir Matthew Hale was a Christian, too. Christianity has never assumed to include scientific illumination.'

'No ; and that is just my point,' I said. 'If it had ! If it had given us a test by which we could judge of the unknown by the proved !'

'In which case there would have been no room for faith. And without faith there is no religion.'

'Is there no religion is heaven, where we are to know even as we are known ?' I returned. 'The ultimate of religious enlightenment precludes the necessity of faith according to the conditions of our state.'

'Precisely. Then we shall have know-

ledge, which is the fruition of faith,' he
answered, with a certain kind of compassionate disdain for my ignorance. 'It is the
seed and the flower—the root and the tree;
the one cannot exist without the other.
Here we have faith and the higher series of
religious research—there we shall have love
and knowledge. The two are different notes
on the same string—a simple question o^f
vibration.'

'And for those who have not faith?' I
asked.

'The loss of time consequent on straying
on wrong roads—the condemnation due to
wilful ignorance.'

'Is any ignorance wilful, Mr. Grahame?' I
asked. 'Do we not all do the best we
can?'

'No ; some do the worst, and some ignorance *is* wilful,' he answered. 'As with you
now. You have the truth offered you and
the light is all around you. You will not

accept the one nor open your eyes to the other.'

'Will not or cannot ?'

'The one is only a mask to hide the other. "Velle est agere." You say that you cannot, and I, that you will not. You might if you chose. It is because you will not choose that you do not. You are not the first half-educated youth who has fallen into the sin of unbelief through presumption—who has lost his better reason through the pride which accompanies ignorance so dense as to mistake itself for knowledge. And I suppose you will not be the last. It is a spiritual disease which has to be gone through, like measles or small-pox. Pity that sometimes the eyesight goes for ever and the scars remain ineffaceable to the day of death! Absit omen! Be wise in time and heal yourself while you can. I fear, however, you will not. I know your kind; and your training has been too disastrous.'

This was the first time that Mr. Grahame had spoken to me with harshness. In general he had dealt with me tenderly, as one in error truly—but, though erring, one sincerely desirous of knowing the truth, and therefore to be in a certain sense respected. And this sudden dogmatic condemnation wounded me to the quick. For I could not feel that I was wilfully wicked. I was merely conscious of a desire to know the truth and the corresponding dread of believing a lie. If I were in the wrong, might God forgive me and lead me aright! I had not intentionally gone astray. And if it is part of the function of Divine Grace to keep souls straight, why had mine been abandoned ?

There was no more impiety in asking this question than there was in acknowledging the fact. If faith comes by grace, and divine illumination is necessary for salvation—is it the wilful fault of the individual when this grace is withheld, this illumination denied? Is not God more powerful than the thoughts of man?

I was far as yet from the materialism which makes certain thoughts the necessary results of certain conditions of the brain. I believed in mind as a thing apart from and uninfluenced by matter—the soul as something that both controlled and was determined by thought. And the shape of my head, the depth of the convolutions, the arrangement of the molecules and the quality of the grey matter, together with the state of my blood and nerves, had no part in that which I held to be essentially spiritual and super-sensual—inspired by heaven or dating from hell.

Hell? Was there such a place as hell? —such a being as the devil? I began to doubt even these two points, cardinal as they had hitherto been. The Incarnation, the Atonement, Eternal Punishment and Satan—these four corner-stones of the

Christian Church had loosened so much that the slightest movement more would shake them down altogether. And then— what would be my state?

CHAPTER VII.

ABOUT this time, however, came a lull in my speculative troubles, for trouble of another kind began to possess me. There had lately settled among us a certain Mr. and Mrs. Dalrymple, who had already won the goodwill of the neighbourhood by their charm of manner and general delightfulness. They had established themselves on a scale of what was to us rather unusual luxury; and, as Mr. Dalrymple was known to one of our magnates, there was no cause to doubt the solidity of their condition. We had had before now our jackdaws pranked in peacocks' feathers, and we had been punished pretty severely for our want of discrimination; but here we stood on safe ground, and no one hung back because no one was afraid.

It may be that the idealizing power of youth created more than existed, and that the golden mists of time have added their magic to that idealization; but even now, with my imagination sobered by age and chastened by experience, Mrs. Dalrymple stands in my memory as something unapproachable and supreme. Her image is that of the most exquisite creature under heaven— of a woman more like an impersonate poem, or embodied music, or a spirit half-transparently incarnate, than a living, solid flesh-and-blood reality. She was about twenty-seven—tall, slender, with a cream-white skin, and dark eyes full of inconceivable pathos and a kind of far-away spiritualized listening look, as if she saw what we did not. Her eyelashes

were the longest I have ever seen, and she
had a fabulous abundance of jet-black hair.
She dressed, too, as no one dressed in Eden;
with more elegance and refinement than that
to which we were accustomed from even our
grandest ladies. She had lived much abroad;
and from her Polish mother she had inherited the subtle charm which is given
by the foreign element, as well as having
that which comes from home good-birth
and perfect breeding.

She was in delicate health; languid in her
movements; indolent in her habits; but she
had an almost feverish activity of mind, an
almost dangerous energy of thought. She
could do everything. She was an admirable
linguist, and spoke the principal four Con-
tinental languages as well as she spoke
English itself—which, by the way, was
coloured with the daintiest little dash of
foreign accent—a certain Italianized lingering on the letters that was like a caress.

She was a musician of rare force and an artist far beyond the average. She could talk of men, books, places, things, ideas. She knew all that others knew and worlds beyond. She was the most graciously-educated and the most gracefully-minded woman I have ever seen—I use the terms advisedly—and from my father to myself we all yielded to her charm and adored her.

From the first the Dalrymples were very friendly with us. We saw a good deal of them; and the more we saw them, the more we loved them and the more they seemed to like us. For myself, it soon came to be that the day when I was not with them seemed to be blank and colourless—a day of deadly dulness, to be lived through only for the sake of the morrow, when I should go up to Windy Brow, where they lived, as a half-frozen creature creeps to the fire to be warmed back into life. Gradually these new arrivals became the world to me. When I was not with them, I was thinking of them—longing, pining, restless, dissatisfied; oppressed with untranslatable sorrow; burning with hidden fever; finding no pleasure save in the books which Mrs. Dalrymple had lent me, whereof I learnt all the marked passages, and repeated them to myself with somewhat the same reverence as that with which I said my prayers. Or I made Edwin or Ellen play again and again the music she played and had given them —certain pieces of Mendelssohn and Beethoven which were to me like poems or pictures—as full of thought and dramatic fervour as the one, and of visible beauty as the other. Or I begged for that long-drawn sigh of Pestel's prison-hymn, which I cannot hear even now without a swelling at my heart and something that feels like tears behind my eyes.

When they played these things to me I

used often to find, to my own surprise, my eyes wet with real tears as I sat, my elbows on my knees, my face buried in my hands, lost in a dream of nameless yearning— a kind of nebulous haze of formless sadness, where nothing was distinct save sorrow— which yet was also beauty.

Then I used to dash out of the room, generally leaping through the window into the garden, to hide from my brother and sisters the strange effeminacy that had over-taken me. My abrupt departure naturally enough offended them, and was counted to me for ingratitude, after they had done something to please me ; so that when I re-turned I received a lesson on my sin of rudeness and bearishness in general, which, with my fiery temper, was sure to involve me in a quarrel.

I was both too intense and too inex-perienced in those days to realize how things must necessarily look from the outside. I was only conscious of what I felt. And when looks and feelings were at variance, I took my stand on the latter, and held myself unjustly treated when condemned for the former. Were more allowance made for this inability to realize the world outside one's self—this inability to understand that we are not so transparent as we imagine ourselves to be, and that what we do and not what we feel is the rule by which we are measured—life would be far better for us all, and especially for such young creatures as I was;—young creatures of impulse and sincerity, as yet incapable of that ethical diagnosis which can criticize self.

Our new friends did us all good. Mrs. Dalrymple helped Edwin and my sisters with their music and lifted their taste into a higher sphere ; and Mr. Dalrymple led them to practise drawing on a better method than they had done before. He taught them to sketch from nature and to draw from the round, and he gave them hints about their colours and perspective; so that their efforts grew to be of better quality all through than when they had been content to reproduce in pencil, with smooth and servile fidelity, this stag's head from a wood-cut by Bewick, or that child and dog from a steel engraving after Corbauld.

To me, neither a musician nor an artist, they lent books—chiefly the poets in various tongues—which widened my horizon and added to my knowledge. I had always been passionately fond of poetry, so that I had felt as if our common possessions had belonged by right of appreciation to me alone ; but it seemed to me that I had never understood the true meaning of even those I had loved best until now. Shakespeare and Schiller and Goethe, Shelley and Byron, Dante and Tasso—all took a different mean-ing and gained an added value after Mrs. Dalrymple had repeated such and such pas-

sages, or given a new interpretation to such
and such thoughts.   And whatever I read
now, it was with her voice, her inflection
sounding in my ears, and her divine eyes
following mine on the page.   Her mental
influence was about me like the sunlight,
and there was no hour of the day when I
forgot her—no occupation which made me
unconscious of her.   She was the soul of all
things to me; and I felt like that picture of
the half-uprising man in whose nostrils she
was gently breathing the breath of life—
like the dumb Memnon when the first rays
of the sun touched the soulless stone.

All the thoughts which had hitherto held
me, and which I had elaborated for myself,
seemed to me crude, unformed, unbeautiful;
without life or artistry—all but my love of
Liberty, and that I think must come from
the formation of my brain from birth.   I
had been such a rude clod up to now; and
now I was fining down, like Dryden's

Cymon—was I becoming the inversion of
Pygmalion's statue?

Again another help onward. Mrs. Dalrymple taught the rest new steps and new
dances. I say the rest, for though she tried
to teach me as one of them, I could not
learn. Yet she took as much trouble with
me as with them, and I did my best to do
as she told me. But something held me.
' A spirit in my feet' kept me stupid and
clumsy.

I could have walked safely over a foot-
wide ledge with a precipice on each side of
me, but my head swam when Adeline Dalrymple laid her long white hand on my
shoulder and I put my arm round her
supple stayless waist; and I was faint and
giddy before I had made a couple of turns
round the room. What anguish it was to
stop, and yet how impossible to go on!
Why was I so weak? I, the strong one,
par excellence, of the family—the young

lion of the brood—the Esau, the Nimrod, the savage—to be unable to waltz twice round a room not more than twenty-four feet square ! It was inconceivable and humiliating ; but also it was unalterable ; and I never conquered the strange physical weakness which touched me only when waltzing with Mrs. Dalrymple, but which overpowered me then.

She too was sorry. True to her Polish blood, for all her delicacy of health and general indolence of habit she was enthusiastically fond of dancing ; and she would have liked me for a partner, she said with her faint sweet tremulous smile, and that look in her eyes which was like the very glory of the heavens opening.

If, however, I could not waltz, I could talk and listen. And in our little evenings together, when I was finally pronounced hopeless, not to let me feel neglected and shut out, Mrs. Dalrymple generously forbore to dance with the others, so that she might sit and talk to me on the window-seat. And on the whole I felt that I had the best of it.

Up to now I had never known the sentiment of jealousy against Edwin. He was the family favourite, caressed by all where I had ever been cold-shouldered and repulsed. At an age when education was the one essential of my life, and idleness the ruin of my whole future, I had been sacrificed in my best interests and denied my natural rights simply to be kept as his companion at home. Yet I had neither grudged him myself nor been jealous of what the others had given him. I had sometimes broken my young heart over the difference made between us—that was only natural; but I had never carried the blame to him, nor made him suffer because I was wronged and he was favoured.

Now there were times when I almost

hated him for what he was ; though I hated myself much more in that I was not like him. I was furious against myself because I was tall and lean and strong, large-boned, and with a shock of thick brown hair dis- turbed by that unmanageable wave which broke it in heavy flocks that never would lie straight ; while he was slenderly framed and almost as round-limbed as a girl—his head a nest of close-growing golden curls—his skin like a child's—and his blue eyes like limpid lakes beneath the long fine arch of his narrow brows. He was of the Cherubino type, and women treated him pretty much as they would have treated one of themselves. And when I saw Mrs. Dalrymple let him put his arms round her waist while she kissed him as if he had been a child, I confess I was sometimes more really mad than sane. If I could have changed my physique for his, I would at this time. I, who had always gloried in

my strength, would have made myself now
a weakling, if Adeline Dalrymple would
have treated me as she treated my brother.
And there were times when, as I say, I
hated him, and felt that I could have struck
him like a second Cain.

I did my best to conceal this jealous rage
against the one whom hitherto I had loved
best of all in the world. But people who
live together, especially young people, are
quick to note differences of feeling; and
Edwin saw the change in me and taxed me
with it. Of course I denied that there was
any change at all ; and, because his charge
was true, I grew irritable and sullen under
the accusation. But once, when the tears
sprang to his eyes, and his small mouth
quivered as he said : 'I never thought,
Chris, that you would have behaved like
this to me : and what have I done to deserve it ?' I was conquered. After all, he
was my first care, and I would give him

even Mrs. Dalrymple's preference. I would give him, if need be, my life !

For all answer to his reproaches, which meant affection, I threw my arms round his neck, and bursting into one of those violent floods of tears which used to characterize me as a child, I kissed him, as also I used to kiss him when we were children together, and dashed out of the house in a tumult of emotion which made me feel as if I had been caught in a typhoon.

I was in that stage of feeling which makes fetishes of inanimate objects and carries into things the divinity centred in persons ; which energizes symbols and vivifies relics, which then it adores. I remember pushing this fetishism so far as to envy the very clothes that Mrs. Dalrymple wore—which clothes also had a special character of their own to help on my folly. That old wish of being the glove on her hand was no mere literary conceit to me ; it was what I myself

realized. I endued with a kind of consciousness all that belonged to this divinest
woman ; and consciousness included love.
She had a certain ermine cloak, lined with
pale pink satin through which ran gold
and silver threads. If I had made a new
religion, with her for the Paraclete, I would
have taken that cloak for my standard, as
Mohammed took the blacksmith's apron—I
would have venerated it as Catholics venerate
the handkerchief of St. Veronica.

When I look back on the passionate
idealism, the unreasoning sentiment of this
time, and test it by scientific principles, I
can understand how myths crystallize and
religions are made. I dreamt of Mrs. Dalrymple night after night ; but never as an
ordinary woman—always with a halo of
divinity about her which took her out of the
ranks of common humanity and lifted her
heaven-high above the rest. She was to me
what the Madonna is to the Neapolitan—

what his guardian angel is to the young seminarist. She was the divine part of humanity; the incarnation of all its beauty; the last expression of all its poetry and purity and inner wisdom. She was the seraph of the hierarchy; and to worship her as a goddess was the necessary corollary of knowing her as a woman. For her sake I loved the meanest creature that belonged to her; and to meet and speak to one of the servants of the house, to caress one of the dogs in her absence, made me comparatively content. That 'rose and pot'—how true all real poetry is!

Her husband, Mr. Dalrymple, was in his way a clever as well as an eccentric man, at once charming and less than charming. He had a passion for little dogs, which he called his children and made his idols. He had exactly twenty; all of rare kinds and of perfect breeds. It was one of the sights of the place to see this elegant, aristo-

cratic-looking man, dressed in the latest
fashion—light trousers buttoned round his
ankles, light kid gloves, coloured under-
waistcoat showing a narrow band of rose
or blue, gorgeous stock, white hat, hair and
whiskers artificially curled and highly perfumed, scented handkerchief and superb
jewellery, as if he were in Bond Street, not
among the Cumberland mountains—daintily
picking his way on the rough roads, with
his twenty little dogs, all in pairs, streaming
behind him like a herd of miniature wild
beasts. He had the most extraordinary
names for them all; of which I only
remember Zamiel and Lilith for the barking
Pomeros; Puck and Ariel for the graceful
Italian greyhounds; Sambo and Sally for
the pugs; the little female truffle-hunter was
Queen Mab, but I forget the name of her
husband; and the toy-terriers were Oberon
and Titania.

Mr. Dalrymple was his wife's husband,

and therefore I held him sacred ; he was also a man of cultivated intellect, perfect manners, refined tastes, wide experience, and therefore I respected him. But naturally for himself, in view of the man he was and the boy I was, I should not have liked him. He was too effeminate for my taste—and he did not admire his wife as she deserved to be admired. He was essentially a dilettante—just touching the borders of excellence and never attaining it. He drew well, played the guitar well, wrote pretty music and pretty poetry ; but he failed in the full grasp and completion of any of these things. Strange stories of his personal habits, and his devotion to certain occult studies, which terrified the weaker minds among us, crept about the vale ; but we were a scandalmongering set at Eden, and we had those in our midst who would have criticized and plucked out the feathers of the angel Gabriel's wings, had he

alighted at the Town-hall. All the same,
Mr. Dalrymple openly confessed to a belief
in magic, ghosts, and all the higher phenomena of mesmerism. According to him,
both the witches of old and the Indian
jugglers of the present time, had and have
mysterious powers extra to those of the
common run of men ; and he lost his time
and strength in experiments where he was
now the deceiver and now the dupe.

He was never with his wife, save on state
occasions of formal visits and dinners ; and
they lived two entirely different lives under
the same roof. He was a vegetarian and a
Rechabite ; but he drank a great deal of
strong coffee and smoked incessantly ; and
though by no means a confirmed opium-
eater, like De Quincey, he was not innocent
of that strange man's vice, nor of that
other, corresponding, of smoking hachshish.

If his wife did not complain of his neglect,
who else had the right ? Though I some-

times felt I should like to kill him when I saw her sweet, pale face grow paler than before, her pathetic eyes more mournful, as she had to confess that she had not seen her husband for perhaps three days—though we might have seen him, and he had certainly been out and about in the interval—I calmed myself by remembering that I had no right to thrust myself into her affairs, even by my sympathy; and that what she kept secret, I and all ought to hold sacred.

My worship for her was too exalted to be intrusive, too humble to take the initiative. It was she who set the rule and measure of our intercourse; and I should as little have dreamed of going beyond her allowance—of asking a question on things which she had not already explained—as I should have spoken with levity of my dead mother. But I was unhappy all the same, in more ways than one; and, what with my jealous fear of her liking Edwin too much, my indignation because Mr. Dalrymple did not like her enough, and my dread lest she did not like me at all, I was for the most part in a state of torment which nothing soothed. but her voice and presence, and nothing effectually charmed away but some signal act of gracious kindness and special distinc- tion.

In the midst of all this feverish unrest I had some divinely happy hours. As time went on, and our intimacy in- creased, not a day passed when we were not with the Dalrymples—with her more often than with him, and seldom with both together. We used to row across the lake and land at some favourite spot where there was a fine view, or a waterfall, or perhaps a rare fern or orchid to look for and never find ; and where there was sure to be one of those wide wet tracts which require some amount of courage and activity to pass dryshod. At such places Mr. Dalrymple, if he came at all, had enough to do to take care of himself, having the most extraordinary horror of dirt and damp. My sisters were mountaineers born and bred, and needed as little help as a triad of goats ; but Adeline Dalrymple was different. She was like a hothouse flower where they were field daisies ; and what was child's play to them was an insurmountable difficulty to her. Such a feat as springing from one loose stone to another over a mountain ghyll, or picking her way from tussock to tussock through a bog, was simply impossible. And I was glad that it was so. For then I used to take her in my strong young arms and carry her safely across and far on to the dry ground. I could not dance with her, but I could bear her through difficulties such as these, and feel as if I had the very universe in my arms. It was the epitome of all divinity— the possession of all humanity. It did not make me faint nor giddy, but strong, invulnerable, unconquerable—like an old Israelite to whom had been given the sacred ark to defend — the very essence of God made helpless to guard.

I used to want to kneel to her, to kiss the hem of her garment, to make myself her footstool, her slave, so that I could be of use to her. I would have liked to have spent my life in ministering to her, as if she had been a living goddess in a temple and I her sole servitor. Sometimes I had the criminally selfish half-wish that some great loss should befall her, when the world would desert her—all but I—and I would carry to her the same homage, the same reverent worship as before. Discrowned by evil hands, she should ever be sole queen to me! And sometimes I had a morbid kind of wonder, if she would be sorry were I to die, and if she would ever come to look at my grave and lay flowers on the turf. If she did, I knew that down there beneath dead and dumb as I might be, I should know the touch of her hand, hear the tread of her feet, and feel on my face the quick-drawn breath of her parted lips. I could never die so that I should not be conscious of her ; and I could only die in her service. To know her, to love her, was of itself the warranty of immortality. She was already, herself, immortal ; for the body which held her spirit was emphatically only a veil, a shell, a medium of communication. The true reality was the angel within her form.

The strange deifying reverence that I felt for Mrs. Dalrymple was due partly to my age and temperament, and partly to her own philosophy. She belonged to a school of thought quite unlike any I had ever met with. And, as she interested herself in my religious difficulties, she naturally gave me her own views to help my cruder thoughts. She was emphatically a transcendentalist, and in a certain sense a pantheist. To her

the things of the spirit—the unseen world
of the souls that had once been men, and
of the angels who had neither been born
nor had died—spiritual experiences and
realizations, and the all-pervading presence
of God, were more real than those things
we call time and space. She believed in the
interfusion of souls—soul with soul in spiritual blending more lasting than any earthly
tie, more potent than any physical circumstance of disruption or removal. She
believed in the oneness of God with life,
of God with matter, with thought, with
emotion, with the cosmic forces of the universe. Like the atmosphere which surrounds us, like the ether which interpene-
trates all space, God is the universal
medium, the spiritual ether in which we
float, the energizing sense by which we recognise and love each other. Soul inter-
fused with soul, and both lying cradled
in the Heart of God—minds touching each

other in the dark, and seeking each other through long ages and across interminable distances, welded together for all time and through all eternity—welded together by and with and in the very substance of God!

She was also in a sense a metempsychosist, and believed that we had all known each other in another life—all of us who loved in this. For she maintained the absolute indestructibility of love, and the impossibility of sundering those whose spirits had once met each other and been united by love. Her beautiful face took the rapt look of a sibyl when she spoke to me, as she often did, of the glorious joy and sense of freedom and invulnerability contained in this conviction ; and how it dwarfed all the pains of life, and life itself to a mere short day's dream not worth lamenting while it was passing. Eternity was behind and before us. Why fix our minds only on the one troubled hour?

'Those who believe as I do,' she said one

evening to me, when we were sitting in the twilight, watching the last of the day fading from the sky and the first of the stars coming out; 'no—not who believe, but who know—are never really separated from the beings they love. Time and space may divide us from each other, and circumstances may be stronger than our will; but thought overrides matter, our souls are ever one and inseparable, and the bond of the spirit once made is indissoluble. Love is in itself immortality. It cannot die; it cannot change; and no force in nature can kill it.'

She laid her white and scented hand on mine, so brown and large and bony—and bent her head till she looked full and straight in my eyes. I was sitting on a low stool by her side; she was on the window-seat made in the embrasure.

' You, dear boy, will go into the world far away from all of us here,' she said; and—was it my fancy? or did that sweet voice which always reminded me of pearls tremble, and something as tender as tears come into her glorious eyes?—' but, wherever you go, my spirit will go with you, surrounding you, guarding you, one with your very breath, your very life. Never forget that, my child. I am with you always—like God and with God—in the future always, as I have ever been in the past.'

Her hand closed on mine with an almost convulsive grasp. It burnt like fire, and the diamonds on her fingers and at her throat flashed as if by their own internal light. Her voice had sunk almost to a whisper, and something seemed to pass from her to me which thrilled me like electricity. I could not speak. My heart suddenly swelled so that it strangled my voice and cut short my breath. I only felt a dumb kind of desire to carry my life to her hands and worship her as I would have worshipped the Eternal Mother of men and things. She was beyond womanhood to me—she was the casket that embodied and enclosed the Divine.

As I looked at her, she still bending down her head and looking into my eyes, I felt a strange rapture and loss of myself in her personality. Her eyes were as mysterious as those stars overhead—worlds where I was, as it were, engulfed, but wherein was contained all the beauty, the love, the secrets of the universe. It was the unveiling of Isis to her priest—the goddess revealing herself to man. I scarcely lived ; I did not breathe; I was as if spiritually carried away into another sphere; and for the moment I was not human but immortal. It was a sensation beyond mere physical excitement; and it would have been appalling from its intensity, had I had enough consciousness left to examine or reflect.

What was in my face I do not know, but there must have been something which did not displease Mrs. Dalrymple. One hand still clasped mine, the other she laid on my forehead, pushing back my hair and bending my head a little backward.

'Dearest child,' she said, 'God has given you to me. You are mine in spirit now and for ever. Never forget this moment, Christopher, when our souls have met and recognised each other once again across the long ages which have separated them.'

She stooped her gracious face to mine, and lightly kissed me on the eyes and forehead.

It was the first kiss any woman, other than my sisters, had given me since I was a child ; and it was the birth-hour of a new life to me. Henceforth all things were transformed for me, and life meant a new existence as it had a new message. The sunrises and the sunsets, the song of the birds, the flowers in the fields, the shadows of the clouds on the mountains, the reflections in the lake and the ripple of the blue waves, the voice of the waters making music in cascades, the budding and the fall of the leaves of the trees—all were the circumstances of a more beautiful world than that in which I had hitherto lived. Nature had a secret language which was revealed to me, and I understood the hidden meaning of things which hitherto had had no meaning at all. I, like Adeline Dalrymple, felt and saw God everywhere—but when I thought of God, she stood ever foremost at His hand.

How I lived then, I do not know. I remember nothing very distinctly outside my being with Mrs. Dalrymple — our sunlit noonday walks in her garden—our speculations beneath the stars—her eyes, which looked more eloquently than words — her words, of which I sometimes lost the meaning because her voice filled my ears with too much music. When I was not with her, I was away in the lonely mountains, where I could think of her without interruption and associate her with the beauty of all about me. I carried my secret joy like a bird in my bosom, hidden from the eyes of all ; and not even to Edwin did I reveal what was in my heart.

Of him I was no longer jealous. I had no cause. For I noticed that of late Mrs. Dalrymple had ceased to treat him so familiarly as she used to do in the early days; and on this side I was at peace. I lived in my enchanted island, so far as I knew alone and undiscovered. And if any one suspected my state, no one spoke to me about it. But indeed I have forgotten all the details of my family life at this time. I suppose I ate and drank and slept and lived among them as usual ; but I do not remember the fact nor feeling of a day, save once, when I looked at Edwin and thought: ' How much I know that you do not—and how different the world is to you and me!'

The strain at this moment must have been severe. I had not done growing, though I was six feet as it was—but I am six feet two now; and my big bony frame took a great deal of rest and nourishment to keep it in serviceable condition then and to make a strong man of me in the future. Under the excitement of my present rapturous life I lost both my sleep and my appetite, and became as thin as a grasshopper. It was impossible not to see that I was changing; and my sisters were always commenting on my eyes, which they said looked as if they had been picked out by hawks and put in again by a chimney-sweep; while my face was whiter and leaner than ever, and I was altogether uglier and even more like Don Quixote than I used to be. But as I was certainly less violent and less irascible, they were too glad of a change which was a respite to fall foul of the cause, whatever it might have been.

By degrees the rapture of my first content faded and the old unrest took possession of me and ruined all. To be with Mrs. Dalrymple was ecstasy, but to be away from her was torture and despair. And how could I be always with her? Still, absence from her was like passing into the darkness of the grave; and my old impatience of sorrow made me furious and wild against the obstructions which kept us apart. I used to get out of our house at night by a side door that no one ever looked after, and wander about her garden on the chance of seeing her at the bedroom window, or perhaps of seeing only her light, burning far into the dawning day. There was no danger of being discovered. Mr. Dalrymple slept at the other side of the house altogether, and the big watch-dog knew me. I used to stand among the laurestinus bushes, looking

up at her window; and I was grandly rewarded when, as she sometimes did, she
came all in white and drew back the blinds,
opening the window, and sometimes stepping
out on the balcony and looking at the sky.
I never let her know that I was there.
That too was my secret which I kept
sacred; till one night, as if attracted by
some magnetic influence, she came down
the outside steps which led from her bedroom to the garden, and walked straight to
where I was standing in the shadow of
the bushes.

'I knew you were here,' she said, as she
came up to me. 'I was conscious of you,
and could not sleep. Child! what have
you done to me to draw me to you? What
strange power have you over me?'

I trembled as if in fever.

'Have I any power over you?' I said.

'You see it,' she answered simply.

I cannot describe the curious sense of inversion which these words created. I, who had been the slave, the worshipper, the subordinate, to be suddenly invested with power—to be even so prepotent as to compel obedience from the one who had hitherto been supreme—it was a change of parts which for the moment overwhelmed me with a sense of universal instability ; and to the end of my life I shall never forget the strange confusion of pride and pleasure, of pain in loss yet joy in the sensation of a newborn power which possessed me, as the goddess thus became a woman, and made of me, who had been her slave, her master and a man.

I did not speak, nor did she. It was like an enchanted spell which words would have broken ; and we walked in the dark alleys of the shrubbery in a silence that was at once divine in its blessedness and painful in its vagueness, and more like a dream than a fact. I did not know what it meant, and yet I dared not break it; and she did not. We went into a small summer-house at the end of the garden, and sat there hand in hand, till the morning broke. Then the faint flush on the mountain-top and the first stirring of the birds told us it was time to part.

'See how I have trusted you!' she said as she stood up to go. She laid both her hands on my shoulders, then drew my face forward and kissed me as she had done once before, on the forehead and the eyes. 'Your consecration,' she said; 'the seal of our eternal oneness.'

Overpowered by an emotion so powerful as to be physical pain, I knelt on the ground at her feet; and I think that for a moment I died.

This was the first and only time we met thus by night in the garden. But after this I passed the best half of every night in the shadow of the laurestinus bushes, praying

for her to come down to me as she had
done on that night of ecstasy and silence.
And as the hours passed and she gave no
sign, I used to feel as if I must inevitably
die as I stood there—as if this agony of
vain longing and ruthless disappointment
took from me my very heart's blood.

At last the strain grew too intense, and
nature gave way. I had a sharp attack of
brain-fever, when I was for many days in
danger. Through the dark tempestuous
trouble of the time, I vaguely remember a
sudden influx of peace and rest when there
came to my bedside some one who spoke to
me softly, in what seemed to me a language
I had once learned and now vainly tried to
remember ; bending over me and breathing
on me. I remember how my face was
cooled and refreshed by what I thought was
water from a Greek fountain, and how, with
a subtle scent of roses, it was softly dried.
I thought it was my mother who had come

out of heaven, or poor Nurse Mary who had returned; then that it was the Divine Virgin who had made me her second Christ; then that it was the goddess Isis, she whose awful beauty no man had unveiled; and then I had a confused dream of Diana and Endymion, which changed into that of Juno and Ixion, as the vision faded and the form melted away into mist.

It was none of all these. It was Adeline Dalrymple; and the tears on my face, which seemed to have fallen from some divine source, were those shed because of the sorrow which had no healing—because of the love which had had no past and could have no future.

When I recovered I found that the Dalrymples had left Windy Brow, and no one at Eden knew where they had gone. Years after I heard of them as living at Venice, where Mrs. Dalrymple was a confirmed invalid and never seen, and Mr.

Dalrymple was wholly given up to mesmerism, opium and poetry.

Thus then, began and ended the first love of my life ; and in this manner the Great Book was opened and the page turned down—half-read but ineffaceable. And ever and ever a fragrance steals from that closed page which neither length of time nor deeper knowledge of life can destroy. Adeline Dalrymple remains in my memory as the impersonation of all beauty and all delight — a woman more heavenly than human—ever the saint in her shrine, the goddess in her temple, her white robes unstained and her divine glory undiminished through all time and for all eternity.

CHAPTER VIII.

WHEN I had fully recovered, it seemed to me impossible to go on living at home. I had lost all that made life sweet on the outside, and the monotony of existence within was intolerable. If I had had the hope of a settled future and the occupation of preparing for it, things might have been better; but even such lame endeavours after self-education as I had made now failed me, and I seemed to have lost the key to all the holy places of the past, and to have let the fire on the sacred altar burn out.

I was listless, inert, uninterested. All

hope, all joy, all secret ambition of future
success, all passionate thrill of living, all
delight in books, all intellectual vitality,
had gone from me. I wanted but to be
left alone, not spoken to and not noticed.
Even the companionship of Edwin was dis-
tasteful to me ; and their cheerfulness under
what I felt to be our irreparable loss made
my sisters seem the very incarnations of ingratitude.

Everything had gone from me. I could
have shrieked for the torture given me by
music. I dared not read a poem which
was associated with Mrs. Dalrymple—and
all were associated with her—and the zeal
with which I had dug down into the arid
wells of the ' Encyclopædia Londinensis ' for
that fantastic learning with which I had
crammed my brain, had gone with the rest.

What a wretched time this was to me !
I had recovered my life and lost that which
had made it beautiful. It was the husk

without the kernel, the shell without the pearl ; and I was like the Garden when the Lady who had been its Soul had died. I have gone through the fire more than once since then, but I have never had a more painful period than this of that drear dead winter, down among the mountains, after Adeline Dalrymple had left.

The Grahames did what they could to help me. I think they saw what was amiss and were sorry for me. But I had lost all interest in those subjects which had been common to us, and cared nothing for the theological difficulties which, a year ago, had so much disturbed me. Things might be, or might not. What mattered it to me ? I went back to that languid acquiescence in doctrines as they are taught, which is neither faith nor voluntary acceptance. It is simply letting things slip and taking no trouble. I had lost, too, my political ardour; and from passion and enthusiasm and turbulence all round had passed into the silence of indifference, the quietude of death.

Thus I droned through the days, dreaming rather than doing ; sheltering myself behind the false plea of study, because I wanted to be left alone, but, destitute of either purpose or vigour, in reality doing nothing. My books lay open before me, but I, with my face in my hands, was thinking of all that Adeline Dalrymple had ever said to me—recalling all that she had ever done—remembering her eyes, her voice, her hair, her hands—till I broke down into such tempests of despair as frightened even myself. The consciousness of her was my universe, my inseparable second self—like another soul possessing me. I carried her always with me ; and my heart was like a perfumed vase filled with the ashes of the dead.

She was the spirit that animated Nature

—Nature, who had always been my Divine Mother, my Eternal Friend. I saw her in the stars and found her in the skies; I heard her in the voice of the waters and traced her outline in the misty foldings of the silent hills. She was as beautiful as the snow-crystals on the window-pane, as pure as the frost that fringed the dead leaves of the trees. She was everywhere— everywhere; the one unchangeable circumstance traceable behind all different forms. In the night and in the morning and through out the day, she was my ever-present thought —sometimes strong and vivid as a solid fact, sometimes pale and vaporous as a distant cloud, but always there—always!— always! She held me and possessed me— as she had said she ever would. She stole between me and heaven, and when I prayed to God I thought of her. She was fire in my veins and ice in my heart; but I should have been poorer through life had I not known her. I can see now the good of the pain she brought me.

'When winter went and spring came back'—how I love that beautiful copy of Shelley which she gave me! I have it yet, and can still repeat almost all the minor poems I learnt as a lad, blistering the pages where I learnt! — my blood once more began to stir in my veins and my natural energy to re-assert itself. I gradually got back my old feeling of power and invulnerability—my old sense of certainty in the future and my ability to conquer circumstances and compel happiness, no matter what the obstacles to be overcome. Heart-broken though I might be, I was still master of fate; and I had always the fee-simple of the future.

Yet, as this sense of power returned, so grew ever more masterful that which was its reflex—repugnance to my home-life, and desire to go out into the world on my own account, to work for myself and be independent.

But how? What could I do? I had learnt nothing thoroughly and nothing useful. Even my languages, which were my battle-horses, were merely so much literary furniture, and were useless for the more practical purposes of either writing or speaking. I had amassed cart-loads of useless knowledge — including heraldry and pre-scientific mythology—but I knew nothing that represented money - power—nothing which touched the fringe of any professional robe, or included the price of a plate of meat at a chop-house.

It had been intended that I, like my brothers, should go to Cambridge when I should come of age. My father would have given me a reading-tutor for the year previous to matriculation; and after that he would have held me responsible for my future, and himself acquitted of all obligation. But I was too impatient to wait even the short two years that stood between me and my majority. I was now past nineteen; and those two years seemed to me an eternity of ennui. Besides, what could I do after I had taken my degree? I could not take Orders; and the Bar was beyond my means. Where was the good, then, of widening foundations over which I could never build? and why delay the more restricted building which should be begun now at once?

Then it was that I returned to my old love, Literature—that waste-pipe of unspecialized powers, which no one thinks demands an apprenticeship, and wherein all believe that fame and success are to be caught like wild goats, at a bound! Besides—it would be my means of communication with Mrs. Dalrymple. If I could but write things which she would repeat, as she repeated that poem of Shelley's, that sweet

music of Heine's—if I could make those
beautiful eyes moist and stir that lofty soul
with generous emotion, she remembering
the boy who through her had become great!
—if I could! Yes: I would be a literary
man, pure and simple; and I would leave
home.

Of late I had blossomed into poetry. It
is the natural expression of love and
sorrow, and minds, like all other things,
obey fixed laws and exhibit the same phenomena under the same conditions. And
being only a Philistine, without real insight
into the true meaning of the gift of Song,
I thought that, because I had been able to
set down a few passionate couplets with
tolerable flow of rhythm and harmony of
rhyme, my path was clear before me, my
tools were sharpened to my hand, and my
chaplet of bays was already sprouting on
the tree. I wrote a short poem, which I
resolved should determine my future. If

accepted, I would at once take up my parable and begin my career; if rejected, I would accept the verdict as final, and go to the colonies as a sheep-farmer, or I would go to sea as a sailor before the mast, or enlist as a private in the army—trusting to myself to be recognised as a gentleman, raised from the ranks in less than a year, and made an admiral or a general while still young. I was such a mere child in some things, even yet!—and in nothing more than in my ignorance of the ways of the world, and the impotence of the individual when brought into contact with systems. Meanwhile, I would try my fate with literature; poetry and literature being to me, in those days of darkness, inter-changeable terms meaning the same thing.

At that time the two magazines in greatest favour among us youngsters at the vicarage were ' Ainsworth's Miscellany ' and ' Doug-las Jerrold's Shilling Magazine.' My father patronized Blackwood, of which some articles were delightful to me and others made me rageful. With the superstition of youthful hope and fear, I determined to do a little bit of private vaticination for my better guidance ; and to make the best of a certain number of catches on the point of cup-and-ball determine the magazine to which I should send my poem. I caught forty-nine out of the fifty for Ainsworth, and only forty-seven for Jerrold. To the former then I posted my rhymes, with a boyish letter of entreaty which must have amused him by its fervour.

To my joy he accepted my poem, and sent me an honorarium of two guineas ; together with a kind and encouraging letter, assuring me of success if I would persevere, and promising to accept all such work as would suit the ' Miscellany.' So now things were plainly ordered, and my future was fair before me.

Literature, as a profession, was a thing which went dead against our family traditions—our inherited ideas of respectability and what was due to our gentle birth. To write in the quiet dignity of home a learned book like Burton's 'Anatomy of Melancholy,' or a profound one like Locke 'On the Understanding,' was one thing ; to depend for bread on one's pen was another. The one shed increased lustre on the noblest name ; the other was no better than fiddling in an orchestra, acting in a barn, or selling yards of silk across the counter, all of which were allied disreputabilities. It was a low-class *métier*, let who would follow it ; but for a gentleman and the grandson of a Bishop, it was degradation.

So at least my father said when I opened fire on him one day, and propounded to him my notable scheme for leaving home, going to London, and supporting myself by literature. He was opposed to the scheme from first to last, and tried to deter me from it by sarcasm.

'I thought, with your fine ideas, you had more ambition than to make yourself a mere newspaper hack, a mere Grub Street poet,' he said, throwing into his words that galling emphasis which impetuous youth finds so hard to bear. 'Do you think you can do nothing better for yourself than write poems for Warren's blacking, or scratch up Bow Street details for a dinner?'

'I do not intend to write poems for Warren's blacking, nor to scratch up Bow Street details for a dinner,' I answered—I honestly confess it—insolently; for my father had the fatal power, as some others have also had, of rousing the worst passions in my nature. 'And if to be a literary hack now is the way to literary fame hereafter,' I continued, 'I will serve my apprenticeship as others have done. Sir Walter Scott was not a literary hack!'

' There is no good in talking to such an obstinate young puppy as you,' said my father angrily. ' I am sick to death of your whims and affectations! The best thing for you would be a good thrashing to knock some of the conceit and wilfulness out of you. If you go to London, as you propose, you go without my consent—do you hear ? —and the curse of God rests on disobedient children to the end of their lives. Now leave the room, Christopher, and never let me hear of this ridiculous rubbish again.'

Here then I was at the junction of those two roads of which either determines the whole after-life. Opposition of my father's unreasoning kind was naturally, to a boy of my violent temper, so much oil on flame and so much strengthening of resolve. All the same, obedience to parents is a duty ; so also is the perfecting of one's own powers and leading the life for which one is best fitted—for we all have duties to ourselves as well as to others. At this moment the two clashed and made my choice very difficult. For underneath the fierce temper which I could not deny, was always conscience and the desire to know the right;—and to do it when known.

Finally, my personal ambition conquered. I reasoned the thing out in my own way, and came to the conclusion that, although self-sacrifice for the good of others is absolute and imperative, the sacrifice of a real vocation for no one's good and simply because of the arbitrary opposition of a parent, is not ; and that in my case self-assertion was not selfishness. The permission then, which my father would not give me, I prepared myself to take ; and I was on the point of running away from home, as my grand-father, uncle, and brother had done—keeping quiet for the moment only because Edwin was not well—when, fortunately for us, Mr. King, our family solicitor, came down

from London to pay us a visit, and proved
the ' deux ex machinâ ' by whom all difficulties were arranged.

Mr. King took a fancy to me.   A sharp
practitioner in his office, outside his profession he was a kind-hearted man enough, fond
of young people, and always ready to assist
undeveloped talent and help on the schemes
of honourable ambition.   He thought that
I was fit for something better than a
parson's petticoat, he said with his cynical
contempt for all forms of faith ; and, as it
was not possible to send me to the Bar, the
next best thing was to give me the run of
the British Museum, and leave to prove of
what stuff I was made.   He would help
me with his advice ; and he promised my
father that he would look after my health
and morals.

But, first of all, he said to me : ' Could
he see what I had already done, beside that
prancing poem in " Ainsworth's Miscel-

lany," which was—well—which was pretty
fair, but vastly young ?'

Full of the pride of ignorance and the
confidence of youth, I gave him some of the
things I thought my best; and never
doubted of his verdict. Poor Mr. King !
Such a turgid, upheaped, colossally clumsy
style as mine was in those early days !
—'like a wood where you could not see the
trees for the leaves'—like a confused mass
of ornamentation, where not a figure was detached nor a volute truly drawn. But to
me they were all monumental—chaos, en-
cumbrances, bad drawing and all.

Mr. King told me quite candidly what he
thought of my productions. In consequence,
he went near to drive me mad by what I
took to be his prosaic aridity and deadness
of touch. He cut out all my finest passages ;
ridiculed all my best descriptions ; gravely
demanded what I meant by my sublimest
ideas ; put my most high-flown phrases into

flat prose, and then asked me if that was not much better?—certainly it was more intel-legible!—and reduced the whole thing to pulp.

But it was protoplastic pulp, after all his hacking and pounding—pulp with the germ of life and the potentiality of development in it—pulp out of which, with care, might be evolved some kind of vertebrate organism —for, though he edited me severely, he ended by saying he thought I had 'stuff' in me; at all events, enough to justify me in my choice of literature as a profession and him in his advocacy with my father. And after he had thus waded through my literary Niagaras, he addressed himself again to my father and discussed the matter with him philosophically.

It was evident I was doing no good at home, he said. I was too big for the house; too vigorous for such a life as we led down here. It was power wasted—vitality running to seed—and it would be far better to send me up to London, as I wished. Let me have a year's grace to see what I could do. The question of permanent settlement might come after. When I should come of age my small fortune would simplify matters —until then, could I not have an allowance?

Mr. King was one of the few people who had a decided influence over my father. His sharp, brisk energy; the trenchant audacity of his theories; his worldly knowledge and business capacity; his respect for society, appearances, success; his absolute self-confidence—all naturally impressed a man whose indolence was his bane, and who had to be stirred up if he were to be made to move. And as Mr. King swore by all his gods that his sisters—he was not married— should look after me and keep me out of the destruction into which my father made sure I should run, the thing was at last

arranged. My father gave his formal consent to my going up to London for a year
for the purpose of studying at the British
Museum, and writing the book on which I
had set my heart. And he agreed to furnish
me with the funds necessary for that year's
experience.

'After that,' he said kindly, and yet
severely ; 'you sink or swim on your own
account. If you fail, as I fear you will, you
have your home to come back to. It will never
be shut against you, unless you disgrace
yourself so that you are unfit to enter it.
If you succeed—my blessing be with you !
It will be a pleasant surprise if you do—but
all things are possible to God ; and to His
care I commend you.'

My leaving home in this sudden and
erratic manner created a tremendous stir
among us. Poor dear Edwin cried like a
girl, and said that he did not know what
he should do without me, and that it was

hard, after I had accustomed him to lean on me all his life, for me now to leave him alone.

And when he said this, for a brief instant I felt the joints of my resolve give way, and I thought I would throw it all up and be content with him and home. But, like another Pharaoh, I hardened myself afresh, and, instead of yielding to him, did what I could to comfort him—especially promising to return before long, and to write to him every day, faithfully.

As for my sisters, they were half-relieved and half-sorry, as now the prospect of greater peace by the withdrawal of my turbulent personality, and now the loss of a useful kind of servant, was uppermost. As pretty Ellen drawled out in that quiet naïve way of hers, by which she was able to say the most wounding things with the greatest serenity, and not get into a quarrel as the price to be paid for her frankness :

' We shall have no one now to do things for us ; and I think, Chris, you are very selfish indeed to go away. Who is to go down for the letters on the wet days ? and how dull it will be for Julia and me to walk out by ourselves when Edwin has a cough and cannot come ! How can we go up the mountains alone ? Who is to drive away the bulls ? and how can we sail without you to manage the boat ? And what is Edwin to do without you?—you, who have always pretended to be so fond of him too ! I must say I think you are very wicked and selfish for leaving us all like this, just to go and amuse yourself in London. But you always were a selfish and ungrateful boy ; and it is not to be wondered at.'

' Am I really selfish, Nell ?' I asked.

' Of course you are,' she answered, lifting her soft eyes to mine with her candid look. ' You were never anything else.'

Well, perhaps. Still, I thought that to

give up such a chance as I had now, that I might go to the post on the wet days, take care of my sisters in their mountain walks and amuse my brother when he was not well, would be a disproportionate expenditure of my own life in view of the gain to theirs.

And more. With the return of the old strength and hope had come back the old theological troubles ; and my 'unsoundness' had by now become so patent as to make things less than ever harmonious between my father and myself. His method of reconversion was not of a kind to bring us into closer union. Leland's 'Short Method with the Deists,' which he insisted on my reading, only made me angry ; and his unstinted abuse of all Unitarianism, Deism, and even Dissent, made me angrier still.

When the 'Vestiges of Creation' came out, our fight was serious. Giving, as it did the first idea of cosmic continuity, and the consequent destruction of the bit by bit creation of Genesis, it was a priceless treasure to me, to him a deadly and diabolical sin. And in the controversy between Whewell and Sir David Brewster, we of course took opposite sides—and mine was not that which adduced as the convincing proof of the centralization of intelligent life on the earth alone, the astounding argument that Christ had died for man only, and that no other world could, therefore, be peopled with creatures of intelligence, soul, or spirit like ours.

For all these reasons then, I felt that it was best to go. I had outgrown the dimensions of the old home; and fission is the law of families as well as of animalculæ. I was the one inharmonious circumstance within the vicarage walls, and all would be better without me. The die was cast. My choice was made. Selfish, or only self-respecting, I took my place with Mr. King in the coach which was to carry us to the railway station; and thus and for ever broke down my dependence on the old home and set my face towards the Promised Land —the land where I was to find work, fame, liberty and happiness.

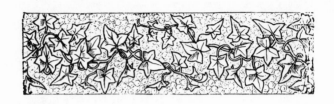

CHAPTER IX.

MY first year in London was one of strange alternation of feeling. Sometimes I longed for the old place—the lake, the mountains, the rivers, the woods, the faces I knew when passing up the street, and my own people—with that sickness of desire which grows into a real malady, culminating in death if continued long enough. And then again I was in a world of enchantment as my mind opened to new impressions and my heart warmed to new affections.

This total change of scene, and the influx of fresh interests included, did for me what nothing else would have done. My certainty of endless heart-break for the loss of my first love began to be as a grave-mound which gently covers itself with moss and flowers as it sinks down almost on a level with the plain, while sweet birds come to sing above the dead.

I read daily at the British Museum, gathering material for my magnum opus, and making raids into all manner of strange regions—according to my old habit of amassing unusable cartloads of perfectly worthless learning. Among other things, I remember how nearly I made shipwreck of myself in the fascinating whirlpool of Analogy. I improved my knowledge of classical times and circumstances, and blessed Becker and Winckelmann; and I lost myself in the mazes of comparative mythology and Higgins's ' Anacalypsis.' Turned loose in this rich pasturage, with only the limitation of subject which came from the main lines of my book, I ran great risk of losing my time by the very fact of over-filling it.

The consciousness of living in the midst of such boundless stores, and of being the potential possessor of all this wealth, acted on my brain as a stimulant—sometimes as an intoxicant. I was never weary of that badly-lighted, ill-ventilated and queerly tenanted old room, with its legendary flea and uncleansed corners. The first to come, the last to leave, and always surrounded by a pile of books, of which the number brought down on my young head many a good-natured sarcasm from the attendants, I soon became known to the officials and habitués, whom my youth interested and my enthusiasm amused. All were kind to me ; but one attendant was especially my friend. The habitual readers of the Museum from some forty to a few years ago will recognise my man.

With his heart in the country, and his

hope of leaving his hated service in the reading-room to once more establish himself as a gentleman-farmer in Norfolk ever flitting, like a Will-o'-the-wisp, before him, he had to live on those narrow lines for the remainder of his life. The post which had been accepted as a temporary stop-gap when he was ruined by that unlucky speculation of his had to be his permanent office; and the discomfort of a few months crystallized into the discontent of a life. Honest as the day, true as steel, tender-hearted as a woman, he was gruff in manner and of superficial surliness of temper to men; to women he was always both courteous and considerate, so that he grew to be the recognised ladies' attendant of the room. His delicate little wife, for whom he had the most chivalrous devotion, knew his real worth; and I too learnt the intrinsic value of his nature. He and his wife were my good friends, and I used often to go and see them on the Sunday afternoons, when they lived out by Stoke Newington.

From the first—partly owing to the habit of mixing with all classes, proper to a clergyman's family, and to the familiarity natural in a small country place towards the children whom the elders had seen grow up in their midst; partly to my own nature—I have been as democratic in my ways as in my principles. I have ever chosen my friends for their worth and not for their station ; and, taking society vertically as I have done, I have counted friends in all the strata, from those born in the purple down to fishermen and servants. And I began as I have gone on—starting off with this real friendship made with the family of a simple attendant in a public library.

In those days Mr. Panizzi—not yet Sir Antonio—was our Deus Maximus ; and on more than one occasion he showed how far ahead Italian astuteness looks, and how wise it is to have your traps in order when you suspect that vermin may be about. He caught and caged one of these vermin in the most masterly way in the world. The thing was done as neatly as a conjuror's trick, and has left on me the impression of a nightmare. It was my first introduction to the Italian character, whereof I have had wide experience since.

Mr. Panizzi took great notice of me. He had a watchful eye over his small world both of readers and officials, and not so much as a mouse squeaked behind the skirting-board but he heard it and tracked the run from end to end. Who did his work of espionage no one ever knew ; but some one must have been his ' mouse-trap '—for this accurate knowledge of all things within the domain of the Printed Book Department could not have been had by direct personal observation, even granting those ' eye-holes ' of which there was a

dark tradition and unpleasant consciousness.

One day he gave me a little wise advice
about my friendliness with this good attendant, of whom I have spoken. He had seen
me shake hands with him on coming into
the reading-room, and he knew that I
visited him and his wife at their own home.
And as he knew from Mr. King something
of my inherited social position, and saw for
himself how young and unformed and
impulsive I was, he thought himself justified
in warning and reproving me. As a reader,
I was so far under his jurisdiction; and his
position gave him seigneurial rights.

'You are a gentleman,' he said; 'he is
only a servant. Make him keep his place,
and do you maintain your position. These
familiarities with low people always end
badly.' Then he bent his head and levelled
his eyes at me from under his broad bushy
brows. 'You are very young,' he said with

a peculiar smile; 'and you think that you can revolutionize society. You will find that you cannot; and that if you knock your head against stone walls, you will only make it ache and alter nothing.'

But he talked to the winds. What can heady youth do, when temperament and principles combine to push it in one direction, but stick to its own sense of right and earn its own experience ?—with bitter weeping, if need be, but always earned through constancy and conscientiousness. The young fellow whose course of action or mode of thought can be changed or modified by the first dissident he comes across will never be a man, morally, but will remain a bit of jelly to the end. For weakness of will and plasticity of conviction, however pleasant they may be to live with, make but a poor job of life on the whole; and while one is young, moral steadiness is more honourable than intellectual amiability. Wherefore, acting more or less consciously on these ideas, I gave no heed to Mr. Panizzi's counsel, and continued my friendship with these good people as I maintained it to the end.

My chief friends however, at this time, were naturally Mr. King and his family, and their house was like my home. I have often wondered since, how they could have been bothered with me as they were; but they were wonderfully kind to me—at least, some among them. There were two sisters who did not like me; so we will let them pass. It is not in human nature to speak very enthusiastically of those who dislike one and make no secret of their feelings; and I wish to remember only things pleasant and of good repute in connection with my old friends and quasi-guardians.

They were a strangely united family; not so much in personal affection as by the feeling of family solidarity. When I first knew them

they were five in all; and all were unmarried.
The eldest brother was the master; the eldest
sister was the mistress. The youngest two
sisters were respectively the beauty and the
invalid; and the younger brother was the
family pet and subordinate. He was one
of the best fellows that ever lived—kind,
unselfish, devoted, faithful; but he hated his
profession, and he was emphatically a round
man in a square hole. He was a great
athlete and fond of all country exercises.
He had wanted to go to sea, but had been
prevented for reasons of family ambition
never fulfilled; so he had to sit at his desk
instead of climbing up shrouds and handling
stays; and his brother found, when too
late, that to coerce a life out of its natural
direction does not always ensure a successful
settling in another form.

This brother, George, and I were great
friends; and for years we spent every Sunday together. We used to take long walks

into the country, about London, and through
the parks and public gardens; and, utterly
unlike in every thought, feeling and instinct,
we were nevertheless chums as close as if we
had been brothers together.

The eldest sister was the great feature
of the family.   She was a tall, large,
strikingly handsome woman, almost stone
deaf, and of a singular mixture of qualities.
With certain virile characteristics—witness
her personal courage and her constancy; her
strong sense of family duty, which led her
to self-sacrifice for the sake of her own;
her self-respect, which ran into queenli-
ness of pride and dignity; her power to
command and her ability to obey—she had
the most ultra - feminine notions of propriety, and for certain transgressions felt
a loathing amounting to horror.   She, as
well as my special chum, were curiously
conservative; and it was impossible to make
them believe that anything which had not

been in their forming-time of youth was valuable or respectable. I was devotedly attached to this noble creature — 'Queen Betty' we used to call her; and she made a kind of pet of me, and protected me against the animosity of her sisters.

For Mr. King himself I have only kindly tender recollections; and I will not dwell on the clouds which came over the future.

In these days I lived at a small private boarding-house kept by a dear, good woman with a magnificent contralto voice, formidable eyebrows, a decided beard and moustache, and hands as large and strong as a man's. In spite of these masculine accompaniments, Miss Smith had a heart as soft as swansdown and as large as an elephant's. She was totally unfit for any undertaking in which she had to resist encroachments and defend her own rights. Anyone could talk her over. She was influenced by her affections more than by her interests ; and where she took a liking she would sacrifice her gains to please the favoured him or her by extra liberalities. She had generous instincts, refined tastes, indolent habits ; and she kept a loose hand on the domestic reins. Hence she made the most comfortable home possible for those who lived under her hospitable roof. But our comfort was her loss ; and, when Christmas brought its bills, the two ends gaped ever wider and wider and were less and less able to be strained together.

I knew all this only afterwards. At the time everything seemed to stand on velvet.

This house was a queer experience to me. The tremendous love-affairs which budded and blossomed, but never set into the permanent fruit of matrimony ; the friendships which began, continued, and then suddenly one day went pouf ! in the smoke of a blazing quarrel ; the fights of the old

ladies for the footstools, the favourite easy-
chair, the best place by the fire, and the
stratagems and wiles put in force for victory
and prior possession — how odd it all
was! And what extraordinary people came
and went like shadows, or stayed as if they
were coeval with the foundations of the
house, and as little to be moved as these!

There was the bull-necked, bullet-headed
bon vivant who kept the bill-of-fare up to
the mark, was inexorable on the subject of
breakfast-bacon and soft-roed herrings, and
allowed of no stint in quantity nor scamping
of quality.

There was the dissipated young clerk
who did nothing but count returned notes
at the Bank of England, and had no intellect for higher work had he been put to it.
He had a private income in excess of his
salary ; was given over to music-halls and
late hours ; spent his money as if it were
water running through his fingers ; dressed

gorgeously and wore a small counter-full of jewellery ; and, among other things, bought a fine carved mahogany bookcase, which he stocked with novels, all in showy bindings, uncut and never read.

There was the well-conducted young solicitor, silent, reserved, methodical—the best of them all ; and the loose-lipped young fellow, who spluttered when he spoke, and asked counsel of unmarried girls whether he should put on his thick trousers or his thinner.

There was the uxorious couple who made embarrassing love in public, and the quarrelsome couple who were just as embarrassing in their fierce disputes ; the maiden lady of good family, whose feature was eyebrows, and who would have sniffed at Venus herself as plebeian, had she not had the exact arch held by her as a sign of birth and breeding ; and there was the mincing prude who objected to Cromwell 'because he was not a gentleman,' kept a sharp look-out on the young men and was a very Cerberus to the girls.

There were the girls themselves—the pretty, touzled, mop-headed ones, who turned the heads of all the men, and had their own loves out of doors ; the earnest ones who had something in them, and the frivolous ones who had nothing in them ; and one—that girl who was my special friend and studied with me at the British Museum. She was one of the vanguard of the independent women ; but she did her life's work without blare or bluster, or help from the outside; and without that weakness of her sex which makes them cry out when they are hustled in the crowd they have voluntarily joined — which makes them think themselves aggrieved because they are not aided by the men to whom they have placed themselves in opposition and rivalry.

Then there were the women of sixty and

upwards, who chirped like birds and dressed like brides; the mother and daughter, who came no one knew whence, did no one knew what, were pleasant companions and charming entertainers—but kept at a distance; the buxom widows of forty, smiling, debonnaire and ready for their second bridal; and the sad-eyed ones of the same age, whose weepers were as big as sails, and their crape of phenomenal depth and blackness. There were the half-crazed members of well-known families planted out to insure that peace at home which their odd ways disturbed; and sometimes there were people whose antecedents would not bear scrutiny, and whose dismissal had to be summarily given. Like the shadows of a magic lantern these memories pass before me, and I ask myself: Was it really I, the man I am now, who lived there as one of this strange menagerie—myself, perhaps one of the strangest of them all?

Impulsive, shy, eager, enthusiastic, sensitive at all points, revelling in my sense
of liberty but scarcely knowing how
to use it, I was like some big bird as yet
unfledged—some huge puppy as yet untrained. My kind landlady, however, liked
me, and did her best to warn and direct me
as to my conduct in the house and the
intimacies to be formed or avoided among
her people.

'It is a pity you should be spoilt too
soon,' she said to me one day with a sigh.
'Boys are so nice, and men are such
wretches! I wish you could be a boy
for ever, then you might be worth something.'

'I shall be worth more when I am a man,'
I laughed. 'You shall be proud of me
then, Smithy. Wait till my book is published, and then you will see.'

'I would rather keep you as you are,'
she answered. 'When you are a man I

shall have lost you. Now you are like my own boy.'

'You shall never lose me, Smithy,' I said. 'I am not of the kind to change.'

Dear, good, generous Miss Smith ! She was only a boarding-house keeper ; but she was the most of a mother to me of any woman I have known—save poor Nurse Mary. I got to like her and confide in her so intimately that it seemed strange I had not known her all my life; and to the end we remained the perfectly good friends we were now, when she 'mothered' me and looked after me, and kept me, so far as she could, from making mistakes and falling into mischief. If I have seemed to give too much weight to this comparatively unimportant tract in my life's journey, it is because it was my first field of personal freedom ; and like all first things it has left an indelible impression on my mind.

CHAPTER X.

BY the end of the covenanted term I had accomplished my purpose and written my novel. It was an ambitious undertaking for a 'prentice hand, but it met with that kind of reception which means promise and opens the door to better things. It gave me no money. On the contrary, the publication cost me fifty pounds, which sum, advanced by Mr. King on the faith of my majority, was Mr. N——'s standing price for first books by young authors.

I shall never forget the day when I read the first favourable notice of my book, which, strangely enough, was in the *Times*. I seemed to tread on air, to walk in a cloud of light, to bear on me a sign of strange and glorious significance. I felt as if I must have stopped the passers-by to shake hands with them and tell them it was I who had written the novel which the *Times* had reviewed so well that morning. I thought all the world must be talking of it, and wondering who was the unknown Christopher Kirkland who, yesterday obscure, to-day famous, had so suddenly flashed into the world of letters ; and I longed to say that this veiled prophet, this successful aspirant, was I ! I remember the sunset as I went up Oxford Street, to what was not yet the Marble Arch. For I could not rest in the house. I could not even go home to dinner. I felt compelled to walk as if for ever—not like that poor wretch, for penance, over a dreary and interminable plain, but through an enchanted garden of infinite beauty

—to damp down the glad fever in my veins. I could only breathe out in the open. I should have been stifled within the four walls of that house in Montague Place.

Since then I have watched with breathless emotion the opalescent skies of Venice; the westering light which streams like visible prayer through the windows of St. Peter's as you stand on the Pincio; the gorgeous sunsets of Naples, with that burning bar drawn all across the horizon, stretching from Vesuvius to infinitude; but I have never seen one to match the splendour of that sunset in London, on the evening of the day when I first achieved success. For the moment I was as a god among gods. My veins were filled with celestial ichor, not human blood; and my mind saw what it brought—the infinity of glory because of that intensity of joy.

I turned into the Park and sat down on a bench, looking at this resplendence which

was to me like a message—a symbol of my
own strength and future lustre.   Suddenly,
as distinctly as if she had been there in the
body, I felt the presence of Adeline Dalrymple.   It seemed to me as if she stood
before me, enveloping me in her personality
as in the old days.   I seemed to feel her
arms about me—as if she drew me gently to
her bosom ; and I felt again her lips on my
forehead and my eyes.   Then she seemed to
sit down on the seat beside me, and I heard
the murmur of that marvellous voice, saying
softly : ' By the power of Love you have
come to the possession of Fame !'

The full chord of divinest harmony was
now complete.   All my life and being were
swept away as by one great rush and flood
of rapture, unfathomable, irresistible.   It
was as if I heard the primal harmony
whence all other music flows—as if I saw
the archetype of all beauty, and felt the
essence of all love and joy.   For that brief

moment I was in what we mean by heaven; when a heavy hand was laid a little roughly on my shoulder, and a harsh voice said rudely :

' Come, none of this now ! You mustn't sleep here, you know. Or is it drunk you are ?'

The angel with the flaming sword who turned me so unceremoniously out of Paradise was a park-keeper ; and poor Icarus, my spirit, had a headlong tumble from the empyrean to the dust !

When the agreement between us came to an end, my father again wanted me to give up my present life, go to Cambridge, put away my foolish doubts and take Orders like a rational being. He ought to have known this last was impossible, granting me the very elements of honesty. But he was so convinced, for his own part, of the truth of Christianity and the perfectness of Anglican Protestantism, that he felt sure if

I read in the orthodox direction I should be
also convinced. Thus he hoped that, by
studying for the ministry, I should by force
of better reasoning abandon my errors, and
at one and the same time redeem my
worldly position and save my soul.

Naturally I resisted this plan ; for I was
more than ever in love with liberty and
literature. And as there was really nothing
in my choice injurious to my family nor
derogatory to myself, I at last bore down my
father's opposition and won his consent :—
I am bound by truth to add, never his cor-
dial approval. Still, he consented ; and I was
thus saved from the pain, as well as the disgrace and wrong-doing, of flat disobedience
to his will ; and my home-ties remained
intact. And after my people had got rid of
the daily irritation of my presence, and I
myself had learned more self-control by
contact with the world, and had also become
less sore, because not so often wounded, we

were better friends than we had ever been before. My bi-annual visits to the dear old place were purely harmonious; which my life there had not been; and our mutual affection was strengthened, not weakened, by the loosening of the links and the lengthening of the chain.

My life, then, was finally arranged on the lines I had so long marked out for myself. Now I had only to show of what stuff I was made. For the rest, my future was in my own keeping.

The first necessity was to get steady employment outside my novel-writing, which was to be the sweet after the meat; and my ambition was that of most young writers not specialists—to get work on the press. This gradation of aim was the natural result of experience. From poetry to novel-writing, and thence to newspaper work—what an epitome of young ambition is here! I could not begin by reporting, as Dickens and Beard and Kent and Hunt and, if my memory serves me, George Henry Lewes, had begun. I did not know shorthand —which yet was easily learned. But I was too ambitious to like the idea of work so unindividualized and a position so subordinate as are the work and position of a reporter. I wanted to be a full-fledged leader-writer at once. Wherefore I tried my hand at what was really a social essay rather than a leader, on the wrongs of all savage aborigines. This I sent down to the office of the ——, with a letter stating the full presumption of my desires; and waited for the result.

Poor dear ' Smithy ' had a bad time of it for the next few days. For that fatal quality of concentration which has intensified every feeling and action of my life was then more potent than it is even now ; and there was nothing in heaven nor earth, the past, the present, nor the future, save the acceptance or rejection of that essay. The four days which intervened between my letter and the answer were four days of restlessness amounting to agony—of alternate hope and fear rising into insanity. There was no treading on air nor walking in a cloud of light now ! It was going through the Valley of the Shadow ; with perhaps that fatal abyss at the end !

On the fifth day I had wrestled through my torment and come out into the upper air once more. My proof lay on my plate at breakfast ; and with it was a letter from the editor, bidding me go down to the —— office to-day, at four o'clock precisely.

I was punctual to the moment ; and with a beating heart but very high head, went swinging up the narrow, dingy court into which the ' editor's entrance ' gave ; and then up the still narrower and still dingier stairs to a room whence I could not see the street for the dirt which made the windows as opaque as ground-glass. Here I was told to wait till Mr. Dundas could see me. In about half an hour the messenger returned, and ushered me into the awful presence.

For in truth it was an awful presence, in more ways than one. It was not only my hope and present fortune, but of itself, personally, it was formidable.

A tall, cleanly-shaved, powerfully-built man—with a smooth head of scanty red hair; a mobile face instinct with passion; fiery, reddish-hazel eyes; a look of supreme command; an air of ever-vibrating impatience and irascibility, and an abrupt but not unkindly manner, standing with his back to the fire-place—made half a step forward and held out his hand to me as I went into the room.

'So! you are the little boy who has written that queer book and want to be one of the press-gang, are you?' he said half-smiling, and speaking in a jerky and unprepared manner, both singular and re-assuring.

The little boy, by the way, was as tall as he—and that was two inches over six feet.

I took him in his humour and smiled too.

' Yes, I am the man,' I said.

' Man, you call yourself ? I call you a whipper-snapper,' he answered, always good-humouredly. ' But you seem to have something in you. We'll soon find it out if you have. I say though, youngster, you never wrote all that rubbish yourself ! Some of your elder brothers helped you. You never scratched all these queer classics and mythology into your own numskull without help. At your age it is im-possible.'

' It may be impossible,' I laughed ; 'at the same time it is true. I give you my word, no one helped me. No one even saw the manuscript or the proofs,' I added eagerly.

On which my new friend and potential

master startled me as much as if he had
fired off a pistol in my ear, first by his
laughter, and then by the volley of oaths
which he rolled out—oaths of the strangest
compounds and oddest meanings to be
heard anywhere—oaths which he himself
made at the moment, having a speciality
that way unsurpassed, unsurpassable and
inimitable.   But   as   he   laughed   while
he blasphemed, and called me ' good boy '
in the midst of his wonderful expletives,
he evidently did not mean mischief.   And
I had fortunately enough sense to understand his want of malice, and to accept his
manner as of the ordinary course of things.

This pleased him ;   and after he had
exhausted his momentary stock of oaths,
he clapped me on the back with the force of
a friendly sledge-hammer, and said :

' You are a nice kind of little beggar,
and I think you'll do.'

Then he told me to go into the next

room to write a leader on a Blue Book
which he would send in to me. It was the
report of the Parliamentary Commission on
the condition of the miners relative to the
' truck ' system.

'I give you three hours and a half,' he
said, taking out his watch. 'Not a minute
longer, by ——. By that time your work
must be done, or you'll have no supper
to-night ! You must take the side of the
men ; but—d'ye hear ?—you are not to
assassinate the masters. Leave them a leg
to stand on, and don't make Adam Smith
turn in his grave by any cursed theories
smacking of socialism and the devil knows
what. Do you understand, youngster? I
have had the passages marked which you
are to notice, and so you need not bother
that silly cocoanut of yours with any others.
Keep to the text ; write with strength ; don't
talk nonsense, and do your work like a man.
And now be off.'

To my great joy and supreme good luck, I seized the spirit of my instructions, and wrote a rattling, vigorous kind of paper, which pleased Mr. Dundas so much that he called me a good boy twenty times with as many different oaths, and took me home to dine with him. And from that day he put me on the staff of the paper, and my bread-and-butter was secure.

The next two years followed without any change in outward circumstances. I worked hard for very moderate pay; but I was young, strong, energetic, and temperate in my habits. To live was of itself good enough for me. I did not want the adventitious excitement of dissipation nor luxury. My work was my pleasure, and to do well was its own reward. I had that appetite for work which is the essential of success on a newspaper; and I was to be relied on at a pinch as well as for the day's steady routine. I filled the office of handy-

man about the paper—was now sent down
to describe a fête ; now given a pile of books
to review ; sometimes set to do the work of
the theatrical critic when this gentleman
was away ; and given certain social leaders to
write—but never the political.

For a young fellow as I was then, unfit
for responsibility because wanting in experience, this was all that I could expect.
And occasionally it was more than I was
fit for. Twice I got the paper into trouble
because of my unsound political economy,
and the trail of the socialistic serpent,
which made itself too visible for even
the —— ; for all that this was one of our
then most advanced Liberal journals. But,
as I was a favourite with the irascible
editor—to whom also I was sincerely attached, though I stood in wholesome awe
of him into the bargain—my sins were
forgiven. A sounder man than I was told
off to reply to the attacks I had drawn

down on our heads ; to explain away what
could not be retracted; and to carry the ——
out of the fire.   And I had nothing worse
to bear than an outburst of imprecations
which let off the steam and broke no one's
bones.

All the employés of the journal did not
come off so well when hot water was about ;
and some ran rough risks :—as, for instance,
that poor fellow who brought in either a
wrong or an unpleasant message—I forget
which—at whose head Mr. Dundas hurled
his heavy metal office-inkstand.   The man
ducked in time ; but the door was cut and
indented where the sharp edge had struck,
and blackened by a stream of ink from the
centre panel to the floor.   Mr. Dundas
showed me the place with a peal of laughter
and a volley of oaths, in no wise discon-
certed by this narrow escape from committing murder.   He made it up to the man
with a couple of sovereigns; and when the

door had been scraped and re-varnished, no more was heard of the matter. The men in the office were used to his ways, and dodged him when he let fly—waiting till the dangerous fit was over. All forgave his violence —some because they really loved him, and some because he paid them handsomely for their bruises.

Mr. Dundas was a bad writer and a poor classic, and not especially well-informed on any subject; but after Delane he was the best constructive as well as administrative editor of his time, and knew how to choose his staff and apportion his material with a discrimination that was almost like another sense. He was indefatigable in his office, and finally broke down his iron constitution by sheer hard work. What made the pity of it was, that this hard work was often more superfluous than necessary. But this minute attention to details was his point of honour, and he would not be beaten off it.

He used to wait at the —— office till the first
sheet was printed off—till five in the morning—and often he was so exhausted that he
had to be almost carried down the stairs.

For all his violent temper and frightful
language, he was able to dominate himself
with certain of his staff—two of whom are
especially in my mind.   They were men of
very different calibre and standing.   One
was the publisher of the paper—an extremely timid man, who looked as if he
would have died outright had he been
brutalized in any way; but he remained in
absolute peace with Mr. Dundas all the
time the —— lasted, and moved with him
to those other offices where the great weekly
paper was established; and the other was
his co-editor—a sensitive, refined, cultured
scholar, whose pride of gentlehood would
not have brooked affront nor submitted to
insolence.   To neither of these, so different
as they were but each so valuable, did Mr.

Dundas ever go beyond the nicest line of moderation; and the last, like the first, held with him to the end, and finally took the sole charge of that sharp-tongued Weekly, when the fiery spirit which had first ruled it was laid to rest under that melancholy monument on the Cornish coast he loved so well.

To me, younger and in some sort defenceless, I confess he was at times exceedingly brutal, though he was substantially kind and did what he could to give me work. But his oaths used to curdle my blood; his violence was at times appalling; and once he forget himself so far as to shake his fist in my face. That was when trouble had come between us; and it may be easily understood that this day saw my last visit to the office. It was the rift which was never mended.

But this furiousness was his habit. He forgot himself in the same way even with

18—2

ladies—witness that well-known scene, when he ran along the platform as the train was moving out of the station, cursing and swearing with all his might at the women he then loved best in the world, because they would not do something he wished.

All the same, he had his grand good points. He was generous and affectionate; utterly devoid of all treacherous instincts; and he bore no malice. He was brutal, if you will; but the core of him was sound; and his fidelity to his friends was very beautiful. With so much that can be said less than laudatory of this fierce Boanerges of the press, it is pleasant to record that which makes for his renown and claims our more tender memories.

I remember two notable crowds in which I found myself in these early days. One was when my old friends the Chartists marched through London twenty thousand strong, and I followed—not as a special constable. And the other was when Baron Rothschild addressed the people from the balcony on the day of his futile election. He began his speech by these words:

'I stand here by the will of the people.'

From the dead silence of the dense throng rose a voice clear and strong:

' So stood Barabbas!'

But, Barabbas notwithstanding, after a fight of years the Jews won the day; as the Roman Catholics had won theirs before them; and as Agnosticism will also win in the near future.

At this time I went much into society. My social place was that which naturally belongs to a youngster of good birth, who, if he has not quite won his spurs, may yet some day do great things—who knows?— and who has good names at his back. The tower of strength my grandfather the Bishop and my uncle the Dean were to me! What humiliating snobs we are! I became ac-

quainted with a few of the leaders of
thought already established, and some
who were still preparing for the time
when they too should lead and no longer
follow. Among others, I fell in with that
notorious group of Free - lovers, whose
ultimate transaction was the most notable
example of matrimony void of contract of
our day. But though those who floated on
the crest of the wave, and whose informal
union came to be regarded as a moral merit
even by the strait-laced, had the more genius
and the better luck, he who made personal
shipwreck, and from whose permitted tres-
pass the whole thing started, had the nobler
nature, the more faithful heart, the more
constant mind, and was in every way the
braver and the truer man. The one whom
society set itself to honour, partly because of the transcendent genius of his companion, partly because of his own brilliancy
and facility, was less solid than specious.

The other, whom all men, not knowing him, reviled, was a moral hero. The former betrayed his own principles when he made capital out of his 'desecrated hearth' and bewildered society by setting afloat ingenious stories of impossible cere- monies which had made his informal union in a certain sense sacramental, so that he might fill his rooms with 'names' and make his Sundays days of illustrious reception. The latter accepted his position without ex- planation or complaint, and was faithful to his flag, indifferent to selfish gain or social loss. And whether that flag embodied a right principle or a wrong, his steadfastness was equally admirable, and the constancy which could not be warped for loss or gain was equally heroic.

It must never be forgotten too that he who afterwards posed as the fond husband betrayed by the trusted friend, was, in the days when I first knew them all, the most pronounced Free-lover of the group, and openly took for himself the liberty he expressly sanctioned in his wife. As little as he could go into the Divorce Court for his personal relief, because of that condonation and his own unclean hands, so little did he deserve the sympathy of society for the transfer which afterwards he put forward as his own justification and that friend's condemnation.

This I say with absolute knowledge of the whole series of facts, from the beginning. And I say it for sake of the truth and in the interests of justice—though it be but justice to the dead.

At the time when I first knew these people they were living in a kind of family communion that was very remarkable. Sisters and cousins and brothers—some of the women married and with yearly increasing families, to which they devoted themselves ; others single, and of general domestic utility all round—clubbed together their individually thin resources, and made a kind of family Agapemone which had its charm and its romance. Among them were some who practised no divergence in their own lives, and allowed of none in theory :—such as Samuel Lawrence, who was then vainly giving his strength to discover the Venetian method of colouring ; and that handsome Egyptologist, George Gliddon, who might have thrown his handkerchief where he would, but who was true to his first love, and married her when her youth and beauty had long since gone, and only her truth and her lovely nature remained. These and some others went with the broad current of ordinary morality. But also there were, as I have said, certain Free-lovers mingled with the orthodox rest ; and of these the most remarkable was that faithful and lovable man, that generous and patient, loyal and devoted friend, of whom I have just spoken, and whose individuality many still living will recognise.

I also became as intimate as a son with a father with the most famous poet-scholar of our generation ; the ' old man eloquent,' whose mind was more Greek than English, and whose hatred of political tyranny on the one side, was balanced by his aristo-cratic exclusiveness and personal pride on the other. He was of some use to me in helping me to polish my style ; and he indoctrinated me with an enduring horror of slang. But the crowning misfortune of my character, intractibility, which has marred so much of my life, prevented my gaining as much as I might by his lessons. I could accept only such things as commended themselves to my own judgment. I could not accept them simply on authority—even his. I therefore profited intellectually by this friendship less than I should have done had my mind been more plastic and more apt to subordination. But I gained all the same.

I always look back to the times when I visited Mr. Landor as the most valuable for lessons in self-control. I reverenced him so deeply and loved him so tenderly, and the difference between our ages was so great, that I should as little have thought of contradicting him as I should have thought of irritating a lion. If I did not accept all he said, I never presumed to oppose him ; and his fiery temper subdued mine by the very force of my own love and respect. Had he declared that the stars shone at mid-day, I would have answered: ' Yes, dear father, they do ;' and he would have returned, with his sweet smile : 'My good Christopher !—my good son !' Thus his temper, notoriously short in tether and leonine in its wrath as it was, was never once ruffled during the whole of our thirteen years of close and constant friendship ; and the self-control I was obliged to exercise was of incalculable service to me.

The affection between Mr. Landor and myself was very true and deep, and it began at first sight and through my own enthusiasm. His 'Imaginary Conversations' was one of my most cherished books. Edwin gave it to me when he came of age, and I loved it better than all else I had—save Adeline Dalrymple's 'Shelley.' When I was introduced to an ill-dressed and yet striking-looking old man—with unbrushed apple-pie boots ; a plain shirt-front, like a night-gown, not a shirt ; a wisp of faded blue for all kerchief round his neck ; his snuff-coloured clothes rumpled and dusty— but an old man with a face full of the majesty of thought, with a compressed mouth capable of the sweetest tenderness, and an air of mental grandeur all through, and was told that he was Mr. Landor— WALTER SAVAGE LANDOR—I broke out into an ardent exclamation of joy, and showed such boyish delight as pleased him, and, in a sense, took his heart by storm.

' And who is this young fellow, who cares so much for an old man ?' he said, holding my hand, and perhaps not understanding what joy it was to me to see in the flesh one of the great gods of my intellectual world.

From that hour the thing was done. I became to him like his own son, and he was my father. And as he loved me in that I was his child as well as his scholar—and loved my love for him as much as he took interest in my professional career—and as we agreed in our abstract politics, and harmonized in our hatred of tyrants—we got on together, as I say, with perfect accord—to the surprise of everyone who knew my dear father-friend's peculiarities of impatience and my own natural indocility.

If some marvelled, others envied. Among these latter was John Forster—that literary

Ghebir who worshipped all the suns that shone, and grudged that any but himself should bask in their rays. He never forgave me my intimacy with the Samson who had already generously endowed him with the copyright of his books, and whose kindness, he was afraid, would be diverted to me. Probably he thought I was as self-seeking as himself. In the days to come he made me feel his enmity ; and of all the queer things in my strange life, one of the queerest is the determination with which he, first, and then subsequent biographers of Mr. Landor, have agreed to ignore my friendship with him. This grudgingness has gone on to the end; and I was deprived of his bequest to me on a plea which was either a false pretence, or an act of selfishness.

In this fair city of palaces, where my dear 'father-friend' had made his home, lived a clever old lady who had once been a schoolmistress and had written a very pretty little story. She was cleverer than her works; seeming to need the friction of conversation to bring out her own latent fire. She was a picturesque old lady, and always dressed in very light, soft grey with a profusion of white lace. After seventy, she said, all women should dress in light grey and wear much white lace; so, giving the sense of freshness and cleanliness. After fifty and before seventy they ought to wear black. She was a great friend of Mr. Landor's; but she one day offended his susceptibilities, and he broke with her, never to renew his acquaintance. Courteous as he was to women—taking them downstairs and standing bareheaded by the door of their carriages, according to the manners of the old school, and of Italy—he could be as vehement to them as to men when he was offended; and to affront him once was to lose him for ever.

My first friend in the city was that learned and fastidious Dr. Devise, who had read too much for any good work of his own to be possible. He had, as it were, smothered his originality by the enormous mass of other men's thoughts with which he had loaded his brain. He was intent on writing a book which should demolish all religious superstition; and he had already been many years about it. The first chapter only was finished. This he had had printed as a ' brick,' for private circulation. I cannot say that I was impressed by it. Seeking to be comprehensive, it was wire-drawn and diluted. It read like a list of synonyms, or a catalogue of intellectual processes; and in the matter of literary style it was singularly poor.

Dr. Devise was a man who had extreme fascination for some people. One of our greatest celebrities, when in the Ugly Duck stage of her existence and before she had joined her kindred Swans, had wanted to dedicate her life to him. But too many other feminine interests were already established to allow of the introduction of an outsider; and the friendship came to a stormy end, after a more than ordinarily ardent beginning. His house was my first sojourning-place in Bath ; but I annoyed him too, by my confessed preference for the 'Father'; and I fear he thought me both ungrateful and a fool.

Anyhow, he gave me one of those moral shocks which are the birth-hours of new experience to youth, when, one day, he gently chid me for loving Mr. Landor better than I loved him. Still gentle, but cynical as well as half-compassionate, he went on to remind me that Mr. Landor had no money to leave ; that he had even given the copyright of his works to John Forster—as I already knew—and that his very pictures, of which he was so proud, were for the most part rubbish.

I never forgave this insinuation. And it did not mend matters when he spoke of his own ampler means, and how he was able both to leave his family well provided for and to remember congenial outsiders into the bargain. I never cared for him after this. At no time of my life have I been self-seeking in friendship; and legacies have come into my calculations as little as the chance of a peerage or an offer of the Garter. And if this be so now, when I have learned the value of money, what was it then, when I was still too young and impulsive to calculate or foresee anything whatever? For all his learning and hospitality and undoubted qualities, there was ever in my mind after this a repugnance to Dr. Devise which lasted to the end.

But I liked his cheerful, patient, blind wife, with her graceful little courtesies, pretty flatteries, and craving for sympathy. And her energetic sister-in-law, with her strong brain and heart of purest gold, was 'Aunt Susan' to me, as she was to some others. She was a passionate propagandist of freethought, and was never so happy as when giving away the small tracts and bigger books which were her artillery against the strongholds of superstition. Mr. Scott, of Ramsgate, found her a valuable auxiliary; and she welcomed every new light with almost youthful enthusiasm. She was one of the bravest of the morally brave; for she suffered keenly from that kind of local ostracism, consequent on her unorthodox opinions, which in a manner isolated her and reduced her society to a few—fit, if you will, but few all the same. Yet she never relaxed her propagandism, which was as much part of her philanthropy as was her more direct benevolence in the matters of food and flannel; and she dug her own social grave unflinchingly, if with some sighs and not a few heart-aches.

Dr. Devise's soft - voiced, fair-skinned daughter was also one of my chosen friends at this time. Her charm lay in her marvellous power of sympathy and almost godlike strength of consolation. She was like a younger daughter of Demeter, in whose soft white arms the troubled might lie and be at rest. In my own dark hour, which came upon me a little later, she was of divine and infinite consolation. And others found in her the exquisite charm that was so patent and potent to me.

A kind of outlying member of this remarkable group was a certain refined and thoughtful man who was in those days the ideal poet and student—as he is now the ideal scholar and philosopher. He was of all the men known to me one of the most graceful in mind, most cultivated in intellect, most modest in bearing, most accurate in learning, and of the purest kind of morale incarnate in human form. He was then in Orders. Subsequently he broke his chains and came out into freedom and the light.

There were also two learned sisters who lived near my doctor friend, and carried to him a chilly worship like incense smouldering in a censer of ice. They awed me by their fearful superiority. They were women who had the most extraordinary power of dwarfing all other pretensions and degrading you both in your own esteem and in the eyes of others. And they used this power unsparingly. They had not lived down the softer follies and tender frailties of youth, for they had never had any to live down, being of the tribe of the 'unco' guid'—the 'prigs in petticoats'—from the beginning. Self-centred, bloodless, intellectual, sarcastic, unemotional, they had no sympathy with the sorrows which sprung from passion and no compassion for failure. They were like a couple of old Egyptian

goddesses shot through with Voltaire—
Pasht for the one, the Sphinx for the other—
while behind the mask of each peered the
keen satirical and mocking face of the
author of 'Candide.' They thought me
abominable, and I thought them dreadful;
and there was always war between us, such
as Tieck or Hoffmann would have made
between a couple of Ice-maidens and the
Fire-king.

Here, I made the acquaintance of Mr.
Empson, that pre-historic æsthete who did
his best to create a taste for minor ornamentation by skilfully combined and original
adaptations, and whose bric-à-brac shop was
a favourite lounge with the best people in
Bath. My dear old 'father' was frequently
there, and I with him. Mr. Empson was
eager for lengths of old brocades with which
to line the covers of his more valuable books,
or to drape as curtains about his statuettes.
He was wonderfully sleek and silky in his

manners; but I saw the reverse of the polished medal when, one day, he turned on me with a sudden outburst of astounding ferocity, because I compassionated him for some rheumatic ailment of which he complained.

'How can you, a strong young fellow in the beautiful morning of life, care for what an old man like me suffers? I hate humbug!' he said savagely.

On which I fired up and told him that he was both impolite and inhuman, and that he had no right to question my sincerity unless he had found me already less than honest. But these sleek, silky, smooth-mannered people are so often savage when touched beneath the skin!

Then I knew the charming family of that delightful Irish actor who went down in the ill-fated *President*. The mother had a mania for birds and small dogs, and the girls were among the prettiest in Bath.

They were of three distinct types—'petillante,' statuesque, elfin—Rosina, Galatea, Fenella; and each was perfect in her kind.

There was also one man of whom I will only say that I thought him then, and I think him now, one of the Best I have ever known—one of those who make the honour of their generation, and who help to keep society sweet and pure, because entirely governed by principle. With him it was religious principle, which he translated into practical and vital morals. He and my brother Godfrey stand side by side under the measuring standard of human worth. The one has touched the heights by faith, the other by honour. The one has learned self-command by obedience, the other by self-respect. Neither could commit a dishonourable action, were the noose knotted and life to be the forfeit; but the one would gather his strength from religion, the other from heroism—the one would die with the fervour of a martyr, the other with the fortitude of a Stoic.

All the same, differences of method notwithstanding, they stand shoulder to shoulder on the green plot of human nobleness; and no one can say that the one is higher than the other—the one better or braver or stronger than the other. They have come to the same point by different roads; and the modes of faith for which graceless zealots fight are emphatically of no account with such as these, whose lives are so eminently in the right.

END OF VOL. I.

BILLING AND SONS, PRINTERS, GUILDFORD.

G., C. & Co.

THE AUTOBIOGRAPHY

OF

CHRISTOPHER KIRKLAND.

BY

MRS. LYNN LINTON,

AUTHOR OF
'THE TRUE HISTORY OF JOSHUA DAVIDSON,' 'PATRICIA KEMBALL,'
'THE ATONEMENT OF LEAM DUNDAS,' 'UNDER WHICH
LORD?' ETC.

IN THREE VOLUMES.
VOL. II.

LONDON:
RICHARD BENTLEY AND SON,
Publishers in Ordinary to Her Majesty the Queen.
1885.

THE AUTOBIOGRAPHY

OF

CHRISTOPHER KIRKLAND.

CHAPTER I.

 WILL go on with my general reminiscences of persons, not keeping strictly to chronology.

I became as a child of the house in the family of Captain Maconochie, that great and good inventor of the Mark System. He had then just returned from Norfolk Island—the penal settlement of the penal settlements; the lower deep of the lowest

depths; that veritable hell upon earth
which he had made human and possible.
He had been deprived of his governorship
by those at home who thought that to provide for the moral improvement of criminals
was to offend against justice, which should
be simply punitive.

The whole question of prison discipline
and the final cause of punishment has under-
gone revision since then; and it was Captain
Maconochie who started the change. He,
who after Howard had the most compassion
for convicted criminals, had, even more than
Howard, breadth of view and administrative
capacity. But the grand idea of giving
prisoners an interest in their own good conduct, and of making Hope an element in the
process of self-redemption, was unpalatable
to the official world. The actual system
was founded on the basis of punishment
pure and simple, plus the deterring of others
by example; the method was that of unin-

dividualized and unelastic coercion; and the new view of self-reformation by rewarding voluntary well-doing was looked on as offering an educational premium to vice, and making crime a profitable moral investment. For do not minds follow the law of all the rest? and is it fair to reform criminals and let honest men go wrong for want of better teaching?

It was the same in other things. When Captain Maconochie advocated certainty of detection as more deterring to crime than severity of sentence, he was laughed at as a dreamer; when he said: ' Reform while you punish, and turn out a possibly useful member of society, rather than a confirmed gaol-bird, sure to come back to his foul roost,' he was ridiculed as a crazy philanthropist who had lost the just distinction between vice and virtue; when he wished to do away with short-time sentences, he was met with the rights of the ratepayers; and everywhere he fell upon the dead wall of negation, and found himself opposed and baffled.

He was one of those men who fail in their own persons, but whose principles take root and fructify—not to their own profit. The Home Office negatived his scheme; but afterwards they allowed Sir Walter Crofton to try his Mark System, modified; and the ticket-of-leave now granted is also only a modification of his more comprehensive idea. It was painful to watch the uphill fight he carried on against inertia here and active opposition there, and to know that all this while a grand truth was being arrested and nullified by prejudice.

His wife, as firmly convinced as he, and as good and sincere and earnest, went for a little in this opposition, because of that fatal quality of exaggeration which makes women such unreasoning partisans and dangerous auxiliaries. Thus, she was an

ardent homœopathist; and when she visited
the sick female prisoners in the borough
gaol afterwards given her husband to ad-
minister, she slipped surreptitious globules
into their pockets, to the discrediting of the
orthodox system and the encouragement of
rebellion against the appointed healers. Her
doings, when the medical authorities discovered them, brought the whole thing
down about their ears ; but she comforted
herself for the loss she had occasioned by
the consciousness of the good of her cause ;
and the sentiment of martyrdom upheld her.
She believed too in mesmerism; she was
a born proselytizer ; and she had that kind
of fervour in her conviction which denies
honesty to all opponents.

My friends were full of interesting stories
about the criminals whom they had tamed,
subdued and reformed by kindness; among
whom, I remember, figured one notorious
ruffian, Jacky-Jacky, who had almost homi-

cidal mania. Him they made their gardener; and Mrs. Maconochie spoke of a certain creeping of the flesh when one day she stood alone with Jacky-Jacky by the fruit-trees in their compound—he armed with a bill-hook, and she defenceless. They had a family of delightful boys, of whom the eldest was singularly handsome and good; and Captain Maconochie used often to speak of this young fellow's purifying influence over the roughest of the men, and how they checked their ribaldry in his presence because of respect for his youth and purity, and listened to his Bible-reading without a word that would have shocked a girl.

It was the Christian law of kindness all through, rather than the old hard lex talionis; and it answered so far as the men were concerned. But practical Christianity is the worst investment a modern Christian can make; and to follow the example or obey the precepts of Christ is even more disastrous than to doubt His divinity. And so my friends found to their cost.

In those days I held, with these dear people, that capital punishment was a barbarism, and that the 'worst use to which you can put a man is to hang him.' Now I am not quite so sure. Life is only valuable for what it gives to the individual or contributes to society; and life-long imprisonment cannot do much for the one nor the other. And as there is always that inevitable 'must' at the end, it makes little matter whether it comes a year or two sooner than need have been, when the intrinsic worth of life has gone and there is no more hope for the man himself. I did not think this then. I was too strong, too fully vitalized, to regard death with other feelings than those of dread as well as pity. But when the coloured glass of vigorous youth, through which one looks at the large landscape of life, has been broken, one sees things more in reference to the whole, and less with regard to the individual.

But in those olden times we were warm anti-death punishers at my dear friends' house, and just as warm believers in the restoration to righteousness of life for those criminals who were properly directed. We were all humane, religious, believing and unscientific. We had no faith in heredity, and we gave no weight to environment. We believed in mind and soul and spirit; in heavenly influence and divine grace ; and we thought that miracles of moral healing could be worked if only a pathway were made for this divine grace to enter and take possession.

If Captain Maconochie had been a less religious man, and if Mrs. Maconochie had been a less logically sincere woman, they would have done better for themselves and their great ideas than they did. The sword of the Lord and of Gideon is a difficult weapon to wield at any time ; and, on the whole, biological facts and the hard common-sense views of men make more practicable handles than faith in the influx of the Holy Spirit and the answer of God to prayer.

I knew the famous American actress who then divided London into two camps—the one of admirers, the other of detractors.   I will not say on which side I am.   Things cling about her name which it is as well not to disturb, and the grave, though dumb, is the most potent of all advocates.   And she had some superb qualities, if she also had some that were low and mean.   Of these last she had jealousy—that lowest and meanest of all in the moral catalogue ; and, for another, she had ingratitude, and knew how to kick down, with consummate address, the ladder by which she had mounted a stage higher. Her mother was the vulgarest old woman I have ever seen.   I remember a brief conver-sation with her which ran thus : The

subject was an underhung, wriggling terrier
pup:—

'My !' said this old lady, looking
curiously at the dog. 'Why, it's wopper-
jawed !'

' "Wopper-jawed"? What is that ?' I
asked.

' Why, don't you know!—like a wiggler!'

'But what is a "wiggler"?' I asked
again.

'Oh my ! Not know !—du tell ! A
wopper-jawed wiggler—just like a pollywog
out of a hydrant !'

The first time I heard the expression
'talking the fifth wheel off a coach' was
from her ; and the way in which she used
to eat lemons was what she herself would
have called 'a caution.'

Associated with her and her two
daughters, in my mind, are a certain medical
man and his beautiful young wife. I knew
this rather odd, as well as famous American

triad through them, and so the association comes about. What charming days I used to have with these dear young people ! How handsome they both were!—and how young and happy we all were ! As for her, she was one of the most beautiful creatures under heaven, and as good as she was lovely. I have seen the whole theatre turn round to look at her, and she could not walk in the street without attracting more attention than she cared for. She had the carriage of a young goddess or an old-time nymph; and her character corresponded, in its fearless truth and unflinching honesty with the wonderful nobility of her bearing. He too was a right good fellow; but though she, alas! is dead, he is alive—and I do not like to mention the names of those still living.

Also I knew the 'Raffaele-faced young bookseller' whose hopes were so high and whose aims were so lofty ; and in his house

I met many of those who, then young and unknown, have since become world-famous. Herbert Spencer ; Marian Evans—our future incomparable George Eliot ; William Smith, or ' Thorndale' as he used to be called ; Dr. Hodgson ; Charles Bray ; Dr. Brabant ; Edward Pigott ;—these were among the stars rising or risen to be found at that house. There too I met Froude, one of our best, if most prejudiced, historians, master of style and eloquent Devil's Advocate as he is ; and I remember once seeing Mrs. Gaskell with her beautiful white arms bare to the shoulder, and as destitute of bracelets as were her hands of gloves.

Above all, I remember one special evening when Carlyle and Emerson were there, and each had his own little circle of adorers clustered round him as he harangued and perorated. The two great men did not speak to each other—only each to his own special gathering; which was for all the world like a swarm of bees clustered round their queen. I sat apart with that soft-voiced, fair-skinned daughter of Dr. Devise of whom I have spoken before, and wondered at the mental servility of these two groups —a mental servility which I confess was to me more sickening than worshipful.

Morris Moore's newly discovered ' Raffaele ' was then almost as much a matter of bitter controversy as it has been since; and the recognition of its genuineness got somehow mixed up with party spirit and became a sign of identification. It was engraved by Linton in the *Leader* newspaper ; and perhaps that was the reason why it was taken as a test of Liberalism.

The establishment of that newspaper, by the way, was to all of us ardent youths like the beginning of a moral and intellectual millennium. How ardent and eager we all were ! How bravely Thornton Hunt and

George Henry Lewes and other young lions roared in its columns!—and how confident everyone was that it would supersede the *Examiner* and the *Athenæum*, become a monumental success, and transform to its own likeness all divergent public opinion! Oh! those fair false hopes of youth!—those baseless visions of enthusiasm! What 'strengthless heads' of dead loves have half the pathos that lies in these dead faiths! What a glorious castle too, we built when the first International Exhibition was reared, and we all believed that the reign of universal peace had begun, and the death-knell of international strife had sounded! And how all these brilliant hopes and iridescent faiths have gone into space, with nothing left as the residuum save disappointment!

About this time came to all of us who were known to be unorthodox a certain private and confidential circular bearing Thornton Hunt's name. It had for its object the foundation of a quasi-masonic community—a kind of cryptic church of free-thought, where the unpublished members should be able to recognise each other, and by their aid and counsel support such as were weak before the social trials inevitable to denial. This scheme also fell to the ground, and never went beyond that printed appeal.

With others, I became an intimate in the house of Mrs. Milner Gibson, that large-hearted woman who opened her doors to all the exiled patriots that flocked to England as their only safe asylum, and who was as a crowned Queen wandering through Bohemia. She was one of the most prominent features of London society in her day, and went through the appointed phases of the widest Liberalism, the most marked Bohemianism, the most mystical spiritualism, and the most fervent Catholicism, proper to her kind. But in each and all the generous heart, the loving nature, the wide, full charity of divine sympathy and pity, remained unchanged.

At her house I met, in their due time, Mazzini, Louis Blanc, Kossuth, Klapka, Pulszky, the Sicilian exiles—notably the Scalias—to mention only a few of the most famous. But when the well-known floating medium got hold of her, her salon was given up to table-turning and séances, wherein she herself was the most deceived and the most credulous. Great efforts were made to convince me of the truth of the phenomena exhibited. I was young, ardent, and a press-man; hence I should have been so far a valuable ally. But though I went diligently to these séances, and was quite prepared to believe in their genuineness, I never saw anything that might not have been done by trick—neither there nor elsewhere.

I was at this house when the notorious

levitating medium was said to have floated to the ceiling. The story is simply this. Mr. Hume was in his usual place at the end of the chain of experimenters, where the circular-table touched the jamb of the window—leaving a free space between him and Mademoiselle, the governess, who always sat opposite to him. Our hostess was always on his left hand. The room was almost pitch-dark—lighted only from the distant lamp in the mews, which this window faced. Suddenly Mr. Hume left his seat and came over to where I was sitting. He leaned over my chair and spoke to my neighbour and me, saying that the spirits were preparing something, he did not know what. The next moment we heard the sound of a piece of furniture moving across the room. It was a light *chaise longue*, which stood by the wall in a line with our chairs.

'The spirits want me to get on this,' he

said; and forthwith he sat down on the couch.

There was a certain man in the company, called Smith, of Peckham, who had been an atheist, but whom Mr. Hume had converted to spiritualism and Christianity. To him this medium was a Christ. He clasped his hands and knelt on the ground.

'Let me go too!' he said, praying the Lord rather than making a request to his brother man.

His High Priest gave a rather ungracious assent, and the two moved off; but Smith of Peckham was found to be inconvenient, so was soon sent back to his old place at the table.

There was a large mirror over a console-table at the end of the wall, facing the window; and near to this was a heavy old-fashioned ottoman, with a strong and serviceable centre-piece.

In a short time Mr. Hume said he was

floating up to the ceiling; and in the dim light of the room we could see that a dark body was between us and the mirror. The voice seemed to ascend, and we heard the sound of a slight scratching. Then the voice came down. Mr. Hume said he had scratched a cross on the ceiling, and called for lights. There was a great hunt for the small grains of plaster on the floor, and the case was recorded in the spiritualist journal as an undoubted instance of floating.

There was nothing to have prevented Mr. Hume from drawing the *chaise longue* to him by means of a string round the front two legs; moving it by his own feet and muscles; standing on the centre-piece of the otto-man; and, with a knife tied to the end of a stick, scratching a cross on the ceiling. The rest was easy to ventriloquism and certain to credulity.

At other times he showed the hands— luminous hands—which Mademoiselle, the

21—2

governess, said she felt forming themselves in her dress. These hands played with the tassel and strings of the blinds, and were phosphorescent. One, coal-black, was the emblem of superstition; another—covered with what they all said was a spiritual veil or refulgent kind of mask, and I a cambric pocket-handkerchief—was the sign of faith. But as no one was allowed to investigate, and as to express doubt would have been impolite, things were received with acclaim by most of those present, and only a few of us had the honesty of silence.

Capable of being made into a useful ally, could I but be caught, Mr. Hume arranged one séance for my benefit. This was the first at which I was present. I must explain the foundations. One of my friends had had a little child of which I had been passionately fond. It had been named after me; I had adopted it for my own; and the whole story was patent to the world.

At the time of which I write the child was dead, and the mother was a hopeless invalid. By all my own people I had always been called Chris, or Christie. By our hostess and the whole group of her friends, who were mine, and by this group only, I was called Crishna. The child had been christened Christopher, and was called Christie.

In the midst of the usual array of luminous hands, this night, came a round shining thing which Mademoiselle, the governess, and Mr. Hume, the medium, both cried out at once was a child's head. For whom? The guests were numbered, and the spirits rapped when I was indicated. This spiritual child was for me. This was my first personal experience of a thing of this kind, and for the moment I was overcome.

'This means a little child of whom I was very fond,' I said in a half-whisper to my neighbour. 'It was called after me and dedicated to me.'

' Yes,' said Mr. Hume, as if speaking in a dream. He was in a trance. ' This little child was Crishna on earth, as it is Crishna in heaven, and its mother thanks you in heaven for your loving care of it on earth. She is standing by you now, blessing you and watching over you.'

She was in her own bed, poor body, incapable of either blessing or watching over even herself!

This bad shot saved me from all after danger of credulity, and left me with a clear mind and untroubled senses to watch and weigh all that I saw.

Robert Bell was one of the most convinced of Mr. Hume's dupes. He expatiated warmly on the supernatural power which enabled a pencil to lie—on a clinging velvet cloth—without rolling off when the table was tilted to a certain angle. I tried the experiment at home, and found that by careful manipulation I could tilt my own table at even a more acute angle than the medium had done, and that neither the pencil nor the glasses would fall.

When I said this to Robert Bell he was exceedingly angry, and what had been a very pleasant friendship came to an abrupt and sudden end.

Poor old Dr. Ashburner too, had it much at heart to convert me to the faith; and at his house I saw, among others, the medium who writhed like a demoniac when the spirits were writing in red letters on his large white fine-skinned arm a name that should carry conviction to the soul of the unbeliever.

This man had two tricks—that of this skin-writing, which was soon found out; and that of reading with the tips of his fingers the names written on small pieces of paper, folded up into pellets and flung into a heap on the table. This sleight-of-hand was respectable; but I caught the trick, and told

Dr. Ashburner what I had seen. The dear old man did not believe me and he did believe Mr. Foster, the medium, even after he found out that he had been in prison for felony.

I could fill a volume with my spiritualistic experiences, suspicions, and silent detections of imposture. I have never seen anything whatever that might not have been done by trick and collusion, and I have seen almost all the mediums. Never, anywhere, has there been allowed the smallest investigation, nor have the most elementary precautions been taken against imposture; and the amount of patent falsehood swallowed open-mouthed has been to me a sorry text on which to preach a eulogium on our enlightenment.

Yet all the time I was yearning to believe—to be forced by irrefragable proofs to accept one undoubted authority, which would have ended for ever certain gnawing pains. Those proofs never came. On the contrary, with every séance at which I assisted came increased certainty of imposture. And yet, now, at the end of it all, though I have never seen a medium who was not a patent trickster, I believe that there is an uncatalogued and perhaps undeveloped human force, which makes what the Americans call a magnetic man, and which is the substratum of truth underlying the falsehoods of spiritualism, the deceptions of hysteria, and the romances of religious fervour. We have not said the final word yet on the development of man; and this uncatalogued force may be one of the chief factors in the sum of future progress.

So far there may be truth in what we hear; but when heavy women are brought bodily through the air and dropped clean through roofs and walls; when notes fly from India to London; and when spirits materialize themselves and put on hair which is made up of cells and fibres and pigments like growing human hair, and dress in clothes well-cut and stitched together with ordinary thread, beside being loaded with Manchester dressing—then, I think, the common-sense of the world should revolt in indignation at these patent falsehoods and frauds, and the weak should be protected from the cruel craft of the unscrupulous.

What will not people believe ? I remember poor old Dr. Ashburner telling me a story of how once, when he was sitting alone at night, in sore perplexity as to ways and means, a knock came to the street door. He opened it, and saw on the pavement an unknown man bestriding a black horse. Without a word this visitor silently thrust into his hand a packet of Bank of England notes, then dashed off down the street and was no more seen. The notes were to the value of five hundred pounds, and were given by the spirits.

If so, were those spirits thieves or forgers? For these Bank of England notes must have been stolen, either from the Bank itself or from some private person; or, if made by the spirits themselves, they were forgeries and the Bank would have to suffer. But, because the transactions of the Bank of England—like those of nature—are so large as to appear illimitable to us, we do not realize that not one single five-pound note is issued without the utmost accuracy of registration and balance; and that therefore a spiritual theft or forgery of five hundred pounds would as certainly be detected, and would as certainly result in the loss of some individual, as if it had been money taken out of one's own private purse.

It was, however, like arguing against the miracle of the loaves and fishes because corn is made only by translation of material through assimilation, and is built up cell by cell—and fishes cannot be fashioned without milt and spawn and development, save at the cost of upsetting the whole balance of everything. The dear old man only lamented my blindness, which far exceeded his own, he said sorrowfully. But my Sadduceeism was immovable, and I could not see my way to the spiritual origin of those bank notes— if indeed they ever existed out of the realms of fancy at all. For after he became blind, and his imagination was neither checked nor controlled by his senses, Dr. Ashburner fell into that state of mental haze where the boundary lines between fact and fancy are clean swept away.

What crowds of people, and what multitudes of drawing-rooms come before me, like shapes and shadows passing over a mirror ! Handsome Harrison Ainsworth, with his choice little dinners at Kensal

Green ; Dr. Quin, that prince of diners-out and king of good fellows ; Douglas Jerrold, keen, witty, sarcastic, yet kind-hearted ; those Sunday evenings at Thornton Hunt's, where used to be met that Reader, who always reminded me of the Spanish proverb which bids you beware of the man who speaks softly and writes harshly; for Mr. Williams, with the softest, sleekest, silkiest manner in the world, had the most trenchant pen, and could cut your very heart out when he refused your manuscript for his firm:—All are gone now ; and of many almost even the very remembrance has died out.

Who now remembers that fine old lady, in her quaint old-world costume, who had been married to one of the notabilities of his day, and was herself a notability in her own? whose son-in-law was also a celebrity? and whose daughter is still one of the standing marvels as well as one of the charms of London society ? How well I remember

her friendly interest in me, and how, when
I once kissed her hand, she patted my face
and thanked me.   At her daughter's house
I first met one of our since most famous
painters.   He was a mere lad then, very
handsome, and very unused to society.   He
wore a frock-coat buttoned to the chin ;
black gloves ; and his boots showed that he
had been walking, and that the streets were
muddy.   The whole *mise-en-scène* of his life
is rather of a different character now !

Then there was that celebrity-loving lady
who was always supposed to have been the
original of Mrs. Leo Hunter.   Her husband
had lost his large fortune in some South
American mines, but they still ' saw people.'
At her house I met poor Miss Pardoe, who
took the substance for the shadow, and
spent on society the proceeds which she
should have husbanded for old age, to find,
when too late, that fashion is about the
worst bank in which you can invest.   She

had very small feet, of which, woman-like, she was proud; and I can yet see the dainty coquettishness of her pale blue satin slippers and the art with which she kept them well in view.

Here I met the two Misses Strickland —Agnes, with her ringlets and look of faded prettiness, accepting homage as one who had been used to it all her life; Elizabeth, sturdy, plain, devoted, self-effacing, the one who did the real work while giving to her sister all the honour. She lived only for that sister's pleasure and in her success; and she really idolized her. I shall never forget my own surprise when one day she turned to me, with a look of supreme devotion on her good, plain, hard-featured face, and said—every word like a caress—' How pretty Agnes looks to-day !'

Once I was taken to see Miss Jane Porter, then living in a little street in Bayswater. She was in her bedroom, dressed in black, and I think she wore a white cap underneath a long black scarf over her head. I was considerably awed by her presence and manner, and I felt as if I had been in one of Mrs. Radcliffe's rooms. She was an eerie, ghastly old lady, and she had that stagey and stately manner of the old school which impresses young people so painfully —impresses and crushes them.

Then there was that pretty little wife of the Q.C., with her trim figure, childish shoulders, youthful manners, and plain-featured daughters—whom she suppressed. She was one of my social godmothers, and stood sponsor for me in more houses than one. She took me, inter alia, to Sir Charles Babbage's, telling me on the way that he admitted to his evening parties only pretty women and distinguished men. The compliment was two-edged, and pleased both her and me alike.

Her sister was that famous widow who

spent her substance in searching for the remains of her still more famous husband. But, as was often said, she built her own monument when she manned her ships and organized her expeditions ; and she wrote her epitaph in her conjugal constancy. Nevertheless, I believe it is an open secret that when they were together she and Sir John did not live quite like turtle-doves.

Then there was the barrister, so well known in society, who has now become a legal power and has attained high dignity. What charming parties he gave in his pleasant chambers! He got together notorieties of every kind, and levelled social distinctions as smooth as a bowling-green. I remember one evening when he introduced sherry cobbler, then a novelty, and when we tried our skill in guessing the face, whereof we saw only the eyes through two holes in the curtain. We all knew Mr. Urquhart's and Chisholm Anstey's.

A strange little drama was then goin ong behind the scenes of that barrister's life. It was not so much behind the scenes, however, as to be concealed from the whole world; and there were many of the initiated who assisted at its representation. The curtain was rung down one evening, when, pale as his own white gloves, he stood by the door of a certain pretty and popular woman's drawing-room in Belgravia, and saw enter the lady of his long-time love, leaning on the arm of his triumphant rival and accepted successor. He took his public displacement like a gentleman, and effaced himself without a word of complaint or reproach.

I went to the house of Serjeant Talfourd, to whom women owe so much, and who added heroic poetry to his legal reforms and well-considered Bills; and I remember how he kept up the traditions of the then past generation, and came into the drawing-room with a thick speech and unsteady legs.

Then, in strong contrast to all this, I was proselytized by Mrs. Schimmelpennick, whose mystical piety oppressed and chilled me—taking, as I thought it did, all the colour and backbone out of life. I was too full of the fire of youth to accept her quietism and self-suppression—which had not in it the active force of voluntary stoicism. Nor had it the etherealized passion, the sublime poetry, which had characterized the spirituality of Adeline Dalrymple. This had been the fiery essence of passionate love purified from all earthly grossness; but here I felt only the congelation, the paralysis, the death of life.

The most intrinsically remarkable of all my friends at this time was a certain Mrs. Hulme—a woman not in the fore-front anywhere, though she was incomparably the cleverest, the most brilliant, and the most original of my whole circle of acquaintances. She wanted only that energy

which springs from respect for humanity
and consequent regard for success—that
energy we call ambition—to have become
as famous in her own way as a second
Madame du Deffand or another De Stael.
She was a distant cousin of the Kings, and
she therefore felt bound, she said, to be
dry-nurse and bear-leader to all their
cubs.

'And as you, my dear,' she said to me
one day, with her curious little smile, cynical
for the one part, humorous for the other,
' are a cub who want a great deal of licking
into intellectual shape, I shall be glad to do
what I can for you. So come to all my
Tuesday evenings, and as often as you like
in the week besides. I shall be always glad
to see you, for you amuse me—I might
almost say you interest me.'

And of this permission I was not slow to
avail myself. If society were my favourite
primer, I had nowhere such queer pages to

decipher as here.   All the other people I
knew were tame and common-place compared to those I met at Mrs. Hulme's ; and
I date many of my after-views in life to my
acquaintance with her and hers.

CHAPTER II.

THE people who crowded Mrs.
Hulme's unaired and undecorated drawing-room were, to
say the least of it, oddly mixed. Among
good, steady, high-nosed folk, with whom
conventional propriety was as sacred as
the Decalogue and the religion of white
kid gloves that for which they had the most
practical respect, were to be found seedy
foreigners who had no investments outside
their sharpened wits; obscure artists whom
the Academy rejected and the picture-
dealers would not endorse; shabby literati,
said to be capable of great things but

achieving only small ones, and living by methods unknown to men of letters in the mass ; handsome women, with invisible husbands and curiously constant male friends ; unengaged actresses, whose jewels, fine dresses and pretty little broughams did not suffer from their enforced want of work ; and every shade and kind of Bohemianism extant. There were no limits to the breadth and depth of Mrs. Hulme's hospitality; and as there were no restraints, from dress to certificates, and the only stipulation demanded was the power to amuse or the capacity for being amused, she got round her what Mr. King called a 'job lot'—and a job lot of even more unscoured character than that which Silk Buckingham drew into the net of his famous Institute.

Her evenings were singularly pleasant. There was always good music by professionals, for whom this was a kind of unpaid and unfruitful advertisement. Sometimes

there was an impromptu charade; or a pretty
aspirant gave the walking scene of Lady
Macbeth, or Juliet on the balcony, as a
proof of her powers—if only that stout
sleek impresario in the huge white waistcoat and heavy golden chain would make
her the leading lady at so much the week.
Or a clever imitator reproduced Buckstone,
or O. Smith, Paul Bedford or Webster, Wright
or Liston, Farren, 'Little Munden,' or
Robson, to the life, and the stock catch-
words 'brought down the house' as at
the real thing.   Sometimes there was a
spell of table-turning, or of mesmeric experiments, when young sensitives acted
according to order, and proved the truth of
craniology by showing love or hate, devotion or disdain, as this bump was touched
or that indicated.   And always there was
plenty of wit and laughter, with a subtle suspicion of garlic and tobacco, and an ever-
present sense of hunger and impecuniosity.

The steady folk were scandalized by the free-and-easy tone of these evenings, as well as by the slightly ragamuffin look of some of the guests, and the more than slightly doubtful antecedents and conditions of most of them. But as Mrs. Hulme was a woman of good birth, passably rich, heirless, and of an age when scandal had ceased to make merry with her name—it had made very merry indeed in times past — she somehow managed to hold on with respectability, while she towed her queer cargo behind and kept her own head above water.

She had lived a great deal abroad, where it was supposed she had adopted her loose ways and put off more than her English stays. And the pernicious influence of all that bad foreign example to which she had been subjected was her excuse with those who could not approve yet would not renounce. Thus, nothing

worse was said of her, by even the strictest
of the Pharisees who consorted with her,
than :

'What a pity it is that Mrs. Hulme
knows such very odd people ! She is
really too kind-hearted and indiscriminate !'

If they were odd, however, they were all,
according to their hostess, personages of
latent distinction and the unrecognised
geniuses of the future. What a hot-bed of
compressed talent it was !—the crozier heads
of forth-coming far-spreading fronds ! What
nameless Raffaeles in long hair and threadbare coats discoursed learnedly on 'method'
and ' touch,' ' technique ' and ' morbidezza;'
on Turner's skies and Stansfield's seas ; on
Chalon's grace and Etty's flesh-tints; on the
power of Maclise and the versatility of
Mulready ! What cotyledonous Beethovens
sprung the notes and broke the strings of
that Broadwood ' grand ' which was Mrs.
Hulme's most important bit of furniture !—

and what fascinating Malibrans that were
to be sang ' Robert! toi que j'aime !' looking at that stout impresario in the big white
waistcoat, who had their fortune in his
pocket if only he would put his hand therein
to find it!

And those black-bearded counts and fair-
haired barons, with coats buttoned to the
chin and not a line of linen to swear by—
they were all great men in their own country,
and most of them were inventive geniuses,
with that potential wealth beyond the
dreams of avarice we have heard of so often
before, in the shape of unpatented inventions
—wanting but so few pounds to set agoing
for the certain realization of those dreams!
Among them were some good ideas which
have since been taken up and worked out
into practicality. But it is sad to think that
many a germ of what is now an accomplished
fact, bringing an enormous fortune to the
manipulator, had its origin in the brains of

these poor unfriended foreigners, who scarcely knew where to get the bread and meat that should keep body and soul together.

Mrs. Hulme herself, always sitting in her own especial arm-chair by the fireplace, was not the least remarkable in an assembly where no one was common-place. She was a woman of about seventy, whose love of personal ease had conquered all that personal vanity some vestige of which most women keep to the end of time. She was loose and stout, and with no more shape than the typical sack tried round the middle. Her grey hair was thin and wispy, and brushed straight off her bold full brow; and she wore no cap, as do other women of her age, but only a small black lace kerchief, tied round her face and knotted under her chin. She was always dressed in black stuff, with a grey woollen knitted shawl on her shoulders. She wore black mittens on her soft white flaccid hands; and among her numerous old-fashioned rings was one large onyx. This she said held her quietus.

'The day when I can no longer laugh,' she said to me quite cheerfully ; 'the day when I have to confess that I am beaten, that life is at last played out, and that humanity has become to me more revolting than ridiculous—then I shall open this and bid you all "Good-night."'

She made no secret of her intention to commit suicide when life should be no longer enjoyable. She had no fancy for dregs, she used to say, with her strange laugh, at once so cynical and so pleasure-loving, so mocking, so sensual and so humorous. And the knowledge that she could die when she chose, without pain or confusion, helped her to live. It was her staff of strength, without which the road would be both rough and tiresome — and perhaps already too long.

I may as well say here as later, that she

carried out her intention, and did one night take that great leap into the dark which she always said she would take when tired of the light. When she found out that she had an internal tumour, which would probably become cancerous, she put her affairs in order; gave her last Bohemian evening, where she surpassed herself in the audacity of her speech and the brilliancy of her wit; and then, with her finger between the pages of her pocket Rabelais, she drew down the thick curtain between herself and the House of Life, and so ended the play for ever. She left all she possessed to the Society for the Prevention of Cruelty to Animals, and other kindred institutions; dumb brutes being, according to her, less bestial than men.

She was the first person I had ever heard speak of suicide in this philosophical manner —as a thing to be discussed like any other —an act of free will and intelligence, good

or evil according to conditions, but not
necessarily a sin, a mystery, a shame, a
dread. And her words made on me one of
those ineffaceable impressions which are the
birth-hours of thought.

Of course the first time she spoke to me
I was shocked—and more. My father had
never mentioned the subject without horror,
as murder of the worst kind—impiety of
the most damnable character—the one sin
which could never be repented of. Cato
might be pardoned, because Cato was a
heathen; but a Christian who had the true
knowledge was outside the pale of forgiveness—and God Himself had limited His own
power. But the thing was altogether forbidden; and even discussion was an irreligious tampering with evil. It was to be
simply abhorred in silence, like any other
infamy. Yet I remember when a poor
fellow, a clergyman, cut his throat not
far from Eden, my dear father would not

allow a harsh word to be spoken of him, but said only:

' The mercy of God is infinite. Let him who is without sin cast the first stone.'

For here, as so often in his life, personal charity was stronger than dogmatic harshness, and the man pitied what the theologian condemned.

Of this teaching I naturally retained the impress, and looked on self-murder as one of those crimes which have no two sides and for which there is no kind of palliation. And now, here was Mrs. Hulme calmly upholding not only the moral right, but even the social value, of suicide, and proclaiming her own intention of one day practising what she professed!

Two years ago a new arithmetic would have seemed to me as possible as a new moral code. Theology might be, and was, an uncertain quantity, but morality was as fixed as the everlasting hills. But now, I confess it, my absolutes were beginning to dissolve. My old principles were laughed out of court by my Paphian friends the Free-lovers, with whom the sanctity of marriage was effaced in favour of the imperialism of love—by the hedonism of Mrs. Hulme, with whom duty was a superstition and pleasure the final cause and great end of existence.

Yet these people were neither criminals nor savages. They were thoughtful, kindly, cultivated, conscientious; and the ordinary theological writ about the depravity of the human heart did not run among them. Still, they made morality discretionary and not compulsory; and changed the granite stability of right and wrong into a nebulous kind of individualism, where all was convertible according to convenience, and nothing was radical and superior to conditions.

Thus it was that I first began to see the

moral law as a question of evolution and social arrangement, void of extrinsic divine ordination—that, while recognising some laws as better and making more for progress than others, I had to confess, also, that nowhere has been said the final word, and that nothing has received its last and unchangeable form — that everything on earth is relative—from colour by juxtaposition, to crime by the circumstances surrounding it.

In manner Mrs. Hulme was kindly, brusque, unconventional, familiar. She never rose from her chair, let who would enter the room ; and she kept a seat immediately behind her for her favourite of the evening, to whom she laughed and talked over her shoulder. That beside her was for the last comer, who was expected to vacate it when another visitor entered. If he delayed, he was ordered off without ceremony. She called women by their Christian names, and men by their surnames, without prefix or distinctive title ; and she treated all young people like children, rebuking, encouraging or caressing, according to her mood, as if these young heroes had been so many boy-babies at her knee.

In religion an atheist ; in theoretical politics a socialist ; despising human nature, and therefore tolerant of its weaknesses and indifferent to its vices ; mocking, cynical, irreverent ; without tenderness of sentiment to make her sympathetic with earnestness, yet marvellously kind-hearted and generous to excess, she stripped every question that she touched of all sacredness, all mystery, all poetry, all divinity, and reduced it to a standard as prosaic as the market-price of a pound of tallow-candles. She scoffed at the idea of hidden mysteries, and denied the peculiar sacredness of things because they are unknown. She saw no difference in kind, only in degree, and

23—2

swept the whole universe into the same abyss of contempt.

' The Divine Life to be found in bugs and blue-bottles ?' she said with her mocking laugh when I, still under the influence of Adeline Dalrymple, spoke as I had been taught. ' So you make yourself a deicide every time you catch the one or scrunch the other ?   The Divine Life energizing itself in a stinging-nettle or a dandelion ?   What rubbish!   Reduce your pretty fancy to reason, and you will find that your divinity means, on the one hand, bigness and com-plexity of organism—on the other, that which pleases and profits yourself.   You vapour about the beauty—a condition of the Divine Life—of a lily ; but you will dig up and destroy that stinging-nettle aforesaid. A beautiful woman is of course very divine —but that flea biting her neck ? that midge making a bump on her forehead ?   Pshaw ! You have a great deal yet to learn, my dear boy, and a great deal more to unlearn. We shall have to scrape those brains of yours clear of all the superstitious whitewash plastered over them, if you are to do any good in life or see things as they are.'

' Say what you will,' I answered, ' there must be something at the back of creation; and life did not come of itself.'

' How do you know that?' she said drily. ' If you do not know one thing you do not know another ; and one unlighted candle is as good as another when you are in a dark room and have no matches.'

According to Mrs. Hulme, we come from nothing and return to nothing—or, rather, we are simply old material re-combined and re-incorporate. We are mere phenomena of the hour — mere phantasmagoria in time and appearances flitting though space—no more stable than clouds, no more indivi- dually valuable than so many melon seeds. If any secret meaning lies at the back of life, we have not found the key yet, and never shall. But she denied any secret meaning at all, and treated the whole thing as a huge cosmic joke and energized satire.

' A fortuitous concourse of atoms—creatures bound by the material circumstances which have formed them—brought into the world without their own consent and by no action of theirs—dependent on time and place, food, parentage, and weather for what they are and do—and then credited with an immortal soul to be punished or rewarded for deeds done in the flesh !—those deeds as necessarily the result of material conditions over which the individual has no more control than has the acorn when it springs into an oak and not an ash—than has the piece of wax when it is moulded into the likeness of Jupiter, or battered out into the mask of Silenus ! What logic ! What reasoning ! And this is the nineteenth century ! And you are one of those who

" lead public opinion." The blind leading the blind, with a vengeance, and the ditch as the consequence !'

'But what do you make of free-will ?' I asked. 'We all have free-will, and can choose the bad or the good at pleasure ; we are not the mere slaves of material conditions.'

She measured my head with her two hands. Among other things, she was a phrenologist, and believed in George Combe as well as in Lavater.

'A simple question of proportion,' she said. 'Intellectual, moral, animal :—which of the three is largest, there will be the thing you call "free-will"; that is, self-governance through the preponderance of the intellect —passions which are uncontrollable because of the weight of the cerebellum—or the higher range of social instincts because of the size of the coronal region. The mind is like a muscle—it cannot go beyond its own power. A weak arm cannot raise a heavy weight; a small intellectual and moral development cannot overcome a large animal region. The doctrine of free-will, like all the rest of human life, is a delusion. It has its economic uses. So has the belief in heaven and hell—in the eye of God and the claws of the devil. But economic uses, because men are ignorant and therefore superstitious, do not make a lie the truth, nor delusion a reality.'

' Then you would destroy the conscience?' I asked.

' What is conscience?' she returned. ' The public opinion and fleeting ideas of a certain time and era individualized. Is that an absolute?'

' If it is not, then all human virtue goes to the wall,' I answered. ' Your theories leave us neither spiritual influence nor eternal laws of right—neither truth nor conscience.

She laughed in her mocking Voltairean way.

'Eternal laws of right, spiritual influence, truth, the absolute, conscience!' she said. 'And pray, my dear, what do you make of any of these, outside external conditions? Point me out one virtue which has not been merely the expression of the needs of the time, cherished because of social exigencies;—tell me of one that has been absolute from the beginning anywhere, and in all stages of civilization—and then we can talk of the divine illumination of conscience and the eternal rule of right. Go over the list. Truth, which is the most necessary of all as the mutual defence-work and protection between man and man—the concordat of society and the basis of association; Chastity, on which the family is founded, the family being in its turn the foundation of society; Justice, which is the taproot of law—these, the very elements of all the rest, are es-

sentially geographical, chronological, social.
So also is magnanimity; so charity, liberty,
patriotism, temperance—and all the rest.
The whole fabric from end to end is a
matter of growth and modification ; and
this absolute rightness, this divine illumination of the conscience, about which you
ecstatics talk such egregious nonsense, is
the mere result of external education, like
proficiency in mathematics or clever combinations in chemistry.'

' Then right and wrong do not exist ?' I
said.

' As unchangeable principles ?—no !' was
her answer. ' Where do you find them ?
In the Bible ? Surely there least of all !
But in no place—none ! Polygamy, honoured as well as lawful in the East, is
prostitution in the West. Mohammed
sanctified what David and Solomon and the
patriarchs had all practised and what Christ
and later Judaism forbade. Who is to

choose between the two systems, and pro
nounce arbitrarily on either? Slavery, supposed by the Jews to have been expressly
sanctioned—and limited—by Jehovah; practised by all barbarous peoples and a main
feature in the civilization of Greece and
Rome ; upheld in the United States as
morally allowable, divinely ordained, and
valuable for the general good—has become to us of late years an accursed
thing, and we have put it away from
us. But the doctrine of a man and a
brother is one of quite modern growth. It
is not even essentially Christian. Yet
before the rights of man were preached you
cannot say that slavery was a crime. There
can be no fault where there is no better
knowledge. You might as well say that
belief in dreams, touching for the king's
evil, or any other foolish outcome of superstition, was a crime. It was only ignorance. And he who would condemn

ignorance must begin with the new-born babe.'

' You make life very uncertain, and leave no solid foot-hold anywhere,' I said.

' Do you think so ? I do not. On the contrary, I find in my belief the greatest certitude,' she answered.

' How ? Where ?' I asked.

She laughed again.

' In a paradox, my dear—in the universal phantasmagoria and mirage that it all is—the universal delusion and maze of everything,' she said. ' There is no reality except illusion. There is no absolute standard—only the opinion of the day ; and morality, truth and right, change their names and dresses according to time and place, just as our winter is the Australian summer, and the despised donkey of the London costermonger is the honoured ass of the Eastern dignitary. We are no better than blind puppies abandoned by their mother, and we know very little

more than they. We do not even understand the material of the basket in which
we find ourselves, nor our relations with
the rest of the stable where we have been
littered.'

'I cannot push God out of the world,' I
said. 'He is the Absolute; He is the Truth;
the Life of the universe and the Soul of the
soul of man'.!

'All in capitals?' she said, lifting her upper
lip, but with no sting in her good-tempered
contempt. 'All right; I congratulate you,
my dear boy. You have found the key to
the riddle which the world has so long
sought in vain. Give me your talisman.
Teach me your method. It is worth knowing.'

'My talisman?—Love!' I answered fervently, thinking of Adelina Dalrymple.

'Yes? love? Love of what?—of whom?
Love between the sexes?—sometimes not a
very celestial matter,' she said.

'Love in Nature,' I repeated.

'So!' she said drily. 'The Divine may be there for you, but for myself, I cannot for the life of me find God in a stagnant horse-pond, nor in a ploughed field spread over with dead fish. And I confess I see Him no more in hawks and tigers, bogs and weeds, than in this bundle of passions, weaknesses, appetites, treacheries, and impulses we call man. But your Pantheism, to be logical, must include man as well as beasts and roots and stones and trees.'

'And why not?' I answered. 'Man is the base of our ideal God—he is the best we know.'

'In which case all I can say is—bad is the best, and very bad too; and your divine tabernacle is wonderfully in need of repair, and a very ramshackle concern all through.'

'That which He has made must have something of Himself in it,' I said. 'Nature, and with nature man, are both the expression of the thought and power of God.'

' You believe in direct creation ?' she returned, as if with surprise. ' You believe that we are consciously and intentionally made as we are, by a Supreme Being who could have done so much better for us if He would ? How odd! If I were to think so, I should go as mad as if I were locked up in a torture-chamber where I had to witness the agonies of others, and be twinged myself as a gentle reminder of consanguinity. To believe that this world, with all its pain and misery, its disease and death and ignorance, is the deliberate work of an Omnipotent and Omniscient Deity, seems to me the most blasphemous assumption—if there be such a thing as blasphemy—the most illogical and self-contradictory idea, as well as the most derogatory to the character of the God proclaimed, that the mind can conceive. No, my dear, I make no God responsible for all this misery! It was not by the direct act of a Supreme Power that Pompeii and Herculaneum were destroyed—that we are born by torture and have to die in agony—that we have to protect ourselves from the elements which else would annihilate us—that we have to labour if we would live, and to suffer if we would enjoy—no Conscious Power is responsible for all this. It is the Law—that thing of which we know neither the origin nor the issue—Law without consciousness, without favour, without discretion, without individualism—Law as cold and stony as one of the old Egyptian gods, sitting through all eternity, their hands resting on their knees, deaf to the cries of men, dead to their prayers, and unmoved by all that passes before them, whether it be the blood of slain men or the laughter of little children.'

All this kind of talk fascinated while it half-terrified me. It had on me the same effect as conjuring up the devil and the practice of the Black Art must have had on a mediæval student. It was peeping into forbidden places and listening to forbidden sounds. The boldness of Mrs. Hulme's negations; the cynicism of her morality; her contempt for all those things which have ever been most sacred to man, and which were then my holiest treasures of faith; her keen wit; her kind heart and the barrenness of her spiritual nature—all made her a study of singular interest to me. But my interest was mixed with dread and my affection for her was dashed with reprobation. I was in a new world when with her; and I had not yet polarized myself. My enthusiasm was pitied as the fever of youth; my principles of deepest root were shown to be unworkable in actual life; the 'counsels of perfection' to which I yet clung were set aside as moral fairy tales, without substantiality or reasonableness; my faith in the essential qualities of vice and virtue was treated as a superstition on all fours with Aubrey's astral spirit, the properties of the herb moly, and the gift of invisibility lying in fern-seed. When I spoke of the absolute, I was met by the relative, the evanescent, the apparent; and I was becoming familiarized with the doctrines which made all life mere vapoury phenomena, where nothing is new, nothing is true, and nothing signifies.

As I have said, Mrs. Hulme's contempt for humanity made her latitudinarian all through. She was philosophically tolerant of lying and deceit, of selfishness, treachery, unchastity, and all the rest, because she expected nothing better.

'They have broken the eleventh commandment and been found out,' she used to say. 'Everyone does the same, but some manage better than others, and fasten their doors with a closer lock. It is all that question of the lock—you may be sure of that, my dear! Behind the door everyone is pretty much alike. An Archbishop is only a chevalier d'industrie made honest because he has no need to cheat. Take away his lawn sleeves and put him into a jockey's jacket, and in place of a saint you will have a blackleg. It is only a matter of dress and assignment.'

'Do you allow no good in human nature?' I asked, a little impatiently. 'What do you leave us?'

'Well, I leave you Nero and Domitian and Caligula and all that lot—Lucrezia Borgia and the Marchioness de Brinvilliers —Gilles de Retz and the whole crew of in-quisitors—and a crowd more; all own brothers and sisters, founded on the same ground-plan as your saints and heroes, and all divine tabernacles according to you. What more do you want?'

'Oh, Mrs. Hulme! how can you live without faith in God or love for man?' I

24—2

said with real pain. ' I should die if I were out in the wilderness as you are—if I were so desolate and deserted.'

A sudden look of tenderness came into her face and moistened her eyes. She leaned forward in her chair and took my hand between both her own.

' What a child you are still, my six-foot-two dreamer!' she said. ' When you were a little fellow, did you not suck your thumb before you went to sleep? I am sure you did! You suck your mental thumb still. It served you then for comfort—was as good as a lollipop. So are your beliefs and aspirations, your vague adorations and base-less certainties, now! It is almost a pity to take them from you prematurely. The day came when of your own accord and by the law of growth you left off sucking your thumb and yet went happily to sleep ; and the day will come when you will cease to idealize human nature, and yet you will find life tolerable when you have left off believing in its pretty fables.'

'And I am to find no one good, no one true or faithful?—not though I know and love you?' I asked, masking emotion under playfulness.

She patted my head.

'What a pretty speech!' she said. 'I despise flattery, my dear, but I love it all the same. When I hear beautiful music, I know it is only a cunning combination of sounds made by lifeless material. But it stirs my blood, for all that it comes out of the bowels of a cat and the wood of a tree— nient' altro! So thank you for your nice little bit of humbug, which is pleasant to hear and which I do not in the least believe. So far from thinking me good, you think I am a horrible old woman, given over to the devil and all his works, and destined to be damned to all eternity.'

'I do not,' I answered. 'I do not agree

with you, but that does not prevent my respecting you.'

'How should you agree with me?' she said, with her mocking little laugh. 'I am old, you are young; I know, you believe; I have proved, you hope. We are not on the same platform. It is impossible. But you will come to me in time;—that is, if you are made of stuff that matures and ripens and does not wither green—nor become fossilized before it has fructified.'

'And then I shall despise humanity?' I said.

'Yes, my dear — despise, pity, aid and not condemn it,' she answered. 'It is a poor thing; but it cannot help itself, any more than a snake can help its poison-fang or a jelly-fish its want of backbone. It is so, and no one is to blame. But, being this poor thing, do not talk to me of the divinity lying within it, nor of the omnipotence, the love which energizes this grossly cruel and imperfect world.'

This was the kind of thing which Mrs. Hulme perpetually said to me; and I wonder now how my belief in goodness and the right survived her efforts to kill it. It did. I could not be brought to that terrible contempt which seemed to her the key of all wisdom—the awful mirror bought of truth by knowledge. I must love. I must be able to feel reverence, and to trust; and to live among the dry bones as she did would have ruined me for ever. If I had doubted those whom I loved, I should have doubted of God. And this was to me that mysterious sin against the Holy Ghost on which my young imagination had been so often exercised.

No; Mrs. Hulme was wrong. There was more than blind Law under which we lived—there was Divine Providence ever leading us, like little children, step by step, higher and higher. There was more than the irresponsible animal in man—there was his soul, his conscience, his love, his aspiration, his truth. And there were always some who were absolutely good—had I not loved Adeline Dalrymple ?—and right and wrong were facts, not fancies.

So I fortified myself against my old friend's cynicism, and for her dead negation substituted my own fervent affirmation, and made sure that I had the Truth in front of me. And I was still actuated by principle, and did my best to put into practice those counsels of perfection which had always stirred my soul and, so to speak, fired my spiritual ambition. But I made a terrible fiasco of my worldly matters in the process, and put back the dial-hand of fortune for as many degrees as it had gone forward.

For instance : I had written a novel, for which Mr. Colbourn, one of the great publishers of novels of that time, had agreed beforehand to give me three hundred pounds. Now, three hundred pounds, in those days of hard work and narrow gains, was a small fortune; and I had reckoned on it with the satisfaction of certainty. But my book was an unconventional and daring sort of thing ; and when it was finished I began to think it was not quite the kind Mr. Colbourn had anticipated when he bargained for it. He came to me on the day when I told him it was completed; and he had the three hundred pounds in his pocket-book. When he took out the notes I laid my hand on his.

'No,' I said ; ' let it stand over. Take the manuscript ; and if you do not like it, I let you off the bargain.'

He did not like it, and I lost my money. But I kept my sense of honour, of truth, and fair-dealing ; and was not that better ?

When I told Mrs. Hulme what I had done, I really thought the end of our friend-ship had come. She raved at me for my folly, my absurd pride, my presumption

even, in pretending to arrange Mr. Colbourn's business for him. What right had
I to teach him the lesson of not buying a
thing he had not seen? Who was I, to
think myself wiser than a sharp man of
business who knew what he was about a
great deal better than I could tell him?
So she stormed. But at last she ended by
taking my face between her large, soft,
flaccid hands, and kissing me on the forehead.

'You are a fool,' she said in her queer
cynical way; 'about the biggest out of
Bedlam. But,' she added more softly;
'you are a good fool—which is something.'

CHAPTER III.

NATURALLY all the Liberals, and even the Freethinkers who cared nothing about the intrinsic merits of the question, were on the side of Mr. Gorham in the controversy about baptismal regeneration which took place between him and 'Henry of Exeter,' that diluted representative of Hildebrand, or, more properly, Thomas à Becket modernized. It was easy to foresee the tyranny of the High Church, should it ever have supreme power. For though Tractarianism was only in the protesting and struggling stage, a condition of things for which

Liberals have a constitutional sympathy, yet we knew then, as we know now, that it was the effort of tyranny, happily restrained, to place its yoke on the necks of men. It was like Sinbad's Old Man of the Sea, apparently helpless and ill-used and asking leave only to live like the rest. Once seat him on your shoulders and you will never know intellectual freedom again!

Men suffer individually from the moral grip of the Low Church ministers; yet, as this grip is more congregational than organic, it can be shaken off when desired, and is by no means so dangerous as that other. The ' sin of Erastianism,' which the Tractarians denounce, is the only safeguard of national religious freedom; and while the Church remains national, and holds in its hands any kind of directing power over the lives of citizens, it ought to be essentially, not nominally, Catholic; that is, it ought to include in its bounding line as much diversity as may be without self-stultification.

For all that, and in spite of the part which I, and others like me, took in this Gorham affair, the Evangelical section was, and always has been, profoundly abhorrent to me. The constricted human sympathies of these people—their hostility to science —their superstitious adhesion to every word of the Bible, whatever geology or philology may say—their arrogant assumption of absolute rightness—their greater reverence for certain mystical and unprovable doctrines than for active and practical virtues—their unnatural asceticism, which has none of the manliness of stoicism in it, but is founded on the crushing idea of Sin, that pallid spectre everywhere, even in our affections—in a word, their sanctimoniousness, gave me in my early youth a repulsion for the whole school, which I retain to my cooler and soberer old age. I have had a wide personal experience of this section, and when I speak of them it is according to knowledge;—which is the only excuse I can offer for a prejudice I confess to be both illiberal and unphilosophical.

Amongst the full-flavoured Bohemianism and scoffing Voltaireanism of Mrs. Hulme —the practical honesty and unreserve of my uncovenanted friends, the Free-lovers —the sharp and brilliant, but not always modest, wit of Mr. King's lawyer guests, to whom nothing was sacred save success —was wedged in the Evangelical straitness of the Honourable and Reverend Mr. Caird, the Low Church incumbent of the parish in which my boarding-house was situated. My father had stipulated that I should attend the church and make the personal acquaint-ance of the clergyman, whoever he might be, within whose jurisdiction I might be placed ; and, of course, I kept my word.

This intercourse was my penance for the pleasure of the rest.

The Honourable and Reverend Mr. Caird was one of those ecclesiastics whose very personality sends one's blood the wrong way. Manner, look, voice, enunciation, gestures, all are studied and artificial with these men, who talk of glōry and knōwledge, saving grace, the blood of Jesus, and the new birth, as others talk of the crops and the weather. Everything is subdued, nothing is spontaneous about them; and there is the ever-present con- sciousness of superior holiness, like a visible varnish, over them. The thin lips, tightly closed, seem unable or unwilling to take a deep draught of vitalizing air. Who knows what sobbing breaths of sinful passion may not have profaned it ?—what rude impulses of vigorous life may not have stirred it ?— unlawful for those whose castigated pulses may never throb beyond the chill regulation beat.   The smooth clean-shaven face is as impassive as if cut out of wood.   No generous flash of quick emotion brightens the cheek nor softens the eye, dilates the pinched nostril nor dimples the sterile mouth.   You   detect   the   clerical   impress   on   that   impassive   face   the   first instant that you see it ; for the episcopal laying-on of hands has left the thumb-mark for ever.   The eyelids are generally dropped over eyes which may not see too much of Nature,   that   robust   child   of   goat-footed Pan, with its bold glances roving free and wild over all the mysteries of life, and its ruddy mouth, red with the juice of fruits, laughing up to the sun, its creator and preserver and destroyer in one.   Nature, which is unredeemed—humanity, which is unregenerate—are both among the things inhibited to the ' saved ' sons of the Gospel. To them Love itself is a snare and a sin ; and the very passion of a mother for her

child is deprecated as an idolatrous preference for the creature over the Creator.

As for Nature, the word itself is re-
dolent to them of impiety and indelicacy.
I remember how once, when my sister
Ellen, protesting against the arid teachings
of one who it was then thought would be
her mother-in-law, said warmly : ' It is not
natural,' received for her rebuke : ' Natural,
Ellen ! how can you, a Christian young
woman, use a word at once so indelicate and
profane ?'

Still, the men themselves are often so
good, so conscientious, that it is impossible
not to respect them as individuals, how
much soever one may shrink from them as
officials. And this was the case with me
in my intercourse with Mr. Caird.

He lived only to do his duty, as he conceived it, and to spread what he thought
to be right principles. But what principles
they were ! He sanctioned no kind of

social pleasure and found sin in the most innocent amusements. Cards were always the 'devil's books' with him; a theatre was the equivalent of hell, and those who went there were predestined to eternal damnation as surely as those who sunk in mid ocean were doomed to be drowned ; and dancing was also synonymous with damnation. He once found himself at a lady's house where a small impromptu dance among the boys and girls was got up. They were only children, none counting over ten years of age.

Mr. Caird routed up his wife, took her on his arm, and went straight to the hostess.

' Madam,' he said severely ; ' I cannot stay here to see these young souls led down to hell. Either this sinful pastime must be stopped, or I and my wife must leave.'

As the lady refused to stop that in which she saw no kind of harm, and thus make a whole roomful of innocent little people unhappy, as their sacrifice to this Moloch of superstition, Mr. Caird acted on his threat, and buried himself and his wife in the cloak-room until his carriage came to take them away.

Another time his wife went out with a cameo brooch in front of her dress. Seeing it for the first time as she came from the cloak-room, unshawled and bare-necked, he peremptorily bade her take it off, saying, with more prudent prevision than substantial delicacy:

' Take that off. It attracts the eyes of men to a part of your person it is not desirable they should look at too closely.'

He was a man as incapable of understanding or discussing a religious doubt as was my father himself. He might, perhaps, have scraped up as much moss of tolerance from among the boulders of his convictions as would have enabled him to discuss variorum readings of certain texts ; but any doubt cast on the bases of his faith—that was beyond his limit; and to have entered on it at all would have been to him like holding a candle to the devil, where the torchbearer would have been as damnable as the demon he served.

To him and all his school the devil is a personage as real as that next-door neighbour the Socinian, and hell is as actual a place as Paris or Rome. Logical and literal, they admit no refining away of words nor enlargement of sense by the doctrine of development. The worm that dieth not and the fire that is not quenched are material and existing things. They cannot accept the softening exegesis of ' tropes,' ' parables,' ' speaking to the people in the language which alone they could understand,' ' doctrine according to the learning of the times, and not permanent and fixed in the face of better knowledge,' with which the Broad Church smooth out difficulties. The words are final and of cast-iron; consequently the material personality of Satan and the topical reality of hell are matters of absolute certainty which nothing can undo.

I was once present at a very painful scene in the house of one of these fervent believers in the personality of the devil and the physical pains of hell—a scene which made a great impression on me and drove me farther and farther from the line of orthodoxy. The eldest son of the family had lately died. He had been a wild outward kind of young fellow, who had enjoyed his youth too freely and flung his cap too far over the windmill. He had been thoughtless, extravagant, pleasure-loving; and he had done a great many things which it would have been better to have left undone. But he had harmed no one but himself; and his worst offences had been due to temperament rather than to any obliquity of moral nature.

One day, about a month after his death, I was dining with the family, when the father suddenly laid down his knife and fork, covered his face in his hands and burst into loud weeping. We saw the tears run down below the palms of his hands and ooze through his fingers. His eldest daughter got up, went over to him, and put her arms round his neck.

'Dearest papa,' she said; ' what is it ? what troubles you ?'

'Ah, my dear !' he sobbed ; ' I was think- ing of poor Jim in hell !'

The strange incongruity of the thought, so ghastly and so grim, with the prosaic circumstances of the meal, made a contrast that I have never forgotten.

Poor man ! How often I have thought of the needless agony of that moment; and how often I have wished that I could help in breaking once and for ever all these cruel chains which bind men to misery and falsehood. We deprecate the sacrifices made of life and manhood to Juggernaut; are ours of spiritual peace and courage made to Satan any more respectable? By my own early torments I can gauge the misery felt by others; by my own early terrors I know the strength of that mysterious fear which possesses the souls of those who believe and tremble.

I was brought into even closer personal relations with this section of the Church. My sister Ellen was engaged to be married to the son of one of these Low Church clergymen, and I was naturally a reprobate and accursed to the family she was about to enter. Mr. Smith, her father-in-law elect, made it a condition of the marriage that she should give me up as completely as if I were dead—that she should never see me, hold no intercourse with me, and that she should abandon me entirely, as the plain and manifest duty of a Christian woman.

We were a strange family and full of apparent contradictions. We might quarrel among ourselves at home, as we did; I might be reprobated and considered abominable by the rest, as I was; but we were too strong-willed a race to submit for submission's sake to king or kaiser. And Ellen, who had never specially loved me and had always trounced me when she could, refused to accept any husband in the world on these terms.

'Christopher may be quite wrong in all he thinks—and he is quite wrong; that I admit,' she said; 'but he is my brother, and I will not give him up. And if Morley'—her lover—'has not courage to stand by me, he need not.'

He had not the courage; and the marriage was broken off, to my intense trouble. But Ellen did better afterwards; so that burden of unavailing regret was rolled off my shoulders. And indeed I doubt if she would ever have been happy in a family where it was considered indelicate and un-christian to say that a thing was unnatural, and where the theatre was considered as one of the Halls of Eblis.

In later years another sister discarded me of her own free-will for my unsound-ness. This was when she had become a believer in the theory of the Ten Tribes—in universal Jesuitism, so that a Freethinker, a Socinian, an Evangelical, a Tractarian, have each and all been supposed by her to be so many emissaries of the Jesuits—in secret poisonings as matters of weekly occurrence—in the Apocalypse, and the Seal now being opened (witness thereof the potato disease and the phylloxera)—and in ghosts, apparitions, presentiments and warnings as among the ordinary phenomena of this solid earth.

Not all these Evangelicals are sincere ; or, if they are sincere in their convictions, they have odd irregularities in practice. A certain great provincial light in these days was the leader of the Evangelical school where he was stationed. An eloquent preacher, he longed to get to London, say-ing : ' I am an oak in a flower-pot here '— though his place was in the second city of the kingdom, and his fame and following were as great as if he had had St. Paul's for his pulpit.   Among his hearers and friends was a very charming young married woman, with that kind of mental activity which made her go into religion as she went into society ; study the esoteric meaning of texts as she studied Balzac and Georges Sand ; and long for peculiar enlightenment as she longed to be received at court and to work her way into the houses of the great.   It was one part of human life to her ; and she had a feverish desire to know all the parts, and to possess herself of everything by which her mind would be filled with new ideas, as a balloon is filled with gas.

Mr. —— was a handsome, well-favoured man, also desirous of new ideas, and not disinclined to lead blind white souls into the light, nor to set dainty tripping feet on to holy places. He and his fair friend often read the Bible together. He expounded and she took in. How it really ended I do not know, for she did not tell me more than this little anecdote. When they were sitting together in the summer-house, with the Bible open before them, he suddenly re-enacted the drama of Francesca and Paolo—they were studying the Song of Solomon—broke out into a declaration of love, and, when she repulsed him, reminding him that both were married, flung piety to the winds and said :

' Let us then go down to hell together.'

This is all I know; and I know this only

by the voluntary confession of the lady herself. The Oak in the Flower-pot I never saw;
and I never told the story against him. But
I used to laugh to myself when I heard
his name, and think how odd it was that
I knew so much of him, while to him I was
not even the shadow of a name.

Hearing so much of sin from Mr. Caird,
and seeing how he conjured up this pale
and ghastly spectre everywhere, I set myself
to think out the matter and to clear the
question, so far as I could, from all con-
ventionalized interpretations, going down,
more meo, to the foundations of things. And
going down to the foundations here, I made
it clear to myself that elemental sin does
not exist, and that the whole thing is a
question of proportion. Cut away the base of
anything—even of murder—and you cut
away a necessary and integral part of human
nature. Exaggerate this absolutely necessary base, and you come to disproportion

and selfishness—that is, to sin; as in the
instinct of self-preservation, of which anger
or revenge, culminating in murder, is the
excess, the exaggeration, the disproportion,
the crime. Also I made it clear that
certain virtues rest on a physical basis; as,
the value of chastity in woman for the sake
of the purity of the race—the value of
temperance in man for the sake of the health
of the offspring.

When I had reasoned this out for myself,
I can scarcely describe the relief I felt; how
much more manageable the whole question
of human life became; how much wider
the horizon, how much clearer the
light. Instead of that maddening mystery
of the origin of evil, and why God, who is
Omnipotent, causes His creatures to be
born in sin and conceived in iniquity, I
came to the simple equation of comparative
excess and conditional ignorance, of which
the results must be dealt with as severely

as may be, but whereof the cause is remedi-
able, and will one day be removed. It
seemed to lift me out of the depths, and
to invest humanity with a hope and power
forbidden while I believed in the inborn
wickedness of the human heart. I saw law,
crime, and punishment as the logical conditions of human society—society conscious
of its needs, and acting out the law of self-
preservation by repressing excess and
punishing inordinate selfishness. But this
was a very different thing from the doctrine
of elemental and intrinsic sin which the
Low Church holds so strongly. And, as I
say, the freedom, the light, the hope, the
cheerfulness which resulted from my conclusions made a new moral world for me.
So far I owe gratitude to Mr. Caird and
his followers. That powerful stimulant of
opposition, which has ever worked so
strongly in me, led me to the examination
of the whole matter; and I burst into

freedom through the very contemplation of
bondage.

It was about this time that I met Robert
Owen, then an old man, but still full of pith
and vigour. His belief and enthusiasm
were in no wise damped by disappointment,
and he still held on to his idea of philosophical communism as the ultimate outcome
and regeneration of society. I became his
ardent convert, and had there been a
' phalanstery ' founded on philosophical
principles I would have gone into it. In
some form or other I felt sure that these
principles of co-operation would ultimately
prevail; and we see their partial working
at the present day, under a new name
and an altered shape. But I should have
liked to have seen the question fairly tried,
and to have proved for myself what was
the moral hitch to prevent smooth running.
We can live peaceably together in hotels
and pensions—why not in a community,

where we should simply enlarge the principle, and still further restrict that bane of life and progress—selfishness?

Together with Owen I knew Dr. Travis, the delightful man they used to call his Paraclete. He was one of the loveliest flowers of humanity; but he wanted magnetic force and vitalizing energy. Handsome, well-read, singularly well-bred and as pure as a good woman, he was content with holding sacred the faith that had been bequeathed to him, but he made no valid efforts to spread it. He might not have succeeded if he had; but I have always thought that if a more supple intellect, a more worldly-wise and experimental man, had taken the management of Robert Owen's ideas, we might have had co-operation sooner in time and more radical in organization than we have. It seems to me very certain that the thing has to come sooner or later, and that mutual support will some day be the rule of society, rather than what we have now, universal competition.

The strange variety of thought and view found among the people I most frequented made a moral and intellectual dissolving view or kaleidoscope which sometimes a little bewildered me; and I often asked with Pilate: 'What is Truth?'—that question which no man answered then, and no man has answered since ; and yet we all believe that we ourselves have this Truth. And I in those days thought that I had it in faithful belief in God's Providence and power; in the ultimate good of all things; in the perfectibility of man and the rapid advance of society towards that perfection; in the sure progress of the soul after death; in the elimination of the devil from the scheme of the spiritual world; in the sweeping away of hell ; in the divine life within us ; in the universal Fatherhood of God—God above and beyond us all—God revealed in the mind of man—God untrammelled by church or creed or formula, neither Christian nor Jewish, neither Mohammedan nor Brahmin, but everywhere, in all beliefs, in all heroic deeds, in all faithful effort, wherever a prayer went up to heaven or an act of sacrifice was done on earth. For though I had got rid of sin in the abstract, I had not relaxed my hold on good; and of all arguments, that which maintains there can be no good without evil was the one I most passionately repudiated. Light was light to me, and I could not admit that it needed darkness to enable it to exist. And in like manner God was God, and needed no devil as His shadow.

CHAPTER IV.

ALTHEA CARTWRIGHT lived
with her aunt, Mrs. Pratten,
in a pretty house in South
Bank, where, for all that South Bank was
then looked on as so much in the country
as to be almost beyond the reach of Lon-
doners, they saw a great deal of society
and attracted many well-conditioned people.
Ladies certainly grumbled at the distance,
and made that and the possibility of foot-
pads on dark nights their excuse for keeping
away; but men found the weekly receptions
delightful and the more intimate association
full of charm; and Mnemosyne Lodge, as

the place was somewhat strangely called,
was never without its attractions and its
visitors.   It was a kind of social honeypot
round which the flies continually buzzed, and
no man who once went there ever failed to
put in a second appearance.

There was a mystery in Mrs. Pratten's
life which no one understood.   When a
young woman she had married a man apparently her suitable match in every way ; and
she had kept with him four days.   On the
fifth she went back to her mother's house,
and never left it again.   What happened to
divide these wedded lovers no one knew.
It was one of those well-kept secrets on
which all may make theories at pleasure ; for
no one can either disprove or verify, and
one hypothesis is as good as another.
Neither the husband, who was still alive
and who enjoyed life as a bachelor in Paris,
nor Mrs. Pratten herself, told more than the
mere fact betrayed :—They had married a life

time ago, and they had parted after four days, never to meet again.

Since that time the one ever spoke with the bitterest contempt of women—the other with the profoundest horror of men. To Mrs. Pratten all men were marked with the Sign of the Beast; and she was accustomed to say that nothing tried her faith in God so severely as the creation of such monsters as men. To Mr. Pratten, whom I afterwards knew in Paris, women were mere jointed dolls, and there was no hope for the human race, doomed to the degradation of being mothered by such unredeemed and absolute fools.

Being so uncompromising a man-hater, Mrs. Pratten was, of course, a misogamist. She lectured every girl of her acquaintance on the sin of matrimony, as if this were indeed a crime; and, though she accepted women who were already wives when she knew them, she repudiated those who took to themselves husbands after she had known them as girls. She professed for them a horror only equalled by that which she felt for the men themselves.

With Althea she was explicit enough. If ever she were to fall away from grace and virtue so much as to marry, she would be cut out of her aunt's will as irrevocably as she would be banished from her aunt's house. If she remained unmarried, as a good and modest woman should, she would come in for all. And as Mrs. Pratten was a wealthy woman, who lived up to about half her income and put out the other half to interest, the bribe was considerable, and so far had proved successful. Althea Cartwright was Althea Cartwright still ; and everyone knew that she would not marry, and indeed could not, unless she got hold of a millionnaire.

When I knew her she was some way past thirty—a tall, fair woman with an almost perfect figure, at once generous and graceful,

where the outlines were long and flowing
and the filling-in rich and firmly modelled.
Her face was not strictly beautiful, and yet
she was more attractive than many con-
fessedly beautiful women. She had an
abundance of shining flaxen hair, with a
shade of red to be sometimes seen in the
sunlight, and her skin was of that clear but
not unhealthy pallor which generally goes
with flaxen hair. What would else have
been its exquisite transparency, however, was
marred by freckles, which were the standing
sorrow of her life. Her eyes were light-hazel,
large, finely-shaped and wonderfully brilliant; her nose was short, rather blunt, but
beautiful in profile; her lips were curved,
flexible and delightfully expressive of her
emotions; her hands and arms were simply
perfection; and she was singularly soft
in manner, speech, voice and texture.
Indeed, her main characteristic was softness. Yet she was not weak: still less was

she flaccid or without grip. She knew what she wanted, and she took it and held it for so long as it pleased her; and when she no longer cared for it she let it drop, and walked on without it. She had the most consummate ability that way, and was no more to be held against her will than a mermaid in the water—no more to be constrained than the cloud which once looked like Juno. More Ixions than one knew this; and no one had yet found the charm which could compel her to maintain any kind of relation whatsoever when she wished to abandon it. From friends to servants, she held while she would and took the good while she could; and then she slipped aside and discarded without a second thought. No; Althea Cartwright, the softest, sweetest, and apparently the most pliant creature in the world, was certainly not weak nor yet flaccid.

Her central point was her devotion to her

aunt, whose moods she divined with almost intuitive perception, and to whose humours she adapted herself with marvellous plasticity. For among her other qualities she had the temper of an angel, and a power of sympathetic receptivity which made her the favourite confidant of all who had anything to confide. But though she was thus devoted to her aunt, she managed to live her own life with tolerable breadth of margin; and, while Mrs. Pratten never went out in the evening, Althea was never at home, save on the nights when they themselves received. Popular as she was, everyone wanted her. Women seemed to love her as much as men admired her; and when once a house-door was opened to her it was rarely shut again. The oddest part of the whole thing was, she always seemed to have some strange power in those houses where she was intimate. I think she did a good deal for her lady-friends as well as for the men;

and I know that she sometimes screened
them and sometimes helped them. At all
events, she was useful; and she was far too
good-natured to refuse a request, whatever it might be. But these concentric
circles revolved round and never broke into
the standing duty of her life; and her aunt
had no cause to feel herself neglected.

Mrs. Pratten was a kind of palimpsest of
all the crazy faiths that float about the
world. She had gone through the whole
cycle of religious experiences, yet had
learned no self-distrust from her repeated
failures. Her last state was always her
final revelation; and for all that the voice of
God had already spoken to her in so many
different dialects, she was invariably sure
that this last was that in which He had
spoken to Moses on Mount Sinai. 'Guided
by the Spirit'—that was her phrase. Were
this so, it cannot be denied that she had
been guided into many queer corners

and landed among many odd heaps of
rubbish. She had adopted every mystical
creed extant, and was now in the full swing
of the most mystical of all :—it was before
the days of Theosophy and Occult Buddhism.
She was a Swedenborgian, and a 'spiritist'
of the school known a few years afterwards as that of Alan Kardec. His ideas
had been in the air before he consolidated
them into a system ; and Mrs. Pratten, who
caught all floating theories as boys catch
moths, had adopted them for herself. She
believed in successive incarnations of the
spirit, and amused herself by tracing back
the pedigree of her friends' souls, and locating
each in its special tabernacle.

Of her own incarnations she was never
weary of talking. She was a frail, meagre
little woman, with a mousy face, a nervous
manner and a temperament as timid as a
hare's ; but she gave to herself all sorts of
heroic and spiritually splendid antecedents,

and jumbled up her pre-incarnations into an olla podrida of the oddest kind. She had been Miriam and Judith, Joan of Arc and St. Theresa, Queen Elizabeth of England and Queen Elizabeth of Hungary, Dorcas and Elizabeth Fry, besides others which I have forgotten. She added to her impersonations so often that she herself got somewhat 'mixed,' and lost all hold of a dominant idea; and I, among others, was hopelessly muddled.

Her niece, Althea, had been a whole string of interesting frailties; among whom I remember figured Bathsheba, Aspasia, Fair Rosamond and Mademoiselle de la Vallière. Her penultimate incarnation had been Marie Antoinette, as a sign of progressive improvement. But Mrs. Pratten spoke with pride of the moral superiority of her present condition, and the cleansing fires through which her soul had manifestly passed. This avatar was better than all the others. Even Marie Antoinette was married :—Althea, thank heaven! was husbandless, and one of those divinely marked on the forehead.

Me she called Nero. Certainly, in the daguerreotype taken of me, I had a curiously Roman look, not visible, I fancy, in my real face. But I did not feel conscious of my identity with the imperial madman who, she said, had been my former self. When I objected on the ground of non-recognition, she became more than ever positive that she was right, and assured me that this was the best proof I could give, both of my identity and my spiritual advance. I was ashamed of my former self and therefore repudiated the connection. I had forgotten my then cherished sins, just as we forget the angry passions of our childhood. So far I too was cleansed, and by just so much was nearer to ultimate regeneration. Perhaps this was my last incarnation, as it was her own and Althea's. She was certain of these; and she hoped, but was not quite so sure, of mine. She thought I had in me still too much of the original red earth of which the first man was made. And while we had any of that left in us, we were too heavily weighted to soar upward to the New Jerusalem.

Another of her amusements was to find out the correspondences of her friends in the animal world, and to determine whether they were the further evolution of that energy, the enlargement of that idea, which had initially expressed itself in beasts of prey or beasts of burden; in the animals which are the sustaining sacrifice or in those which are the companions and servants of man; in singing birds which delight him; in insects which torment him; in reptiles which destroy him. She subdivided even these divisions, as when she gravely pondered on the question whether I was a setter or a retriever.

She finally settled it by a spiritual ukase:—I was a retriever. For herself, she was the solitary unpaired female eagle—the third of the nest; and Althea was a butterfly—that which had crawled having now learned to fly.

Also, it cost her many hours of anxious thought to determine to which organ of the Great Man, which she and her co-religionists say makes the shape and conditions of Heaven, we should all be assigned when we had done with our re-incarnations, and had finally shaken off the last grains of that red earth which was the cause of our bondage and the chain of our darkness. She placed herself in the eye, 'seeing' being her faculty. Althea was in the great sympathetic nerve; but she moved my locality from organ to organ as she shifted her ideas of my character—and when I last heard of myself I was in the nerves of the tongue, as the discriminator of spiritual food.

Odd as she was in all this, Mrs. Pratten was not substantially insane. She was on the borders, I admit; as must needs be when a woman with an active brain of small size, and more imagination than critical faculty, has allowed her reasoning powers to become practically abortive, while she has cultivated indiscriminate belief as the alpha and omega of spiritual insight, and passes her whole time in hunting out analogies. This search for analogy is neither more nor less than so much spiritual patchwork—piecing together forms and colours which harmonize and make a pretty pattern. For even religions follow Mrs. Pratten's own law of analogy ; and some are simply mental amusements, as was hers.

Queer as she was, yet, being withal rich, hospitable, of good family—and the aunt of Althea—people flocked to her dinners and suppers; assisted at her séances and expositions; and laughed at her afterwards as their compensation for time wasted. It was as much as their good-breeding could compass not to laugh at her to her face when she told them of the spirits who had visited her and the revelations which had been made to her. For really, to hear what Napoleon had to say about the celestial bell-shaped tent in which he lived—in the palm of the right hand—and how Marlborough and Gustavus Adolphus and the Black Prince, and all other illustrious warriors, were also living in bell-tents within a stone's-throw of each other, was rather strong meat to come between the roast and boiled! People who walk habitually in spirit-land do undoubtedly scatter a few of their wits by the way; and poor Mrs. Pratten had scattered some of hers, like the rest.

Her favourite scientific craze at this time— for she prided herself on her science equally with her religion—was the Odic Force and

mesmeric clairvoyance. She had been one
of the first in society to follow after
Reichenbach and to believe in the Okeys.
Now she had elaborated a medium for herself. This was her maid—a certain sharp-
witted little Welshwoman, called Sarah
Jones in the parish register. In Mrs.
Pratten's blue book she was Ruth. The
extraordinary ' sensitiveness' which this
young person possessed—the way in which
she exemplified and even went beyond all
Reichenbach's experiments, and the certitude
with which she discovered magnets in the
dark, owing to the light which played
around them and streamed in purple filaments from the ends—were matters of
constant wonder to the world which
witnessed. The sceptical did not know
how it was done ; the credulous were all
agape at the marvel.

I noticed that Althea avoided discussion
on the topics which made her aunt's whole

happiness and filled her mental world from centre to circumference. She believed in them, of course. She accepted her former doubtful incarnations and her present progressive improvement with her customary serene grace; was quite sure of her eventual lodgment in the great sympathetic nerve; had not a doubt that Sarah Jones, the black-eyed, sharp-witted girl from Wales, was once the sweet and patient Ruth; was convinced of her ability to see a magnet when hidden in a cupboard, and of the purple filaments which streamed like flames from either end when the armature was removed; convinced also of her obedience to orders transmitted by thought from Dover to London; of her knowledge of the word written on a piece of paper and placed inside a hazel-nut or sealed up in an envelope; of her being able to travel to the exact spot where Sir John Franklin and his men were lying stark beneath the snow;

27—2

of her interpretation of the mystery of the
Foley Place murder; of all the things which
'sensitives' do and know. All the same,
out of Mrs. Pratten's presence Althea never
talked on these matters. When pressed, she
used to refer her interlocuter to her aunt,
who understood these things so much better
than she herself did! She was only in the
place of an ignorant believer. How indeed,
could she be a disbeliever, when such marvels
were daily enacted before her eyes? But
she was neither an expositor nor a teacher.
She left that to her aunt ; and she did not
care to talk about the thing at all. It was
beyond her ; and she felt lost and bewildered.

If she did not actively support, she never
showed the faintest doubt as to the genuineness of the phenomena ; and to the last no
one knew what she believed and what she
discredited. For if Mrs. Pratten had dropped
a few of her wits by the way, Althea had
kept all hers intact. And, said the sceptical

and squareheaded: 'How could she possibly believe such rubbish?'

From the first both aunt and niece showed me much kindness. Mrs. Pratten looked on me as a future certain convert. She recognised my love of truth; and, as she knew that she had the 'true truth,' she said she was as sure, as of to-morrow's sunshine, that I would come to the light wherein she stood. It was only a question of time and teaching. She knew that I was still too full of red earth; but sometimes the work of winnowing went on at rapid speed, and I might be one who, when the sifting once began, would get rid of all that clogged the spiritual machinery in less time than one could count. Also, as a literary man, I would be a valuable convert. I never blinded myself to the extrinsic importance given me by my profession; and I understood from the first that the hand of the pressman was of more account than the still further purification of the spirit of Nero. This, therefore, was why Mrs. Pratten made so much of me and had me so often to her house; and Althea naturally followed her aunt's lead in this as in other things.

With Althea was another reason to lend additional force to these—I filled a gap. She was one of those women who have always on hand a 'brother' or 'son' or 'uncle,' according to relative age, with whom they go about—to the opera, the theatre, sometimes down to Richmond, to Greenwich, on the Thames; whom they take into society and introduce to their friends; and whom the world agrees to accept as adopted relations according to nomenclature. I was presented to her by Mr. King, who in his day had been her uncle; and I was presented at the time when she was looking out for a new kins-man. She had just lost her 'favourite boy'—a young barrister who had gone out to India; and she was therefore, as she lamented, sonless. And as she was now growing an old woman, she said with her seductive smile and a peculiar softness veiling the glitter of her greenish-hazel eyes, she preferred sons to all other relations. She was so fond of boys! They were such dear fellows with their funny fresh ways; and men were such dreadful creatures! Hence she adopted me, in the place of Ronald Ray removed; and I was quite willing that she should.

She was of immense use to me in every way. She took me with her into society, and introduced me freely to all the best people she knew. And she knew a socially higher and more fashionable set than even that to which I had been taken by my pretty patroness with the childish shoulders, or than I found staring at luminous hands in the house of the friend of Mazzini and the believer in the Floating Medium. And of itself this was a valuable experience. She polished my manners as much as the material would allow ; taught me the shibboleth ; instructed me in those microscopic minutiæ which only the initiated can see, but the absence of which they detect at a glance and resent as a crime; and she wanted to make me a fine gentleman from head to heel, in character as well as in bearing. She found fault with me as I was—chiefly for my want of small change in conversation—for my want of all badinage and lightness—for my vehemence when I talked on those things wherein I was really interested — for the frankness with which I gave my opinion when I was called on to say what I thought and what I believed. And above all, she found fault with my superabundant earnestness.

'Glissez mortels, ne vous appuyez pas,' was her motto; and she found my step too firm and my grip too close.

So did her lady friends; some of whom seemed to consider me good fun because of the 'simplicity,' the 'naïveté,' the 'innocence' which they said more than once was 'delicious.' But I was not of the stuff which makes fine gentlemen nor courtiers; and through all my gratitude for their kindness, and a certain inevitable dazzle of the senses by reason of the rank, beauty and wealth of those by whom I was caressed, I kept my head steady, and the core of me was never reached. There was something about these grand ladies which intellectually repelled me, for all that personally I was attracted. There was a certain insolence of egotism to which I could never reconcile myself, and which came out in all they did and said and were. The wretched stuff which passed for Art with them; the miserable daubs; the flimsy writing; the idea-less music; the hideous jingle called poetry which they displayed to each other with pride, and for which they received such lavish commendation! What good did their education got by foreign travel do them, if, after having seen the galleries in Florence and Rome, Dresden and Madrid, they could think simpering masks were human likenesses and tea-board abominations landscapes according to nature!

I got an ugly glimpse into something worse than self-contented incapacity, through the offers made me by more than one great lady who wanted to appear as an authoress without the trouble of writing, and who thought to buy my brains as she would have bought so many yards of silk. Did not the then famous Baroness —— come to me with a bundle of woodcuts for which she wanted me to write a story under her name? —and did not Lady —— and Mrs. —— both ask me to take their manuscripts and put them into readable shape for so much down? And were they not all offended because I

refused? And did not Althea herself say
that I was twin-brother to that Huron of
old time who stands as the ideal of unpractical folly, and that I would never
make a man of the world?—never!

Again, the lives of these grand ladies
struck me as so fragmentary, and the scope
of their energies as so small and thin! An
hour in the morning given to the acquirement of an art which takes for years and
years the whole day's working-time of him
who would be a proficient; the importance
of fashion, of etiquette, of the artificial rules
of conduct by which living human nature is
checked and stifled; the sense of individual
and social superiority to the commonalty, and
one's own consequent inferiority evidenced
by their very condescension; the consciousness that any man out of their own social
sphere is to them a mere toy or tool, to
be used for their pleasure and cast aside
when they are tired of him; their want of

thoroughness and humility, and their unbridled egotism—all this created in me a
certain moral and mental revulsion which
kept me from the self-abasement of social
ambition.

Young as I was, I was determined that
it should not be said of me, as was said
of some one else : 'He is smothered in
Countesses.'

I went among these grand ladies because
Althea Cartwright wished it ; but I went
as an outsider ; and I was never anything
else. I was too proud of my own order
and too essentially democratic to wish to
shift my place or to shine by reflected
splendour. And all Althea's endeavours to
make me understand the value of being
seen in certain drawing-rooms failed. From
the first days up to now, grand folk were
and are nothing to me but curious studies.
While they cannot confess to equality, I
refuse to kowtow to superiority, such as is

given by mere name and fortune. Not inheritance, but acquirement, is, I think, the only true gauge of merit ; and the name that is won far surpasses the lustre of that which is bequeathed. And these principles are not those which harmonize best with fine ladies and fine drawing-rooms.

Notwithstanding this stiffneckedness, Althea's kindness to me did not diminish. On the contrary, it increased, and often became so great as to be a little startling and bewildering. She called me her boy and presented me as her new son. She found out my tastes and ministered to them, even to providing for me a special kind of cake that I liked, and to giving me a certain champagne glass, which I fancy had gone the rounds. She worried newspaper editors, and all those who had the power, for boxes at the theatre and stalls at the opera ; and as she had her own little brougham, these evenings cost neither her nor myself anything beyond the flowers and the ices which were then de rigueur. She loaded me with small presents, which embarrassed me to receive and were utterly useless to keep ; but she would take no denial; and when I remonstrated, she would tap my face with the tips of her fair, soft fingers, and say, with mock anger :

'Naughty child ! may not a mother do as she likes with her son ?'

But in the midst of all this undeserved kindness, as the days came and went a certain strange unrest and impatience seemed, as it were, to line her satin-like softness—a certain core of almost fierceness, almost harshness, to lie within the outer envelope of her habitual tenderness. She was always kind to me in word and deed —caressing, indulgent, ' spoiling '—and yet she seemed dissatisfied with me, as if she had secret cause of grief against me. And she was so strangely distrustful of me—so

exacting of assurances, protestations, promises! She used to make me swear every
time I saw her, she holding both my hands
in hers, saltier-wise, that I would be faithful
to her—quite, quite faithful ; that I would
never have another friend like her—never
take one so near to my heart, nor give to
any living woman the affection I had given
to her. She used to torment me—not all
unpleasantly — with her jealousy, which
overflowed at all four corners. In that pale
pink room off the first landing, where she
made her private nest and received her own
especial guests, she made me go through
many an agitated half-hour by jealous
accusations flung broadcast, and as aimless
as so many arrows shot in the air for any
chance quarry that might be about, although
unseen.

After I had sworn and vowed and pro-
tested with sufficiently strong emphasis to
satisfy her, we used to have a grand recon-

ciliation—if that could be called reconciliation where the fracture was all on one side;
after which things would go smoothly for a
day or two, and the sky would be cleared of
its phantoms.

It was after one of these scenes, when she
had been angry and I had been contrite for
absolutely nothing, that we came to an
understanding.

She took my hand and pressed it against
her heart.

' Feel that, you naughty boy !' she said
caressingly ; ' think how dear you must be
to me, when you can make my heart beat like
that for fear you do not love me as much as
you ought !'

' But I do love you!' I replied. ' You
know that I do ! How could I help loving
you ? No one has ever been so kind to me
as you, and no one is so delightful.'

' Is that true ?' she asked.

' Yes, absolutely true,' I said.

Her breath came with a quick little sob.

' If I could believe you!' she said softly; and as she spoke the scales fell from my eyes.

True, she was many years older than I; but what of that? She was beautiful still, and delightful in every way. I was young and could work; and her certain disinheritance when she married me would free me from all suspicion of fortune-hunting. I had my own future in my own hands, and fortune would be the friend to me she always is to the self-reliant. She loved me. There was no vanity in thinking this; it would have been stupidity not to have seen it. And I—I loved her, and had forgotten Adeline Dalrymple:—of whom, by the way, I had never spoken to her.

I took her in my arms and kissed her upturned face. She closed her eyes, and, dead white as she was, I thought she had fainted, till half a smile and half a tremulous little movement of beseeching came over her colourless lips, as she whispered tenderly:

' I love you !'

I forget now what I said or did, for I was swept away by the emotion of the moment. I only remember pouring out a whole torrent of love and thanks and violent delight, ending by a picture of our lives when we should be married and safe in our love together.

And when I said this Althea opened her eyes and looked at me as if I were something strange and comical—something she had seen for the first time, that amused her.

She raised herself, stood erect and firm before me, and threw back her head.

' You extraordinary child !' she said, with a light laugh that jarred on me like a false note in music. ' Marry you, caro mio ? No ! anything but that !'

So here was another tumble for that

unlucky Icarus, myself, and a new draught
of that (poison or elixir ?) experience.

My friendship with Mrs. Pratten and
Althea lasted for some time. At my age,
in the very morning of life as I was, with
all to learn and so little to forget, it
was a novelty to me, as delightful as it
was new. But though so much in it was
pleasant, there was also much that was
painful ; and many things grated on my
sense of truth, and made me sometimes
feel as if the whole earth were void and
humanity but a simulacrum that held nothing, if indeed it were not a mask to conceal deformity. When I learnt from Althea
the truth, which I had resolutely refused to
suspect because I was afraid to believe it,
that all the manifestations and proofs of
sensitiveness, which passed as the unregis-
tered data of a new science and a living
truth, were made up between herself and
the maid, and when, in answer to my

28—2

remonstrances, she only said, in her calm, clear, soft, but immovable way :—' I am doing no wrong. What harm is there in making a poor old woman like my aunt happy ? She likes it; why should she not have it? It is better than dram-drinking, and answers the same purpose,' I felt as bewildered as if I had been suddenly blinded, and I mentally staggered as if I had been struck.

'But truth?' I said. 'Does that count for nothing? Do you not think it wrong to aid and abet what you know to be a lie ?'

' What a Puritan you are !' she answered, laughing. ' As if you did not know as well as I that the whole world is one huge false-hood! You dear innocent old fellow—or you dear old hypocrite. Which is it, Crishna ? You will never open your eyes, if you are really an ingénu. If you are not, you are the cleverest young Tartuffe out !'

'Well, I do not think I am a Tartuffe,'

I said, just a shade nettled. ' And is opening my eyes, as you call it, synonymous
with tolerance of falsehood and disbelief in
rectitude ?'

She looked at me a little oddly.

' I do not think you need ask that,' she
said drily. ' Who lives on the house-top?
Do you ?'

It was so much the recognised thing,
as I have said, for Althea Cartwright to
carry about her boys, that no one made any
remark when she and I went into society
together as if we had the right of close
companionship by blood-relationship. A
few women certainly looked at me askance,
and some men laughed, as it were, behind
their hands. But no one said anything,
except a certain Colonel Hinds, an old
' brother ' of Althea's. And he one evening,
hitching his arm into mine as we left
Mnemosyne Lodge together, said, in a half-
bantering, half-warning manner :

'So, you have the box-seat now? All right, my boy! Give everything but your heart, do you hear? If that goes into the abyss, you may drag for it in vain. You will never fish it up again !'

Also, as time went on, Mr. King gave me a long lecture on the folly of too much sincerity. To take the world as we find it and make the best of our portion; to enjoy all that is set before us and never to examine the material; to understand men and women and not to expect more from them than they can give, but to profit by what they have, and to be always gallant and grateful and discreet—and never in earnest :—this was his advice and the lines on which he had constructed his own life. But he was sorry, he said, to see that I was too hot-headed to be wise, and too fatally in earnest to be diplomatic for the one part or on the defensive for the other.

My relations with Mnemosyne Lodge

came rather abruptly to an end. All Althea's favourites had to go by the same road; and it was interesting to watch the difference of their methods.

Among my friends was a certain James Tremlett—a splendid young fellow, handsome as a Greek god, the heir to a fine estate, with nothing to do but to enjoy life as fortune had ordered it. To do him justice, he did this to perfection. I was one day walking with him in Bond Street, when Althea passed in her pretty little open phaeton, the forerunner of the victoria. She stopped her ponies to speak to me. While she spoke to me, however, she was looking at Tremlett in that fixed, full, yet not bold way, which was one of her charms. With her exceedingly sweet and gracious manners, her low soft voice, her atmosphere of tranquillity and sympathy, that long fixed gaze had in it something indescribably alluring. It was irresistible.

She told me of a water-party for the next week which she wished me to join; and, looking at Tremlett, then back again at me, she said with a smile, and slowly:

'Gentlemen are always valuable at such times. Will you bring your friend?'

Whereat I presented Tremlett and left him to answer for himself.

The answer was in the affirmative; and after a little more talk she shook hands with us both—she shook hands to perfection—smiled in her sweet caressing way, and drove off; as she went, turning back her graceful head as if unconsciously, with one last look at Tremlett. He on his side looked after her with a strange smile. Then, turning to me, he said carelessly:

'Your friend is very taking. Tell me about her.'

I told him all I could; and all that I said was in her honour. But some vague impulse of jealousy made me less enthusiastic than I should have been had I been describing her to a woman, to an old, or to an unpersonable, man.

When I had finished, Tremlett said carelessly:

'You are fond of her, I see. If I were you, I would not trust her with too much of my heart. I know the kind.'

'You do not know her. She is to be trusted, I assure you,' I answered eagerly.

'Yes?' was his indifferent reply. 'Well, you see, you know her and I do not; you ought to be the best judge.'

Events proved that I was not so good a judge as he; and that he had read at sight what I had not learned after months of almost daily intercourse.

This introduction was the beginning of the end; and it is not necessary to trace the process. I was dispossessed in my place as favourite, and James Tremlett was elected in my stead. If I were to go through the whole story, day by day and step by step, until I came to the final moment when I was refused admittance, while—as I stood by the door—Tremlett, dashing up to the house in his private cab, was taken in without delay, I could say nothing more than this :—My fair friend had tired of me ; the play was played out ; the lights were turned down ; the curtain was lowered. And I had to accept my silent dismissal with such patience and philosophy as I could command—such patience and philosophy as others had shown.

But I was too young, too untrained and passionate, for this. I made scenes and had quarrels, followed by false assurances and false reconciliations—in each of which I felt that I had lost and that she had receded, and had become by so much the more intangible. I knew that I was doing myself no good by all this, and that I was shouldered out and could not reinstate myself. Yet I could not help trying in the beginning—knocking my thick head against a stone wall while running after a fading rainbow.

Then, when I finally recognised that I was absolutely dispossessed, and that I could not recover what I had lost, I grew savage and sulky, and refused to go to those general At-homes which was all the intercourse that was left me. This naturally made Althea angry, inasmuch as it gave cause for gossip and forced her to find reasons. She resented that I had not let her slip gracefully and quietly, as others had done. Open breaches are such nuisances; and who on earth keeps always to the same set of friends ?

My present savageness, however, was a proof of past sincerity; and so far ought to have pleased, because it flattered her. But the Althea Cartwrights of life do not care for sincerity. They want only the amusement of the hour, without having to pay the piper when the dance is over. And a savage like myself is both a blister and a danger.

Undoubtedly it would have been more polite, more manly, better breeding altogether, had I accepted my fate with the same stolid indifference which, to all appearances, others had felt. But it must be pleaded in my self-defence that I had really loved her. Perhaps those others had not. She had played with me, but I had been desperately in earnest. And the strange manner in which she slipped away from me gave me no purchase, no point by which to hold her, but melted away like a cloud—the masterly cleverness with which she effaced and obliterated all the past, and stood like one of those German Ellewomen, unmoved by all I suffered, untouched by all I said, was beyond me to bear with equanimity. But my turbulent despair and then my sullen resentment cost me dear, as I found afterwards.

The friendship between James Tremlett and Althea was of briefer duration than mine had been. It came abruptly to an end when Tremlett married, as he did suddenly, and broke with Mnemosyne Lodge as cleanly as a champagne glass is snapped at the stem. He saw Althea one day; the next, he wrote her a letter of eternal adieu ; the week after, he married ; and when he returned home with his bride and met his fair friend with her ponies in the Park, he did what no power should have made me do—and what no true man could have done—looked her full in the face and passed on without recognition. I was there, a witness to the whole thing; and for the first and only time of my acquaintance with Althea, I saw her fair clear-skinned face and rounded throat dyed crimson.

Just at this time Althea became acquainted
with Mr. Dundas, my irascible editor, who
was as susceptible to the power of a pretty
woman as he was violent with men ; and
from the first day of their acquaintance my
star in the office declined.   What was said I
do not know.   All that I do know is, I
suddenly failed to please.   I, who up to this
time had been a kind of cherished seedling
who might some day develop into the very
roof-tree of the office, now could do nothing
that was right.   Day by day my independent
articles were rejected and my routine work
was undone ; while I myself was rated with
the peculiar force and fervency with which
our chief knew so well how to flavour his
displeasure.   Finally, I was abruptly dismissed, and told to go to the devil, but never
to show my face in that office again ; and for
his parting blessing Mr. Dundas hurled a
wild world of invectives against me, amongst
which I distinguished ' a presumptuous and

ungrateful young brute, who does not know how to treat a lady when he sees her, and who thinks, because she has patronized and been kind to him, that he can ride roughshod over every decency of society!'

So here I was adrift on the great sea of life, with a dragging anchor and no harbour in sight!

As to Althea Cartwright, to whom I shall not recur again, I need only say that when her aunt died she found herself, as she had been always promised, supremely well-endowed, and the owner of everything, save a handsome legacy to Sarah Jones, the re-incarnate Ruth—by which this clever young person was enabled to marry the inn-keeper of her native village, and live as a lady in her degree to the end of her days.

As soon as her affairs were settled, Althea went abroad, married an Italian Marchese and became a Roman Catholic. Her husband died about two years after the marriage; but she is still alive and well, a white-skinned, flaxen-wigged old lady, fond of tea and cards, and enjoying life in her own way. That way is the close companionship of priests, monsignori, papalini of all kinds; and the consideration which surrounds a wealthy English widow and convert in the Eternal City, where the Pope is still able to dispense social honours to the faithful, and to float on the crest of the wave those whom he favours—no matter what the secrets whispered to the discreet ears at the other side of that grating of the confessional.

CHAPTER V.

MY anchor did not drag long. I was too energetic to be demoralized by my first failure; and my fall in nowise maimed the hope and resolve which are the best pioneers of certainty. Casting about for a continuance of press-work, which was the substance, while my independent writings were the decorations, of my income, I happened on a Parisian correspondentship just then vacant, and went over to the Brain of the World as one of 'Our Own.'

Here I entered on a new set of experiences and broke fresh ground everywhere.

I had several introductions, both private and
official; and some to the confraternity. But
I did not find these last very useful. I do
not know how these things are managed
now, when telegraphy has equalized endeavour, but then the whole system was one
of rivalry. In the interests of his paper,
each man wished to be first in the field and
to have the practical monopoly of private
information. Hence, brotherly kindness, and
doing to others as you would be done by, did
not obtain among men whose professional
loyalty lay in misleading, tripping up the
heels of and outstripping their competitors.

One man, however, was free from this kind
of class-jealousy; thinking that the world
was broad enough for everyone to move freely
in his own place, and that it was better for
the public at large to receive true information
than for even his own paper only to have the
truth and all the others to be stuffed with
' ducks ' and lies. The man I mean

was Frazer Corkran, that generous and genial correspondent of the *Morning Herald,* whose hand was ever open to his friends, who knew neither grudging nor jealousy, and whose house was such a pleasant rendezvous for both the floating and the resident literati. In him I found a willing guide and ready helper in my salad days of inexperience; and many a time he put me straight when else I should have gone astray, and filled my notebooks which else would have been half empty.

I found as true a friend in his bright-witted and sympathetic wife—a woman always glad to enlighten me with advice, to introduce me to those whom it was good for me to know, and to give me information where I needed it. Theirs was one of the pleasantest houses open to me—mixture of the home and the salon as it was; and I soon became like an outlying member of the family, round whom the children clustered as of right, and who was admitted farther into the penetralia than were most.

I also had the entrée to the salon of that sharp and amusing little woman who not long since passed over to the majority at a far riper age than most of us attain. When I knew her, Madame Mohl was already old—or at least she seemed old to me in the insolence of my luxuriant youth ; but she was in the perfection of her mental powers. I cannot say in the perfection of her beauty, for she never possessed the very faintest suspicion of good looks. Nor did she care to make the best of herself as she was, but despised even such grace as comes from trimness and conformity. Shall I ever forget the extraordinary figure she made when once, as I called by appointment, I found her in dressing-gown and slippers, sitting in the middle of the salon, reading, while the little girl whom she had adopted was pulling at her scanty frizzled hair till

it stood on end about her head—like a tra-
vestied aureole, from glory brought down to
burlesque ?

This was a pleasure to her, she said. She
liked nothing so well as to have her hair
gently pulled while she was reading; but
she might have remembered the comical
effect to those who saw her. I remember
standing in the doorway for an instant,
terrified, thinking that she had gone mad.
But she called me to her in her smart, short,
dislocated way; and I sat there, while she
gave me lessons on worldly wisdom and the
little girl continued to pull out her staring
locks.

Her good ponderous husband was also
kind to me. He was a very dungeon of
learning—I use the word intentionally—for,
like a dungeon, for the most part he kept his
treasures under lock and key, away from the
daily light, and only at stated times made a
grand gaol-delivery in his books. Still, he

was gentle and human and knew when to unbend; and though he did not take the initiative, he gave me valuable advice when I asked for it, and such information as I wanted, and in all things treated me like a rational being—though I must have been to him terribly embryonic and inchoate. At that time I was still lost in the pathless morass of comparative mythology, where, for want of the knowledge of Sanscrit and the true scientific method, I did no good to myself nor to others. And to M. Mohl, whose intellect was eminently practical and void of mysticism, my then fondness for 'views' and 'theories' must have been wearisome enough. In looking back over the past, the one thing which strikes me above all the rest is the wonder of the kindness I received from men and women of matured minds and well-plenished intellects — I, so crude, so fluid, so unformed as I must have been!

All who knew Parisian society then, and

for many years after, will remember the famous salon in the Rue du Bac, with its tea-table to the side; its pretty little Frenchwomen in smart white bonnets, well-fitting black silk gowns, and graceful cashmere shawls—which last they hung over the back of their chairs, thus avoiding the need of a cloak-room; its more formal English ladies in conventional evening dress; its wits and literary celebrities of all nations; its leaven of dull respectability to tone down the brilliant Bohemianism which sometimes filtered through the more orderly pores; its learned pundits and frivolous beauties; those three exquisite Americans—the mother even more beautiful than the daughter, and the sister and aunt the fairest of the triad, as the great Italian physician—he who afterwards became a senator in Rome—found to his cost; that high-couraged English girl, then one of the vanguard of the advanced women, and now left behind in the rush of the movement; and the eccentricity of the hostess herself, equalled only by her goodness of heart and vivacity of brain. No one who was anyone at all was left out of that hospitable menagerie across the Seine; and perhaps no room has been the birthplace of more important private events than that of M. and Madame Mohl.

For myself, I met there many notable people and made some good friendships; among others that of William Rathbone Greg, one of our most brilliant men of the immediate past. His ' Creed of Christendom' had had an immense fascination for me, and his sparkling talk and pleasant personality completed the charm already begun. Certainly, he often rasped me by his tremendous assumption of superiority and the accusation of my own correlative folly. But he was so much older than I, so much more experienced in all matters of thought and observation, and I was personally so sincerely attached to him, that I could bear his high-handed way of dealing with me with the equanimity befitting the inferior. Even when he said to me, with that smile we all know—half playful, half satirical:—'You have no right to hold another opinion when I have given you mine—I, one of the wisest of men— you, the most foolish of boys'—even then I did not take fire, as it was in my nature to do, but accepted the antithesis as accurate in all its parts.

For which piece of good humour I earned his good will, and, as time went on, a more valuable measure of friendship. But to the last he counted it to me for blame that he could not influence me more than he did, and that I still cherished thoughts and hopes, specially about human progress and perfectibility, which he gave himself some trouble to destroy.

Earnestness in searching for truth has always this penalty to pay:—Everyone who is convinced of the rightness of his own views thinks he has but to put these views before you — clearly, forcibly, with the authority of his conviction—and that you will at once adopt them and go over to his side. When you do not, he is disappointed, displeased, and possibly changes his opinion of you altogether and ceases to be your friend.

This has been my experience again and again. I do not suppose many minds have been more laboriously worked over than has mine by those who, convinced in their own persons of this or that unprovable truth, have tried to make me see that light which for them has put out all the rest. And I never could! I was never able to see more than the spectroscopic lines which revealed constituents.

It never came to the point of severance

with my dear friend, the political Cassandra who thought he had found a satisfactory answer to so many of the Enigmas of Life, and that those which he could not explain were essentially insoluble. To the last of our intercourse he was an indulgent kind of Mentor, though I made but a recalcitrant and unsatisfactory Telemachus; and, if he never changed his opinion on my illimitable foolishness, he honoured me with his trust, his confidence, and in some sort his affection; and he knew, as he once said, that I was as true as steel to him and all other friends, and that my heart was sound if my head was not.

I also met the famous poet-couple, the husband and wife, of whom whereof in those days she was the more popular and famous. Now the 'whirligig' has reversed their respective positions, and his star is in the ascendant, gibbous and rough-edged as it is, while hers has comparatively declined. She was always very genial in manner to me when I saw her, but she did not like me. She wrote to a common friend, poor Fanny Haworth—she who just touched excellence at so many points and never quite achieved it — and her adverse verdict was rather severe.

'I have seen your favourite boy, Christopher Kirkland,' she said ; 'and I do not like him. He is not true.'

When she talked to me she used to look at me through the dropping curtains of her long ringlets as if she would have read my secret soul. I used to feel as if I were on a moral dissecting-table, while she probed my thoughts and touched speculative tracts which probably seemed to her hopelessly wrong and corrupt. She did not show that she disliked nor distrusted me, but something about me must have jarred her highly strung sensitive nature.

I was very sorry when I knew what she

had said of me. I cannot remember anything of the kind which pained me more,
and nothing has stung so deeply. If she
had shown me her mind I would not have
felt it so much; but she did not; and
in those days I was young enough, and
sincere enough, to take things as they
seemed to be and to believe in appearances
as realities. And, naturally affectionate as
I was, with my heart on my sleeve, I credited
those who acted towards me with kindness
with the same sympathetic instincts as I
myself possessed.

I had another adverse verdict flung at me
at this time. There came to Paris a certain
Dr. Hughes, who had taken for me one of
those unfounded dislikes which sometimes
blind even good men to the sense of fairness and justice. I had never seen him nor
had he seen me; but I suppose he had
heard something against me; and what he
did not know he imagined—which does just

as well for that kind of antipathy which is based on conjecture, not intercourse. Finding that I was a friend in the house of some of his friends, he spoke of me strongly and bitterly, and made the husband at least believe that I was an atheist, a socialist of the worst type, the propagandist of all sorts of immoral and subversive opinions, and in no wise a safe nor fit comrade for young people.

Alarmed by this evil report, the husband wanted to forbid me the house; but the wife stood by me with all a good woman's courage of charity, and I was thus saved the pain of ostracism without knowing my offence. I was ignorant of the skirmish at the time, and only heard of it when the danger was past. Meanwhile, by my dear friend's clever management, I met Dr. Hughes in her salon and was straightway introduced to him—he, thus taken unawares, being unable in common politeness to escape.

One of the strangest revulsions of feeling I have ever witnessed took place that night, and through my whole life I have never known so great a personal triumph. Frankly, it is to 'peacock myself' on this that I tell the story at all.

Knowing nothing of his hostility, and speaking to Dr. Hughes without suspicion or embarrassment, and as respectfully as I would to any one else of whom I had heard only good things and worthy, I won him over from enmity to liking, not conscious of what I was doing. To this hour I can see his eyes, deep-set, glittering, penetrating, full of fire and thought as they were, turned on me, doubting, questioning, and then with kindly glances, as we stood together for a long two hours on the balcony beneath the stars, and discussed many things of life and faith. And I can yet feel the touch of his broad hand on my shoulder when, as I turned to go back into the room, he half held me so that I should look at him squarely, and said, smiling—and for all the sternness of his face and character his smile was sweet almost to pathos :

' I am glad I have seen you and talked with you face to face. I know you better now than I thought I did.'

Dr. Hughes was as unorthodox as I was myself. But he made up in increased moral austerity for his abandonment of old theological restraints. He was a political economist of the hardest, as he was a philosopher of the most ascetic, type. A broad strain of Scotch Puritanism ran through his nature, and he allowed no margin for ' slopping over,' no excursions into the forbidden regions of unlawful passion. He had forsworn Hades and he did not believe in the devil ; but in his code materialism was virtually Satan, and looseness was the true region of damnation. What he had heard or imagined of me made him believe that I slopped over at all four corners; that I was a rank Materialist and a frank Epicurean; and he felt bound to testify to the cloven foot he made sure was hidden within my boot.

In those days I was a fervent Deist and by no means an ethical latitudinarian; though I confess I was so far a hedonist in that I thought happiness a human good, and pain and misery evils which it was our duty to avert from others when we could, and our wisdom to avoid for ourselves.

Besides those whom I have mentioned, I knew slightly Ary Scheffer; I was once presented to Béranger, who was too closely surrounded by his intimates to give much thought to an outside stranger; and I knew Daniele Manin. With this last indeed, my relations were friendly almost to intimacy; and I used often to go and see him at his meagre rooms in the unfashionable quarter where he lived. He was always wrapped in cloaks and blankets, and complained much of the cold ; but he was ever dignified and noble. His daughter was then in bad health. It was the sad beginning of the sadder end ; for when she died all that was essentially Manin died too, and the broken heart of the father put the finishing touch to the ruined career of the patriot.

More than anyone I have known Manin made me feel the disadvantage of domestic affections when a man is the leader of a cause, and how far wiser it is for those who are self-consecrated to the service of humanity to keep free from family ties. This loneliness within allows of so much the more activity without. It made part of the secret of Mazzini's enduring power ; and Manin, without the heart-break of his desolated home, might have been for years longer an active agent in that Italian

Unity which came too late for him to share in its glory and its triumph.

At this time I was poor rather than well off, and I had to live modestly if I would live honourably. Hence I had my eyrie on the fifth floor, where I shared the apartment of a young fellow a few years older than myself. His French mother and Irish father were dead—the latter quite lately—and his sole inheritance was the lease of this apartment for the five years it had to run. We lived a rough kind of life; but at our age roughnesses did not count. An old woman used to come in the morning to 'faire le ménage' for the day; after which we were left to ourselves. We had to take our meals out of doors, save the 'premier déjeûner' of bread and coffee; and we had only two rooms—one each. But our friends used to toil up those five flights to visit us. Men of note, women of condition, young fellows like ourselves—they all came to make merry or to talk seriously, as the humour took them. Among the rest I remember Mr. Thackeray coming here to see me; and the good-humoured way in which he sat on the flat-topped black box, not to disturb the mass of papers heaped on my second chair, was especially delightful. Mr. Greg also used to come; but he generally fell foul of my hundred and ninety steps; and it was here that I first saw Henry Wills, who, with his wife, afterwards became one of my dearest friends.

My young landlord, Léon O'Byrne, had a small employment somewhere—I never knew what it was nor where. His only sister was governess in an old Legitimist family of high rank and fortune—the Marquis and Marquise de Boiscourt. Through Léon I became acquainted with these charming people, whom I was fortunate enough to please. Madame la Marquise was specially good to me; and we soon became fast friends. She always wore a broad gold bracelet, which one day she took off and showed me. It contained a lock of hair, underneath which was engraved : ' Mon roi. Henri Cinq.' There was also a date, which I forget. Perhaps it was that of his birth, or of his visionary accession ; in any case it was a sacred memory. The outside of the bracelet bore the crown of France surmounting the letter H,—both wrought in diamonds.

I often went to the Boiscourt Hotel in the Faubourg St. Germain; and I met there the then famous Jasmin, the Provençal barber, whose 'papillotes' were the fashion among the fine ladies, somewhat as the works of Barnes, our Dorsetshire poet, were the fashion here in London a few years ago. Jasmin had been invited to give a reading of his poems to a select circle, wherein I had been generously included. All the ladies wept; and Jasmin himself wept more

copiously than did they. He was begged
to repeat one of the poems—the one which
had most moved his audience and himself;
and I was rather amused to note how his
voice broke on exactly the same words,
how he wept at exactly the same passages,
and how the whole of the second reading
was the precise echo of the first. Not an
intonation, not a gesture, not a look nor
emphasis was in any way changed; and
this second reading, in destroying all appearance of spontaneity, destroyed all vestige
of illusion.

Madame la Marquise was naturally a profound believer in the saints. She told me
that if ever I lost anything I was to pray to
St. Anthony of Padua, and he would find
it for me. She instanced the truth of this
heavenly interposition by telling me how,
a week ago, she had lost her diamond necklace. She had been out to a soirée, and
when she left her carriage and went upstairs,

her necklace was gone. They searched everywhere for it, but in vain. Then she prayed to St. Anthony of Padua, and promised him a candle if he would help her. The next morning her diamonds were found in the courtyard, just there where she had stepped from her carriage. If that was not confirmation strong, what was or could be ?

She was kind enough to ask me to spend some time at her country house, where I went with Léon, and where I enjoyed myself immensely. But perhaps this was more on account of the novelty of all I saw than because of the intrinsic pleasantness of the arrangements. Things to which I have become accustomed now, and which are as natural to me as old home habits, were then strange and unusual ; and my faculty of observation, always alert, had enough to occupy it.

The family, Legitimist and devout to their finger-tips, lived in that quasi-patriarchal style which only exists in families of high rank where relative positions are too sharply defined for any kind of blurring to be possible, and which is clearly a survival of serfdom and seigneurial prepotency. The upper servants had lived all their lives in the family; and the younger ones, who were the children of peasants on the estate, training under the direction of their elders, would not have dared to have given up their places, to which they were also destined for the whole of their natural lives.

These old upper servants were familiar and affectionate, but never disrespectful nor presumptuous: they were simply the inferior members of the household, but always integral to the family. The old butler used to mingle in the conversation at table while handing round the dishes. He would confirm what M. le Marquis said, and put Madame la Marquise right when she blundered; or he would contradict M. Wilfrid when he spoke at random, as boys will; or he would tell me what I ought to eat with a kind of humane condescension to an outside barbarian and heretic that was infinitely amusing. Every day, after the second breakfast, at twelve o'clock precisely, he, the lady's-maid, and the housekeeper, used to go out for a formal walk down the avenue. This was as much part of the day's doings as that second breakfast itself. The lady's-maid sat with Madame la Marquise in her bedroom; and the two talked together as they sewed in concert more like sisters than mistress and maid. Madame la Marquise, always superbly dressed, did not disdain a host of unseen economies never practised by Englishwomen of a certain status. But one of her many complaints against Englishwomen was their extravagance in the unseen parts of dress, such as linings and the like. Another was the wicked way in which they crumpled their skirts and spoilt them generally by unhandy usage.

That bedroom of Madame la Marquise was a great rendezvous for us all. She had been in England, and she had instituted four o'clock tea—not then so general as it is now—where we had buttered toast 'à l'Anglaise,' which they all preferred to cake. M. le Marquis and the young men used to come to these symposia in shirt-sleeves, and without waistcoats. And it made no difference that Mademoiselle Sara, Léon's sister and the governess to Mademoiselle Berthe, the only girl, was there; or that Madame la Marquise herself was in a déshabille startling in its buttonless intimacy or what Italians call 'confidenza.'

M. Wilfrid, the youngest son, did not often join us. He was still under tuition, and in the care of M. l'Abbé, who literally never let him out of his sight, never allowed him to be away from him one moment, day

nor night, except when he was with his
mother. The boy was then seventeen; and
I think our average schoolboys would have
set him down laconically as an 'awful
duffer.' I used to pity him for what was
substantially a life of slavery, for a strictness of surveillance beyond that which we
think necessary for our girls. It seemed to
me an enervating, emasculating thing all
through. and ill-calculated to make a man
of the best type.

Indeed, I did not think much of the
essential manliness of any of the young men.
They were all 'petits maîtres,' dissipated
rather than energetic, and with the strangest
mixture possible of indifference, unbelief
and superstition in religious matters. I remember my unbridled contempt for the little
round kind of summer-house in the garden,
wherein the sportsman shuts himself, with
loop-holes for sight and aim, whence, after
having scattered seed all about for the birds,

he can pot them comfortably as they feed on the ground. After our honest sport on marsh and moor and stubble-field, this miserable pretence was cousin-german to a crime.

We 'made maigre' three times a week—Wednesday, Friday and Saturday—and we were devout members of the Church in every way. Since a dangerous illness of Mademoiselle Berthe, when she was 'vouée au bleu et au blanc' for two years, with great gifts promised to the Virgin should she recover, Madame la Marquise had 'entered into the way of religion,' and she carried her family with her. This did not prevent some frightful scandal attaching to one of her sons whose name was never mentioned, and who had gone across the seas, heaven knows where; nor the dissipation of the eldest; nor the want of moral principle in every direction of the nephew whom she had brought up as her own son, and who combined the most extraordinary amount of 'fastness' with the most wonderful apparent docility to 'ma tante'; nor the Jove-like gallantries of M. le Marquis, whose amourettes were as notorious as they were numerous. The pretty post-mistress of the village, whose appointment was owing to him, for all that he stood aloof from the Emperor and all his works—the curly-headed children he danced on his knees and set to hunt for bonbons in his capacious pockets—this young girl and that young wife—M. le Marquis indemnified himself in lordly manner enough for the enforced asceticism to which Madame la Marquise condemned him!

And no one thought the worse of him. He and his wife were perfectly good friends; and what she knew was her own affair only. Her blameless life did not allow of recriminations, even if she made reproaches, which it was very likely she did not make;

and the two went on together in apparently perfect harmony and accord, and ' ma femme' was the first care, consideration, and centralized authority with M. le Marquis, who, while he amused himself, took care not to hurt her.

I was at first amused, but soon became bored, by the limp invertebrate pleasures which diverted the household. Ecarté, where the stakes were bonbons; billiards, without science or precision, and merely so much child's play—these were the two great resources of the evening. But when they were alone the young men indemnified themselves by their talk, which was all of Paris, the Boulevards, the theatres, Mabille and women, flavoured with a ripeness of experience as strong as the absinthe of which they had a secret store not sparingly used. This was the first time I heard it plainly stated that the virtue of women is not man's affair, and that he is a fool who

does not profit when and where he can.
A girl ought to be looked after by her
mother ; a young wife by her husband ; a
woman of maturer age must take care
of herself. In no case does it fall within
the duty of a man to protect or respect
her. When I had first heard of the extraordinary precautions taken by French mothers
and gouvernantes for the efficient protection
of young girls, I had been both indignant
and amazed. It had seemed to me an insult
to everyone concerned. But I have somewhat modified my views since then; and I
think a few barriers in early life not quite
needless, even among ourselves.

On the whole, I was not sorry when my
prescribed fortnight came to an end. I had
got all the good I could get out of the
novelty of the thing, and I was tired of the
flaccidity of life as laid down in that un-
picturesque, dead-alive old place. But I
was sorry to part from Madame la Marquise,

whose kindness to me had been almost maternal; for all that I knew she was afraid of my freer English habits and more independent modes of thought, and would as soon have thrust Mademoiselle Berthe into a lion's den as have trusted her to me for one minute alone. Still, she was so thoroughly well-bred and so good that she never made me feel uncomfortable because uncovenanted. I divined, rather than was shown experimentally, the state of her mind ; and, though naturally it was not pleasant to me, it was only what was to be expected from her.

I remember, however, being considerably exercised one day by the contempt with which she spoke of the English for their 'romantic marriages.' Marrying for love without sufficient means, preferring the person to settlements and affection to ambition, was to her one of the seven deadly social sins for which was no forgiveness. A runaway match with a detrimental was an infinitely worse crime in a girl than was the most flagrant infidelity in a wife ; and the unpracticality of romance counted for more than the immorality of vice.

This too, was one of those new views which, when first heard, make an ineffaceable mark on the mind. They add a strand to the skein, certainly ; but at the moment they shock, repel, and give a general sense of instability to everything. And when Madame la Marquise first launched forth against love in favour of convenience in marriage, I seemed to be listening to the wildest kind of moral treason, and wondered how any good woman could hold such awful principles. Now, in my old age, I have come to think that a great deal is to be said for the French method of marriage-making, tenderly and judiciously carried out ; and that the blind impulses of inexperienced passion are not quite the solid foundations for happiness it is the fashion in England to assume them to be ; but that knowledge and reason and foresight come in here, as in every other fact of human life ; and that niceness of daily habits, and ease from the carking cares of impecuniosity, go far to render existence endurable, even in the absence of the ideal.

CHAPTER VI.

WHEN I went back to Paris, I fell in with that beautiful and most unhappy woman whose head and neck were so strangely the human representation of the Ionic column, and who was one of the most pronounced of the man-haters and woman-defenders of her time. Sex with her determined everything. To be a man was to be a monster; to be a woman was to be probably a saint and certainly a victim. The most manifest perjury, if of a woman against a man, she received without examination and believed without doubt; and she justified all

viragoes on the ground of the provocation received by the sex, if not individually by themselves—a provocation which
called for and glorified reprisals and
revenge.

Through her I knew one who had been
in her day the most famous of our tragic
actresses, till she married and made herself
the most miserable of wives, and her husband as wretched as herself. The deep
voice and stage-stateliness of manner, the
assumption of supremacy and really cruel
strength of this lady, crushed me flat. The
way in which she levelled her big black
eyes at me, and calmly put her foot on me,
was an experience never to be forgotten.
The pitiless brutality of her contradictions ;
her scathing sarcasm ; her contemptuous
taunts, knowing that I was unable to
answer her ; the way in which she used
her matured powers to wound and hurt my
even then immature nature, gave me a

certain shuddering horror for her, such as I fancy a man would feel for one who had flayed him in the market-place. I am thankful to Fate which never threw us together again.

Years after, I knew her yet more gifted sister in Rome. She was a very different person—as womanly as this other was virile; as sweet and generous and sympathetic as this other was arbitrary, insolent, and inhuman. A characteristic little trait of the former was told me, instancing, to my way of thinking, the stony and unyielding quality of her mind. She was used to number all her dresses and hang them up in rows. If it came to the turn of her gold tissue to be worn, she would wear it, though she might be going to a simple family dinner ; if it were the turn for a morning silk, she would wear that, though she had to appear at a stately ball. This was her method of expressing order; and in this

apparently insignificant little habit may be
seen the germ of all she was and did, and
the cause of all she suffered and made others
suffer.

My lady the Ionic column was continually going over to Paris, which she
anathematized when she got there. She
used to say with vehemence that it was
the worst city in the world ; and I have
seen her shudder with horror as she
spoke. As I had not then peeped behind
the screen, I thought her both prejudiced
and fantastical, as well as illogical for
voluntarily living so much in a place she
held to be good only for fiends and satyrs.
I used to listen to her with frank amazement. Taken up as I was with my work,
and satisfied with life as it came to me on
the broad highway, I had neither time nor
inclination for excursions into dark passages
and shameful byways. Therefore I had
seen nothing of all the vice she so strongly

deprecated, and I did not believe in it. Moreover, I thought it then, and I think it now, the wisest plan to take the apparent good as it offers itself, and leave untouched those hidden evils which do not of themselves leap to our eyes, and with which we have no official concern.

Certainly I went about a little to doubtful places, as all young people do. Mabille was then in its glory; La Closerie des Lilas was just opened; and the Bals de l'Opera were also things for strangers to see. The students and grisettes who danced the can-can and did their extraordinary steps at these places, seem to me to have been different from the men and women who haunt the public dancing-halls to-day. The fun and frolic, if decidedly fast and more than 'risqué,' was more spontaneous, less professional, less commercial and calculated than now, and the whole style of thing was simpler. It was all the difference between the grisette and the cocotte—the student of the Quartier Latin and the 'petit crévé' of the Boulevard Italien.

One painful and horrible face dwells in my memory. I forget the man's name, but he had been the wealthy son of a master-baker, who had ruined himself at Mabille and all that this represented. He was now an old man, penniless, and supported by the charity of the Administration on which he had spent his large inheritance; but, old as he was, he danced with the lightness of a youth and the look and bearing of a satyr. His face was entirely that of the legendary satyr; and I looked for the pointed ears and goat's legs. He was the most suggestive and degraded specimen of European humanity possible to see, and might have been taken as a living text for any number of sermons you will.

My greatest pleasure, however, was not found in dancing-places, but in the quiet

country about Paris. I used to go for
long walks and excursions to Vincennes
and Versailles, St. Germains, and Fontaine-
bleau, Asnières, Ville d'Avray, and the like;
and I was never so happy as when noting
some new aspect of nature. For among the
contradictions with which my life is full is
that of the most passionate love for nature
and voluntary residence in towns. From
quite early childhood I had this delight in
nature, and I remember things which struck
me even when I was so small a boy that I
was frightened by finding myself alone in
the garden :—as, that dark cloud which hung
over our 'burgomaster' mountain to the
north, while the vale below and the hills
around were bathed in sunshine ; that double
rainbow which spanned the whole vale ;
those big drops of the thunder-shower ;
the revelation of folds and secondary peaks
in the mountains opposite by a sudden outburst of sunlight, and then the sinking back

into an undifferentiated mass when that sunlight passed. I cannot date the first times when I noticed these phenomena; but they were in quite early days, standing out from the chaotic darkness of the rest. I remember when I first noted the different shapes of certain buds of trees, *e.g.*, the difference between those of the horse-chestnut and the lime; I can yet put back certain rosebushes and honeysuckles found in the hedges; and, if it still exists as a field, I could walk straight to that corner of the field where I once found what I suppose must have been an oxlip. But it is more than fifty years since I have seen the place.

I remember the smell of the laurestinus and the bay-trees the first evening we arrived at my father's Kentish home; and the kind of awe with which those two cedars in the shrubbery opposite inspired me. I remember certain days of snowstorm when the fast-falling flakes were driven before the

pitiless wind, and I gave them the pain of
hunted creatures as they were hounded on
—now in eddying circles, and now in straight
lines. I remember how the rain one day
came down like a white sheet at Eden;
and I can still see my father going through
the garden gate to Sunday morning duty,
struggling against the wind, and half
shrouded within the cascade of rain, of
which also I remember thinking it was a
return of the Deluge. Certain sunsets are
yet plainly visible to my mental eye; and
the new flowers I found in the fields and
woods and waste places about Paris are
photographed on my memory, as are the
sunsets and the flowers of later years, seen
and found in beloved Italy.

And yet, the rush and grandeur of human
life in London and Paris, and the sense of
being in the heart of all this emotional and
intellectual movement, were more fascinating to me than even the beauty and the

peace of nature.   Hence the want of consistency which has marked my career from
first to last has its part in the apparent
contradiction of delighting in every circumstance and manifestation of nature, and
electing to live in cities.

Through Léon O'Byrne I became acquainted with a typical Frenchwoman of
a certain kind—one Mademoiselle Cléonice.
Though in a small way, she was the real
'femme de commerce' of Paris; and to know
her was to know a whole class.   She was
about thirty-five years of age, trim, neat,
plump, tight, sharp.   She was not pretty
when dissected bit by bit, but she was
'arranged' with such faultless taste as
to be charming and attractive on the
whole.   She was always dressed in black
silk or soft black stuff, without frills
or furbelows of any kind ; and her gowns
had that wonderful look of having been
moulded on her, like a second skin, which

is so peculiarly French. She wore linen collars and cuffs of scrupulous whiteness; round her neck was a small narrow handkerchief tied in a bow; and the smartest and prettiest kind of cap, made of filmy lace trimmed with pink ribbon, took off the severity of her smoothly braided blue-black hair. She was the trimmest and best got up little woman of the quarter, and was never seen with a thread awry.

She lived in the small room behind her smaller shop, where she sold laces, caps, embroidery and other feminine finery; and her room was as neat as herself. The mahogany bed was in an alcove concealed by curtains; the toilet apparatus was in a dark closet to the side. The mahogany furniture and crimson velvet chairs; the white muslin curtains tied with pink ribbon, hour-glass fashion; the ormolu clock and candelabra on the marble chimney-piece; the chimney-glass and marble-topped mahogany drawers; the red velvet sofa and the red velvet *fauteuil*—all were signs of *bien-être*, approaching to luxury for one of her class; and all were of a cleanliness, an order, that was of itself artistic poverty and scientific beauty.

Her way of life was typical. She lived absolutely alone, without a servant or assistant; but a 'femme de journée' came every morning to sweep and dust; a man from the street took down and put up her shutters; her food was sent in from a 'traiteur's' hard by; and when she wanted a holiday, she put up her shutters, locked the door, took the key in her pocket, and was free of all restraints. Thus she kept her apartment intact and undisturbed, and where she hid away her loose ends was a marvel.

In manner she was at once fascinating and provocative, petulant and caressing. She had a high-pitched voice and an irrit-

able way of speaking, as if always somewhat injured by some one and always com-
plaining of something. Her temper was
uncertain and easily ruffled, though it was
never violent and as little enthusiastic;
and her whole life was based on calculation.
Passions, affections, chances, duties, sins,
self-restraint, or the reverse, all made a sum
in the living arithmetic of her days—so
much to be gained by such and such an
action, so much to be lost. She could not
have loved nor hated without this balancing
of her mental books ; and of all the people
ever known to me, she was the least spontaneous. She was also slanderous and spiteful
to an appalling extent, and could not speak
well of anyone. According to her, all the
women she knew were ' drôleuses,'—all the
men ' coquins,' when not ' vauriens' nor
brigands. She despised the English, now
for their mathematical coldness, now, like
Madame la Marquise, for their unmathema-

tical romance.   The Italians she considered sinks of iniquity as fathomless as the Pit whence they came and whither they would return.   But her own people were even worse; and of the ten righteous men who might have saved Paris, could they but be found, she denied the existence of more than one.   Of one person only she forebore to speak evil, though she also never committed herself so far as to speak good.

This was a certain M. Bolivard, an elderly man, who wore very loose clothes and a very white waistcoat ; obese, loose-lipped, sharp-eyed ; with a skin like yellow ivory, and a black head, clipped close like a clothes-brush.   He was the landlord, patron, and book-keeper of the trim little 'lingère,' and came regularly on Wednesday and Saturday evenings to inspect her accounts and see how she was getting on. On these days she was always in an atrocious humour, and Léon, who was a pet of hers, was forbidden her place after four in the afternoon, as if he would have brought the plague.

From Mademoiselle Cléonice I learnt a good deal about the commercial class all round ; and if half she told me were true, and the present is like the past, Zola has not exaggerated. The corruption of the ' petite bourgeoisie ' is as complete as that of the ' haute volée ;' and no strokes are too broad, no ink too black, by which the inventory of their vices is made. But her own vice of slander made me hesi- tate before I believed all the rest, and the homely old saying about the pot and the kettle took off a good layer of soot from the latter. Still, she was a bright little companion, so far as she went; and if she went no deeper than the froth in cham- pagne, it was always champagne that frothed; and her repartee was as smart as her mind was shallow.

The most important of my Parisian friends, however, was Madame de Clairvaux, a Parisienne born and bred, who knew Paris and the whole art and mystery of life there, as she used to say, 'comme sa poche.' Her revelations were even more startling than those of Mademoiselle Cléonice, and more trustworthy, because neither spiteful nor made for the purpose of a disguise. She made them quite freely and impartially, almost scientifically. As I was young, a man of letters and a student of humanity, she said I ought to know the truth of things. And though I thought I did, pretty accurately, I certainly did not know so much before Madame de Clairvaux undertook to enlighten me as I did after.

The apotheosis of the demi-monde was just then beginning. The 'Dame aux Camellias,' with Madame Doche and Fechter as Marguerite and Armand, had made all Paris weep, and had still further loosened

the joints of its never too stiffly buckramed
virtue. But it seemed to me impossible to
know where the demi-monde began and
where it left off, save in the matter of
public notoriety. Of Madame de Clairvaux's
own friends—all women of good family,
good social standing and apparent repute—
there was not one who did not belong to
that famous basket of speckled peaches—
not one who had not qualified herself for
condemnation on account of that Damyan
of hers hidden among the leaves.

Some of Madame de Clairvaux's stories
were wonderfully graphic and romantic;
and some read hardly like truth as we
have it in this sober age of prose and commerce. For instance, that anecdote of
Madame de Niemand—who kept her lover
for six weeks in secret in the loft of her
country-house, while her husband was
absent, and only she, her child and her
sister, were at Ville Saint-Jean; the droll

32—2

expedients she had to adopt to give him food, fresh air and exercise ; her foraging expeditions in the kitchen at night, after the servants had gone to bed ; the cook's amazement at the disappearance of his stores, and the awful burden which that midnight appetite of ' Mademoiselle Marie ma sœur ' had to bear ; the rambles in the woods and grounds, under the stars, of the two lovers who more than once were taken for ' lutins' and ' les dames blanches,' and once ran great risk of being fired on as robbers ; and the wild mad happiness of the time— it was a romance from preface to colophon. But had it been written in a novel, the critics would have been down on the author as an absurd bungler who imagined things out of the line of possibility. Yet it was all true; and Madame de Clairvaux knew it. Another time Madame de Niemand, who was as beautiful as an angel, slipped away from a ball where she was and her lover was not. He was a poor artist, by the way, and lived in a garret. Suddenly there appeared before him a vision which, for a moment, he took to be unreal. Madame de Niemand in her ball-dress of pale pink and silver, her cloak thrown off, her hands held out, stood there in that dingy garret like the incarnation of beauty, love and riches ; and for a moment he lost his senses and swooned at her feet. The contrast between his poverty and her splendour was too great, and the joy, so unexpected, was too strong.

The little daughter born of this intrigue was the husband's favourite of the whole family, and the one in whom he took the greatest pride. As for suspicion of his wife, he had not the faintest trace. On the contrary, with this child on his knee he said to his friend, the lover in question :

'Of one thing I am perfectly sure, Emmeline has never deceived me.'

' You may swear that by the life of your mother,' said the lover calmly, laying his hand caressingly on the child's fair head.

' So much for the pretty theory of natural affection and the instincts,' said Madame de Clairvaux when she had finished, with an odd smile, and a rapid glance at Henri and Alphonsine, playing demurely in the corner —Henri the rosy blondin, the very counterpart of her fair Norman husband, while his little sister was as black as a morella cherry.

She told me many other things—always on the same lines ; till I began to feel that no such thing as womanly virtue nor manly constancy was left in the world, and that Mrs. Hulme was right:—It was only a question of the eleventh commandment and the comparative security of the door.

During my stay in France I went to a pension near Tours, where M. and Madame de Blainville, and M. and Madame Saint-

Georges, were living. M. de Blainville was, and had been for many years, 'le bon ami' of Madame Saint-Georges. Meanwhile, he had married and she had cooled. He had not. He had married for money, and his love remained intact. As for principle, that did not come into the arrangement. In this house I fell into the heart of mysteries and intrigues, where I was used now as a tool and now as a mask; and where, in the beginning, I understood nothing, neither what I did nor what I concealed, nor yet what was passing around me.

It was emphatically diamond cut diamond with M. de Blainville and Madame Saint-Georges; a game at chess with lives and hearts for pawns and queens, a duel 'à outrance,' where the rapiers were none the less deadly at the points for being covered with velvet at the hilts. Madame Saint-Georges had transferred her affections from

her old lover, whose marriage she had never
forgiven, to a handsome young fellow in the
neighbourhood, to whom such an adventure was a godsend.   M. de Blainville,
suspecting what was going on, set his
wits to work to prove what he feared.
He had the light tread and the supple
spring of a panther, and no one ever knew
where he was nor where he might not
appear when least expected.   He used to
say that he was going away for the whole
day, but he would conceal himself in the
branches of a tree which served as a kind
of watch-tower whence he could see all
that went on; and night and day he stole
about the house and grounds, noiselessly,
untiringly, watching with the vigilance
of jealousy for the moment of conviction.
I lived on the ground-floor; and I slept
with my windows open; safe against intruders by strong iron stanchions and bars.
Often at dead of night I used to be awakened

by M. de Blainville suddenly calling me by my name; and two or three times during the morning, as I sat there doing my work, a shadow would fall across my paper, and I would look up to see those dark gleaming eyes shining from beneath the broad sombrero as M. de Blainville said to me curtly 'Good-day,' and passed on, satisfied that I at least was innocently employed.

At last he was rewarded. During one of his nocturnal prowls, when he was believed to be in Paris and had been hidden all day in the woods, he saw a rope-ladder hanging down from a certain window, not too high for a courageous man's leap. Up this ladder he crept like a cat, and sprang lightly into the room. There was a woman's smothered cry; a dumb struggle between two men; then a bold leap into the dark; and Madame Saint-Georges had lost the game.

That winter in Paris was a tremendous thermometrical experience. The water used to be frozen hard in my tub, and I have often cut myself as with a knife with the icicles in my sponge. One day my milk froze on the top of my inefficient stove; and I never knew cold as I knew it then. But it was all experience, both moral and physical, both social and ethical.

After about two years of this strange life I was summoned back to England at a moment's notice; and I had to leave just in time to escape some unpleasantness to this day unverified. A general illumination had been ordered for the Emperor's birthday, and each householder had been warned to light all his lamps and candles, and make as brave a show in his window and on the balconies as was possible. In my Republican pride and youthful folly I declined to add my quota; and my special window remained dark. The next day I was summoned to appear at the Prefecture. As I was leaving that night, and the summons was for the next day, I could not go.

So the thing passed, and I heard no more of it. I knew that I had committed no crime and broken no law; though now I acknowledge that I had offended against good-breeding in refusing,to conform to the regulations of the country which gave me hospitality. The fact, however, of being 'wanted by the police' was in itself a little disturbing, and I was glad to be out of it. The Empire had a long arm and a heavy hand; and if I was hot-headed and absurd, the Government was tyrannous and unscrupulous; and between the two it was I who would have got worst off.

CHAPTER VII.

M Y Parisian experiences changed my point of view in more things than one, and in nothing more than on the marriage question. People would say those experiences had corrupted me. Perhaps so. For sure it is that from this time I have thought the laxity which reigns in society comes less from the corruption of the human heart than because life is too monotonous here, or the laws are too strict there. That is, I have learnt to condemn results less than to reason on causes.

With belief in direct revelation dies out

the divinity of laws as they stand. One gets to see that all society is built up by experiments, and that the final word has not been said on anything. One gets to see too, that, although to obey existing laws is the duty of every citizen, to change them is the right of the community and to criticize them that of the individual. Without doubt there is a better and a worse, a higher and a lower; but nothing is absolutely final; and that 'fourth dimension' may be applied to society as well as to space, and to morals and even matrimony as to other things. I saw that in Roman Catholic countries the sublime theory of the sacramental quality of marriage is wholly inoperative in practice, and that this is none the more sacred because it is indissoluble. On the contrary, the unyielding nature of the tie forces consideration for human weakness; and adultery is condoned because divorce is impossible.

The matrimonial ideal of the one love for life, beginning in youth, enduring through maturity to old age, and ending only with death, is of course the purest and noblest basis of the family. Extremes meeting, we see this condition fulfilled in those elemental states of society where wants are few, the intellect is undeveloped, the sphere restricted, and the instincts, satisfied, leave no room for vagrant imagination—where in fact, there is no imagination to go astray. But in a complex and widely differentiated society like ours—where men cannot marry when young and women cannot marry where they would; where the highly developed nervous organization of the race makes compatibility difficult to find and incompatibility impossible to bear; where women's domestic life is cramping and monotonous, the development of trade having robbed it of half its duties and all its variety—post-nuptial dissatisfaction is fatally common for both men and women alike. Hence, facility of divorce by robbing inconstancy of its falsehood and substituting the honest confession of incompatibility for the shameful detection of crime, is not only a just relief, but is also an accumulation of virtue for the community. Thus, though I have never gone so far as those who would have no bond outside inclination, I have, since my Paris days, gone as far as those countries which allow of divorce by mutual consent and without the necessity of committing a crime to procure relief.

These views are not considered now so subversive as they were when I was young and before the passing of our own Divorce Law, which at least gives easily to the poor what had been possible only with difficulty to the rich. Liberty of opinion has made great strides since then, in spite of the persecutions which have lately disgraced us; but we must never forget that these strides

were first marked out by those who had
the courage to speak plainly and aloud,
and the constancy to submit to the moral
obloquy which was their reward. Every
time has its fetishes which must not be
touched with a profane hand, nor discussed
as to their meaning or substance. To the
Greek, his sacred Xoana were mystical
representations of the unseen gods and not
battered old blackened blocks of wood ; to
the Catholic peasant, the Miraculous Virgin
of the Santuario is the direct Giver of
Health, the Healer by its own intrinsic
power, and not a hideous daub with as
little art as divinity; to the seminarist,
his guardian angel is a fact and not a
poetic dream ; to the pious savage, thunder
is the voice of his god and the doctrine of
an Impersonal Force would be impiety and
patent falsehood ; and to us, our existing
laws on marriage—not to go farther afield
—are as sacred and as unalterable as are all

those material fetishes to their worshippers ; and he who discusses the one or the other from the ground-work of development and the point of view of expediency is an infidel and profane.

And yet my old friend Mrs. Hulme was right. There is no absolute; and we shall have to try back and go forward many times yet before we reach perfection.

No man can say that all things are perfect as they are, even in Protestant monogamous England ; and the cuckoo-cry of the wickedness of the human heart is an excuse, not a reason. The worst possible legislation is that which multiplies unnecessary restrictions, and thus creates artificial offences. The best is that which leaves the individual unchecked liberty up to the point which harms no one. For legislation, like everything else, develops and matures, passing from the absolutism necessary for infancy to the freedom of the full-grown man. So it will some day be with marriage—when the command : ' You shall not, how much soever you may desire,' shall give place to the wider line : ' You are the best judge for yourself.'

I have dwelt on this subject so long because it was one of those which had the most fatal influence over my future life. I was more or less a moral derelict everywhere; but here I was not only abandoned, but actively accursed as well.

The young man's fancies that we know of ran lightly in those days in the direction natural to my age. My position was sufficiently good to make marriage possible, and I had begun to feel the lodgings into which I had gone when the old boarding-house came to grief both lonely and oppressive. To be sure, all that Parisian experience had been a little deterring, not to say intimidating ; but who believes that his neighbour's history will be his own? All women were not discursive, and faithful wives and honest mothers were still to be found. I set myself, therefore, to look for that which never comes when sought, and I did my best to fall in love with one or other of the girls I knew—chiefly, of course, amongst the advanced class.

Somehow, each failed to satisfy my taste all through. I was a Republican, granted ; but I was also a gentleman. I did not think then, and I do not think now, that Republicanism or Freethinking exempts us from the obligation of the most perfect courtesy, the most exquisite moral refinement. On the contrary. The more you respect yourself, which is the key-note of Republicanism, the more you will respect others ; and the less you recognise divine command in the things of life, the more you will be careful to maintain the very minutiæ of moral delicacy. It is laid on you to prove to others that this spotless grace and delicacy—this stately moral heroism—is the natural development of the moral sense, human and intrinsic, not taught from without. Far from brutal disregard or slipshod license, the Republican and Free-thinker is bound to be more courteous and more self-restrained than others. He has only himself for his own diploma. It be-hoves him, then, to be careful of both parchment and endorsement.

But, I confess it with a certain sense of shame—a certain sense of ethical unmanli-ness in a fastidiousness which looked like disloyalty to my flag—all these girls of the emancipated class sinned, or in grace and good breeding, or in the more serious quali-fications for domestic life. They were clever and bright-witted; some were pretty and some were good ; but either they were not conventionally ladies or they were not trustworthy as future wives.

There was Henrietta,. tall, handsome,

brilliant, vigorous—a fine kind of nineteenth-century Diana in a duffel coat with
big buttons and outside pockets. She gave
music lessons, to help her mother's narrow
income. So far, this was to her honour.
But the life of the streets, and the independence, freedom and breaking up of all
domestic habits engendered thereby, were
destructive of more than regularity of hours.
She was a brave accentuated creature ; an
ardent Republican ; a passionate woman's
rights woman ; a potential martyr for
liberty of thought and freedom of action ;
the kind of woman to be of priceless value
in a revolution, when she would have ridden
fifty miles at a stretch to carry papers, at
the risk of her life, past the enemy's lines ;
a woman to take the lead and keep it ; a
woman in her own right—'maîtresse-femme'
from head to heel ; good for action, for
courage, for devotion and a hundred other
heroic virtues. But for the monotony of

domestic life? for the small submissions of wifehood? the larger self-sacrifices of maternity? No! she was not fitted for these! When custom should have staled the first freshness of love, and the inevitable reaction should have set in, she would then have gone back to her old habits, to her vagabond life, to her delight in her sense of freedom and self-support, to her quasi-masculinity of custom, and her independence of hours and duties. And her own home would be the place where she would be seen least.

Then there was Laura, good, sweet-tempered, orderly, conformable. But she had not a thought higher than the lowest mole-heap of practical utility. She would have steeped herself in her domestic duties till nothing else was left. Her soul would have simmered away in the stew-pan; and that basket of needlework would have engulphed every vestige of her intellect. She would have sunk into the place of a fair and gentle servant; and I wanted my wife to be my companion, not only my hand-maiden.

Again, there was Kate, that passionate and desolate little virgin disgraced by fortune and worthy of a better fate. She was lame, but very sweet and lovely in the face; a spiritual, self-consuming, enthusiastic flame of fire, with a soul that wore out her body and hidden passions that burned her as it were alive. I was very fond of her, and she liked me; but she was my friend, not my lover, and never could be.

For worldly advantages Miss Daniels was the largest prize in the lottery; and I knew, without vanity, that I had only to stretch out my hand, when she would put herself and all she possessed into it. She ' called cousins,' as she expressed it, with my old idol, King Dan, but—those buts!— she was seven years older than I, and of portentous plainness. She was perfectly well-bred and extremely well-educated; and she had fifteen hundred a year. But it wanted only one or two little lines to make her face that of a dromedary. And with my sensuous temperament some share of beauty was an essential.

Theresa, sweet and seductive, had not quite a clean bill of moral health; and I did not care to come second. Mary was grace incarnate, but she was mad about display, and thought the only propaganda of advanced opinions to touch the world was to be made by diamonds and dinners. No! none of them would do. They were all deciduous; and my fancies fell like autumn leaves. I was desperately in love for four-and-twenty hours; and then I came out at the other side and recognised the impossibility of things.

This happened so often, that I began to believe myself incapable of anything like a serious or sustained passion. Had I then exhausted my heart in that one early out-flow? was I now nothing but a bit of moral thistledown, ever floating and never able to root?

When I saw Cordelia Gilchrist the whole panorama of my life changed, and I fell in love with her in that intense way which is almost like possession. It was not because of her beauty, for, save a tall and grace-ful figure, perfect hands and feet, and large deep blue or rather violet-coloured Irish eyes, she had no beauty, properly so called. But she had that irresistible fascination which is more than mere loveli-ness of feature. To see her was to love her; to love her was more than a liberal education—it was to touch the sublimest moral heights. Had I been able to forecast all that had to come, I would have done as I did, in spite of the anguish involved. I loved her as a man of my character would perforce love the woman he found in every way supreme, and whom he rejoiced to own his superior. I loved her with tenderness and reverence combined; with the love of a man and the worship of a devotee; with the same idealizing fervour as that which I had given to Adeline Dalrymple, and with more consciousness of myself. And she loved me. It was a thing that came at first sight on both sides, a sudden recognition of affinity for which neither was responsible and which neither could resist. We were made for each other. Each was the half which together made the completed human being.

And yet, what hope was there? None! Cordelia was a Roman Catholic, sincere, convinced, devout. And I was a Freethinker, a Deist, whose God was scarcely Providence so much as the Universal Mind; a sociologist, unable to see society as other than a series of experiments, where even marriage, which

to her was a divine sacrament, was nothing
but a human convention to be righteously
dissolved if it failed its appointed end.

To Cordelia all that I thought was fearful
blasphemy; and it is a marvel to me now
how her love withstood her horror. But
the fact that it did lifts my feeling for her
into a kind of divine gratitude, which keeps
her ever in the place of my holiest and
my best. In spite of her religious repugnance she loved me, the human being.
She would not abandon me, and she clung
to the hope of my conversion. Her director,
too, was merciful, and suffered her to continue the understanding—which was not a
distinct engagement—in the belief that
I should be turned to the true faith by love.
As I was still notoriously unanchored,
denying more than I affirmed—and mere
negation is supposed to be a kind of
Götterdammerung which only wants the
presence of Freya to disperse and make

into living light—it was not impossible
that love should work this reformation in
me, as it had in others before me, and that
I should come to my own happiness and
make Cordelia's, as well as save my soul
alive, by giving another convert to the
Church which alone is the true Ark of
Faith.

But, as I could not accept the foundation,
the superstructure had never a chance.   If
Protestantism had been rejected for its unprovable assertions, what could I do with
Catholicism, which makes larger demands
on our faith and adds stone upon stone to
the great temple of superstition?   How
could I speak of the Virgin Mary as
Deipara?—take part in her Litany?—
believe in her own Immaculate Conception?
—call her ' Mother of our Creator,' and ask
her to ' deliver us from all dangers?'   I
went to mass with Cordelia because she
wished it, and I was with her.   Had I

believed in hell, I would have gone there too, could I but have been with her. Ah! there could have been no hell where she was! Francesca da Rimini must have carried heaven with her had Paolo loved her as I loved Cordelia! And I let her chosen priests talk to me, because it was her wish; and also because I learnt more clearly what she thought through their teaching. But I was never stirred a hair's-breadth. Though I should lose all, I could not command belief in what seemed to me mere fables from end to end; and even against love I must be faithful to truth.

What argument was it to me, when Father Nolan spoke of authority and the long line of tradition, miracle and inspired counsel, which had remained unbroken in the Romish Church from the establishment of Christianity to now? Their traditions are not evidence; their miracles I disbelieved; and the Councils presided over by a John XII., a Benedict IX., an Alexander VI., did not seem to me to carry with them strong assurance of divine inspiration. For unbroken succession of teaching —have not Indian jugglers also this? Does that make their juggling miraculous according to its seeming? Could all the authority of all the popes and cardinals that ever lived *prove* the truth of the Incarnation?—or manifest more than their own belief in it?—or reconcile stories which oppose the laws of nature and deny all that science teaches? Could authority and tradition harmonize impossibilities? or make the distinct assertion that this generation shall not pass away till such and such things be fulfilled, aught but a promise which failed to justify itself? Could any number of Councils, of the same Church which condemned Galileo, verify the standing still of the sun upon Gibeon and of the moon in the valley of Ajalon?—or the

going back of the shadow on the dial ten
degrees for a sign of healing to Hezekiah?
Who will keep the keeper? and who will
verify the verifier?

The great cardinal who then ruled over
the Romish Church in England—whose appointment had so fluttered the Protestant
dovecote, and whose gigantic 'guy' I had
seen not so long ago as the expression of
that fluttering—he, like Father Nolan, found
me impracticable; and what love for my
darling could not win from me, arguments,
flawed from the base upwards, could still
less! For I loved her! I loved her!—how
deeply, to my enduring sorrow I alone knew.
I would have died for her as willingly as
other men would have received their supreme
honour. I would even have seen her married
to another, if she had loved him and he had
been worthy of her. I loved her beyond
self, beyond jealousy, beyond passion itself.
Her happiness was dearer to me than my

own; and to have known her blessed would
have been more to me than any joy that
could have befallen myself.   I loved her till
I sometimes felt as if my heart would break,
as when something is overloaded—it may
be with golden treasure; all the same, it is
overloaded;—and it breaks.   I loved her
beyond life and fame and repute; and all that
I had or desired of fortune was valuable
only so far as it regarded her.   I would
have accepted a title only to give it to her;
and wealth would have had no charm for
me if I might not have shared it with her.
I read her into the universe and saw all
things as the reflex—the shadow—of her.
But I could not lie—even for her!

When I parted from her it was absolutely
as if my heart were taken from my body—
as if my life were torn away physically.   It
was acute bodily suffering; and more than
once I had to use conscious self-control not
to shriek like a man in agony.   Whenever

she left me it was no longer life, it was death—but death which retained the consciousness of pain. I would have made myself her helot, if that would have done her good. I would have sacrificed my whole position and have worked for her on the roads, in the mines, at the lowest and vilest occupations, if she would have gained thereby. Had she been stricken with leprosy, I would have taken her in my arms; had her breath carried with it death, I would have kissed her lips till I died. It was for no want of love. No man, living nor dead, in fact nor in fancy, ever loved with more wholeness of devotion than I. But the Truth, as I conceived it, was my Sacred Mother whom I must not betray. Let my heart break—let my life go down to ruin— let me lose all and stand a beggar and an outcast instead of the glad possessor of love and happiness—let me sit for ever among the ashes and live to the end in the black midnight—but I must not lie; and I could not! And had I still to make the choice, I would rather commit personal suicide than, even for Cordelia, stand up in the market-place and say ' I believe' what I hold to be a fable.

On her side she was as firm as I was on mine, as passionately convinced of the truth of her creed as I was of its false-hood. She had no alternative but to refuse to marry me. How else could she have acted? She believed with the intensest fervour of conviction all that I rejected with the vehemence of denial. It would have been sacrilege to *her* Mother, the Church, and blasphemy to God, had she married me, unbeliever as I was. Indeed, her Church would not have sanctioned our union, nor could any priest have been found who would have given us the blessing. And to her— a simply civil ceremony would have made her, not my wife, but my concubine.

' If only you would believe !' she used to say to me with tears in her beautiful eyes. Oh, those eyes ! they haunt me still ! those tears in them, which were like blood drawn from my very heart ! And yet both truth and honour forbade me to dry them. My heart ! my heart ! how was it that you did not break?

One day she laid her hand on my arm.

' Become simply a believer in the Divine Incarnation,' she said. ' Be a Christian of any denomination, and I will get the consent of the Church to marry you. But how can I be the wife of one who disbelieves in the Divinity of the Saviour?—who rejects the message of love and the means of reconciliation sent to a fallen world by God through Christ ? How could I ever say my prayers again, after having committed such a deadly sin? and who would give me absolution while I went on living in it?'

And what could I say but repeat the old sad cry?—

'I cannot believe, and I cannot lie, even for you!'

But almost worse than my theological unbelief was my moral unsoundness; and specially on that marriage question. There seemed in this a certain kind of personal contamination which touched her own purity. My want of belief in the sacramental quality of marriage seemed to rob it of all sanctity, and to make it—on my side, at least—nothing better than a veiled and decent sin.

'What security,' she once asked, 'have men or women with wives or husbands who think as you do? If marriage is merely a civil contract, dissoluble at pleasure—a social convenience without intrinsic sacredness—what security is there? Yourself, Christopher —if I have no stronger hold on you than your fancy—is that inalienable? We

all know that people change. How could I
be sure you would not ?'

It was in vain I pleaded the worth of a
man's word and the security lying in a
steadfast nature. I had never yet proved
false to an affection nor a principle ; and
speculative opinions have nothing to do
with practical honour nor living conduct.
Because I thought marriage a civil contract
and not a divine ordinance—because I
would give relief to those who had made a
mistaken choice—that did not imply I would
change in my love for her, nor fail in my
fidelity. Was no reliance to be placed on
the proof afforded by the past ? Was the
whole run and set of a character valueless
as evidence?

She shook her head when I spoke to her
like this.

'The only safeguard of conduct is religious principle,' she said. ' Outside belief
in God and His commands there is no security
—no sacredness!'

We soon ceased to discuss the question of the sacramental or experimental character of marriage. It was too painful for her to hear; and I understood her sensitiveness. And I loved her for it; as I loved all that was hers, how much soever opposed to myself, because of the saintly purity and the saintly constancy with which she held to her convictions. If I could have changed her and made her a Freethinker, like myself, I would. As I could not, I loved her for what she was. But this marriage matter was the colouring thread that ran through the whole web of our mourning. And though after a time we left off open controversy, as being worse than useless, I knew what she felt; and she knew that I had not changed. She held fast by her points of faith and I by mine of denial; and there was no middle term where we could meet.

Year after year we went on in the old

ways, and time brought us no nearer to a settlement than we were at the beginning. She did not give me up. She had always the pious believer's faith in the power of God to work a miracle in my behalf, and in His goodness to turn my soul from the darkness to the light. I, on my side, prayed earnestly for better guidance. I besought the Power who over-shadowed and influenced all life to be shown my wrong, if I were in the wrong ; to be convinced of error if I were wandering and astray. Passionate, extreme, thorough, I would have submitted to any public humiliation had I been convinced of the truth, as Cordelia saw it, and of my own error, as she believed it. No recanta-tion would have been too complete—no penitent reconciliation to God too humble. I would have devoted my life to the service of the Church I had slandered. And had it been the Mother's will, and Cordelia's, I would have foregone all personal benefit from my conversion, and would have gone into a monastery to expiate my former sins instead of to the marriage altar to profit by my present grace.

But no light, if light it were, came to me. The whole thing still continued to be a mass of beautiful but unreal superstition. And the idea that the Great Incommunicable Spirit beyond and above all sense had ever been localized and individualized was more and more to me the outcome of that ignorance which made the earth the cosmic centre—the outcome of that vanity which supposes man to be the supreme object of divine thought and care.

But we loved each other. Deeper than all faiths, stronger than all doubts, lay that deathless love of which irreconcilable principle was just strong enough to prevent the translation into deeds. It was not able to kill the spirit! Oh! those long years of ever-increasing denial of those things which it was my life's happiness to affirm! —of ever-decreasing trust in the power of love to bridge over the gulf dividing us! It was like a long death-agony, where Hope and Fear stand by the watcher, now the one chanting a hymn with a smile, now the other wailing a threnody with a sob.

And the whole thing was such a contradiction; and yet it was inevitable! The ardent desire to benefit humanity, which is the very tap-root of my moral nature, urged me to combat everywhere the organized mental tyranny and debasing superstitious ignorance of the Church of Rome—that deadliest enemy to human progress which the modern world possesses. Yet the person for whom I would have died—for whose good I myself would have gone down into infamy—was a Roman Catholic, and from her faith drew half her moral beauty. From that very religion which I would have de-

stroyed, she got that supreme spiritual loveliness which bent me to worship her as
something beyond the normal heights of
humanity. She was like some faultless
masterpiece turned out by misshapen work-
men;—for never on earth lived a purer soul, a
more conscientious, high-principled, faithful
nature. If her land of departed souls be
peopled with such as she, purgatory is an
unnecessary halting-place, and hell would
emphatically be empty!

For her dear sake, to this hour I have a
strange feeling of tenderness for the Roman
Catholic ritual — for all who worship in
sincerity as she worshipped, love what she
loved and believe in those to whom she
prayed. The sweet faint lingering scent of
incense in the churches recalls her pure and
lovely image to my mind as clearly as when
I saw her cross herself as she knelt, watching her in her prayers, and loving her all the
more for the faith I could not share. And

I am not ashamed to confess that more than once in these later years, for all that has come and gone between now and then, I have wept like a child when I have heard the mass and seen the symbol which stood between me and this well-named ' servant of Christ.' Hating the system with the whole force of my intellect, I love the worship with that idealization of sentiment which is so pathetic in its impotence to influence the conduct.

My love for that best and holiest of women was like one of those ground-springs which are too deep to stop, yet are impossible to utilize; but they always keep that one spot green where forget-me-nots grow and summer roses fall. I loved her as a man loves when life and death meet in mingled passion and despair—with heart and soul and adoration—with the kiss that was heaven and the tears that were torture—with all that I had of poetry, of sentiment, of aspiration, of

desire—with infinite yearning, with boundless reverence, with tenderness, with devotion, with trust and with faith—with all
that is human LOVE in its fullest sense.
But the Crucified Christ stood between us
with the force of Death; and the Church was
the angel with the drawn sword who drove
us forth from Paradise.   And so it must be,
while I could not worship nor she deny.

Thus the thing continued for many weary
years, and at the end of all our struggles
and all our agony, we were just where we
were on the first night when we had met
and recognised our mutual fitness to our
mutual sorrow!   Only this difference was
between now and then—Hope lay like a
dead child between us, and youth had faded
from both.

We still saw each other at intervals.
Cordelia had taken the habit of calling me
brother, and wished that I should call her
sister.   Sister Cordelia!   No living human

sound has in it the music of this to me!
Sister Cordelia—the heart of all beauty, the
soul of all grace! The name seemed to keep
us together in the invisible bond which we
could neither break nor draw closer. And
by this time society had accepted our relations as fraternal, and had ceased to busy
itself about our future.

One day we were walking in the fields
together. It was the early summer, or rather
the late spring-time—that time when love
has yet in it the eager stretch of future hope,
and when nature reminds one of nothing so
much as a bridal and a blush. How well I
remember that day—the unstained blue sky;
the dazzlingly white cumulus clouds hanging like milky fleeces in the upper air; the
interpenetrating sense of freshness, of joy, of
life that laughed, of love that had won,
everywhere in creation save with her and
me! And yet we were together. And to
me, with my passionate temperament, the

presence of the beloved and the joy of the moment were so much!

The fields were full of flowers—here silvered with daisies; there golden with buttercups and paler cowslips; and here again delicately shaded with the pale purple of the cuckoo flower. The air was full of subtle scents from root and blade and leaf and flower; from the teeming earth and the freshening water; from invisible substances brought from afar, and mixing their unknown sweetness with those we know at home. It was full of yet more subtle music from the thousand unseen creatures which hummed and quivered and sang their songs to each other in words we could not understand, but the theme of which we knew by the interpretation of our own hearts. A lark was soaring overhead, and singing as it soared; birds all along the hedgerows and from the trees were calling to their mates; a couple of white butterflies were fluttering above our heads—everywhere it was the same—happiness and love—life, happiness and love!

We sat down on a bank under the lee of a hedge, and close to the gate. I took from my pocket Moore's 'Lalla Rookh' and began to read aloud the 'Fire Worshipper.' She was fond of that poem, representing as it did both her faith and her country. And at all times she liked my reading to her. When I came to those lines in the first canto, beginning: 'Hadst thou been born a Persian maid,' something as real as a touch seemed to pass between us, and more than the spoken words had been said. My voice broke and I stopped, while she looked into my eyes with an expression in her own that was at once a prayer and a confession, an entreaty and a lament; then suddenly she turned her face to my shoulder and burst into tears.

'Why will you not come to me?' she

sobbed. 'How can you still deny Christ and crucify Him afresh? How can you reject me—who love you so tenderly?'

I cannot relate that scene; as little could I catalogue the death-throes of my favourite child. It was the last despairing effort to win me over that she made, the last time I had to endure the rack I had voluntarily prepared for myself. She was as little near to yielding to my prayer to marry me, despite all, as was ever Saint Agatha near to denying her Lord. And I could not forswear my truth, nor join in the ranks of those who worshipped idols and cherished fables as living facts.

We stood together and watched the last of all things fade away between us. And Death came up where Love had been, and settled down on our hearts for ever. The long agony of years culminated in one supreme hour of anguish; and when the evening came, all was over. I knew no

more than that she had left me—that she
had gone with Father Nolan, who had
seemed to come out of space to where
we sat, and who had spoken to her words I
scarcely understood, but words which she
obeyed and which severed us for all time
and eternity.

When I came back to life and the things
of the earth and the senses, I was alone.
The sky was overcast; the night had come;
the hoarse cry of the goatsucker vibrated
in the mournful air; an owl hooted from
the wall; and the passing bell told of the
death hour of some poor soul cut off from
all its love. Christ and the Church were
victorious; and there were only two desolate
hearts the more, and one ruined life, to add
to the count of the martyrs made by Faith
and Denial.

But, set on a pedestal unattainable by
any other stands the image of this sacred
woman in my heart. Whatever of grace

and glory others have, she had more. Perfect in purity, in goodness, with a conscience that was as firm as adamant and crystal clear; perfect in loyalty to her creed and in loyalty to love, irreconcilable as these were; full of the majesty of moral beauty, of the splendour of human virtue— she is unique and apart from all I have ever known. She is the enduring loss and the unhealed sorrow of my life; and when I die, her name will be the last on my lips as it is the first in my heart. Whatever loves I had before, or have had since, lie in her shadow. The aureole round her memory eclipses their noonday brightness. Were she to call to me to go to her, I would stride over the grave of my fortune and my fair fame, and I would go. Were she to hold out her hand to me, I would step down the golden stair into the abyss to take it. And I lost her for an idea—for an unprovable belief and an undemonstrable negation. I lost her because I could not lie, nor could she. But if I saw the print of her foot in the sand to-day, I would kiss the mark, and the bitter dust would be like rose-leaves on my mouth.

Life was never the same to me after this. Something had gone from me which could never be replaced. I felt like one who has received some unseen and irreparable hurt which maims, but does not kill. I was not visibly disabled, but living was more difficult. My affections had lost their centre and I was unfocussed everywhere. I had to live without personal hope or love in my life, and with only work, humanity, and thought to fill up the void. It was a colourless kind of thing for one like myself, strong, impassioned, fully vitalized, unable to exist under the blight of passive melancholy, whose impatience of gloom made it necessary to kill his sorrow or be killed by it. But it had to be borne; and I did what I could for the sake of self-respect, and to vindicate the claim of character and philosophy to give the power of endurance. For I have always said that resignation to the inevitable is a question of natural strength and not of religious principle. The endless despair and passionate insubmission of many sincerely pious Christians show that they do not 'forgive God' for having afflicted them; while those who have no belief in the direct and deliberate will of an All-good Father, take their courage in both hands and bravely bear that cross which no tears can remove.

For myself, I buried my sorrow out of sight, and flung myself more and more into active life. Cordelia was dead to me, but humanity was left alive, and still suffered. There was so much to be done for the world! And after all, what were my individual sorrows compared with those of the race? What we now call altruism was then as much a fact under another name. And altruism is integral to my nature, born as it is of passionate sensation and keen imagination, by which I suffer in my own person and understand that others should feel as I have done.

'Your vice of pity,' said old Madame Mohl one day to me, reprovingly.

For all that it has cost me I would rather have this vice than the alternative virtue of indifference.

Meanwhile, great changes had taken place in the old home. All my sisters were married, and my brother Edwin was also married. His wife was somewhat older than he and well endowed. She was almost maternally fond of him; and in every way his lines had fallen in pleasant places. Hence he was off my mind, and I had neither duties nor regrets on his account.

My father was dead; and the three old homes had passed into the unsympathetic

hands of strangers. Mr. Grahame too was
dead, and the new incumbent of St. Mark's
belonged to the most exaggerated section
of the Evangelical school. He was simply
' old priest writ large,' who had narrowed
the universe down to his own microscopic
point. He was the sworn enemy of science,
literary breadth of view, freedom of speculative opinion, change in any direction; and
the grossest superstitions of Rome—to him
the Scarlet Woman of the Apocalypse—
were run hard by his own.

Thus my relations with Eden were broken
at the root, and I never now went down
among the mountains which had seen my
youthful struggles and my boyish despair,
the first waking of my mind to doubt and
my first experience of love and loss.

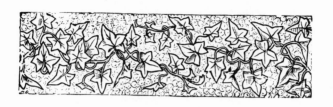

CHAPTER VIII.

Y personal happiness in its fullest sense was lost for ever. What these late years had taken from me could never be regained; and the hope of my manhood, like the certainties of my youth, had gone down into the grave of those dead illusions which we bury one by one as we pass along the highway of life. I should never now be the conqueror of fate and the controller of circumstance, as I once used to believe— happy, successful, triumphant, by the very force of my will—the very vitality of my courage. Like the rest, I must bear the cross rather than wear the crown; and no more than Prometheus could I free myself from the vulture at my heart. But, if joy had gone from me, I could still be faithful to the right as I had made it for myself; and I could always be strong.

And I could never become one of those anæmic worshippers of sorrow who are content to mope away their lives in sad-eyed dreams of 'what might have been, had things been different.' My life must ever be active and objective—before me, not behind. To lie down by the open grave of our dead hopes seems to me both cowardly and insane; for the forces which are not utilized become poisonous and destructive.

Like all of my character and temperament, at once resentful and compassionate, I was both a philanthropist and a fighter. I would have bound up the wounds with the Samaritan, but I would have broken the heads of the Priest and the Levite. And

the one action would have been as justifiable
as the other. It has taken many years of
much chastening to get this fighting blood
toned down to moderation, and to dissolve
my strong conceptions of the absolute into
a more tolerant and a wider acceptance of
the relative.

But in my youth and early manhood all
this passion was in the harmonious ordering
of things. Revolt was in the air; and
public events had added fuel to the original
fire of my temperament, and set the tow of
my imagination ablaze. Many facts in living
history had seemed to me like modern repro-
ductions of the old time 'Acta Sanctorum'
of liberty. Thus, while I was yet a boy,
Frost had repeated for me the part of
Camille Desmoulins, with that Newport gaol
for a minor Bastille and Henry Vincent
as a translated and anachronistic Hampden.
The Rebecca riots had been a righteous
Jacquerie; the trial of each leader in those

riots had been the ostracism of a true
Aristides — the punishment of nobleness
because noble; and I firmly believed that
Sir James Graham, when he opened Mazzini's letters, was the paid and authorized
spy of that House of Hapsburg of which, as
of our own Stuarts, no evil was too great to
be believed.   My old idol, King Dan—
the modern Gracchus who had embodied
all the praises lavished on Grattan by
Byron in the 'Irish Avatar'—had died,
like the worn-out wounded old lion my
fancy had depicted him.   Broken in health,
enfeebled in mind, pitifully repentant of
faults which had sprung from the grand
and glorious vitality of his nature, he had
sighed out his last breath in the bosom of
his Mother in Rome; but, if he had gone,
Ireland still lived, and her wounds were yet
unhealed and bleeding.   And when the
United Irishman preached its gospel to
young Ireland, and Smith O'Brien, Meagher

and Mitchell came to the front like new Emmetts and Fitzgeralds—I too contributed my small brick to the building of the temple, and felt twice the man I was before.

I had seen the Chartist movement quenched in its original form; but the Corn Law League and the Reform Bill had already given us more solid gains than my poor friends and brothers could have granted had they even had their will. I had seen the French Republic proclaimed, and I had believed in the formula, ' Liberté, Egalité, Fraternité,' as a new gospel against which the gates of hell itself would not prevail; and I had seen the murdered corpse of this fair hope lying beneath the heel of Louis Napoleon, and the empire established on the basis of perjury and murder. I had witnessed the trial of Orsini, noted the care he took of his long white finely shaped hands—even there in the dock—and I had thought, between the two it was a pity this one had been the victim! So that the ' Sturm und Drang' period of my own life had been in a manner repeated, as well as justified, by public events; and, as I say, revolt and excitement had been in the air all round.

Now things were modifying ; and my own thoughts, like politics, were taking a new and more practical shape.

The miserable condition of the poor; the injustice of existing arrangements, both in the tenure of the land and in the relations between labour and capital; the need of ' levelling up'—of inculcating greater self-respect among the masses by improved education, by increased political responsibilities, by better material conditions in food and dwelling—these were the subjects which now sat nearest to my heart. They made the more mature phase into which had passed that crude academic ideal of

Liberty with sword and banner, wild hair and floating plumes, crying, ' Death to the Tyrants!' on the ramparts, and shouting the ' Song of the Greeks' to the winds, which had been my dream in the boyish days of romance. This kind of thing had gone for ever; and I had come to the knowledge that reforms, to be lasting, must be legal, and that true liberty comes by the slower process of growth and gradual fitness, rather than by the sudden leap into supreme power of men unused to responsibilities and incapable of self-government. To be sure, armed revolution has been, and still is, necessary where supreme power is backed by the army, where abuses are maintained by the law and peaceable reforms are impossible. Then there is nothing for it but a hand-to-hand fight for the freedom of the many against the tyranny of the few; and the sacred right of insurrection cannot be proclaimed too loudly nor too loyally upheld.

But under a constitutional government, where liberty of speech, association and remonstrance is already won, armed rebellion is unnecessary; and bit by bit reform, so loftily despised by heady youth, manhood learns to respect as the only revolutionizing method fit for rational people.

'Ohne Hast, ohne Rast' is the best motto for the political reformer. But there must be that 'ohne Rast;' and the nuisance to be carted away must not be left to obstruct the highroad.

Thus, making a wide leap onward, the Education Bill was a better measure than would have been the Chartist demand for the payment of members, whereby working men, who did not know their real needs nor the best way of supplying them, might sit in the House and put back their own cause by ignorance and unpracticality. And again, limitation of a proprietor's power over the land, and the enforcement of the doctrine of duties as a substitute for that of rights—so that he shall not be able to evict whole villages at his pleasure, nor to convert arable land into deer-forests because these let better than fields and farms, and shall be forced to build and maintain labourers' cottages on his estate, at convenient distances from the centres of work ; limitation of the acreage to be held by individuals ; abolition of plurality in estates as in ecclesiastical holdings—of the law of entail and of the power of willing away property, so that a man shall never more be able to disinherit his wife and children, thus carrying his enmity beyond the grave—all these would be wiser as first steps and thin edges, than sudden nationalization, even with so many years' purchase as the solatium. And these things have to come. They too, are in the air ; as is limitation of the powers and a change in the processes of the House of Lords

—to be obtained peaceably but inexorably.

Violence, the ugly side of reaction against wrong, is the enemy which we Liberals and iconoclasts have to contend with in ourselves. It has already done as much to retard the birth-hour of true liberty as bave both Russia and Rome. Where the gospel of the knife, of dynamite, of the guillotine is preached, there liberty loses, and by just so much wrong and oppression gain. Threats are of no use unless they can be carried out ; and the attack which does not frighten and subdue irritates instead. The salvation of society will come only from that kind of philosophic and scientific Radicalism which sets itself to mend the evil of things, not by cataclysms and coups-d'état, but by the gradual education of public opinion, by orderly organizations, by the exposition of causes, keeping free of personal rancour, and by the steady and sustained pressure of argument, rather than by appeals to the passions or even the emotions of the multitude.

This would have been the work of the Positivists, had Dr. Congreve's social formula been wider and freer. He missed a noble opportunity, by which, however, the other section has profited. Yet, in spite of the perfect truth in part of the teaching of this other section—in spite of all Frederic Harrison's eloquence and glorious humanity—the world refuses to go over. Positivism, as given in the beginning, was too truly 'Catholicism without Christianity'—that is, mental subjection without spiritual consolation; arrested development without the beauty, the poetry, the finer fancies by which the elder sister gratifies the dwarfed intelligence of those for whom the last word has been said, the final revelation given, the finishing touch laid. Scientific reform—

philosophic democracy—are what the world
wants ; remembering that science includes
the element of growth and the possibility of
mutation, and that life is perpetual flux and
interchange of force and form.

Anything that made for liberty was sure
of my poor support. I sympathized with
all the movements afloat, and knew something of them all as they rose and swam,
then sank and were lost in the depths of
completed things. The Christian Socialists,
with their brave leader, Parson Lot, at their
head, spinning golden webs which drifted
away into nothingness, fastened as they
were to nothing more solid than the mere
poetry of Christianity—the Republican
formula canonized:—The Secularists whose
very name frightened respectable folk,
though they were so dry and formal and
severely moral, and whose blameless chief
stood as a kind of diabolic Demiurge who
would create a Pandemonium where had

been an Eden, though now he is looked on as a fossilized kind of Conservative by his successors and overtakers:—The dreamy and unpractical Republicans, whose ' organ' was printed down among the mountains, with no public to buy it when done, and with only the ruin of the enthusiast who manipulated the whole matter as the net result :—The eloquent, if not quite satisfactory, Unitarian who preached on Bentham and the Holy Spirit—poetry to-day, and free-trade to-morrow—and who, utilitarian from head to heel, ' would bless a river for its beauty, and bid it turn a mill ':—Kossuth, Mazzini, Garibaldi, Victor Hugo—the men who had written words which burned the hearts of those who read them, and the men who had fought behind the barricades as their practical commentary thereon :—The French who had escaped Cayenne, and who cursed the Man of December:—The Russians who had escaped Siberia, and who cursed

the Czar :—The Hungarians and Poles, the
Lombards and Venetians, who had put Spiel-
berg and I Piombi behind them, and who
swore vengeance to the House of Hapsburg,
like so many Archangel Michaels against
Satan :—The Italians who had fled from
the Neapolitan dungeons and the Papal
prisons :—The new Luther and the modern
Tell :—The unsuccessful conspirators of all
nations—I knew them all.   And I believed
in some, while I confess I gravely doubted
the sincerity of others.

For though exile was a bad business, say
for those Sicilian gentlemen and noblemen
who sacrificed place and fortune for the
rational liberties of their country, it was a
means of living, like any other, for those
shady patriots who were less martyrs than
adventurers, and whose politics were a profession rather than a principle.   And even
among the best of the sincere—always excepting such men as the Scalias and their

friends — there was a notable absence of good sense and workable methods, and a great deal of childish noise and bluster.

I did my best, however;—myself not being exactly qualified to sit in the seat of the judge condemning exaggeration; and I gave both my strength and my substance to the cause of freedom in general. I was still hopeful enough to believe that we were on the threshold of a new development, at the fork of a new departure. The echo of the high hopes with which we, the young men of that time, had greeted the establishment of the first International Exhibition, that precursor of universal peace, still lingered in the air, and turned to noble music every little scrannel pipe that squeaked. We looked to all four corners of the earth for deliverance from the social and economic ills which oppressed our poorer brethren; and our Saviours of Society were as many as there were ingenious men to draw out a pro-

gramme and bold ones to take the
initiative.

Our belief was, in a sense, omnivorous,
and adapted all that came as food.
Schemes for the regeneration of the world
strewed the ground like golden dust, and
Vidocq himself could not have gathered up
all the ends which formed the tangled skein
of our hopes. But I can never be sufficiently grateful for the small grain of
caution, which lies like a two-pennyworth
of common-sense in the midst of the intolerable quantity of impulse with which I am
handicapped, that I forebore to join any
association, and refused to become a member of any of the secret societies by which
I was surrounded and solicited.

What a crowd of memories surge around
me as I write! Kossuth's triumphal entry
into London, matched for enthusiasm only
by that of Garibaldi's still grander apotheosis some years after :—The assault on

Haynau by the sturdy brewers who resented the presence among them of the
woman-flogger:—and our own piano-wires
in Jamaica vibrating in the near distance !
That crowded meeting at St. Martin's Hall,
where Kossuth and Mazzini sat on the platform—the one so showy, so brilliant, so
like the hero of romance, the other shy,
reserved, silent, intense—the one phosphorescent, the other hidden fire :—The
establishment of the Whittington Club,
which was to be the beginning of all social
good and the grand refining influence and
' leveller up' of the ' second set,' where
ladies were to dance with shopmen, and
gentlemen were to squire, but not flirt
with shopwomen :—The great lights of the
literary world, Macaulay, Carlyle, Ruskin,
Grote, Tennyson, Mills, the Brownings
—in his own degree, Arthur Helps—
George Henry Lewes, Miss Martineau, ' Jane
Eyre' and Mrs. Gaskell, together with

Thackeray and Dickens:—all are heaped up in my mind without order or chronology; and I could not without some trouble lay these memories in line nor arrange them in their sequence. I only remember the seething time that it all was, and the hope which was born into the world, to be extinguished by fear—even as that divine child, lying in a blaze of light in the cradle, was killed by the frightened nurse as a thing of horror, not cherished as a gift of glory.

Other things come before me as I write. I remember the evening when news of the Czar's death flashed into London. To me it was the forerunner of peace and the redemption of thousands of lives through the loss of one. Therefore it was a thing rightfully welcome to England. Yet Nicholas was a man of whom his worst enemies must speak with respect for his person, how much soever they may hate the system of which he was the crowning

symbol. I was in a state of boiling excitement and could not remain at home, but
dashed out in a hansom, I did not care
where. I remember driving round Regent's
Park in the aimless way of simple emotion
trying to work itself off; and then I went
to the house of some pleasant friends, with
whom I was accustomed to spend many of
my evenings. I thought they would sympathize with my exultation, and share in my
rejoicing over the probable speedy settlement of the war; and I bounded up the
stairs, two steps at a time, bursting into
the room like a whirlwind raised by
laughter.

I found the wife pale and in tears : the
young people sitting about in mute,
desponding, half-terrified distress; the
husband pacing the room in the violent
agonies of despair. What did it all mean?
I was aghast, and not the less so when the
sweet wife sobbed out :

' We are ruined, Crishna! My dear, we are absolutely and eternally ruined!'

Mr. Smith was on the Stock Exchange. He had speculated for a fall; and the sudden death of the Czar had sent all investments up like so many balloons, and swept away his last penny.

This was the first time that I had come face to face with the sorrow of private loss through public gain ; and it made an indelible impression on me. Natural as was this despair of the ruined individual, in face of the general and national good it seemed to me so strangely unpatriotic, so fatally egotistic !

Another strange experience, but before this time, was my introduction to the Queen's Bench Prison. Some friends had got into trouble and were there—the husband as the debtor, the wife as the nurse, admitted on a doctor's certificate. We had a good time, as the Americans say, in that meagrely furnished dingy room, where the height of good company assembled. That handsome Irish notability—I wonder if he remembers those charming little early suppers, where the Sicilian dressed the macaroni, the Frenchman mixed the salad, the nurse-wife supplied the Attic salt, and where we were all as gay as larks?

Among the debtors of that time was a man who had taken his wife's unsecured fortune and lavished it on the famous Phryne of the day. He drifted into the Queen's Bench as the moral of his fable; and his wife, with her little child, came daily to see and comfort him. I always thought this one of the finest instances of womanly forgiveness I had ever met with; and I very much question whether this limp-backed Anthony were worthy of so much consideration from his patient Octavia.

I used to take my caged friends sauces and groceries, and was stopped at the gate,

while the turnkeys drew the corks of the
Lazenbys and Burgesses, to make sure that
nothing less innocent than Harvey or ketchup
was in the bottles. We sat on the bed and
boxes at our symposia, chairs being defi-
cient; and some of the merriest and wit-
tiest hours of my life were spent in that
queer little room, '10 in 12,' as it was
numbered. Perhaps it was somewhat too
much of a 'danse Macabre'; and the ebullient
gaiety of all concerned might have had in it
a certain false ring, as of those who wished
to forget and endeavoured to hide.

But we were all too well-bred to hint at
the skeleton; and indeed some of us did not
see the grinning skull beneath the roses.
For the world is so blind!—and of all qualities extant, perspicuity is the rarest. So we
all went with pretty constant fidelity to
visit the Government debtor and his nurse-
wife; and gaiety turned into a play what
had been assigned as a penance, till the

beneficent hand of patronage did its work, and the authorities came to a compromise which opened the cage-door and set the captives free.

CHAPTER IX.

I HAVE not yet spoken of Morton Cavanagh, for all that he had been for a long time my best and dearest friend. I became acquainted with him during the second year of my life in London, and we made friends on the spot. There was just this little strangeness in our sudden friendship, in that it was made as it were in spite of ourselves. We had been mutually prejudiced against each other by excessive praise. His friends had vaunted him to me so extravagantly that I had made myself sure he was nothing but an overrated and conceited puppy—a jack-

daw pranked in peacock's feathers, and by
no means the phœnix they had painted him.
He on his side had come to an analogous
conclusion about me. I was a pedant, a
bookworm, a dusty, fusty, old-young prig;
and my diligence was a red rag to him as
violent and aggressive as was his brilliancy
to me.

Hence, when we met, we met as secret
enemies determined to hate each other to
the death ; and when we parted, we parted
as mutual friends who knew that they would
love each other for life. It was an odd
little drama; but all life is full of these queer
contradictions of intent and deed.

Cavanagh was one of the handsomest
young fellows I have ever seen. He was
bright, energetic, gallant; a creature whom
all women loved, to whom all men wished
well, and of whom there were as many hopes
as there are stars in the sky. And he
seemed certain to justify the brilliant pro-

phecies made in his favour. He had the
ball at his foot, and the world's oyster was
already half opened. He was an artist, and,
so far as he had gone, a successful one. He
had taken the Gold Medal, been publicly
praised by Sir Charles Eastlake, and he had
sold his first exhibited picture. All that
was wanting now was diligence in work
and industry in self-improvement.

For the first few years his sun shone in a
cloudless sky. While I was making but
a very moderate income by hard work,
Cavanagh was coining money by labour as
light as play. His gains were princely, all
things considered; and he ought to have
saved considerably. But no matter what
he earned, he kept nothing. Generous,
careless, pleasure-loving, extravagant, he
had every quality which leads to expenditure and the melting-pot ; and with all his
gains he never had sixpence before him.
Or, if he had, it was taken from him by some-

one who said he wanted it more than did he himself. Cavanagh had not yet learned how to refuse. 'No' was the hardest word in the language to him, and he would have borne any burden on his own shoulders rather than have given pain to another. As for his openhandedness, it did not matter, he used to say with a laugh. He had a reserve fund where that came from, and his bank was not broken. While he had health and strength he would float on the top of the waves; when he felt himself beginning to sink it would then be time enough to put together a raft and hang on to a buoy.

Although we were more like brothers than merely friends, Cavanagh and I had little mental life in common. He did not care a straw for politics; social questions were dry chaff to him; he never troubled his head about religion. He went to church when he visited his people in the country, because it was the proper thing to do and they would have been hurt had he not gone; but he dropped the habit in London. Not because he did not believe what he heard from reading-desk or pulpit; but because it took up his time and bored him. He liked the sunshine and long rambles in the woods and fields and by the sea-shore better than the dim religious light; and, if remonstrated with, he used to say that Nature was his temple, and a lark singing in the sky was a more devout choir than one made up of any number of nice little boys in nice white stoles, singing antiphonies through their noses. But what was wanting in mental sympathy of the deepest kind was filled in by sympathy of a more generalized sort. We both loved art and nature, music, poetry and beauty. We both loathed vulgarity, and never confounded unconventionality with coarseness nor freedom with vice. And we both profited by the devotion, sincerity and affectionateness which interpenetrated and coloured the character of each.

For my own part, I had reason enough to both love and admire Morton Cavanagh. He was a charming companion ; always ready to enjoy; bright, good-humoured; at once receptive and expansive, playful and sincere. He was entirely natural too—one of the least artificial or self-conscious of men. He was conscious enough of the splendour of life and of his own divine enjoyment therein—conscious of power and pleasure, of what he could do and what he could feel—but he was not conscious of his outer self. He scarcely knew that he was handsome—he, who was as beautiful as Antinous !—and he never calculated on the effect of his personality on others. Perfectly truthful, he did not offend the most susceptible, because what he said was said without either callousness or insolence. It was said simply because such and such things were. Is it an offence to call the hedge wound-wort fetid? or flattery to say that the rose is sweet? This truthfulness was part of Cavanagh's very being. Subterfuge, lying, hypocrisy, all false seeming everywhere, were as far from him as was cruelty or vulgarity; and part of his very manliness was in his sincerity.

In person he was tall, slender, long-limbed. He had dark hair and dark eyes; his skin was dead white, and his whole appearance was un-English. But his beauty was neither French nor Italian, nor yet Spanish, nor again that of any nation with which I am acquainted. It was sui generis. He himself used to declare that he was half a Red Indian, because descended through his mother from the hapless Queen Pocohontas; and he certainly had a curiously long swift stride, and bore himself with a certain savage ease and grace as well as dignity and freedom, which justified his belief. Only, one learns to be somewhat sceptical of these descendants of Pocohontas; they are a little too numerous. Be that, however, as it may, I have never seen anyone like Cavanagh—never one with so much native kingliness of manner mingled with the gallant gay good-humour of an artist and a Bohemian. For he was a Bohemian to his finger-tips—but not of the vicious type.

Such as he was, he was supreme in beauty, in talent, in nobleness, in brilliancy and power ; and not the proudest of us all felt that he doffed his cap too low, or gave up his own rightful pretensions, when he made Morton Cavanagh the king of the circle whom all agreed to honour and none could fail to love.

When I went over to Paris, I naturally lost personal touch of my friend. We corresponded, of course ; but letters are poor substitutes for daily intercourse, and when lives are apart interests diverge. Then there comes of necessity a certain mildew about the intimacy—not in the affections, but in the mutual knowledge of events. And all events more or less mould and modify the character, until it finally sets in its inalterable shape ; when it fossilizes and grows no more.

One day while I was in Paris I received a letter from Cavanagh telling me abruptly that he was married. He had married, he said, the daughter of a lodging-house keeper down at some place in Cornwall—I think it was Bude or Boscastle—where he had been spending the summer. He made no attempt to conceal the real position of his wife, nor to gild the homely russet of her circumstances. She was simply plain Mary, the daughter of a woman who took in lodgers for the summer season in a simple little Cornish village. But she was a good girl, he said, and as beautiful as an artist's wife should be. He was as happy as a king, he

went on to say, and he wanted only his dear
Chris—his fidus Achates—to be as happy as
an emperor.

It was a letter written in the wildest,
maddest strain ; and I was glad that he
was so content. As for a lodging-house
keeper's daughter—well ! the name does
not go for much ; for there are daughters
and daughters, as well as there are lodging-
house keepers and lodging-house keepers.
We sometimes find irreproachable ladies of
good education and small means who pay
their rent by letting their rooms. There is
nothing necessarily degrading in this. A
woman left poorly provided for, and with
children to bring up, must do something to
stretch that narrow margin. Why not this
as well as anything else ? Mary's mother
was surely a lady of this kind ; and Mary
herself was none the worse for the fact that
the drawing-rooms had to pay the rent, and
that a six months' letting had to secure a

twelvemonths' tenement. She must be refined and well brought up. Morton Cavanagh could not have married anything else
than a real, true, genuine, unapocryphal
gentlewoman. With his fastidious tastes,
how could he do otherwise ? The only
thing to disturb me in the matter was that
he had not told me of his engagement, and
that he had sprung his marriage on me so
unexpectedly. But I loved my friend and
respected freedom of action too much to
allow this to rankle in my mind; and I
made no stumbling-block where Cavanagh
had placed none.

When I returned from Paris, Cavanagh
came to meet me at the station. I saw him
striding up the platform with his old swift
silent step, his handsome face alight with
pleasure, his bright eyes shining in the gas-
light as in an instant he had, as he said,
' spotted ' me. But when I stood face to face
with him, at a glance I saw a certain change.

I could not explain it. I could not say where it was, nor in what special tract nor trait. But it was there. It was the same picture varnished with another colour ; and the man I met was not the man I had left. He was stouter than when I had seen him last. The clear white of his skin was obscured and yellowed. His jet-black hair was longer, and the gloss had gone out of it. His dress was shabby, and he had a certain self-neglected look—a certain dash of raffishness which he had never had before ; and as he spoke and laughed his welcome in more vociferous fashion than had been usual with him, his hot breath was heavy with the deadly reek of gin.

When I went to his lodgings I understood matters yet more clearly. A tawdry, ill-appointed young woman, with a by no means appetizing infant in her arms—a young woman with a face like a wax-doll, pink and blue and gold, round and mindless, with nothing in it save youth and colour, and from which maternity had already taken the first bloom—a young woman, fine and slipshod, under-bred and pretentious, ill at ease and affected—this was the landlady's daughter whom my friend had made his wife, and vaunted as his fitting match and willing choice.

My poor Cavanagh! What had blinded him so fatally? Ah! it was the old old story whereby so many young men have been destroyed—a moment's weakness, and a life's sad ruin for expiation! That was the whole thing. When the momentary craze passed, my friend woke to find himself tied for life to an animated log, in no single particular admirable nor worthy of him. I do not mean to say she was actively bad, poor soul!—she was not that; but she was utterly common—not vicious, but un-improvable—not a savage, nor a fiend, nor yet even a mere animal, but just a human doll, mindless, brainless, conscienceless, and worked by curious internal machinery. And she was the millstone round her husband's neck which sank him to the depths.

The sequel is soon told. Disgusted with himself, and not strong enough to bear with patient dignity the consequences of his own mistake nor yet able to remedy that mistake, Cavanagh took to drink, as many a poor fellow has done before him. Neither the claims of his wife and children nor the religion of honour and self-respect, touched him for more than a few days at a time. He had spasmodic fits of repentance, of self-loathing, of good resolve, of refuge in religion, but to no good. The demon of drink had him too tightly in his grasp; and, struggle as he would, my unhappy friend could never set himself free. His wife did not know how to take him. How should she, poor woman? Such a character and such conditions as his required nicer handling than hers. She bullied him, rated, threatened, and publicly disgraced him yet more than he had already disgraced himself. She made his wretched squalid home more wretched by her not unnatural temper, and more squalid by her bad management and unthrift; and he left both her and it for that bitter forgetfulness which only made everything worse.

He grew quarrelsome, too, and suspicious; and it was as much as I or any of his friends could do to keep on fair terms with him, so madly determined was he to find us in the wrong. Poor Cavanagh! Having so much to condemn in himself, it would have been such a relief if he could have found that he was not the only one to blame, and that his griefs against others excused his high-treason against himself! But I never let him quarrel with me. And, painful as it was to go to that sordid home and see the wreck of all that I had once so loved, admired and be-

lieved in, I used to go continually—to at
least ease my own conscience if I could not
lighten his.

Suddenly the whole family disappeared
out of London, and I lost sight of them.
Cavanagh did not write to me, and his own
people refused to give me his address. He
had gone like a faded aurora—something
that had been so glorious and that now had
passed into the mists of night. No one of
our common friends knew more than I; and
I knew nothing. So it continued for some
time, and of this man who had been to me
more like a brother than a friend I knew
absolutely nothing—not even whether he
were living or dead, sane or mad. And I
could not find out.

One night I had a singular dream. I
thought that I was walking on the road
which led to our old rectory when I stumbled
over the body of Morton Cavanagh, lying
half-dead and covered with mud by the way-

side. I stopped, lifted him up in my arms, and cleansed him; then I led him home, hand-in-hand, to my father's house—waking as I passed through the garden gate.

This dream made a deep impression on me, for all that I am absolutely free from superstitious belief in, or reverence for, dreams. Still, it brought my dear friend's image so vividly before me that I could not free my mind from the thought of him. And I resolved at all costs to find out where he was, and in what condition of mind, body and estate.

After infinite trouble and queer, mole-like workings, I succeeded. I found him in a small four-roomed cottage, in a remote village in Essex—separated from his wife and children, and living with a policeman and his wife. His family had taken him in hand, and, as he was now an absolute pauper, they were masters of the situation. The wife and children were cared for separately; and Cavanagh was, as I say, put under the charge of a policeman, with strict orders that he should be kept from drink. He had had delirium tremens more than once, and his brain was by now decidedly deteriorated.

When I knew his address, I went down that same day. I wanted to take him unawares, and thus to be able to judge more accurately than if he had time to prepare himself.

I shall never forget the sickening sensation of the moment when I first saw him in that wretched cottage, amid those gross and mean surroundings that made the reality to which his brilliant prospects had declined. Bloated, blotched—his once bright eyes lustreless, bloodshot, staring—his manner a strange mixture of swagger and shame—his manhood degraded — his whole being debased—and yet flashes of his old purer self traversing this deadly darkness—he was

more awful than a galvanized corpse, more
pitiful than a ghost lingering mournfully
among the living. What a change! what
an awful fall it was!

At the first moment he did not seem to
recognise me. Then, when he did, he
laughed aloud with that false mirth which
is more sad than tears. Then he became
insolent, and challenged my motives for
coming, and threatened me with tragic, half-
insane and impotent bluster; and finally he
broke down into hysterical weeping, which
was a kind of waymark of his degradation.
And then he was conquered; and a little of
that deep crust of moral dirt was washed
away, at least for the moment. I stayed
with him the whole day, and we went out
for a walk in the fields, where he got to be
somewhat more like his old self. We talked
of flowers and art, of pictures and people;
but his brain was weak, and he could not
take in much at a time, and I had to

treat him morally and intellectually as the famished are treated physically—with small spells of talk and long lapses of silence. But my presence seemed to soothe if not to strengthen him; and when I left he pressed me to go again, and often, and very soon; saying, as he stood on the platform, the policeman by his side:

'You have done me good, Chris! God bless you, old fellow!'

I often went after this—generally once a week; but always by appointment. On the days when I was there he was at least safe from degradation; and, indeed, the woman of the house said they reckoned three good days for every visit. He was happy in my company. I recalled him to something of his former brightness, and for sake of the old times he made these pathetic little efforts to rise out of his ruin. But he could not. His brain had deteriorated, his will had been eaten

into, and his morale was paralyzed all
through.   The second day after I had been
to see him, he broke out as bad as ever, and
so he continued till the day before my next
visit was to come off.   Then he kept sober,
for love's sake and mine.

How he got the means, or how he
managed to get the drink at all, was a
mystery.   The only sure thing about it
was, he did manage, and he did get it.   He,
once so honourable, so upright, so straightforward and fearless in the truth, now con-
descended to the meanest falsehoods and
subterfuges for that accursed poison which
had ruined him.

At last the end came.   He died quite
suddenly, in a moment, as he sat there by
the table.   And when he died he was a
mere shell—a mass of used and worn-out
organs, all of which were diseased and
destroyed.   His death was a release from
sorrow shame, and suffering all round; and

I felt that I had gained him again, not lost him, through the purification of the grave. My poor Cavanagh! I never loved any man, save Edwin, so much as I loved him ; but my dream was a lying vision :—I did not cleanse nor save him, nor did I lead him home to the Father's House !

I lost more than Morton Cavanagh about this time—the exact dates and precise order do not signify. My dear old father-friend Walter Savage Landor made the second great blunder of his life, and had to pay the penalty. The law is no respecter of persons ; and those who vault unbidden into the seat of justice have to suffer by the sword they have wielded without authority.

Into the merits of this painful case I will not enter. All I know is the fatal result; and the only defence I make—and to my mind it is all-powerful—is, that age obscures the clearness of the mental vision as it does that of the physical, and that if to those

38—2

who love much much may be forgiven, those whose vigorous youth has been pure and flawless may hope for the reverent veiling of oblivion when they make an octogenarian mistake.

Mr. Landor left Bath, and went back to his own family and the old home he once loved so well at beautiful Florence; and I never saw him again.

But the lives which had been discordant in the years gone by were not likely to be harmonious now; and the love which had been too weak to keep the marriage soldered in the days of youth and maturity could scarcely bring together the jagged edges in old age, when habits had diverged as much as feelings were estranged. After a miserable spell of dissatisfaction, the fire, which had long been burning low, finally burnt itself out, and the old lion lay down never more to rise. There, under the blue sky of Italy, turned to his rest one of the grandest

literary figures and noblest men of his
generation — one who, though his own
worst enemy, was the friend and pane-
gyrist of all things lofty, beautiful and
good.

Too absolutely free from the faintest taint
of vulgarity to be appreciated by the vulgar,
the inner beauty of Landor's nature was not
all men's possession—just as his literary
work itself is only for the chosen few, and
has never been what is called popular.
Sonorous in its melody, but not laboured
nor artificial; suggestive, but not sketchy;
giving the impression of a reserve-fund
unexhausted and of latent force unused, but
never of want of finish nor of neglected
opportunity; never cloying, but never dis-
appointing, his works are among the best
of our literature and language. Nowhere
else do we find such a mixture of grace and
strength, of tenderness and power, of artistic
skill and natural simplicity. The figures

which leave his hands are like the purest Greek statues. There is no violence in their tragedy, no affectation in their elegance, no simper in their beauty, no self-consciousness in their grace. Beneath the smooth surface of the marble the living man lies hidden. His Aphrodites wring the salt wave from their dripping tresses, and know that they have risen to life in the upper air and are the beloved of gods and mortals ; but they are large and free and noble, and art but reproduces what nature created. His Apollos stand secure in their strength, masters of the Chariot of the Sun, lords of life and beauty, who command and are obeyed. There is no posturizing, no effort ; and it is this chastened self-restraint in the midst of his creative activity—this grand command, both over his own thoughts and his material, while infusing life into his dead symbols, which makes Landor so Greek. He sees all beauty and manipulates it to his will; but he never exaggerates and never loses control of his idea. He is the Pygmalion of literature, but his Galateas have always the grave beauty of statues, even while they move and speak. In his intensest love he is free from all trace of licentiousness or coarseness. His Dionysos never changes attributes with Silenus; and his Aphrodite is the Sea-born but never the Pandemos.

For himself, time has dissolved away all the little surface weaknesses—all the thin crust and pellicles of temper which once grew about the outer man, and has left the pure core like shining gold, free from stain and rust. We judge him by what he did and was—by that Ideal which rises from the grave of the dead and is the true man —truer than was he whose brain was influenced by his blood, and his blood by all material things, and whose best self got sometimes lost, clouded and mislaid, like diamonds fallen from their setting, or pearls discoloured by age.

Things had happened in my own history which made it impossible for me to go to my dear old friend in the beginning of this last sad drama at Bath. Had I been able, I knew that I should have prevented much that took place. My influence over Mr. Landor had grown of late years. It was that of a respectful son who has on his side the clearer vision and brisker energies of youth, while always absolutely deferential and obedient.

It was of no use, however, to lament over the inevitable. I could not go to him; and so those miserable Dry Sticks were Faggoted, and the brave life went out without my hand on the one or my love around the other.

I had one satisfaction in the years that came after. When Forster wrote his mean and unsatisfactory 'Life of Landor,' I reviewed it. Two days after the review appeared, I was at a dinner given by dear Shirley Brooks. Lord Houghton was there.

'Have you seen Kirkland's review of "Landor's Life" by Forster?' he asked Lord Houghton. 'It is the neatest thing I know. He has taken the skin off him so—so,' he added, making a movement as if tearing strips along his arm.

Of Forster—'de mortuis' notwithstanding —I can never speak in sufficiently strong terms of contempt. He was bully and toady in excelsis; and the way in which he harnessed himself to the chariot of every manifest conqueror who drove into the literary arena was as degrading as it was loathsome. More loathsome still was his want of loyalty to the man, dead, whose feet he had kissed while living. Landor had been his friend and benefactor—had given him the copyright of his works, and had trusted him with that most sacred deposit, the story of his life. Forster repaid his munificence by emphasizing the weaknesses and faintly depicting the grand qualities of his friend from whom no more was to be expected, and whose last act of generosity had been performed. In like manner his ‘Life of Dickens’ is simply a vehicle for his own self-laudation—dwarfing all other friendships to aggrandize and augment his own. All through his career his one ruling principle of action was egotism and self-advantage ; and of the finer strains of honour he had not the faintest echo.

Another notable man died about this time —Dr. Elliotson—with whom also I had been brought into personal relations. I first knew him through the Maconochies, at the time when his income—so they told me—had dropped plumb from twelve to two thousand a year, as the tax levied on his belief in mesmerism. During his last illness my own dear father had been brought up to London, and placed under Dr. Elliotson, whose prophylactic then was tar-water. Nothing, however, did or could arrest the progress of the deadly disease which was eating away my father's life ; but the friendship which had then been begun, and had afterwards fallen into abeyance, was renewed in later years, between Dr. Elliotson and myself. He was then a Freethinker, so far as Christianity was concerned—a devout believer in God and the spiritual nature of man but not an orthodox Christian ; and we had many long and interesting talks together, after the prescription had been written out and the state of the dear patient upstairs discussed between us in the room below. Years passed after my father's death before I met my friend again. When I did, he was old, broken, penniless and out of practice. A friend —

good be with him and all such!—had taken
this wreck of former power and brilliancy,
and cared for him as a son would care for
a father.   Among other changes which the
years had worked was the old man's
conversion to Christianity by spiritualism.
I met him one night at Mrs. Milner Gibson's,
and he came up to me as soon as he saw
me enter the room.   We talked together for
some time, the burden of his speech being
lamentations that he had ever said anything
to strengthen my own want of orthodoxy,
and beseechings to reconsider the question,
and—as he had done—come over to Christianity by the way of spiritualism and
messages from the dead.   He died not very
long after this ; but his true self had died
long before.

George Cruikshank too, was among the
labourers on the ungrateful field of my
mind.   One evening we had been to West-
land Marston's, and we walked home to-

gether. On the way we passed a group
of rowdy drunken men and women. Suddenly George stopped, and, taking hold of
my arm, said solemnly :

'*You* are responsible for those poor
wretches.'

I answered that I did not exactly see this
and disclaimed any share in their degradation. But he insisted on it ; and hung
those ruined souls like infernal bells about
my neck, tinkling out my own damnation,
because at supper I had drunk a glass of
champagne from which he had vainly tried
to dissuade me.

He got heated and excited when I would
not have what he called enough grace of
conscience to recognise my responsibility in
the drunkenness of these poor sinners. But
we did not quarrel. Sincerity is far too
valuable a quality to be resented, even when
unduly aggressive ; and the good old fellow
had so many fine and sterling moral beau-

ties, one could easily pardon a certain want of proportion in some and want of taste in others. If he had a horror of drunkenness, so had I ; for, though never near to being under the curse myself, had I not seen the misery it had worked with one I had loved so well ?

END OF VOL. II.

BILLING AND SONS PRINTERS, GUILDFORD.

G., C. & Co.

THE AUTOBIOGRAPHY

OF

CHRISTOPHER KIRKLAND.

BY

MRS. LYNN LINTON,

AUTHOR OF
'THE TRUE HISTORY OF JOSHUA DAVIDSON,' 'PATRICIA KEMBALL,'
'THE ATONEMENT OF LEAM DUNDAS,' 'UNDER WHICH
LORD?' ETC.

IN THREE VOLUMES.
VOL. III.

LONDON:
RICHARD BENTLEY AND SON,
Publishers in Ordinary to Her Majesty the Queen.
1885.

THE AUTOBIOGRAPHY

OF

CHRISTOPHER KIRKLAND.

CHAPTER I.

SOCIETY was beginning to busy itself with the question of woman's rights when I was young. Now it is an established cause, aggressive where it was then only a protest. Naturally I was, and am, among those who hold that women, though helpmates, should not be slaves to men; that duties do not exclude rights; and that ' He to God, she

to God through him,' though pretty enough
in poetry, makes but a mighty poor kind of
life for her in practice, and reduces co-part-
nership to serfdom.   My own creed in these
things may be summed up in these three
clauses:—That women should have an education as good in its own way as, but not
identical with, that of men; that they ought
to hold their own property free from their
husbands' control without the need of
trustees, but subject to the joint expenditure for the family; that motherhood should
be made legally equal with paternity, so
that no such miserable scandal of broken
promises and religious rancour as this later
Agar-Ellis case should be possible.   But
these are only the alphabet of the movement ; the main theme goes far beyond.

Things had already begun to move.   Talfourd's Bill, giving the custody of young
children to the mother, had been passed
after a stout resistance from the Law Lords
on the Obstructive side.   One of these said

that, should this Bill become law, the avenues to the Court of Chancery would be choked with applicants for legal separation, as nothing but the fear of being parted from her children kept many a wife with her husband. The prophecy was disregarded; the Bill passed; and married life in England has gone on much the same as before.

The sensational part of the matter was, the story of that man in the Marshalsea prison who took his suckling babe from his wife and handed it over to his mistress—a possibility of action on all fours with the vilest features of slavery.

It is wonderful to think how we supported such hideous injustice; just as it is wonderful now to think how the absolute power of making a will, and thereby leaving all his property away from his wife and children, is still maintained as part of the rights of a man. The argument of trust in the natural softness of the parental instinct is about as solid as a drum. It makes a fine sound when nicely struck; but it is a rickety kind of foundation to build on.

Though the core of this question of woman's rights is just and reasonable, some of its supporters were even then too extreme for my ideas of what was fitting. I could not accept the doctrine that no such thing as natural limitation of sphere is included in the fact of sex, and that individual women may, if they have the will and the power, do all those things which have hitherto been exclusively assigned to men. Nor can I deny the value of inherent modesty ; nor despise domestic duties; nor look on maternity as a curse and degradation—'making a woman no better than a cow,' as one of these ladies, herself a mother, once said to me indignantly; nor do I join in the hostility to men which comes in as the correlative of all that has gone before. On these points I have parted company with the cause. But in the beginning these points had not come to the front.

Also, I have confessed already to the frivolity of finding many of these extremely advanced women antagonistic to my ideas of feminine charm. Most of them then, in the early days, were not only plain in person but ill-bred in manner. The epigram of the time, 'Women's Rights are Men's Lefts,' was truer then than it is now, when the circle has widened. In the first cast the net took in, as by far the largest proportion, the most unpersonable and the least love-worthy of the sex. But this æsthetic dis-taste on my part was what the Americans call 'mean' in view of the gravity of the principles involved, and I was always ashamed of my own childishness of judg-ment.

I tried to make myself tolerant of all this unloveliness, by remembering that the cause, being in the initial stage of pro-test and insurrection, must necessarily be supported by those who had nothing to lose and all to gain, as well as necessarily sur-

rounded by that kind of exaggeration which
is inseparable from the beginning of radical
innovations.   But tolerance is an exotic
with me, got by painful processes of self-discipline and preserved only with care and
watching.   When I was in my fighting age,
it was either the crime of indifferentism or
of time-serving, and I put it behind me as
high-treason to truth.

This is the penalty attached to earnestness—the harsh lining of enthusiasm.

My present intolerance, I am sorry to say,
was even less respectable than this.   It was
simply a matter of taste; and the cause undeniably suffered with me because so many
of its advocates were ungainly and unlovely.

In those days the movement did not include
the political rights which—the rest having
been won—make now the point to be gained.
It was more for the right of a liberal education, such as is given by Girton and
Newnham ; for office-work ; and specially

for leave to enter the medical profession on an equality with men.

In this last I was again at issue with the sect. Unless the demand for female doctors was strong enough to support female schools and hospitals, I maintained, and maintain, the inexpediency of providing a few lady-doctors by means of mixed medical education—just as I dislike mixed drawing-classes from the nude. These two things seemed to me repugnant to every sentiment of morality or decency in either sex; and I have never been able to change my view. For, granting that in the end science and art conquer all sense of shame and bear down all consciousness of sex, then surely the last state is worse than the first—and these young unmarried women have killed within them something more valuable than they will replace by the knowledge of anatomy and the human figure.

As yet, however, mixed life schools were not in force—I only knew of one in those days, private, little known and conducted secretly ; and but few young women had clanked into the dissecting-room. Miss Garrett, the two Misses Blackwell and Dr. Mary Walker are all that I remember. There may have been others, but if so I did not know of them. The aftermath of flirting, touzled, pretty young creatures—foolish virgins of eighteen or nineteen—by whom the ground has been covered, had not then sprouted into being; and as yet the world was spared the oracular utterances by which these Hypatias seek to regulate all the difficulties and pronounce on all the questions of life and science.

Speaking of Dr. Mary Walker, I may as well say here that the Bloomer costume which she wore, with that huge rose in her hair as her sign of sex, did much to retard the woman question all round. The world is frivolous, no doubt, but here, as in France, ridicule kills, and you can force convictions sooner than tastes. When that handsome barmaid in Tottenham Court Road put on trousers as a greater attraction to gin-drinkers, not only Bloomerism received its death-blow, but the cause got a ' shog 'maist ruined a'.' It survived, however ; and now flourishes like a green bay-tree.

Equal political rights ; identical profes-sional careers ; the men's virile force toned down to harmony with the woman's femi-nine weakness ; the abolition of all moral and social distinctions between the sexes;— These are the confessed objects of the move-ment whereby men are to be made lady-like and women masculine, till the two melt into one, and you scarcely know which is which.

Since those early days of which I am now writing, much of what was then agitated for has been granted, and many abuses have been removed. One of the most important was the Bill which raises the age of the child necessarily left to the mother in cases of separation, from Tal-

fourd's three and a half to seven years—
giving afterwards to the child the right
at sixteen to choose between its parents.
This short Bill, of two clauses only, slipped
through the House unnoticed; and I have
always held it for good that the Emancipated
Women did not get wind of it, and by
their clamour draw on it the attention,
and consequent hostility, of the Conserva-
tives.   The Married Women's Property Act
has given the widest range of freedom
possible in any kind of partnership.   Girton
and Newnham minister to the intellectual
cravings of girls and supply stimulus for
their ambition.   Female colleges and hospitals make the study of medicine decent,
and India offers a lucrative and useful field
of practice.   Slade-schools give Adam and
Eve in all their desired nudity, and young
unmarried women exhibit themselves on
the walls of the Academy naked and not
ashamed.   The Post Office and the Tele-
graph Office put money into the pockets o

some hundreds of industrious girls ; and
there is at least one female firm—there may
be more, but I know only of one—which
'devils' for lawyers, and makes a good
thing by its labours. Other women do
other things of a like nature. Some keep
co-operative stores and some breed horses ;
and some again make books and understand
the mysteries of fields and favourites, 'two to
one bar one' and hedging, better than they
understand the science of housekeeping or
the art of needlework. The School-Boards
test the value of their administrative faculty;
and Lady Harberton's divided skirt satisfies
the sentiment and does not shock the taste.

Thus, in all directions, the running has
been more equalized, and women are now
handicapped mainly by their sex. On that
point they have to try conclusions with
nature. To break up the cradles for fire-
wood must be the first step in the series
of transformations; for as long as that obstructive cradle exists, and is filled, there

must be the division of labour and function against which women revolt, and men must fare forth while they bide within.

When the cause was yet young it found its nidus chiefly in the house of one who brought as her contribution a fair person, a good position, money, fervour, sincerity, intelligence, the oddest and most catholic sweepings of adherents, and only just not enough liberality to tolerate opposition. She herself was singularly sweet and charming ; thoroughly feminine, her doctrines notwithstanding ; and without the affectation and exaggeration which characterize the mass of the pretty persons who have gone over to this side in these later days. In those, she was almost the only pretty woman the cause could boast. Her house was the rendezvous for all Liberals of all kinds ; and one of the causes she and her husband had at heart was that of emancipation and the equalization of the negro race. I remember one of her protégés was a certain Miss Redmayne a woman as black as her own American grapes ; who had studied medicine under the Stars and Stripes and who now wanted to practise it under the Union Jack. She was a dreadful looking woman, with a kind of devouring, wild-beast air, oppressive and almost terrifying. Her glittering eyes and tufted hair, wide mouth, white, pointed teeth and jet-black skin, made her remarkable enough in a room full of fair-faced Saxons ; but add to these a curious rapacious manner—an eager, restless, following way in eye and foot, unlike anything seen in ordinary society—and it is easy to understand how antipathetic she must have been to the majority, even of Liberals. I shall never forget the way in which she followed up a fair-haired, slightly - built artist to whom she was talking. He edged away, step by step—she always following close on his track—till he finally edged himself into the corner, where she had him at her will. So there they were, a black

cat and a white mouse ; and the poor white
mouse shivered, while the black cat pranced
triumphant.

My friend, our hostess, thought it mean
and cowardly that no English gentleman
came forward to marry this unlovely
daughter of Ham. I should have held it as
an act of madness if anyone had.

It was in this house that I first met Mr.
and Mrs. Lambert, with whom I made one
of those intimate friendships which invariably lead to sequels and complications.

Joshua Lambert was an artist, shiftless,
dreamy, unpractical, morally self-indulgent,
personally pure and ascetic ; a man who
could live on bread and spring-water, but
who would not work in his studio when he
wanted to be out in the sunshine, and who
exhaled in thought all the strength that
should have gone into action. He was a
man whom everyone loved and was sorry
for—regretting his want of practical grip,
while reverencing the beauty of holiness

which pervaded his whole nature. And yet, between the two, love predominated, and reverence was stronger than regret.

His wife was a woman of like nature, but with more 'go' in her than he had—with an active force behind her wanting to him. He was a dreamer of ideal beauty, she was a worker for ideal perfection. Thus their views were harmonious while their methods were diverse.

She was a Woman's Rights woman from head to heel. A kind of antitypical Louise Michel, doubled with a Madonna, she gathered under the wide cloak of her womanly pity all the suffering and down-trodden, all the oppressed and all the unfortunate. She knew no blame save for the fashionable and the frivolous. The core of her morality was charity; the mainspring of her character, purity; the force by which she worked, belief in the all-pervading Providence of God. Married and a mother, but still almost virginal in her modesties, she abhorred licentiousness as something even worse than murder. At the same time she reverenced love as the true marriage, and when this was real she held other ties superfluous.

Thus, she was one of the guests at that famous supper given to his personal friends and sympathisers by Mr. ———, when, with his wife's hardly-won consent, he brought up his children's governess as his acknowledged supplementary wife, and with but thin ideas of decency called together this cloud of witnesses to celebrate the nuptials. For herself, Esther Lambert was as chaste and pure as ice and snow; but her Liberalism and sympathy supplied what was wanting to her temperament, and she could accept in another an action which she would rather have died than have committed in her own person.

She was a lecturer of some repute; and her platform life was the result, not only of her belief in the righteousness of the things

she advocated, but also of the need there
was for adding to the tale of loaves, which,
at the best, came in but scant numbers for
the many hungry little mouths to be fed.
As it was, the ordering of the household
was narrow to penury and its simplicity
touched on destitution.

The first time I went down to their house
on the borders of Epping Forest, I felt as if
I had got into a new world—one with which
my experiences on this old earth of ours had
no point in common, and were of no use as
guide nor glossary. Playing in the neglected,
untrimmed garden, where never tree nor
bush was lopped nor pruned, and where the
long grass of the lawn was starred with
dandelions and daisies as better flowers
than those which man could cultivate, was
a troop of little children, one of whom was
more beautiful than another. They were
all dressed exactly alike—in long blouses of
that coarse blue flannel with which house-
maids scrub the floors ; and all had pre-

cisely the same kind of hats—the girls distinguished from the boys only by a somewhat broader band of faded ribbon. Nazarenes, even to the eldest boy of fourteen, they wore their hair as Nature ordained, in long loose locks to their shoulders. It was difficult to distinguish the sex in this queer epicene costume, which left it doubtful whether they were girls Bloomerized or boys in feminine tunics; for the only differences were—cloth trousers for the boys, cotton for the girls, and the respective width of the hat-ribbon aforesaid. But they were lovely as angels, and picturesque as so many Italian studies; so that amazement lost itself in admiration, and one forgave the unfitness of things for the sake of their beauty.

The house itself was found and furnished on the same lines. There were no carpets, but there were rare pictures and first proofs unframed; casts of noble cinque-cento work, darkened with dust; superb shells; and all the precious lumber of an artist's home, crowded on shelves of rough-hewn, unvarnished deal set against the unpapered white-washed wall. There were not enough chairs for the family, and empty packing-cases eked out the deficiency. For their food, meat was a luxury; wine as rare as Olympian nectar; and sweetmeats were forbidden as the analogues of vicious luxury. Milk, bread, vegetables and oatmeal, with treacle as the universal sweetener, were the food-stuffs by which the Lamberts believed they should rear a family consecrated to the work of God in the world and the carrying out of the regeneration of society. The boys were to be great artists or divine poets. The girls were to be preachers or prophetesses. One or two might be told off as mothers, to keep up the supply of the Chosen. But, for the most part, their sphere of activity would be the world, not the home—their care, humanity, not the family.

No man nor woman who knew her could have failed to love and reverence Esther Lambert. No matter how little you sympathized with her methods, you could not do other than respect and admire her personality. Her face was the face of a Madonna, behind whose sweetness flashed the inspired enthusiasm of a sibyl. It was the most perfect combination of moral purity and intellectual ardour to be found, and drew all hearts to love, like that Blue Glory of Torcelli. Earnest and religious, something beyond the ordinary thought of humanity seemed to shine in her soft grey eyes; and had she announced herself another Mother of God, she would have found some to believe her by the very force of her own inner truth and purity. As it was, she stopped short of miracles, and contented herself with inspiration.

Her political creed was her religion; the emancipation of woman was her mission; the equalization of the sexes was her shibboleth;

but the supremacy of woman was her secret sacrament. She believed in the regeneration of man by this supremacy, and by this only. All masculine modes of dealing with nature and society were false and futile. No good could come of political economy, of sociology, of science, of statesmanship. All these were of the nature of Dead Sea apes and the Unveracities. But, once admit women into the domain of active politics, and then would come the moral millennium. Deception would be burned out of diplomacy, to leave the pure gold fillet of mutual candour unclogged by dross of any kind; abstract right would take the place of godless expediency; wars would cease; territorial aggressions and annexations would be no more; and the reign of peace and truth, of justice without flaw, and perfect purity of life alike for men and women, would begin. She believed all things of the future and she hoped all things from the present. She had neither fear nor misgiving; and her faith saw in every day so much advance, and in every circumstance a coign of vantage gained and held for future progress. A new society for the advocacy of any form of Liberal opinion was to her equivalent to a victory. A pamphlet was another gospel which must compel assent. A speech was like a judgment of Solomon which no one could repudiate. Her life was the perpetual ascending of a rainbow—an endless mounting of the ladder let down from heaven, with angels before and on each side, showing her the way and directing her steps. Her faith bore her up over all dismaying obstacles; and when bad times were on hand within, as was so often the case—when the family wanted food and the house wanted funds—she would raise her beautiful eyes to heaven, and say, serenely smiling : ' God will provide.'

And so far as they had yet gone, ravens had supplied them somehow; and the children had not starved.

Esther's theological creed was a large loose jumble of Christianity and Pantheism, the chief working tenets of which were:— belief in the direct personal superintendence of God over the affairs of men, faith in the power of truth and the invincibility of the right, with the correlative belief that false-hood would not prevail nor wrong ulti-mately conquer because of this personal rule of God and the ' stream of tendency ' in humanity.

' Men and women want only to be told the better thing—to be shown the higher way,' she used to say earnestly. ' No one wishes to do wrong. It is simply ignorance, not wilful intention, which leads us astray. When all men are taught of God, then they will of necessity act justly. The Truth is God ; and God's laws are the ultimate laws of life. It is only a question of time; and in the end they must prevail.'

For all its vagueness, her enthusiasm gained on me. Her arc was very wide, and though not drawn with mathematical precision and rather sketchy in its lines, it was nevertheless grandly suggestive. Her words were full of that heroic promise, that mysterious magnificence, which surrounds the shining domes of a city seen from afar in the morning light. By noon we shall be there to see with our own eyes the treasure lying therein — to find the lady of our dreams ; the brother consecrated to our friendship from our birth ; the teacher who will show us the meaning of the Great Cabbala ; the hierophant who will take the veil from off the face of Isis. Her words stirred my imagination as much as noble scenery stirs it ; and I felt her to be a kind of dynamic power to which others must apply the direction—but she was always that power.

I used to attend her lectures—I, the declared enemy of the whole tribe of lady lecturers !—and I always vigorously applauded her. I made it up somehow between my consistency and my partisanship by convincing myself that Esther Lambert was essentially different from all the others. She was so real in her self-devotion, her sincerity, her faith in herself and her cause! There was no playing a part, anyhow; just as there was no consciousness, no simper, no affectation and no vulgarity. She spoke well too, and did not offend one's taste by matter nor manner. She did not touch on doubtful subjects; and she had always more the air of an old-time prophetess, re-embodied, than that of a modern lady-lecturer spouting on a platform to a half-curious and half-disdainful audience. She was so completely absorbed in her subject, and so earnest to do good, that she won my admiration all round; and I approved in her what I condemned in others.

For all that, I wished her little tribe had been better cared for, better taught and nourished and more practically handled than they were; that the house had been

less of a squalid and disorganized barrack
than it was ; and that her husband had
been a little more the master and head than
she allowed him to be. Maybe he would
not have guided things a whit better ; but
it would have been more seemly, and his
influence over the boys would probably not
have been quite so emasculating as hers.
I was Philistine enough to feel that the
saint is less useful than the housekeeper,
and that Mary's part is not always the most
profitable.

Still, this fractional want of sympathy
with the fringes of things did not touch
the substance of my respect and liking for
the Lamberts. And as I was not responsible
for the life they made together, and as really
it was not in my right to either criticize or
condemn, I was glad to be their friend, and
to love where I could not follow.

After I had known them about three
years, Joshua Lambert died. He had often
been ailing, and the fatal disease which had

threatened him for so long, and which I
always must think might have been averted
by a little common-sense and care, at last
declared itself in unmistakable fashion
enough. He died of rapid consumption in
less than two months from the first visit of
the mesmeric herbalist who attended him.
For of course the Lamberts were believers in
both mesmerists and herbalists. They were
mystic all through ; and clairvoyant pre-
scriptions, dealing with natural simples,
field-grown, were to them saturated with
a spiritual power wanting altogether to the
coarser therapeutics of allopathists and their
mineral medicines.

Naturally, I was much with my poor
friends at this time. They clung to me like
children, and I was glad to put all my resources at their disposal. Strength and
energy—time and money—I poured all into
their hands, and thought nothing lost which
gained them ease. I was deeply interested
in them. They had fascinated me by their

very strangeness, linked as this was to so much goodness and so much beauty; and feeling myself to be of use to them seemed to compensate me for the loss of her whom her creed—and Christ—had taken from me. The simplicity with which they accepted all I did for them, as of the natural order of things, had also its charm.

Looked at from their point of view, it was better than gratitude; because it was the right thing to do, and if I were a true man I could do nothing else. They would as soon have thought of praising me for not telling lies nor picking pockets, as for bearing the burden of friends too heavily laden to bear it for themselves. Of course, this kind of communism brought about a closer intimacy, and on my side a still deeper affection—the helper always loving the dependent.

At last the end came. Poor beauty-loving and unpractical Joshua Lambert took his last look of the blessed sun, and smiled his last wan smile up to the face of day and all he loved. He died as he had lived, without struggle as without regret; without bitterness, and in love with all mankind; full of faith in his own enduring blessedness beyond the grave and in the Divine goodness for those he left behind; sure that his dear ones would be cared for by the Father—working principally through me.

Not an hour before he breathed his last hard breath he said, with a faint flicker of his old boyish smile and that tranquil assurance which had so often amused me in the difficult moments of past times :

' I leave them to you, dear friend. I have always held that God sent you to us for our good, and I die quite happy, sure that you will accept your charge and fulfil its obligations.'

' Do not be afraid, Joshua,' said Esther tenderly. ' Chris knows his duty, and he has never failed in it yet.'

I need not spread out this part of my life
in detail. In view of what followed, it is
too full of pain to be willingly dwelt on.
So much only I need say:—I was in that
frame of mind which made benevolence my
greatest solace and my only happiness. I
had the desire to sacrifice myself for the
well-being of others, feeling in this self-
sacrifice my purest balm. I had given up
my love for truth:—now I wanted to give
myself as an offering to God, through man.
Believing still in spiritual direction, and in
the moral governance of the world through
duties and chastisements, I believed that I
was indeed specially ordained by God to
serve and save this family. I had come
among them at the moment when they had
had most need of me. Joshua had lived
just long enough to consolidate our friendship; and among all they knew I was the
only one who could really help and practically benefit them. It would be a good
thing to do. If I could rescue a noble

creature like Esther Lambert from the degrading influences of debt and poverty, bring a more rational rule into the household, and set her children well before the world by a more wholesome education, I should redeem the past. If I could not be happy in my own highest and deepest affection, I could at least make others blessed; and in their well-being find my own.

I thought over all this, and prayed for guidance with all the fervour of my boyish days. My prayers, of course, answered themselves, and asking for Divine Direction only strengthened my own inclination. Full of desire to serve one whom I loved and respected—eager to make loyal response to the poor dead friend who had trusted me—seeing only all that was beautiful in Esther's nature and pitiful in her condition—loving the children like my own, and earnest to see them better cared for, better taught, more wisely guided than they were—my common-sense overweighted by religious

zeal and altruistic pity, by affection, by
principle and by hope—I took the irretriev-
able step; and in less than two years from
Joshua's death I married his widow and
took her family for my own.

Behind this strange fact lay contradictions
yet more strange. Personally, Esther failed
to satisfy my taste. She was short, un-
graceful, and careless in her dress, which was
also of notable neglect. She was unthrifty;
without method; and of the two she preferred disorder to regularity. Nothing
could make her punctual nor orderly; and
the love of free nature which left the daisies
and dandelions on the lawn and forbore to
lop the low-growing branches of the trees,
manifested itself in the house by a liberal
dislocation of hours and the want of circum-
scription—of apportionment—all through.
But she was earnest, sincere, devoted, gentle-
mannered; and she had that perilous gift of
loving idealization by which she made one
see one's best and highest self—one's ideal

angel—mirrored in her mind as the work-a-day commonplace human being. And I was blinded by the splendour of the Divine handwriting on the wall, which I thought bade me do this thing; and by my somewhat arrogant belief that I was strong enough to remould and to save.

I do not mean to say that I married with any personal reluctance, but I do say that I married with more sense of duty than of attraction, and that I knew I was making a sacrifice. But it was a sacrifice willingly made—for God's sake and for humanity's, represented by that desolate widow and her children. No action of my life was ever based on more simple religiousness of feeling, on a more entire sense of duty than was this. In none did I ever wish to do so well for others, with so little regard for my own condition.

One thing, by the way, I stipulated for as a sacrifice on Esther's side ; she was to give up her public life and keep to her home like any other wife and mother. What in the beginning had helped to fascinate the friend on the outside of things, revolted the husband who had made himself responsible for the conduct of the family. I confess this frankly. Whatever of egotism, of inconsistency may lie in the admission, I make it, and accept the blame accruing. The home which Joshua Lambert had found sufficient for his happiness would be the grave of mine; and I could no more have lived in the neglect, disorder, unthrift and squalor which had been the normal condition of things in his time, than I could have lived in a wigwam with a Cherokee Indian for my squaw. Hence I stipulated for the abandonment of the platform for the fireside, and for the maintenance of a more conventionally ordered household.

I also urged Esther to give me a list of her debts ; but this I could never get from her. Not because she was ashamed ; nor because she wished to conceal them ; simply because she could not understand the value of financial order, and had always that trust in ravens and things coming right of themselves which despises effort. I could not convince her of the need of method, regularity, foresight, or any other economic virtue. She was sweet in word and acquiescent in manner; smiled; promised compliance—and indeed did much that I wished because I wished it. But I never touched the core. I had modified the envelope for a time; but before I had been married two months, I asked myself the question: ' How long will this last? Will temperament and long usage prove too strong for the new practice? and, Will the bent bow spring back and the strained cord break?'

CHAPTER II.

I HAD furnished my house with such taste as I possessed and such sufficiency as my means would allow; and I had made it what I thought would please my wife to live in, and interest her to keep in good condition. I say 'I,' because she left all the details to me, down to the most intimate arrangements. Our rôles were inverted from the beginning, and I had to be man and woman both. She had no taste, she said. She did not care whether a room were blue or brown, green or yellow. She thought it a pity—and more—to spend on material the time and money which should be given to humanity; and she could not be made to approve of that which she regarded as the maladministration of a trust. But as it was my own money that I was spending, she let it pass without active opposition, and contented herself with being a kind of passive drag on the wheel, neither aiding nor preventing.

Also she allowed me to change the ordering of things for the children. Their epicene costume was put off for the ordinary jackets and frocks of ordinary English children; the boys were sent to school, a governess taught the girls at home. She used to laugh at their studies, but quite good-naturedly, without malice or bitterness—only with a little gentle ridicule; the ridicule of superior insight and higher aims—finding art and literature mere waste of precious time, and woman's work, such as sewing and the like, degrading to the finer functions. Still, she left Miss Palmer, the governess, very much to herself, and did not interfere in her curriculum.   She was indeed very sweet and complaisant in those early days ; and of two threads, the white is as true as the black.

All things in the house, and the house itself, being new and fresh, the radical defects of my wife's character as a mistress were not at the first visible.   Though I objected to the children amusing themselves by carving fancy arabesques on the sideboard, playing at ball in the drawing-room, slitting up the oil-cloth, and the like, things went on with peaceful serenity ; and for the first two months we 'stood on velvet.'   Also, the sense of security from poverty, of rest from strain, of a stable background and a strong arm on which to lean, won Esther to a certain amount of domesticity and made many things in her new life comforting and joyful.   Then she liked me in a way that had the charm of novelty.   She looked up to me as more practical than herself, and as having a surer judgment in worldly matters; and for the time she laid aside her own and accepted my responsibility, which was like taking breath on an uphill climb. To Joshua she had been a goddess, immaculate and absolute. Her will had been his law, and he had placed his honour in his worship and his manhood in his obedience.

'She is my Madonna,' he once said to me. 'I know no higher revelation than her will.'

Consequently she had loved him with that kind of spiritual supremacy, that kind of intellectual condescension, which had sometimes wearied her and made her long for at least equality in her companion.

'If only I could find some one who would say "No" to my "Yes"!' she said to me one day, when she had sought counsel of her husband and had received only acquiescence.

She had found in me what she had often

longed for in Joshua—that is, a strong individuality and a clear will; definite aims and sharply defined thoughts; and at the first, as I say, the novelty pleased her and she enjoyed this new phase of love and life. But——

Though by nature and temperament Esther was purely feminine, by habits of life she had become unsexed in the way of personal independence and political activities; and very soon the restrictions of home began to irk and gall. She submitted at the outset because of novelty and because of gratitude; but she submitted of her own free will, as her gift of grace, not her duty. And what she gave she felt that she could at any moment reclaim. While it was pleasant to her to be loved for her compliance rather than respected for her power and obeyed as an almost inspired autocrat, she was the very soul of sweet surrender. When it should become no longer pleasant—what then?

In the details of the house-management my wife was, of course, absolute mistress ; in the general ordering I was master. That is, I demanded a well-regulated interior, good manners in the children, no debts, and neither insufficiency in the commissariat nor extravagance in the supplies. I interfered not at all in the working of these general laws ; but I was firm on the main points ; and I thought I was in my right to require the niceness and refinements of a gentleman's home.

For the rest, Esther was naturally unhindered. She kept her own friends and asked them to the house when she would ; and I always bade them welcome and gave them good cheer. She went and came as she would, subject only to the necessary restraints of a family life, and I never questioned nor interfered. I, on my side, was as free. But soon she began to object to my friends. She wanted me to forswear them as worldly, fashionable, frivolous, un-

godly ; and when I would not, she made
the house so painful to them that for self-
respect they could not return.

Also she began to disregard those times
and rules without which no home-life can
go on with comfort or decency. For an
eight o'clock breakfast she would come
down at ten ; for a six o'clock dinner she
would appear at eight : and she took it as
unloving—not disrespectful, but unkind—
if we sat down without her. This was
disastrous for us all. For my own work it
was ruinous ; for the children, destructive
both to their health and education. But
remonstrance made matters worse, and the
only way in which I could touch my wife
was by a tender kind of coaxing flattery—
beseeching her to do of her own free, grand,
loving heart that which was the absolute
obligation of her plain duty. And I ask,
how is married life possible under such
conditions ?

Again, I had occasion to be disturbed

on account of the expense at which we
lived. And yet we did not seem to live
extravagantly. The lines on which our
home was based were modest, and well
within my income ; but I had to draw
largely from such savings as the furnishing
of the house had left ; and my hope of
making provision for the future was
merged in the fear that my earnings
would not cover our expenditure. Money
ran away like water in sand. Where did
it go ? This was a subject on which
Esther was strangely sensitive ; and I
could not get her to explain how it was
that we lived so simply and yet spent so
lavishly. Even her hospitalities to poor
patriots and penniless propagandists, large
as they were, did not appear to cover that
ever-increasing margin ; and to this hour
I do not know into what underground
channel the surplus flowed.

Naturally I held that I was in my right
as a partner, to put it no more strongly, to

lay it on my wife's conscience, both for my sake and her children's, to be more careful, more exact. She could not bear the mildest remonstrance on the money question, but turned back on me all that I complained of in her, and said that I was the one to blame, because of the criminally extensive base-lines on which the whole home had been constructed. Poor soul! By this time novelty had worn itself threadbare and the original stuff showed through.

She had grown weary of it all; weary of her part of wife whose husband was at the head of affairs; of her duties as house-mistress, restrictive and necessitating some amount of self-sacrifice as they did; of the order and regularity of a well-conditioned home; of the need of conventional, I should say civilized, propriety, which she confounded with fashionable frivolity—of all that makes the sign-manual of gentlehood in domestic life and personal habits. So long accus-

tomed as she had been to a hand-to-mouth
kind of existence, where Providence had
been her bank and Chance had paid her
dividends, she resented my prosaic precision
as faithlessness, and accounted it to me as
moral cowardice that I should take thought
for the selfish things of to-morrow, when
the altruistic things of to-day needed
doing.

These discussions on money were the
first real rifts in the lute; and they
widened day by day. They precipitated
the end which must have come under
any conditions. For I see now that
my marriage had no real element of
stability in it. Unless Esther or I could
have radically changed, we must have
made shipwreck on one of the many rocks
ahead. And though we struck first on
that of my worldliness, others had to
come.

There crept into our lives a certain
mystery which I have never been able to

fathom. A young Pole, who was said to have escaped from prison, was brought to our house in my absence by one of my wife's political friends, and an asylum was begged for him. Who he was, what he was, what he had done there or was doing here, I did not know then and I do not know now. That he was the centre of some movement and held the strings of some plot was evident; but in what direction, and to what end, were kept from me. I only knew that he was a refugee called M. Boris, and that my wife and he had a secret together which included certain experiments in chemistry, photography, and printing—all of which were conducted in an upper room, whence I was rigidly excluded.

Some of my own possessions disappeared at this time. Letters from eminent political men which had come to me in the way of business, and two Foreign-Office passports, which had served me in my former wanderings, were taken from my writing-table drawers, notwithstanding those patent locks which were pronounced unassailable. I never found a trace of my lost property; and when I accused M. Boris, Esther's passionate indignation was so intense as very nearly to make an end of everything. Finally she sealed my mouth by declaring that she herself had taken those papers, for what purpose she would not say. I might kill her, she said, but she would never confess.

I had nothing for it but to accept her declaration as she made it; though, as I still connected M. Boris with the affair, I insisted on it that he should leave the house. The sequel proved that I took nothing by my action. I only diverted the channel, I did not stop the outfall.

My wife's domesticity gave way as suddenly as a house of cards falls to the ground. The old fever of propagandism,

the craving for political activity, blazed out
afresh. She flung up the reins, saying
that all life was not centred in clean
table-cloths and the accurate adding-up of
butchers' bills; and that the highest
duties of a faithful servant of God and
lover of humanity were not to be found
within the four walls of home. Any
honest maid-of-all-work could do the work
that she was doing now, but that for
which she was specially consecrated was
lying undone, with no one to take it up.
Her sphere was in political morality; her
duty was to preach the rights of the
weaker and liberty for all the oppressed.
To give to one household only, albeit her
own, the energies meant for humanity at
large, was desertion of her flag and infidelity to God.

In vain I argued, pleaded, rebuked,
reasoned—was now, I am ashamed to say,
violently angry, with all the passion and
excess of my old undisciplined days, and

now as violently sorry. Esther was not to be moved ; and, by this time. a distinct flavour of personal dislike to me added strength to her resolve as well as bitterness to her feelings. It was not wonderful then that she went back on the old track, the new having failed to satisfy her. In a week's time from our first stormy discussion my wife's name was placarded on all the hoardings in London, and she was announced as giving a lecture on the 16th —the subject being, 'The Down-trodden Nationalities of Europe.'

I was grieved, disappointed, humiliated and angry. I thought that my wife's affection for me should have been deeper than it proved to be; that, looking at things in the most prosaic light of reciprocity, the friendship I had had for her and hers, the help I had given them in times past, the heartiness with which I had adopted her children and done my best to benefit them, and the sincerity with which

I had sought to build up her ruined home and take her out of poverty into sufficiency, should have secured from her some consideration for me in return. I was wrong. I had not calculated on the force of that nature which, expelled with a pitchfork though it may be, is sure to come back in spite of the prongs. I had no help for it. The strong hand of a husband is all very well to talk about. What if the wife resists? You cannot lock her up, nor create a public scandal. You have to bear what you do not like, or break with her altogether. And as I was not then prepared to do this, I had to take my philosophy in both hands and make the best of things as they were—bad enough as they were in all conscience !

The dyke had broken down just as the pitchfork had failed. My wife went back to her old ways with all the keener zest, because of the cessation which had strengthened and rested her. She was every where but at home—now in Carlisle and now in Falmouth—at Norwich one week, at Swansea another, lecturing and agitating on every conceivable subject connected with Liberal politics, but always sincere—always the Madonna doubled with the sibyl—always enthusiastic, pure, beautiful, religious and unpractical.

The home and the children were thrown entirely on my hands, and I had to do the best I could for them. The young governess, Miss Palmer, was too timid to be an efficient lieutenant and the eldest girl was too young. The house was neglected and ill-conducted ; and the servants were but inadequate mistresses of affairs and unsatisfactory mistresses of themselves. When Esther was by chance at home, the place was like an office with the coming and going of many women and men, her coadjutors. When she was away she billeted on me, in her place, consecrated friends who continued the work and kept up the ball.

Finally, things came to a complete disruption, as was inevitable. My wife suddenly announced her intention of going back to the old house in Epping Forest. She must do her life's work, she said, for she knew that she was called, and that it was God's will she should abandon the flesh-pots of Egypt for the purer manna of righteousness. Our marriage, though not broken by the law—there was no cause for divorce on either side—had been a failure, a mistake, and must be in perpetual abeyance henceforward. She was sorry she had yielded to temptation and gone into the snare of worldliness with me; but she had done so unwittingly, believing that I was as whole-hearted as herself. She had found instead that I was worldly, unregenerate, Laodicean; caring more for persons than for principles; not knowing what truth meant; devoted to pleasure; greedy of praise; a traitor to the cause; shallow rather than broad; a miserable pretence

and a sham, not a reality. God had called
to me as to her from the heights of Sinai,
and I had knelt with the idolators and
worshipped the Golden Calf rather than
the Living and Eternal Jehovah. As she
had expected when she had married to
have found in me a faithful disciple and
not a renegade to the cause of righteousness—a helper and not a hinderer—she
was justified in breaking a social bond
which was antagonistic to higher duties,
and was both a lie and a snare. God was
greater than man, and His laws were
beyond ours. God called her to His work
as He had called the prophets before her.
And, even as Christ had forsaken father
and mother, and life itself, to fulfil His
Father's mission, so must she forsake me
and all the material advantages of our
union for her Father's work. She was
testifying for the truth; and in abandoning
me she was abandoning the world, the
flesh and the devil, which I repre-

sented for the one part and served for the other.

All this she said with the passionate fervour of conviction; and, like Warren Hastings when he heard Burke's indictment against him, I held my breath, and wondered if what she said were indeed true.

Was I really the base and ignoble creature she painted? God knows! I was only conscious of having tried to do my day's work faithfully to be loyal to my principles and true to the light by which I walked; obedient to my conscience, and honest before God and man. When she accused me of this unfaithfulness—this moral dishonour—I remembered my Love, and what my devotion to the truth, as I had made it for myself, had cost me. And I took heart of grace to hope that I was less vile than my wife believed me to be, and that for all my many glaring faults and radical defects she had judged me below my deserving. Rather indeed, than that she left me because she had found me too worldly and insincere to live with—I, whose marriage with her had been a sacrifice in every part, and who had not deceived her in one fact, one feeling of my whole life— I preferred to believe that she had outlived the love which had never been more than fancy. She had gone through the pleasure found in the first novelty of an assured life, and had tired of her very comforts.

She was one of those ascetic Bohemians who frankly prefer poverty and disorder to sufficiency and regularity. Give her the choice, and she would rather have a dish of herbs on a bare table than a stalled ox with glass and silver and damask as the adjuncts. All conventional proprieties irked her; and it was positive pain to her to be brought into line with the ordinary habits of the ordinary world. For though one might well deny her wisdom, no one could doubt her sincerity; and for all the humiliation she heaped on me, I desire only to speak with respect of her.

To illustrate her wholeness of character: I remember the first evening party to which we went after we were married, when she wore an evening gown, how she blushed for shame and wept for sorrow, and could scarcely be persuaded to dress herself in what was to her the livery of sin. It was unfitting, she said; and more—it was wrong. While there was a poor woman in England who wanted a pair of shoes, she had no right to more than was absolutely necessary for decency. All superfluity was robbery; and this silk gown was a crime.

In the children's dress she allowed no ornament of any kind, and she never went beyond grey for the colour. One of our first discussions of an animated kind —not broadening into a quarrel — was, when I bought for the eldest girl a pretty kind of pink stuff I had seen in the shop-window that I thought would suit her age and complexion. Esther refused to allow the child to wear it. The beginning of womanly evil was in personal vanity, she said; and no daughter of hers should learn to take pleasure in dress, nor think twice how she should best win admiration.

These matters, trivial as they are, show the thoroughness of her asceticism, and explain other things which perhaps lie deeper than the mere gratification of the senses. Certainly, they explain the impatience which, after a time, she felt with the order, the very beauty, of the home I had made for her; and how she went back to that barrack on the borders of Epping Forest as one suffering from nostalgia goes back to the old home.

So ended the family life to which I had grown pleasantly accustomed. The children had become as dear to me as my own; I had none of my own, and they took the place of these. I had done my best for

them in such things as I held to be vital to
their interest. But since my wife had
learned to despise me, she had opposed all
my action with regard to them. My
advice was tainted with the sin of worldly-
mindedness. I was the enemy of truth
and the advocate of insincerity; I was,
therefore, not fit to counsel those whom
she hoped to make thorough like herself.
Hence, by the logic of conscientiousness,
she held that she not only consulted the
highest good of her children, but also that
she obeyed the express will of God, when
she repudiated my counsel and opposed my
wishes. Wherefore I had ceased to be of
good to them, and had become only a hindrance instead. I felt that it was better
for her children to be brought up in the
one simple atmosphere of their mother's
influence, than in the storms and dissen-
sions of two such opposing currents of
thought as hers and mine had become.
They were hers too; they were not mine;

and she had the most right to them. So I
let her go first to the old barrack without
me, where she lived after her own rules,
and thence to America, where she said her
life's work was to be found.

Had things been different between us, I
would have thrown up everything in England, and I would have gone with her. I
could have written in America as well as
here, and perhaps with even better results.
Had my wife still loved and respected me,
even while she differed from me—had she
not begun to treat me with systematic
neglect and intolerable contempt—had she
not thought it her duty to oppose me in
everything, merely because it was I who
proposed ; as a saint should deny the devil,
not because he offered evil, but because it
was the devil who offered anything at all
—had she not made her own life apart,
and kept every fact in that life a profound
secret from me—nor stood between me and
the children, teaching them to doubt my

moral worth, my truth and sincerity, and
to refuse my right of rule—I would have
kept with her to the end.   But a continuance of my present life was impossible,
would I retain one shred of self-respect. So
I bade them farewell ; and they started on
their voyage alone.

When my home was finally broken up
and all things were swept away, I found
myself possessed of only a few shillings as
my sole capital.   My last investment was
sold to pay the last of the household bills ;
and the clearance was complete.   I was
just where I had stood twenty years ago,
and had lost in my marriage the whole of
my private means.   This was the least of
my troubles.   I was strong and in the
meridian of my working powers; and I
could always make my way.   But when I
had to ask the most genial and friendly of
my two chiefs for an advance of fifty
pounds to float my stranded bark into
serviceable waters again, I felt as if the

whole thing had been a dream, and that I was once more a boy, with all my life to make anew.

Now that time has dulled the edge of sorrow and dissolved all the bitterness in the cup, I can look back on things as they were and appreciate them at their true value. I blame my wife in nothing. We are what we are, and we cannot act differently from ourselves—at least, not for long. My wife had mistaken a passing fancy for love, and had found out her mistake by use and wear. While she liked me, she believed me good; when she ceased to care for me, she found me evil. Judged from her own point of view, she was right to repudiate me and all my works in the matter of her own life and with respect to the children. Less extreme than she, I was just by so much the farther from the grace of truth; and to keep my pace would have been consenting with sinners. She despised as sensuality and worldliness all that I held essential to gentlehood; and she carried on to me personally the same repudiation, because I was moderately well-born and had both the habits and traditions, the likings and the fastidiousness, of a gentleman. I lost all hold on her imagination, her taste, her esteem, her love.

'You have lost your charm for me,' she said one day, quite quietly, without anger or passion. 'Joshua kept his beauty for me to the end. You have lost yours.'

Yes; I had lost all personal charm for her because I had lost all moral value; and her very repugnance to me was a proof of her own sincerity.

It was strange how deeply the loss of my home-life affected me. I had never pretended to love Esther as I had loved—as I still loved—Cordelia; nor to find in her that idealizing and poetic fascination I had found in Adeline Dalrymple. My first love had been my boyish romance; my second the rooted reality of my manhood ; but she, my wife, had been my friend, my companion, my housemate—my regard for her had been very true—and the sentiment that I had helped her in her hour of need, and done well for her fatherless children, had been one of the holiest joys of my life.

Now, when I stood alone in the desert, I knew that all this past happiness had been illusion ; as I knew that all the future way must be in isolation—that I and the consciousness of disappointment must be for ever one, and that I must live in a solitude of heart more complete than any I had ever yet known. For the first time I asked myself that bitter question : Was life indeed worth the pain it brought ?—Was its joy equal to its despair ?

Days came and went, and weeks passed into months, like clouds over a river rather than as landmarks planted four-square on the solid ground of fact. I looked back on a mirage and forward into vacancy. The present had no comfort, and there was no future to make amends. I was debarred from all hope of love, and I could never rebuild my wrecked and ruined home. Time was too short now to enable me to make a fortune worth having—for I was only a worker, not a speculator; and I had suddenly lost that personal ambition which had glorified my boyish dreams of success. Large as was my volume of vitality—strong as were my energies—with all my passionate determination to conquer fate and make a good thing of life and fortune—to never own that I was beaten, nor to give up the struggle while one hour's sunlight remained —the strain under which I had lived for so many years had told on me; and the disappointment of my last hopes, the frustration of my latest endeavour, completed my temporary demoralization.

I existed only. I did not live, in the true sense of the word. That is, I neither loved nor hoped. I shrank from the world as a wounded animal creeps into the jungle. Indeed, by now I had scarcely any world from which to shrink. The advanced class and all Esther's friends condemned me for my separation; and by the fact of my marriage, and from its outset, I had given up most of my own acquaintances—or the few whom I had still retained had given me up, affronted by my wife's hostile manner when they had called to see us. So that now, save one or two intimate personal friends, I was alone. And society, like fortune, was all to be won afresh.

This stretch of backwater into which I had drifted, by turning my mind inward, brought back over me the flood of speculation which for some time now had been dammed up by action and a certain stability of negation, as well as by a great deal of positive affirmation. Ever and ever in the solitude of the evening and the stillness of the night came thronging about me those

unanswerable questions touching the meaning of the universe; the end of life; the
action of the Great First Cause on this
entangled web we call human history; our
relations with the unseen; the ultimate
evolution of the 'mind-stuff' which lies
behind matter; the self-consciousness of
matter; the destinies of the human race;
the destiny of the individual soul; and
how far the Unknown will be for ever the
Unknowable—those questions which we
cannot answer yet cannot stay, and which
sometimes seem as if they must land the
seeker in the pathless maze of madness.
What did it all mean? In the wilderness
we call life, who can strike the right road?
In the darkness we call faith, who can
come to the light?

One dominant ray had long seemed to
me to be the true illumination—one unassailable fact had been my solid foothold
—GOD! I believed in a Great First Cause,
providential, intelligent, loving; to be

spiritually communicated with by prayer;
informing humanity; directing history; but
unrevealed, save in the mind of man and
physical creation—His act and incorporate
idea. I believed in the truth of the religious instinct, though all religions were
equally symbolic in their structure, and
their iconology was equally untrue as
human fact. Buddhism was as true as
Mohammedanism ; Brahminism was as
real as Judaism; and the Christian Trinity
was no more actual than the Twelve Great
Gods whom it banished from Olympus.
The self-evolved purity of Buddha was like
the Hidden Wisdom of Christ; and both
were the outcome of that human faculty—
that stream of tendency—which attains to
righteousness by endeavour. The aspiration towards a higher life, the belief
in a divine power, which underlies all
religions alike—this was the immutable
and imperishable core. The form, the
name, was the mere provisional envelope.

The only advantage which one faith had over another, seemed to me to be in the relative power of expansion left to the human intellect, the liberality of its formulas, and the smallest amount of historic untruths and scientific absurdities mixed up with its theology. Hence Unitarianism had long been the nearest approach to Truth that I could find—Unitarianism founded on the Christian basis, where denial of the divinity did not include disregard for the doctrines of Christ.

But now, both solid comfort and spiritual enlightenment seemed to fail me here. One of the congregation, I was on the outside of the body and not harmonious with the teaching. That most eloquent preacher of them all, at last ceased to hold me. His sermons were poetic, beautiful, full of spiritual imagination, but there was always in them a limitation of inquiry, and that dogmatism of unproved assertion which prevented my full assent. They assumed their premises too absolutely, and built up the conclusions too arbitrarily, where there was really no Q.E.D. Unlike science, which begins from the unit and from the two and two which makes four proves all the rest, his arguments, however clearly defined, were nebulous and unproved, though arbitrary, and you had to grant too much if you would accept the residue. And they were wanting in that human element in which Stopford Brooke, of all men, is most conspicuous. They touched the stronger passions, the more tragic pain of life, with too delicate a hand, too flimsy a sweep; and gave nor heed nor thought to the more turbulent forces of emotion. They were too etherealized for work-a-day uses; and, though on a broader basis than the Established Church, still the doctrines they taught were always theological—always treating the hypothetical as the absolute— and as if he, the preacher, were afraid of

opening issues which might admit of divergence, and the consequent wandering of the
startled flock—whither ?

One thing, for a time, gave me cause
to doubt the justice of my own dissatisfaction and kept me longer in the
congregation than else would have been.
The spiritual food which did not
nourish me was sufficient for Sir Charles
Lyell, whose fine and thoughtful face was
always to be seen in his place. Yet he
was an intellectual giant where I was but
a pigmy.

Since the failure of my marriage, this
dissatisfaction with my spiritual state and
position had been growing. That thing
which I had done with so much pure
religiousness of feeling—wherein I had
taken counsel of the Lord and believed
that I was doing His will and putting my
hand to the work He had appointed me to
do—that thing had fallen into ruins ; and
God, who had then seemed to be my

leader, had since abandoned me when most needed. No prayers had helped me, no cries for guidance, for patience, for support had been heard. During the dark days of stormy dissension which had prefaced our separation, I had turned to my God, my Father, with all the fervour and passion of my soul. I had carried to Him so much despair, so much bleeding agony of heart, that at last I dared not trust myself in church nor chapel. The passion of it all overwhelmed me with too much violence. And when such hymns as ' Nearer, my God, to Thee,' or, ' My God, my Father, while I stray,' were sung, I more than once broke down, and was too unmanned to dare a repetition of the trial. But to all my seeking I had no answer. None! none! no more than in those early days of youthful violence and unrest; and the dark solitude in which my soul had lived had been terrible and appalling.

This want of spiritual consolation as my

own experience—this seeking and not finding—gave increased stimulus to those
incessant questionings on the meaning of
life and the nature of God by which I was
now torn as on the rack.   I saw dimly the
terrible end which I was nearing.   I would
not confess it, but I was dumbly conscious
in my own soul of the result of all this
frustration of endeavour.   To do in faith
and to fail, to cry and not be heard, to ask
and not be answered, to struggle and not
get free :—there was only one end possible
to such a life, and that was—the abyss.

CHAPTER III.

ABOUT this time I became acquainted with certain scientists of note, and began to frequent scientific meetings as I had not done before. Hitherto I had devoted myself chiefly to politics, history, literature, and various ' views,' which it would be presumption to call philosophy; now a new wing was added to the irregularly built mansion, and science had her home with the rest.

I learned much from what I heard, and sometimes more than the speaker always intended. For the men of that time, so short a while ago, were different from the men of the actual day; and things which are now accepted as incontestable truths were then only in the nebulous or the tentative stage, and you might or might not receive them, at your pleasure. During the last twenty or twenty-five years, science has bloomed and fructified with marvellous vigour and rapidity; but those who did not reap all they sowed, yet sowed well for others to garner. They made the running, if they did not reach the goal.

John Crawfurd was neither a synthesist nor a scientific revolutionizer. He disbelieved in the ' Aryan heresy;' would have no part in the Evolution theory; derided the idea of the Solar myth as in any way incorporated into Christianity; but his labours in ethnology, physical geography and other kindred subjects have helped on the synthesists; and the revolutionizers owe him thanks for at least the use of his shoulders. They sit so much the higher, and know so much the more, for what he has done.

Nor was Sir Roderick Murchison a name wherewith to conjure; yet the palæontologists are indebted to him as much as if the calibre of his mind had been equal to the quality of his discovery, and as if he had been as intellectually great as he was scientifically fortunate. But with him, more than any other scientist of his time, the worth of the work he did was incommensurably beyond himself. It was like the finding of a buried jewel by a child scratching in the garden. The jewel was priceless, but the child had not searched with the intelligence of a mining engineer, and when he had unearthed the treasure his brain was no nearer in weight nor value to that of the engineer than it had been before.

Again, Robert Chambers, though a brave pioneer in the making of the new road, and one of the first to speak the new language, was in a certain sense pre-scientific. He was the dawn but not the full day. He still accepted for granted things which were

not proved nor capable of proof — *e.g.*
spiritualism ; and the poetry of his nature,
while it added beauty to his intellect, took
from the rigid value of his evidence.   Still,
he saw the true shapes of things, if he did
not fill in all the details with perfect accuracy ; and his ' Vestiges of Creation '—
which we may now take for granted was his
—will take rank for ever as one of the advanced guard in the forces of knowledge as
they stand arrayed against those of ignorance.

In cataloguing my memories of twenty
or twenty-five years ago, I see the enormous
span which science and free-thought have
thrown across the abyss of ignorance and
superstition.   Twenty-five years ago, Mill's
definition of liberty was not the household
word it is now.   The doctrine that exact
laws could be applied to that inconstant
quantity, man ; laws of averages as precise
as mathematics ; laws of economic results
as certain as chemical combinations ; laws

governing human conduct and forming the science of sociology as unalterable as those which govern the course of the planets and form the science of astronomy;—this was a new page in the great Book of Life, which many found too hard to read;—and Herbert Spencer's laurel-crown was still growing on the bushes.

Twenty-five years ago too, our greatest man of all, the true epoch-maker and torch-bearer of this century, he to whom our age owes its characteristic value— Charles Darwin—was in the first of the two stages which every original thinker and revolutionizing discoverer has to pass through. He had a few choice adherents who believed in him; but the learned public disputed his conclusions, the unlearned derided his facts, and the theological remnant denounced him as a lying teacher of iniquity.

Now he is in the second phase—accepted as an expositor of common-places:—'What every ploughboy knew generations ago,' as said to me, contemptuously, a certain Roman Catholic Professor, on the action of worms as set forth in one of the last books.

Between Darwin and Sir Charles Lyell— the ' Antiquity ' and the ' Descent ' of man —however, the cosmogony dear to this Professor and others of his creed becomes a handful of dry dust. When the tip of one of Prince Rupert's drops is broken off, what becomes of the body ?   So in regard to the old cosmogony; on which other things, held to be more vital, hang like grapes on a severed vine-branch.

In those days Haeckel and Huxley were not the powers they are now, and Owen was in his zenith.   In that famous dispute between these last two, about the hippocampus minor, how well I remember my eager advocacy of our poor relation, and how I rejoiced in the firm, bold arguments of the younger man !   My state of mind was conviction, not knowledge ; but the want of knowledge did not lessen my ardour of conviction.

Darwin first, and then the spectroscope, opened a new world to me, and one which redressed the balance and recompensed me for all the sufferings and shortcomings of the old. The Unity of Nature was the core of the creed to which I owe my subsequent mental progress—the Doctrine of Evolution that by which I have come to peace. The fact that we have advanced so far already makes all the future possible and reduces pessimism to an absurdity; and the consciousness of fixed laws robs history of all its elements of doubt, incompleteness and partiality. It makes infinite amelioration dependent on man's clear and understanding will; and shows how, by the scientific evolution of morals, systems of government, laws of health, physical well-being and education, we can accomplish things which hitherto have been only the dreams of poets and the fantasies of artists.

Sir Charles Lyell's book had also an immense influence on me; so had Hugh

Miller's ' Testimony of the Rocks'; for all
that this last touched the old faith with as
tender and reverent as he grasped the new
truths with a strong and manly hand. Sir
Charles was in a different category. He
was not one of those who 'builded better
than he knew,' for he looked his own conclusions fairly in the face, and accepted in
its integrity every word of the writing on
the living scroll which unrolled itself before
his eyes. Max Müller's work again was
among the charms of my existence in those
days. I remember what Grote's 'History of
Greece' was to me; also the joy that I
took in Kinglake's ' Eothen,' and, when it
appeared, many years later, in his ' History
of the Crimea.' George Henry Lewes's books
added to the general sum of mental content ;
and George Eliot, just stepping to the front,
was a goddess behind a cloud. But a new
novel by Georges Sand out-ran hers ; and
a poem by Mrs. Browning was looked on
as an event greater than either.

Still, I had not so much interest in pure literature as I had in science. In the former almost everything had been already said. From Æschylus to Shakespeare and onwards, not many thoughts had been left untouched; but in science were FACTS, and these were of the kind to make a new mental era—a new departure of thought for the whole world, as well as for myself individually.

It was all in the air. The emancipation of the human intellect from superstition in the substitution of the scientific method for the theological, was the great event of the time and made itself felt everywhere. Brute absolutism and unreasoning authority were set aside in matters intellectual as they had already been in things social, legal, governmental. That which bestrode the reason was flung off into the dust; and even the Church followed with the rest. 'Essays and Reviews' had brought on its authors the honour of ecclesiastical condemnation; and Colenso's book, which is now a mere letter in the alphabet of destructive criticism, had been stamped in gold by Convocation as 'full of errors of the gravest and most dangerous kind.' And yet how far short it falls of both De Wette and Norton !

Colenso himself was as clear and precise as his arithmetic ; and his thoughtful, handsome, refined face was always a beautiful point in the bald-headed crowd at the Ethnological and Royal Societies, where Sir Edward Belcher and Sherrard Osborne sat side by side like two mastiffs unmuzzled. I used to wonder if what I had been told was true, that Captain Belcher had once been forcibly prevented from hanging Sherrard Osborne up to the yard-arm; and, to indemnify himself for his disappointment, had brought him home in irons.

Strauss's ' Leben Jesu ' had long been known to the English reading public, thanks to the fine translation by Marian Evans, whose first knot in the quipos of her fame was made by this work. The ripple raised by the ' Creed of Christendom ' yet ran to the shore; and Newman's 'Soul,' as well as his ' Sins of the House of Hapsburg,' were moving forces in the world which his brother's 'Apologia ' and reliance on authority have not arrested in later years.

' Ecce Homo ' and Renan—still later —have given pregnant cause for thought and divergence; but these have not roused the anger which has been caused by coarser and more personal attacks, such as Winwood Reade's ' Martyrdom of Man ' and Colonel Ingersoll's leaflets; and Lockyer's popularization of astronomy, with the results of the spectroscope, have lifted freethought into a purer because wholly impersonal atmosphere, and brought the witness of unification against the doctrine of direct and separate creation. Those Friday Evening Lectures at the Royal Institution, when Tyndall experimented or Huxley demon-

strated—or haply William Spottiswoode or
Lockyer tried to bring things ethereal and
celestial visibly before our eyes — what
evenings in the Court of Paradise those
were! How I pitied the poor wretches
who did not come to them! Contrast a
Queen's Ball and a Friday Evening Lecture
—the nothingness of the one and the glorious
communion of the other! I do not think
there was one in the whole audience who
drank in the wine of scientific thought with
more avidity than I. Did my own ignorance make that wine but froth? Perhaps. All the same, it strengthened, warmed,
exhilarated and almost intoxicated me.

What a glorious time it was! Everywhere the ground was being broken up in
preparation for the great superstructure
which has been raised as by an enchanter's
wand. Everywhere was a shaking of the
dry bones, and the clothing of flesh and
sinew on what had been dead and useless
fragments buried in the earth. In art and

science, in literature and theology alike was a confused noise of Life and of the forces which ran together. It was the birth-hour of a new Truth; and more than a few shepherds heard the heralding Voices which announced it. At no time in our history have the mental activities of England been so vigorous as they were now. And to me also, as I have said, came the Promise—which at first I did not rightly understand—and from the desert where I stood I looked over to the fertile land which as yet lay only faintly outlined in the dawning light.

My meeting with John Crawfurd brought me into contact with the long, long ago, and made one of those loops in life which are so full of beauty and interest. When we were young, and while we lived at our father's place in Kent, we were much mixed up with three beautiful girls who lived not more than a mile or so from us. All lovely, yet very different, each was strongly individualized. The eldest

might have been her namesake of Troy.
The second was bright, vivacious, playful,
a kind of English-speaking Euphrosyne ;
and the youngest was the sweetest, gentlest,
dearest of them all.   We called her Dudù,
for indeed she was a very sleepy Venus, and
thinner she might have been and yet not
lose.   She and my beloved brother Godfrey made a summer day's excursion into
that enchanted wood of fruitless love, whence
is no issue save by tears and the heart-
rending of separation.   I was a child at
the time ; but the early friendship of the
families, and the romance of this love-
affair which we all knew, made it very delightful to me to foregather again with those
who were left of these dear people.   My
new old friend, John Crawfurd, had
married the eldest sister of all—one of
the most regal and empress-like women
I have ever seen—whom I can distinctly
remember as one would remember a queen.

There were other members of the family

with whom I was also brought in contact. Let me recall the image of that gracious Lady, just returned from the Drawing-room, as she stood there by the sofa, in her court dress of blue and white and pearls, receiving her guests with the grace and ease, the dignity and the courtesy, of a young queen on her own account. Of all women known to me, Lady —— has the most perfect manner. And it is not only manner. Her heart is as kind as her ways are gracious, and she has proved the worth of her moral courage in more ways than one.

The Dudù of past times has mellowed into a bit of perfection of her kind. The indolent grace of girlhood has become the soft serenity of age, and the sweet temper of the sunny morning has raised itself into the pious pity, the womanly compassion, which makes the evening of life so beautiful, so blessed! Never an old friend lost, and new ones gathering round her, attest her sweetness and give warranty for love.

When John Crawfurd ended his long and honoured life, more than I lost a friend whom to know was to love, to respect, to look up to—a man who, if not one of the world's leaders, yet was one of the world's helpers—a man who had done his day's work gallantly and well, and whose character was as sterling as his intellect. No truer soul ever lived than he; no kinder, juster, nor more faithful friend and father. His tall and powerfully built figure, just touched by the hand of time, and slightly, very slightly, bent—his handsome face with the eyes still bright, vivacious, penetrating, where the lightning-lines of latent passion flashed across the sweeter and more placid tracts—his noble, white-haired head, and that look of a man who has won all along the line, and who enjoys and does not regret—all made him one of the most striking features of the learned societies where no one was commonplace. And when he went, a power passed out of those where he had been most often seen, and had had most influence, which left them flavourless—at least to those who had loved him.

So in these late years, when William Spottiswoode died so long before his time, the world lost more than it will easily regain. Mr. Spottiswoode was perhaps the most ideal of all the scientists. Fortune and place, beauty of person and refinement of mind, an intelligence that somehow reminded one of polished steel, and a character as free from base alloy as gold that has been tried in the fire—we do not often find such a combination as this devoted to the furtherance of pure science and to the good of his fellow-men. And now all these forces are dissolved, lost for ever to man and gone into limitless space. And yet they are not lost. The work he did lives after him and is his truest immortality.

I was in no way up to his subjects—none but the higher mathematicians were ; but I could understand something of what he said. I remember specially a lecture of his on crystals, and how he seemed to indicate that crystals were on the border-land of consciousness—just below the plastic assimilation and active conversion of protoplasm, but beyond the unchangeable rigidity of metals. That lecture was also one of the starting-points of new thought to me— a nucleus whence my mind branched out like one of the crystals spoken of.

How many of our good men have been taken ! James Spedding was one who touched the crown of the ideal student, whose justness of judgment was on a par with his sweetness of nature, whose intellectual force was matched by his serenity, his patience, his self-mastery, his purity. In the midst of the violent clashings caused by the arbitrary and contradictory dogmatisms which afflict and bewilder us, his quiet breadth, his god-like serenity and all-embracing liberalism, were as refreshing as silence after uproar, as shade in the noonday heat. The way in which he died was the crowning act of a life that had never known bitterness, revenge, nor any strain whatever of the darker passions ; and were the world of thought to have its saints, James Spedding would be one of the first canonized.

Very different were the Amberleys, who also were as grievous a loss to the world, though standing on such a different platform. They carried a more complete integrity of purpose and wholeness of action into their ideas than any of their class known to me ; and the brief meteor-like brilliancy of their lives is a subject to me of enduring regret. It would have been well for men and women had they lived and matured ; even though they had changed front and taken a new shape. They were too young and eager as things were to have much influence, and their very wholeness, by the slight exaggeration and want of tact which it included, made fewer proselytes than opponents.

Edward Flower, the handsome Jupiter whose humanity went over to horses after the issue of slavery was closed by emancipation—he also was a man of public note of the time ; and he too was thorough. In the early days of the American Civil War, before the introduction of emancipation by the North—the playing of the black knave as the trump card—I was on the side of the South. I took their part because of the Right of Insurrection which I had always upheld. As all of us who were Liberals had sympathized with the revolution in Italy, and the desire of the independent States to consolidate themselves into one kingdom, so we now sympathized with the States in America which desired to get rid of their Union, and to form themselves into a separate nation. I could not see any difference between the two. In both it was the will of the people that I respected—uninfluenced by the differences of aim.

One day I said this to Edward Flower, as we stood on the hearthrug before dinner was announced; and he very nearly ordered me out of the house, instead of giving me the place at his table destined for me. I think he would have done so, had not Moncure Conway come to the rescue. He defended me, from my own point of view. He condemned that point of view in itself, and showed where it was part crooked and part short-sighted, but, granting my premises as honestly held, he could not see that I was to be condemned. Thus he calmed down the towering wrath of our Jupiter Mecænas, and things went on velvet from the soup to the grapes. But I had skirted by a very unpleasant bit of coast, where I nearly made shipwreck of an old and valued friendship.

Perhaps the two greatest losses to the world—making a wide leap onward; but this chapter deals so much with the honoured dead!—have been the deaths of Clifford and Balfour. Each had showed only a sample of his quality. Neither had done his day's work nor come to the meridian of his power. When Darwin died, he had lived. He had fulfilled his appointed mission, and planted his Tree of Life fathoms deep in the soil of human thought and knowledge. But these two young men went down to the grave before they had more than begun their assigned tasks; and their slips of the great Yggdrasil, by which heaven and earth are bound together, withered in the darkness of their untimely death. It fills one with sorrow to think what great things each might have done, and the loss to the world through their incompleted lives!

All this is a very fragmentary notice of the intellects which then were in their vigour or their promise and now have sunk below the horizon. But I am not writing a history of my own times, nor speaking of things and people with whom I had no relation. I am only writing of those with whom I came in contact personally or intellectually, and who were either friends through love or masters through influence.

As my mind recovered its lost tone by the admission of a new interest, and science worked out the scars left by disappointment, I found a new zest in the work I had never ceased to love. I went as a free-lance under the banner of my old chief, though I never saw him again; and I wrote what struck and made its mark on the things of the time. But my connection with this paper brought me more obloquy than praise. I had something to say, and I said it with what literary force and moral vigour I possessed, indifferent to personal consequences, as I have always been, and as I must ever be now to the end. And those at whom I struck were naturally indignant, and gave me back blow for blow, sometimes hitting below the belt,

with even a few odd scratchings thrown
in.

At this time my portion was a strange
mixture of literary kudos and personal
enmity. I was publicly cut by irate partisans, and no one seemed to think it possible
that I had a conscience and was not merely
an ' advocatus diaboli,' opposing that which
I knew to be good and bolstering up that
which I knew to be evil. But I lived through
it, and got good out of it. For I do not
think anything enlarges the sympathies or
humanizes the mind more than undue condemnation. By what we suffer experimentally we can measure the pain of others ;
and the injustice which we have to accept
we are careful not to pass on.

Besides independent essays, all more or
less dealing with one social subject only, I
did a great deal of reviewing for the paper.
And as I was notoriously beyond fear or
favour, I was trusted with the books of my
known friends as well as with those of

strangers and new writers. My work was always to me impersonal. I said what I honestly thought of the book as an achievement, and no personal sympathy with, nor hostility to, the writer turned me one hair's-breadth to either side. I put my honour in keeping up the high standard of excellence for which the paper in question was then famous. If a book reached that standard, I praised it; if it did not, I condemned it—and who wrote it did not count. This might have been the work of a stranger, that of a friend—to either circumstance I was indifferent; and the personal favour I have not looked for, nor had shown to myself, I never gave to others. I know no other way of dealing with things than on their own merits; and I should care neither to receive for myself, nor to help others to obtain, that ephemeral reputation which is due to private patronage and not to the worth of the work done.

I remember one Sunday dining at the

house of a clever woman who disbelieved
in the general honesty of the press. I
had just reviewed a book which she
had not read; but she knew the young
authoress personally, and believed that she
could not have written anything worthy of
these encomiums—that no good could come
out of this little corner of Nazareth. During
dinner the conversation turned on the corruption and venality of the press, and she
instanced this notice, which had appeared
the day before in the ——, as an example.

' That review must either have been paid
for, or it was done by a personal friend,' she
said. ' In neither case was it an honest
criticism.'

' Neither one nor the other,' I answered.
' I know who wrote it, and I give you my
word of honour that the reviewer had never
heard the name of the authoress before he
received her book, nor was the faintest indication given him of the tone to be taken.
It was reviewed on its own merits only.'

For my own part, I can only say that I know nothing of the venality of the press so often spoken of. One hears of ten pounds paid for this favourable notice and ten pounds paid for that; but I take it these sums are like poor Dr. Ashburner's bank-notes brought by the strange man on a black horse, and never existed outside the region of imagination. So far as I know, those come worst off who attempt to influence to their own favour the authorities in chief or the workers in detail of any paper that respects itself.

I know an editor on whom one day called, unintroduced, a lively scribbler. She had just finished a flashy book, which she was not content to leave to be judged of according to its merits, but thought her social standing should be brought into play as a kind of extra lever whereby her work should be hoisted into notice. When she sent up her card—Lady Fourstars—to one who was only a plain Mister and who lived by his pen, while she got just so much more social consideration by hers, and when, after a few moments' conversation, she asked him to dine with her next day, she expected to have made a supple courtier in the place of an incorruptible judge, and to have bought his favourable suffrages.

The refined scholar who then held the reins of that special journal was revolted by the cynicism of this effrontery; and the lively scribbler gained nothing by her audacity. Her book was dealt with in the ordinary way of business, and neither condemned for spite nor praised for complaisance.

Officially inflexible, personally courteous, this editor, and one other, were models of their calling—past-masters in their craft. Neither ever betrayed his trust to his proprietors, and neither ever offended even the most susceptible of his unsuccessful contributors. Of one—my dear friend, whose loss we still deplore—it used to be said that it was pleasanter to be rejected by him than accepted by many others. For there are editors and editors; and not all are pleasant to deal with. Some bully you, even when you do your best and your article has the place of honour. They think it due to their own dignity, and a useful check on your vanity, to keep your soul low like a weaned child; to cut down your presumptuous imagining that you are necessary to the paper; to make you understand that they could find a dozen as good as you, and half-a-dozen better, to take your place an hour after you had vacated it. Others are dumb dogs who neither growl nor caress. They say nothing of praise nor blame, and let you know you suit only by silent acceptance. Others again, give you heartening words of encouragement when you fail, and the reward of commendation when you do well. They keep the whole thing alive and healthy by their own vitality, and their contributors add personal zeal to their intellectual efforts. These are the best editors. They get by far the most out of their staff; and when they go their place is not readily filled—if indeed it ever is!

But editors are a long-suffering race too, and have their trials like meaner mortals. Not all their young lions roar fitly and in tune; and sometimes, when most wanted, they skulk and do not roar at all. Or they launch the paper into hot water by rash utterances, and the editor has to pay in his own person for the debt of libel incurred by them. That large crowd of ungrammatical folk who believe in private influence rather than in the worth of the work done—who write silly books, then tout for favourable notices—who think that any rubbish whatsoever can be floated by a liberal supply of champagne given to editors and reviewers—and who trust to every reed but good English and something to say for their staff of literary fame—they make one of the many nuisances besetting the editorial chair.

Another is that analogous crowd of incapables who ask for undesignated work without giving the flimsiest rag of performance to certify capacity. They think that a publisher's office is like a charitable kitchen, where are always to be found baskets full of broken meat, and where no other qualification than need is necessary for a share of what is going; or that publishers and editors are so many Michael Scotts, who have to supply their demons with work, to save themselves from being torn to pieces. If either idea were true, there might be some sense in the quest. But, seeing that for every loaf there are two claimants, and far more ropes twisted out of sea-sand than any wizard can stow away in his columns, these uncovenanted outsiders have but a poor claim. And were even the editorial business conducted in this centrifugal way, which it is not, their chances would not be worth betting on. As things are, where I pray you is their peg?

CHAPTER IV.

 HAD known for some time the ordinary Jews of London Society. I had begun with Mrs. Ben Israel, the little woman who bought her social steps by private gifts, graduated in value according to the condition of the person whom she wished to be seen in her drawing-room, and in whose, in her turn, she herself wished to be seen. This was only according to sound commercial principles. But the two queer things in the transaction were the accurate account which she kept of her gifts under the head of 'Charities,' and the way in which she raised the money for them. She borrowed it of young married people on the faith of a will to be made in their favour, wherein she promised to leave sundry Cashmere shawls and rare old laces worth thrice the value of the loan; or to put down the name of their child for double the amount in money. I do not know how many of these wills she had not made, unknown to her husband. After her death, they turned up like stereotyped copies of a bad joke; and who got the initial bequest, or if anyone got anything at all, is also unknown to me.

The sum she borrowed was generally three hundred pounds. This lasted her for a year or two and went in the purchase of the presents—or, if we give things their right names and call spades spades—these bribes for social consideration. She showered them right and left. They were chiefly bits of embroidery very beautifully done, such as handkerchiefs, shirt-fronts, waist-coats, blotting-books and the like, which she said she herself worked in the solitude of her own room on those off-days when she did not receive. Our then greatest living novelist came in for a fine flowered waistcoat, which she presented to him as her own work and a tribute of admiration. She had paid for it at a shop; and I saw the entry in her book, which one day she showed me. Again, a favourite gift was a bit of her old inherited lace, of which she had a goodly store on the back shelves of the bric-à-brac shops.

As her husband objected to this crazy application of their income, and would not give her an allowance to cover this quite unnecessary margin, she raised the necessary funds in the way I have said. And only when she died did her several victims find out the practical joke that had been played on them, and learn the true value of the legacy which was to have been rich enough to go twice round the original loan.

This lady was monstrously proud of her birth. She, Spanish—her husband Arabian

—both were of the tribe of Judah, she used to say, stiffening her small person. All the English and German Jews were her inferiors, being of the tribe of Benjamin; and she looked down on them with the traditional contempt of the elder branch for the cadet.

Her drawing-room was filled with the literary and artistic celebrities of the day. She might have been the model for Mrs. Leo Hunter, had the portrait not been taken before her time from that poor lady whose husband, not content with being well, wished to be better and came to ruin as the consequence. Had our small daughter of Judah been a social circumstance before Pickwick put on his gaiters, the cap would have fitted to a nicety; and her luxuriant shining black hair, of which she was not unreasonably proud, would have received its deserved aureole.

She forbade her step-daughters, whom she frankly disliked, to come down to her

parties.   As she would not have allowed
them to marry Gentiles, she said, she
thought it her duty to keep them out of
harm's way.   Yet one of these step-
daughters was a widow with children; and
so far one would have thought able to
judge for herself, as well as entitled to the
run of the society assembled in her father's
house, where also she lived.   But my
friend did not keep well with her family.
Neither her husband nor his daughters,
neither the grandchildren nor the governess
pleased her; and her details concerning the
various thorns which bestrewed her conjugal pillow were embarrassing to hear.

They were pleasant evenings which
the little woman made; and she was both
a generous and an attentive hostess.   Her
suppers, where was always cold fish cooked
Jewish fashion, were models of good
taste and liberality; and there was that
evident desire to give pleasure which
makes its mark and sets people at

their ease. Her company was certainly on the whole somewhat of a 'scratch lot;' not so odd as Mrs. Hulme's queer menagerie had been, but undoubtedly a little mixed. And people did wild things in her house, as they do in places where the rule is relaxed and they feel themselves delivered from social restraints. But we all felt it was going beyond the broadest line of the loosest social stepper when a certain editor—a man whom nothing daunted, and to whom notoriety was fame and singularity distinction—came late into her rooms, on one of her most brilliant evenings, in a frock coat, a crumpled shirt, a black necktie rather awry, and muddy boots.

We did not meet many of her own nation at my friend's house, and only those of good birth, remarkable gifts, or exceptional position. Against the ordinary Jew of large wealth and small beginnings, superb diamonds and defective grammar, she was as exclusive as the most exclusive Christian

could have been. She would never allow
those she liked to be called Jews in her
presence; only 'Israelites,' or the 'Nation.'
Those whom she did not like, she herself
stigmatized as 'low Jews.' Notwithstanding her social infidelity, she was a
strict conformist, and, when the Feast of
Tabernacles was about, she and her family
lived in green-covered huts built up in the
back-garden. She would have thought it
a sin to have eaten other than 'cosher'
meat; but between the two she would
not have preferred martyrdom to pork nor
even shrimps.

This 'cosher' meat, by the way, beyond
its undoubted merit of superior wholesome-
ness, still remains as a sign and symbol of true
godliness among the Nation. Or perhaps
it were better to say as a fact which in
itself is godliness. I know of one worldly
old fellow who, thinking how he could
best make his peace with Jehovah, whom
he imagined he had offended because

his health and strength had decayed, found nothing more pleasing as an act of submission and holiness than the vow never to eat ordinary meat again, but to be strict and faithful to the cosher butcher and the cosher beef. This little instance shows how deep-rooted in human nature is that mental state we call fetishism.

After our kind little hostess, this black-haired daughter of Judah, had gone to her rest, I got to know more members of the great Semitic family; some of whom I dropped because I did not care for them, while others I count still as among my dearest friends, and love with enthusiasm. There are people whose personality over-shadows their nationality. When with them you never ask whether they are Jews or Christians, English or German. You only know that they are clever, brilliant, trust-worthy, high-minded, beautiful; that you would trust your fair fame and fortune in his hands—your happiness and self-respect in hers; that their society is a lovely charm, their friendship a great gift; and that you have to live beyond your follies if you would be worthy of their virtues. Such as these I have known for some time now; also others who are not up to this height, but are just on a level with the current idea of ordinary Jews; but the quiet, home-staying, Gentile-renouncing Jew was a new experience which came to me at a time when the ferment was again beginning in my mind, and which helped on that ferment to a subsidence very different from what was intended.

In admitting me into their home these religious Jews did me signal honour. Unlike those whose great social aim is to be received by Christians of good standing and old family, these shrink from us still, as Gentiles to whom has been given truly the power of dominion, as was of old time given to the Egyptians, but who are ever outside the courts of Jehovah; while His sons, whom He chasteneth, are His own, even while He punishes and afflicts. And His punishments are mercies in disguise— means of holding them to the truth and of confirming them in faithfulness and righteousness.

I have always done my best to put myself on the outside of things, and to judge of my own standpoint as it would appear to others. If this weakens tenacity it strengthens liberality; and the thinking world knows now that the latter is better than the former in all matters of unprovable speculation, inasmuch as it is the result of that wider knowledge of men and things which makes the whole difference between cosmopolitanism and parochialism. But I confess it startled me as much as if I had received a blow in my face when I first talked with one of these religious Jews—a man as learned as he was pious—and heard him say:

'We are in truth a living miracle—pre-

46

served by God as a perpetual protest against
your idolatry.'

'Idolatry!'

I cried out against the word with a strange
sense of pain and desecration. I had long
ceased to believe in the Divinity of Christ,
but I had that kind of tender reverence for
the faith of my childhood, that kind of
theological patriotism, so to speak, which
made me shrink as if touched with hot iron,
when an alien, an outsider, laid a rude hand
on its mysteries.

'What is it but idolatry?' asked my
friend quietly. 'What else can you call the
religion of you Christians, which makes a
human being of that Incommunicable God—
that Supreme Deity—the Great Spirit of
the universe, Jehovah our Lord, whom we
Jews worship in spirit and in truth? You
pray to a man who, you say, was God Incarnate. You worship one who lived and
died a man like yourselves, and who is still
a man to you now in Heaven—specially

moved to listen to human prayers because of His own human experiences on earth. But we hold that no one has seen God at any time, and that He to whom we pray is beyond all sense. God has been incarnate in man no more than in the Egyptian bull; and your worship of Jesus of Nazareth, the son of Joseph and Mary, is as pure idolatry —that is, the worship of a created and finite being—as was ever the faith which made Apis a divine Incarnation and Dagon a God in whom were light and life and power.'

I repeat these words because of the new view they may give to others who have not thought out the matter for themselves. It is always useful to see ourselves as others see us, and Christians never realize the anthropomorphism of their religion, nor remember that the universal Saviour was but a man, subject to all the limitations of humanity, and that even now He is but the Divine Man deified. Nor do they ever reason out their belief in the Trinity—in those Three Persons and One God; nor ask: Was it always so?—was, as I asked Henry Grahame, that part of the Godhead which afterwards became Christ, always the Divine Man He is now?—or was the essence split and made tripartite when Mary conceived?

To say these things are mysteries is to give no answer at all. Things which come to us through human media, are, I repeat it, to be justly judged of by human reason; and when they are unreasonable they are as justly rejected.

My friend also predicted the persecution against his people which had not then begun, but of which he saw the certainty, as God's way of rebuking the pride, ostentation, laxity and luxury, which had crept in among them. These vices had to be scourged out of them, he said, if they were still to be the Chosen People. He did not speak from political foresight; but only on religious grounds and in faith—believing that the Israelites were, and are, in very truth the Chosen People, and that all which happens to them comes directly from God. When the German Juden-Hetze began, followed as it has been by the still more shameful barbarities of Russia and the late disgraceful trial in Hungary, I remembered what my friend had said.

But I was none the more convinced of the Presidential Authority of God in these matters than in some others. Natural causes, arising from racial, cere- monial and religious separation—from anti- national tribalism, so that a man is first an Israelite and then a German or an English- man—from those classes of business which gather in and do not produce, taking from the hoards of others but not adding to the general store—from a specialized financial faculty, so that they get the better of the slower European intellect—these natural causes are sufficient to account for all that

has been of late, without calling in the aid
of the Divine Hand.

For their earlier persecutions we want
only the reasons that (1) The Jews amassed
portable wealth by the very same methods
as those by which they amass it now,
namely, that specialized financial faculty
already spoken of, which takes advantage of
the duller brains and profits by the more
wasteful habits of Christians. (2) They had
no country, with ambassadors to represent
them and an army to retaliate when they
were evilly entreated. They were the orphans
of the world. And that brutal, blustering,
ferocious world treated them as undefended
orphans have ever been treated.

Between their own self-consecration,
however, and the repudiation of Christendom, the poor Jews are in a state of very
unstable equilibrium. Held by themselves
as miraculously preserved to be the unflinching witnesses of the truth and worshippers
of the one God—by Christians they are

looked on as a standing miracle evidencing the wrath of God, who has hardened their hearts so that they shall neither repent nor believe. Thus they shall be always (right-eously) punished for the sins of those few who, nearly two thousand years ago, shouted ' Release unto us Barabbas'—the sins of the fathers being visited on the children, accord-ing to the Mosaic word. What would have become of the world if this predestined Atonement had not been consummated never troubles those who believe and do not reason. Nor does it come into the order of Christian logic to prove that, far from persecuting, we ought to honour and reward, those by whom this salvation of the world came about.

If only all these theological fantasies could be abolished on both sides, and the whole question treated on its merits!—if only men would cease to be theosophists and learn to be brothers! Ah, then we should have the true millennium, wherein the spirits of Intolerance, Spiritual Pride and

Ignorance pranking itself as knowledge, would be effectually and for ever chained!

The first Friday night supper—which is the Judaic Sabbath first meal—to which I was invited by my new friend, also greatly interested me because of the initial ceremony, when the master of the house, in his quality of head of the family and consequently domestic priest, blessed the bread and wine, which then he distributed to those who 'sat at meat' about the table.   The prayer of blessing was said in Hebrew—all sitting—the men covered, the women as they were. Here was the origin of the Lord's Supper in the Christian Church—the rite which had been practised by the Israelites long before the birth of Christ and for ever after—the homely and familiar 'blessing of the elements' which Christians have adopted, and in their adoption have forgotten the source and claimed the sole monopoly of usage.

Who, in reading the account of the last Supper, ever realizes that Jesus was only doing that which every master of a house was doing at the same time throughout Judea? — which every Jew has always done, from the time of the Babylonian captivity onward, and still does in every house all over the world where the master is a faithful believer and not a back-slider? Who, among ordinary Christians, does not imagine the whole thing to have been specially ordered and ordained—from the verbal blessing to the esoteric meaning and mystic grace still preserved in the observance? It was a strange bit of en-lightenment to me. It had for me the same effect in a minor degree, as I imagine the bodily presence of Christ, just as He lived and thought and talked in those early days of pre-scientific ignorance, would have on the cultured Englishman of the present day. It was bringing the mystic ideal, the symbolic grace, down to the hard and fast lines of realism; and when imagination runs dry at the source, enthusiasm fails at

the outfall.   It took from the celebration of
the Lord's Supper all its eucharistic character, and replaced it among the simple every-
day human events of which we know the
whole genesis, and in which is neither mystery nor sanctity.   It was seeing the future
King as a new-born naked babe, for whom
only a woman's care and a flannel blanket
are needed, and before whom the obeisance
of sages and philosophers is a farce.

Knowing my new friends ever more intimately, I saw ever more clearly the greater
strictness of parental authority and the more
dignified tone of their domestic life, as compared with our own looser code.   The sons
had none of the familiar slang common to our
boys.   The father was 'father' or 'sir,' not
'the governor,' nor 'the pater,' nor 'the old
man,' nor 'the boss.'   The girls, in their
turn, were more obedient to the mother, less
fast, less emancipated, more domestic and
more retiring than ours.   The whole tone
struck me as—unhappily—archaic, with a

little dash of Quaker quietism to intensify the disciplinary spirit. I liked it.

In my own person I had become more than tolerant of all failings which are temperamental rather than deliberate and intentional vices. I never reached the cynical indifference of my old friend Mrs. Hulme, who forgave all things base and bad, because human nature was such a corrupt concern from ground-plan to summit, she expected nothing better. Deceit, treachery, moral cowardice, cruelty, lying, dishonour in money-matters, I held in horror as I have always done. But faults of passion, the ebullition of a strong nature, the excesses of large vitality, seemed and seem to me to belong to another category; and the overpowering force of the physical conditions, of which they are the result, takes from them the evil of deliberate and conscious intention. All the same, I reverenced and admired the gentle and self-restraining virtues when I found them—

those sweet domestic graces which make all the value of home ; and I bear willing testimony to the fact that I found these in more abounding perfection in the homes of the religious Jews than elsewhere.

' A Jewish wife seldom troubles her husband's house,' said one of my friends to me one day, unconsciously using a pure Orientalism of speech when discussing the comparative fidelity of wives—Jewish and Christian.   And :—

' Unchastity before marriage is a thing almost unknown among Jewish girls of good education,' said another, discussing the strange phenomenon of those emancipated women who demand equal rights with men, and discard all the duties of women; who desire knowledge without its consequences, pleasure without its penalties, privileges without their obligations, love without the restraints of matrimony or the self-sacrifice of maternity ; and who make no distinction between the sexes—

seeing no difference between that which is allowed by nature to the one and denied by the best arrangements of society to the other.

Most of us know something of the close solidarity of national feeling among the Jews, proved, inter alia, by the magnificence of their charities, their boundless kindness to their own poor, and the care with which the powerful watch over the interests of the humble. The zealous endeavour to secure a liberal secular education, as well as good religious instruction, for all their poor, and to redeem their young waifs and strays from perdition, is a marked feature of Jewish tribal life everywhere. We also know how learned are their learned men— how to the forefront everywhere is the Jew. In art, science, philosophy, literature, finance —of itself a science—we have to acknowledge the value of the bright Semitic intellect. No hewers of wood nor drawers of water are they ; no helots nor serfs ; but quick, brilliant, irrepressible, they overcome all hostile circumstances and rise to the top in spite of every effort to destroy them.

And we must always remember that these people dwell among us, and know us.

When we think of all this, we may understand a little better than some blind enthusiasts will or can, the mingled folly and impertinence of our costly ' Missions to the Jews,' our ' Societies for the Conversion of Jews,' and the like.   The Jews live in the midst of Christian communities, and have ample means of judging the working results of Christian doctrines in the morality, the philanthropy, the self-respect and education of all classes.   If they saw that the Universal Brotherhood, which Christ taught as the foundation of all faithful human action, gave more satisfactory working results than their own tribal solidarity—well and good.   If they saw that we were more sober, more chaste, more humane, more generous than they, more liberal and more intellectual, they might then think that we had got hold of a higher law than any they know; and that popes, cardinals, archbishops, and bishops, were indeed better priests and leaders than Moses and the Rabbis. But when they give us hospitals and we confine them in Ghettos—when the compatriots of Spinoza, Heine, Mendelssohn, institute the Juden-Hetze, and Rome, the chief seat of Christendom, persecutes them within our own times—when it is only within the limits of the present generation that they have been admitted to full citizenship here in free England—when you still hear, as I have done, Catholic Monsignori maintain that the Jews do sacrifice Christian children at the Passover, and that the story of Esther Solomossy was true—when they know that we have less devotion to our creed than they have to theirs—that they have a purer physical condition because they lead a purer moral life than we—when they watch us in our daily doings and our national

politics, and see the discrepancies between
our preaching and our practice—our efforts
to proselytize fall dead, and are as the
ravings of the idle wind to those who hold
themselves the chosen of God from the
beginning, the inheritors of the immutable
Truth, and the specially preserved for
future testimony.

Once in about half a dozen years or so,
the missionaries get hold of some circum-
cized scamp who has no religion to lose,
and who offers himself for Christian baptism
as a means of living like any other. He
knows those old ladies with their fluffy
brains and comfortable incomes, who are
the mainstays of the converting societies;
and he does not see why he may not profit
by the gold and line his own nest with
the fluff. So he does; and well. The
same man comes up for different occasions
—like one of those veteran stags turned
out time after time for a day's run on
Buckhurst Hill. It is all grist to his

worm-eaten mill ; and Father Abraham has
a broad bosom ; and saints at the best are
few ! But if such converts are considered
worth the making, it is evident that no
better are to be had.

Nothing of all that I have said of those
Jews who believe in their faith as firmly as
ever did Solomon or Isaiah—and perhaps
more firmly than did either Joshua or
Samuel—applies to that loose-lying fringe
of indifferentism which is neither Israelite
nor Christian, composed as it is of men
and women who despise their own race and
do not believe the Christian creed. These
people have nothing of their national characteristics save in feature and the soft
speech which ever bewrayeth them. The
women flirt, the men are dissipated, the
children are out of hand. Scandal mildews
their name and ridicule takes all the starch
out of their pretensions. They found their
claim to distinction solely on their riches,
and think they have scored a point when,

with forced strawberries at half-a-guinea the basket, they refuse their helping in a house of modest expenditure, on the plea of being really surfeited and sated with strawberries—they have had them every day, to please the children, for weeks past! For people of this kind, Jew or Christian, no one can have respect; but for the other two sorts—the strictly religious and tenaciously national, and the sociably catholic and simply well-bred, whose wealth is never made aggressive and who are generous but not ostentatious—all who know them must feel the most profound respect and affection.

This was, and is, the state of my mind concerning the moral and social condition of the Jew; but my intercourse with them had graver mental results than this tabulation according to condition; and it was the nearer contemplation of their faith which finally modified and reconstructed my own. I will do my best to give these results in the order in which they came—making a rough

kind of chart of my thoughts, which may or
may not have value for others. To myself,
of course, it is important.

The unitarianism which a later intellectual development has read into the Old
Testament is grand and majestic. But the
supremacy of Jehovah over a crowd of
other deities, which was the original theology of the Chosen People, was only a form
of polytheism like any other. It was loyalty
to the national God—theological patriotism,
commendable because patriotic ; but it was
not the monotheism of the present day, nor
was it the spiritualized and impersonal
religion it is now. The Being who walks
in the Garden in the cool of the day—who
repents and grieves, and ' goes down ' to
scatter the builders of the Tower — who
appears unto Abram in the flesh, and shows
Himself standing at the top of a ladder to
Jacob in a dream—who comes down upon
Mount Sinai—speaks unto Moses face to
face, as a man speaketh unto his friend—

—who covers him with His hand while His glory passeth by, and shows only His back parts, for no man can see His face and live —this Being is not the God Almighty of the present religious idea.   And this development of idea gives the Jewish religion, which looks so stable, and as from the beginning even to now, the same tentative and experimental character as belongs to all things, all thoughts, all systems.

Again, what is the base-line of this faith?—Partiality and consequent injustice; Egotism and consequent vanity.   The more I reflected on this base-line, the more I was repelled by its egotism.   How intensely selfish is that Litany of Thanksgiving, which else sounds so grand in its confession of trust—so noble in its gratitude!   Analyze it from the human standpoint and come to its real meaning.   God is thanked all the way through in that He has made them, the Jews, better and more blessed than the other sons of man :—Jews and not Gentiles

—freemen and not slaves—men and not women — with acknowledgment of other special mercies bestowed on them, His Beloved Elder Sons. But those other sons, those younger disinherited, condemned by reason of their unconsenting disinheritance—their arbitrary exclusion from Israel —what of them? What justice to them is there in this favouritism shown to these others? Why should the Jews thank God that He has made them freemen and not slaves, so long as slavery exists for their fellowmen? If freedom be His gift and slavery His scourge, why should those innocent black babies born yesterday on the Gaboon be destined to undergo a curse they have done nothing to deserve? And yet, is not this belief in special care and blessing the core of every religion extant? The Jews exclude from equal heavenly rights the Gentiles; the Mohammedans the Giaours; the Roman Catholics all Christian dissenters from their Church, together with those outside the Covenant, in one crowd of the unredeemed because unbaptized; and every petty Protestant sect denies, relative to its own special enlightenment, the pretensions to divine illumination of every other sect. Do not we, of the Church of England, in the plenitude of our self-conferred infallibility, pray for all 'Jews, Turks, infidels, and heretics'? And, indeed, are we not all in turn prayed for by one another in this milder age, after we have burned and been burned in a fiercer?

In truth and fairness, however, I must say that my views, which are entirely my own, gathered from reading and fashioned by reflection, were emphatically denied by my Jewish friend spoken of above, who, after all, by his learning and his position, has the best right to pronounce on his own religion. I will give his own words, which came in answer to a letter of mine, setting forth these ideas.

'You speak,' he said, 'of the Gentiles

who are ever outside the Courts of Jehovah. This sentiment is utterly un-Jewish, and is absolutely incompatible with the belief of the best class of Jews. Also, " His sons," as applied to Jewish in antithesis to the Gentiles, is as wrong as the other.

'With your assertion concerning "the Unitarianism which a later intellectual development has read into the Old Testament," I cannot agree. No Jew, *when Hebrew was a living language*, ever supposed that God walked, repented or grieved, or appeared in the flesh, or spoke to Moses as a friend, etc. Language of some kind must be used to intimate that Adam's disobedience was known to God; that sin is not pleasing to Him; that He inspired Moses, etc. But the expressions used in the text are the mere exigencies of an Eastern language, which clothes every act of the most commonplace nature in the most luxuriant imagery. Even in our prosaic English we say, for instance, " the sun

rises," because it appears to rise.   Shall
the coming New Zealander, when he sits
in the recess of London Bridge, perusing
the disinterred remains of an almanac, be
justified in declaring that the English
nation of the time of Queen Victoria were
ignorant of the elements of astronomy ?

'Your arguments against the "base-
lines" of our faith are even more unjust.
Analyze the prayers, as you say, and what
then ?   Think of the dreadful idolatry of
an incarnate God, and shall not the Jew
thank God for the faith that is in him ?
Think of the life of a slave, and shall not
the Jew thank God that " stone walls do not
a prison make," and that, happen what may
to his body, he is ever intellectually free;
think of the pains of maternity, and say,
shall not the *Jew* be thankful that he is not
a *Jewess ?*   This last sentiment must convince you that when the Jew thanks God for
what he is, he has not the non-Jew in mind
by way of antithesis.   Moreover, your ex-

pression, "His beloved Elder Sons," or
any similar or cognate expression, does not
occur in any Jewish Prayer-book. We
thank God that we are not idolators, but
with no Pharisaic sense of superiority.
Nor are there "other disinherited younger
sons." These words entirely misinterpret
us. The Jewish religion proclaims—and
it is the only one that does proclaim—that
" the *upright* of all nations have their share
in the world to come "—no elder and no
younger, no primogeniture, and no disinherited; and above all, no eternal punishment. We do *not* " exclude from equal
Heavenly rights the Gentiles." We were
chosen, not for the enjoyment of privileges,
but for the performance of duties. I am
inexpressibly pained and grieved by your
words. Moreover, the parable of Dives
and Lazarus does not apply to us. We do
care, and care very much, about other
people's sufferings. For example, we are
about to celebrate the Passover, the anni-

versary of our deliverance from Egyptian bondage. The Feast lasts eight days, during which, in Synagogue, every day certain psalms of thanksgiving are recited. But on six days of the Festival only a curtailed form of thanksgiving is used, because our release involved the destruction of thousands of our enemies, and we may not, therefore, rejoice so fully as if no life had been taken; and this custom exists yet, though thirty-three centuries have elapsed. So, on the Feast of Esther, in whose lifetime the Jews were nearly massacred, no thanksgiving psalms are recited, for the reason that the Jewish deliverance involved the taking of life. We are not really open to the reproach your words convey.'

I give this letter in its entirety, though it condemns what I have already said, and in the minds of many will destroy my whole further chain of reasoning. As a man of honour, no other course is open to me; and, moreover, I have too great a respect for my friend—for his profound scholarship, his sincerity and faithful piety—not to give him this opportunity for refuting me if he has the truth and I am in error.

My friend's arguments did not convince me of more than certain mistakes in fact, which did not touch my main point. No one's arguments do convince me unless based on undeniable proof. By the law under which I live and suffer I have to work out my difficulties for myself; and no personal admiration for the moral results in an individual can carry me over to the faith from which these results have sprung. I am like one standing in a barren centre whence radiate countless pathways—each professing to lead to the Unseen Home. By the very multiplicity I am bewildered, and for fear of taking the wrong way and following after a delusion, I stand still and take none.

The doctrine of a centralized truth, and

therefore of God's special favour to those who hold it, revolts me by its assumption of partiality and consequent injustice.

But the foundation of all religions alike lies in this belief—direct Divine illumination and consequent possession of special spiritual grace—else have they no original standpoint at all. The correlative of this special favouritism and enlightenment is darkness, estrangement, and eternal exile for those who are not included. This state of mind is more emphasized in all other religions than it is in our own laxer and more liberal Protestantism. And the reason why is easy to see. Wronged and ill-treated by man, orphaned among the nations as he is, the Jew clings to his belief in this special favour of God, as his solatium in eternity for his misfortunes in time; just as the long-sustained political supremacy of the Roman Catholic Church, and the tangential divergence of Mohammedanism and the other Eastern religions from Western curves of thought and knowledge explains the exclusiveness of these last.

Going back to Judaism :—When we, who have been taught from our childhood to hold the Jewish race as still under the sentence of Divine ostracism, are brought face to face with its own inherent belief in Divine favour—favour traversing chastisement—we are startled into strange thoughts of comparison and inquiry. And we ask first : What of others ? and then : What of ourselves ?

Contrast this self-complacent trust in God's special favour to ourselves, to the exclusion of our less fortunate brothers, with the generous humanity of those who think that their own best happiness is to be found in the happiness of others. Our poor discredited prophets, the Communists, with their altruistic dreams of a universal Utopia, where shall be no lack and no injustice, have at least a nobler working ideal, if so fatally bad a modus operandi, than any which speculative theology has yet formulated. For them is no exclusiveness of favour—no heights where the beloved stand joyously in the sunshine—no hollows where the disgraced cry out to the empty night in vain—no Heaven for the lambs—no Hell for the goats—no broad lands and goodly heritage for the first-born, with banishment and dispossession for the rest; but a sweet and fruitful elysium for all alike. Poor dreamers, and yet how human! and how far more generous than the covenanted!

The parable of Dives and Lazarus synthesizes the whole matter. ' Leaning on Abraham's bosom—safe in the arms of the Saviour—I and my beloved are happy, no matter who else is in torment. I have made my own calling and election sure; and for the rest, it is not my affair whom God in His infinite mercy and justice may think fit to torture for all eternity. The great gulf fixed between us cannot be passed, and Dives must call out for water in vain. He had his good things when I had my evil days. The balance is now redressed, and the torment of the one who was formerly the pampered favourite of fortune does not lessen my own beatification.'

Why! little children, for all their greed and inconsiderateness, will beg their parents for restoration to favour of their disgraced playmates, even though good gifts are heaped up for their own share. They cannot enjoy their holiday unless John and Jane are there to enjoy it too; and their sweets have lost their savour if these others are doomed to bread and water. But in the creed of the most pious Christian, the angels and the archangels; the blessed saints who still busy themselves with the welfare of the race of which they were once living members: the Madonna whose function it is to intercede; the Christ who came to save; the Holy Ghost who inspires the human soul to good; and God, as Father and

Creator who can do all He will—together with the saved who once loved the lost—they can all rejoice in their blessedness and exult in their glory, while sinful souls weep in unavailing sorrow because grace has been bestowed on the one side and withheld on the other.

It is of no use for advanced philosophers to say : ' All this is elemental. No thinking man believes now in eternal punishment any more than in a personal devil.'

The great mass of people do not think ; and where the men and women who have renounced these superstitions may be counted by units, those to whom they are active influences over life and thought are to be reckoned by millions.

Go a step farther, from generals to particulars, from collective creed to individual prayer. Dismiss as untenable, by reason of its injustice, the theory of inherited blessings because of the faith into which you chance to have been born—

belief in the efficacy and the need, the righteousness of, and the response to, prayer remains. But when I thought of the Jews and their Litany of Thanksgiving—of our own Te Deums for victories gained perhaps in unjust and cruel wars—of all other assumptions of special favour—when I thought of all this as the circumference, and then came back to my own supplications as the centre, I felt a certain shock and conviction of selfishness that was as painful as physical anguish.

If what we call grace is an extraneous gift, bestowed or withheld at pleasure, the bestowal is an act of partiality, the withholding one of injustice. Why should a father need to be entreated before granting that without which his children are less well equipped, morally and spiritually, for the great Armageddon ever going on? That prayer should of itself, by reflex action and by the logical consequences of endeavour, strengthen resolve and calm distress—that is intelligible enough. But that it should be necessary before obtaining a father's favour—of that I began to be sceptical. Benevolence gives un- solicited those things which are needed by the unendowed. A parent feeds his children, who yet do not beg him for their daily bread; a man of average humanity provides for the life and well-being of his dog without being fawned upon. But ac- cording to our creed, God alone demands abasement before He will save—entreaty before He will endow. Can this be true of All Mercy, All Goodness, All Justice? Is it not rather a survival of the old craven times, when the one strong man was the lord and king before whom the people had no rights save such as he granted for favour?—when royal clemency allowed and plebeian humility besought?— when there was no justice, no law, and only his arbitrary will? We see the same thing still in savage countries like Dahomey, where a man may be gradually slain by successive mutilations—mutilations which make him a mere ghastly simulacrum of a man, no more human than a New Zealander's idol—yet where to the last this wretched abject being crawls humbly after his kingly destroyer, kissing the ground and eulogizing his mercy, his goodness and his power.

Again, God does not give His grace even to all who pray. In the continuance of ignorance that might be enlightened, and consequent continuance of the tyranny and cruelty which spring from that ignorance—in the sorrow of pain needlessly inflicted—in the degradation of passions which override resolve—in the fruitless torment of desires which, like scorpions, sting themselves within the circle of fire that surrounds them—in the anguish of untimely death and the bitterness of preventible loss, we see the futility of prayer, whether for spiritual grace or material blessing.

And what a volume of supplication goes
up day by day and hour by hour from man
to that dread Deity behind the clouds, who
Can and Does Not! Surely, were there an
Intelligent God cognizant of our affairs, a
Personal Providence to be entreated and
moved, He must before now have answered
so that all men should hear Him! He
must before now have made the crooked
things straight and the rough places
smooth! We pray—we pray—with tears
and faith, with ardour and despair, with
longing and humbleness of soul;—and who
answers? Who? When our dearest lie
dead and our passions are still our masters
—when the Hand is not stretched forth to
save nor the grace bestowed to help—
where hides the God who has promised
to give to those who ask? And even if I,
in my own person, think that I am answered,
what about my brother still in spiritual
bondage, unenlightened and unredeemed?
There ought to be no peace for me while

one human soul is left without divine guidance. Yet I am but a man ; and God is the Father of all !

All these thoughts haunted and over-powered me. The sins and sorrows of humanity seemed to grow larger as I con-trasted them with the Power which could redeem and would not. Those sins, those sorrows, claimed the Divine as their author by reason of their very existence. ' I form the light and create darkness ; I make peace and create evil; I, the Lord, do all these things.' And the mystery of spiritual darkness seeking light and not finding it, grew till it swallowed up all the rest. I cried aloud for illumination. I prayed with the anguish which no man need blush to feel nor be ashamed to confess, for the Divine Light which should make these dark things clear. No answer came. No voice spoke to my soul, penetrating the thick cloud and showing the living way of truth. None ! none ! But one night as I prayed, I prayed into the visible dark, the felt void ; and my words came back like a hot blast into my face as I realized that I petitioned an immutable and impersonal LAW which neither heard nor heeded—which wrought no conscious evil and gave no designed favour.

CHAPTER V.

WHO that has known the hour when the Father is not, and Law has taken the place of Love, can ever forget it? The whole aspect of life is changed, and a cry goes out from the soul as when the beloved has died—a cry to which is no answer and for which is no comfort—only the echo flung back by the walls of the grave. The blank despair; the sense of absolute loneliness, of drifting on a pathless sea without a fixed point to make for or a sign by which to steer, of floating unrooted in space; the consciousness of universal delusion and phantasmagoric self-creation that it has all been—no man who has gone through that moment of supreme anguish need fear the schoolman's hell.   He has been down into one worse than the worst which terrified timid souls in those Ages of Faith which were essentially the Days of Darkness. Henceforth he has only reason for his guide, with that impenetrable barrier of the Unknown—and Unknowable ?—closing the way at every turn ;—that dissolving power of negation, reducing what had once been solid and eternal to a vapoury mass of conjecture where nothing is sure, save ignorance.

And yet if this darkness, this limitation, this impenetrable barrier, be really the TRUTH, and all attempts at more positive construction be delusions, the pain of the discovery, in the desolation it brings with it, is better for the strong man than the false comfort of a cheating hope.   Before all else let us have things as they are.   If we are in the midst of an untilled waste,

let us recognise its barrenness and its
potentialities; and neither believe that it is
a garden for this part, nor unimprovable
for that. In the one case we have at
least an incentive to cultivate and amend
our holding, and to go on until we come to
something better. In the other, we are
content with our fancied possessions, like
those poor creatures who command the
stars in Bedlam; or we fold our hands and
leave the activities of amelioration to a
higher power and one outside ourselves.

Nothing tends so much to religious
speculation as unhappiness. The believing
strengthen the foundations of their faith;
the doubting plunge deeper into inquiry.
For where there is no outside joy to satisfy
the nature, the mind turns inward on itself,
thoughts taking the place of affections,
and speculations that of emotions. In
these lonely days of my life I went over
again the whole ground that I had traversed
—from my first doubts of the evidence of

the Incarnation to where I now stood—
confessing only the truths of science, and
confronted everywhere else by uncertainty,
phantasmagoria, and the Unknown. I recalled it all, step by step, and how
from the first doubt I gradually grew to
see that the teaching of Christ and His
Apostles was only abreast with the knowledge of the day; and that those things
which have made most for the good of
humanity were hidden from them as from
the later saints and martyrs. I specially
remembered the strange tenacity with which
my mind had fastened on that trivial matter
of failing to eradicate ophthalmia; and how
this had crystallized and drawn to its own
form all the rest.

The impossibility of logically faithful
adherence to the laws of life as laid down
in the Gospels had also been a stumbling-
block. Those laws of life are pure communism in system, with the widest,
flattest, most loving democracy in action.

But put them into practice—call your maid-servant ' my dear,' and shake hands with your footman; forgive an impertinence repeated as often as forgiven; allow yourself to be defrauded twice over by your needy brother who takes your cloak as well as your coat; take no thought for the morrow, but spend your principal on those who want—act out your life on the Christian plan in its integrity, and then see where you will stand, not only in relation to your own fortunes, but in relation to the respect of your fellow Christians.

I could never accept the doctrine of Development, which makes it necessary for man to continually explain and expand the elements of Christianity, so as to harmonize them with the contradictions of science and the necessities of society. This doctrine, which is cousin-german to the uninterrupted stream of inspiration claimed by the Romish Church, is so evidently an ingenious compromise by those who wish to excuse and dare not deny, that the wonder is how any robust thinker can be found to adopt it. It is a clever patch to hide a rent; but the patch was not in the original web.

Again, the sweet and patient moralities of Christianity are not special to Christians, but all, including that sublime command to do unto others as we would they should do unto us, and to love our enemies —which have been held as peculiarly the Master's—are to be found in every other moral code promulgated by every other religious teacher. Buddha, Confucius, the 'Rabbi Talmud,' all taught the same thing. And necessarily;—for the abnegation of private vengeance is the beginning of social law. Just as Judaism was the outcome of Egyptian theology, plus racial sympathy and the supremacy of Jehovah, so was Christianity the outcome of Judaism, plus a more generalized philanthropy than belonged to the close-set lines of an exclusive people. But Christians imagine that

brotherly love began with Christ, as the
Jews imagine that the law of righteousness
was first made known to Moses. And the
evidence of the papyri here, and of the Talmud there, goes for nothing. These beliefs
are on all-fours with that naïve confession
of reverent ignorance made by the poor
Catholic peasant to whom I talked the
other day, when he told me that before
Christ came into the world all was darkness and chaos, and that creation and the
human race began with the Madonna and
her Son.

The story of Buddha, too, had greatly
exercised me because of its parallelism in
self-devotion with the life of Christ.
Buddha, who claims no incarnate Godhead and preaches no impersonate God,
did as much for righteousness and humanity
as did the Son of Mary. A king, a husband,
wealthy, powerful, he abandoned all human
delights to become a beggar and an outcast,
that he might find the Hidden Wisdom and

thus rescue mankind from ignorance and the
sin that lies therein. And—scheme for
scheme—purification by successive incarnations is more merciful than even purgatory,
not to speak of hell; and reabsorption in
the Great Whole is no more unthinkable
than the eternal individuality of a material
product.

We abandon the belief in the unchange-
ableness of law—which is masculine—in
favour of the religious sentiment, shifting,
personal, emotional, subject to the pressure of affection and the relief of compassion—which is feminine. The funda-
mental doctrines of Christianity;—seeking
strength elsewhere than in our own resolve;
humility before a dread power which ac-
cords favour and denies rights; holiness of
life springing from love to or fear of God
and in obedience to His command, and not
because holiness is good in itself and needs no
incentive of reward nor deterrent of punishment; the fear born of hell and the hope

registered in heaven ; Christ, the eternal Man-God, ever willing to save those who come to Him ; Mary, the eternal Mother, ever ready to comfort and intercede for those who pray to her; the saintly hierarchy doing their best for their loving brothers and sisters—all these heavenly advocates standing as merciful mediators between humanity and the Supreme God ; the intense conviction of the personal importance of the individual ;—these are essentially feminine ; and the proof of sympathy is seen in the lines of attachment. It is woman who fills the churches ; as how should it not be, seeing that Christianity idealizes her needs, her virtues, her sentiments ? The virile strength of man has no favour where her timid plasticity has all. Where heathen ethics taught magnanimity, because of the noble pride which would not stoop to parallel lines of baseness, Christianity teaches forgiveness, because Christ forgave His enemies and died that sinners might be forgiven of God. Does not the whole world lie between these two limits ? Surely !—the whole world of masculine self-control and feminine obedience ; masculine reason and feminine emotion. Where heathen philosophy taught self-respect, and Buddhism makes a man's higher moral state dependent on his own will, Christianity sighs out the confession of sin, and trusts to a stronger Hand for help. Where heathendom formulated the great law of Necessity, encompassing and limiting the action of the gods themselves, Christianity confesses an Omnipotence which overloads us with misery here that we may be compensated hereafter, and patiently accepts present sorrow for the sake of future glory, as a woman accepts the mysterious pain of maternity for the sake of the living joy to come. Where heathendom, manlike, credited its gods with the lusty life of love, the pleasures of social intercourse and the varied delights of the senses, Christianity, as the chaster woman, ranks perpetual virginity as one of the supremest virtues, and makes all sensual enjoyment coincident with spiritual degradation. Where heathendom left Hades a land of shadows, and made the sorrow of life after death to consist in the bloodless strengthlessness of the spirits of brave men, neither alive nor yet dead, Christianity accepts, trembling, the ghastly doctrine of eternal torture, to be avoided only through the mercy of the Saviour who gives by grace what cannot be wrung from power—just as the typical woman sues for mercy because she has not the courage to demand, nor the strength to obtain, justice. It is the same through all the clauses. And if not in direct injunction nor in distinct allowance, yet in spirit and sympathy, the apotheosis of woman began with Christianity, because therein are enshrined the special characteristics of her sex.

Here let me ask without irreverence,

and going back on the anthropomorphism of
the Christian faith : Is not the existence to
which the creed condemns our God, or Gods,
inexplicable in its unnecessary and enduring
pain ?   We pray to them for pity and
mercy.   But does not pity include the
sorrow which comes from sympathy ? and
how can there be mercy without the correlative of undue harshness ?   All the cries
and piteous prayers which go up from earth
to heaven, and surround the throne of Grace
like clouds risen from oceans of tears,
if they move the Divine Beings to whom
they are addressed, move them of necessity
through this pain of pity.   And realize
for a moment this weeping, shrieking,
agonizing crowd ; these countless millions
of tortured men and women ; these sobbing
innocents massacred by fate and nature ;—
and the Great Powers looking on, sometimes
helping those who cry to them for aid, and
sometimes not.   Add to this our fratricidal
belief that those who cry for aid to these

Divine Beings under certain names are not heard at all. Christ may help us, but Vishnu cannot help his worshipper. God is our Father, but Brahma, Allah, Joss, are as powerless to save as was ever Ashtaroth or Zeus. It is as if children weeping in a dark room where is some one they cannot see, were left to their misery unhelped, because they beseech the nurse when it is the mother who is there; and the mother will not answer unless called by her right name. The whole thing is human. Ever and ever we determine the ways of Heaven by our own acts. We influence the divine will and deflect the law for our need and by our prayers. Or we create—as in the saints—the aristocracy of departed souls to whom we ascribe special powers, accrediting them as ambassadors whom the Great God accepts as they are sent. Or we give names and forms to angel and archangel, and call one Gabriel and another Michael, with others less popular, such as Zachariel, Anael, Oriphiel and Lamael!

Unitarianism, with its eclecticism, rejecting the miracles, the atonement, a personal devil and eternal damnation, but always retaining that loving reverence for the character of Christ which is due to the most precious possession and perfect outcome of the human race, is naturally the next stage for those who have learned to deny the literal truth of the Mosaic record and the interpretation of the Gospels by the Church. Belief in the efficacy of prayer, in the disciplinary meaning of life, in an overruling Providence and an individual immortality, gives both anchorage and the sense of enlightenment. But here again, though the anthropomorphism of the orthodox creed is softened, and the personality of the Deity is more faintly sketched than in Byzantine mosaic or mediæval fresco, it is always a personality—always humanity — grand, sublime, ideal, even nebulous, if you will, but none the less humanity in excelsis. As how should it not be, seeing that we cannot go beyond our own experience ? Yet are we sure that Unitarianism gives us the truth ? Beyond, and overruling organic forces, are we absolutely sure there is a Power corresponding to our own human nature—pitiful and wrathful; stern and placable; spreading temptations as a net before the feet of the unwary and punishing those who get entangled therein ; able to save and consigning to perdition ?—a Power of fluid resolves and unstable will ; of unjust preferences and inexplicable abandonment ; working a miracle of healing for A, but letting B drag on slowly to the grave by the way of unmitigated torture?—a Power which gives grace to one so that he shall ask for more, and denies to another that initial impulse of godliness so that he does not even desire to have or seed or increase ?—a Power which

saves one soul alive and gives to another
the wages of sin—death ?

If there were in fact any stream of inspiration from the Great Unseen to man,
should we be left to our present blindness,
searching painfully the better way ? Slowly,
toilsomely, urged forward by pain, encom-
passed by difficulties, bit by bit we reform
our laws through the gradual pressure, the
gradual enlightenment, brought about by
the intolerable injustice of the past ; one by
one we unearth those discoveries which
make for the general good.   Are we divinely
directed in all this ?   Have all our law-
givers, inventors, discoverers, been simply
the media of the higher intelligence ?
Where then begins and where ends this providential inspiration ?   Was Volta divinely
inspired ?   If so, then also Wheatstone and
Morse, Siemens and Edison, and every
other adapter of a newly mastered principle
—whether it be electricity, the motive force
of steam, printing from moveable types,

paper made from rags, or any other discovery by which society has been modified and human thought revolutionized.

Unless we accept the creed that man's mental being is governed by the same law of development as that which has produced brain from protoplasm — that the moral sense is as much a matter of evolution as is the intellectual—we are lost in a sea of contradictions. Grant the unseen ultimate to which we are tending, and the hidden origin as well as meaning of life ; grant the whole area of the unknown, and confess the mystery surrounding thought and matter alike ; still, by this creed of mental evolution, we have at least a free sea-board though we may never touch land. But give us Omnipotence which interferes and does not save—which inspires some and does not cherish all—and we come inevitably to Mill's alternative :—Either not Omnipotent or not Benevolent.

The presence of God recedes as science advances. In the ignorant days of fetishism He is incorporate in the trees and the stones, the mountains and the streams, the sun and moon and stars and sky. He then becomes less the individual form, than the active forces, of nature. He is no longer to be touched in His material embodiment, but His power is in the tempest and His voice is in the thunder; He passes by in the strong wind; and when storms devastate the land, it is God who sends them for our chastisement. He gives us gentle rain for our benefit; and again He loosens against us drought and blight and pestilence for our sins. When, by the discovery of physical laws, we come to the knowledge that the forces of nature and all forms of disease are governed by conditions as absolute as those of arithmetic, then we relegate God's dealings with man to the mind, the spiritual sense, to communion through prayer, and inspiration as the consequence. He is the Great Soul; and our soul recognises His.

But when and where does this soul begin in man? when is that something added which is exterior to intelligence? We are one with the rest of living things, just as the earth is one with the sun and the planets. Our moral sentiments and intellectual perceptions have their begin-nings in birds and beasts and insects—differing in degree and grade, not in kind. And thought—which we identify with our spirit, our soul—is no more strange nor incomprehensible than life. Both are in-comprehensible. But that function of the brain which we call thought—life conscious of itself—is as, and no more mysterious than, the selection of its elements of growth by a crystal, the transformation of chemical material into the wood and leaves of a tree, the pushing over a barren space of the underground rootlets seeking their proper pabulum beyond. 'Mind-stuff' is behind and within all matter; but is this mind-stuff providential? is creation self-conscious when as a plant it turns to the light, as a broken crystal takes up material to mend its fractures, as a microscopic speck of protoplastic jelly pushes out a finger-like process to seize some other speck which shall help to its own sustainment? Or is our great distinction in the moral sense? But dogs have a conscience, and elephants a sense of duty and responsibility.

Who does not see that all things are subjective?—all moods and thoughts conditional? Morality is as much a matter of climate, age, sex, education, as is the growth of an oak from an acorn in England, of a palm from a date-stone in Syria. It is as shifting as the thermometer — as local as vegetation. The morality of one age is not that of another. The morality of races is as diverse as the colour of their skins. The drunkenness which carries so little comparative disgrace

with it in England would be a man's destruction in Turkey; the free use of the
knife, which public opinion justifies in
Italy, would be the breaking of the Sixth
Seal in Norway. We have not come to the
absolute even in fundamentals; and Truth
and Justice, incarnate in a Prime Minister,
would make of the empire a wreck and of
himself a traitor; while the polygamy which
is honourable in a Mohammedan is felony
in England, and the public prostitution
rampant in our streets would be the translation of Gehenna to the upper world in
Tangier or Ispahan.

Personally, what we are is determined by
two things—age and sex; and we can no
more go beyond their influence than the
earth can free itself from the law of gravitation. The boy's thoughts and virtues are
not the young man's; nor are the young
man's those of his father in middle age; nor
his again those of the octogenarian who has
outlived both the active energy of his passions

and the plastic power of his brain. Among them which is absolute? What determines the very ground-work of society, and its moralities, but this material fact of sex, with its secondary modification, age? The courage of the man, the self-devotion of the woman; the shame of cowardice and lying—a form of cowardice—with him whose strength includes the salvation of others as well as of himself, and the easy condonation accorded to both with her whose weakness excuses fear; his freer license, her chaster modesties; his sense of justice, which makes laws for the equal good of all, her narrowed sympathies born of the restricted cares of maternity; his reason, her instinct; his philosophy, her religion; his aggressiveness, her compassion—these, and all other antitheses which could so easily be made, are essentially matters of sex doubled with age. And these are the bases of society and morality. How then can things so entirely conditional be treated as absolute?

Again, each man and woman in a community of worshippers has his or her private
spiritual experiences. Conviction passes for
inspiration, and a state of mind proves itself.
We find this in all religions alike ; whether
it be the Christian, the Mohammedan, or
the Buddhist—in a Catholic Trappist or a
Free-Grace Baptist. So that, reason as we
may, we ever come back to the central
point—the subjective quality of all thought,
all belief, all morality, and how what we are
is determined by the material conditions of
inheritance, sex, age, and individual constitution ;—which yet does not explain the
religious instinct, nor catalogue the force by
which it works so powerfully in the world.

Where is that Place of Departed Souls,
so passionately believed in, so fervently
desired ? Always not here — not on nor
about this planet on which we live,
where the ' strengthless heads ' of the dead
lie mouldering in their forgotten graves.
Yet we are made of the same stuff and

governed by the same laws as all the rest
—the difference between us and Jupiter, us
and the moon, us and the sun, being in the
stages of development reached and passed.
The laws of life and motion, of displacement and reconstruction, must be the
same everywhere, though the special manifestations may vary. Everywhere there
must be matter becoming, or already become, intelligence conscious of itself—or,
by the changed relations of material forces,
life in its plastic energy extinct and done
with. Everywhere the form is finite and
the essence eternal—the sum undiminished,
but the place and relation of the units shifting. How can our dream of an unchanging
eternity—a state of stable equilibrium never
displaced—be possible ? How can that individuality, which began and is bound up with
material conditions, exist free from those
conditions ? How can a spirit be always
the same, without change of parts or interchange of force ? Every emotion includes

a change and shifting of atoms; everything we see and feel and hear and touch, and everything we think, sets the molecules of our body in motion—creates waste, reinforcement, an alteration of conditions and a reconstruction of parts. To speak of the soul as something beyond the laws which govern the universe is to assume what reason refuses to accept. A soul must at least be a force, like the flashing of the lightning, or like gravitation or attraction. To say that it is independent of all cosmic conditions is a phrase which simply marks our ignorance of things which are too subtle for our senses:—as the light of the night which the night-birds can see and we cannot—the sounds of the growing grass, the ebb and flow of the sap in the forest trees, the creeping step of the tendrils, the gathering up of material for the building of the germ, the cry of the bursting bud—all of which are there, though we cannot hear them. The organic forces are immaterial, according to

the nomenclature imposed by our own
limitations. But the organic forces include
movement; and movement is displacement.
Is the soul more subtle than electricity ?—
is the heaven of our eternity more stagnant
than a sea of brass ?

We look to a future life as an advance on
this in the perfecting of our intelligence, the
continuance of our affections, the redressing
of our wrongs. Should we have ever formulated this eternal life, had not death snatched
us away in the immaturity or the plenitude
of our powers, before our lives had been
lived out to the end, or our work completed ? Had we all lived out to our ultimate, we should have had only the need of
rest, not the desire of renovation. Our
work would have continued after us—our
real immortality; and we should have been
re-incarnate in our children—our replaced
selves. And when we had sunk to sleep,
after the prefatory slumber of decay, we
should have no more asked for a resurrec-

tion of the body, nor for a continuance of spiritual identity, than for the individual return of this shattered rose and that fallen leaf.

Even those who loved us best would have said : When ? At what period ? Our playfellows, from whom we had been parted all our lives, would have said : As the boy they knew. Our partners in life's work would have said : As the strong and energetic man—strong and energetic because of the conditions of his age and sex. Our children and grandchildren : As the calm and tolerant, just and passionless, sage—calm, just and passionless also as the result of his age and the condition of his sex—that is, as a spirit influenced in its immortal nature by the material circumstances of flesh and food and time. Do you say : As the undated summary of these three states—the individual as he was in the tender freshness of his adolescence, in the energy of his maturity, in the wise tranquillity of his physical

decay ?   You might as well say : ' Give me
the bud, the flower, and the fruit all at the
same moment, enclosed in the same calyx.'

Even while we live, when time has passed
and sorrow is forgotten, is it necessary to
our own happiness, or integral to the well-
being of cosmic things, that our mother,
aged ninety, should be finally convinced
we did not steal those cakes for which we
were unjustly punished just sixty-five years
ago ?   What does it matter now to our
seventy years of peace and patience, wherein
time and thought have taught us the relative value of things and the worthlessness of
going back on the past ?   It is done with—
dead and gone, buried and forgotten.   Let
it lie in its deserved oblivion.   It was hard
to bear at the time ; but now it is as insignificant as the fact that three hundred years
ago the storm came down and wrecked that
poor widow's cottage by the mountain-
stream, and brought her and hers to poverty
for many a day and year.   The ruin was

great in its time, and the poor widow believed in compensation beyond the grave.
Does she want it now? That too is past
and done with, and wiped out of the record
of time and memory; as are the sorrows of
all those who have been destroyed—with
those others consequently left desolate—by
this volcanic eruption and that destructive
earthquake. When, thousands of years
ago, a savage wife was subject to the
jealous test of the ordeal, and, innocent as
she was, died under the ordeal—when
want of food made the men kill the women
and children to keep themselves alive—
when Spartan helots and Roman slaves
were scourged for faults they did not
commit, and Gurths and Wambas were torn
from their kindred swine in the beech-woods
and set up as targets for the foeman's
archers in quarrels not their own—when all
this was done generations and generations
ago, and the very memory of the men and
deeds is lost, must these poor victims be

recompensed now? It was a sorrow while life lasted; and love had the ache of memory to the end of things. But now it is over— like yesterday's fever; and the world—the Great Man—has gone on as if those things had never been. Or rather, these and cognate things have been the ground-work of that amelioration which has come for the successors. They have been accumulated accusations against imperfect conditions, till at last the voices grew so loud that those in power were forced to listen and understand. From their dead selves men have indeed risen to higher things in the concrete; — which is a nobler outlook than that happy hunting-ground for the individual, as compensation for the goring of buffaloes on the prairie.

While pain is sharp and passion strong, we demand justice, redress, compensation, revenge. In a few years we shall have passed out of the sphere of our wrongs; before then we shall have come to the peace of patience. What matters it now? We see how small have been our own individual sufferings, compared with the larger sorrows of the race, the unconscious cruelty of nature, the blind tyranny of ignorance. And we would take shame to ourselves to demand redress or retaliation for that which came and went so long ago, and is so small a fraction in the sum! For we have ever left us—Man. Ever that mighty law of moral evolution unfolds to us greater truths; ever the development of society leads us higher and higher. Just as the physical man has touched the beauty of the Apollo from the narrow skull and prognathous jaw of the brutish primitive—just as Shakespeare has been evolved from that languageless being, half beast, half human, who walked with bent knees not fully erect, for all covering had but his own hairy hide, and for all tools his own huge canines—so has the social man touched the sublimity of Law from the unordered chaos of indi-

vidual strength. We make better enact-
ments ; we spread knowledge ; we apply
remedies ; we improve conditions—all for
others, not ourselves. We realize with
ever clearer understanding the obligation of
living for the future, not only for the present ; for the general well-being, not only
for our individual good. After the practice
of the right of might comes the doctrine of
the duties of power ; after class privileges
come equal rights.

Altruism, far from general acceptance as
it is, is at once our highest duty and our
noblest consolation. To the individual, life
is too often like a huge cynical joke where
he is led by false hopes, mocked by illusive
pleasures, pursued by phantom fears, and
where he loses the joy of his desire so soon
as he gains possession. The length of the
time passed in the preparation of immaturity, the shortness of that of fruition,
and then again the comparatively long
decay—with the brevity of the whole term,

and the fact that each individual, born helpless and idiotic, has to learn all for himself from the beginning, and that he must die, leaving behind him only results attainable by endeavour but not absolute possessions bequeathed to the race like a sixth sense or the power of flying—the sharpness of sorrow and the satiety of love —joy that is pain because of its intensity— pain that makes living intolerable for its anguish—ignorance which brings disaster, yet is of itself part of the inalienable condition of things — all this illusion, this phantasmagoria, this darkness, where the only reality is suffering and the only certainty death, makes life, as I have said, like a farce over-written by a tragedy. And from this suffering, this mockery, this delusion of the senses and painful striving of thought and aspiration, the only mode of escape is forgetfulness of self in the good of the race.

A few tender souls are piously grateful because the grass is green and the flowers are sweet; because the birds sing in the trees, the butterflies are beautiful to the eye, and the exquisite glory of created things delights those who watch it. That is, because their senses are gratified; and the imagination, a function of the emotions, follows the senses. But they forget the strife and death which overarch the whole; and how the general perfection which enchants them has come about only by the sacrifice of the weaker individuality. They forget the ruthlessness of nature, and how that hedgerow and this close-grown turf are but smaller representations of the shambles and the battlefield— Aceldamas wet with hidden blood. When reminded of this wholesale sacrifice for the sake of the selected margin—of the unconscious cruelty of that assemblage of forces we call Nature—they fall back on the pious formula of 'All is for the best,' and how 'the mystery of pain is one of those things which are hidden with Christ in God.'

These tender souls are to virile thinkers
what children are to men; and their
optimism, in view of what lies round them
and the goal for which all sentient life is
bound, is no more serious philosophy than
the schoolman's calculation of how many
angels could dance on the point of a needle
is serious kinematics.

And yet, with this perpetual recession of
the Presence of God, this withdrawal of the
Hand of Providence in favour of an arbitrary Law that is never broken up for miracles
nor set aside for interposition, there is
Something behind matter, whether we call
it Mind-stuff, Intelligence, Life, the First
Cause, or God. What that Something is
we know not. What are our relations with
it and the universe outside ourselves and
our planet—these also we know not. And
the ultimate meaning of our aspirations—
the root and fruit of that religious sense
which is all but universal, and our belief
in individual immortality, also universal—

this ultimate meaning is as dark as the rest.

Why should we be virtuous, men say, when we get nothing by it? 'Eat and drink, for to-morrow we die,' rather than the pale vigils of thought, the painful discipline of self-control, that starvation of the senses we call the higher life, that moral mutilation we call virtue. Why should we forego the present, which is our own, for a future by which we shall not profit nor where we shall be found? Ah, why, indeed! Because of the law of moral evolution, which is just as irresistible as that of the physical—which is indeed the result of the physical. We do not know why this law should obtain, any more than we know how, from the savage chipping his flint, we have come to Nasmyth's hammer and the spectroscope :—we only know that it does obtain. Just as from the lowest forms of life, amorphous, undifferentiated, unconstructive, has been evolved man, so,

from the brutality of primitive communities
where the stronger kill the weaker, and the
mother eats the head of her own child taken
for food because one too many in the tribe,
have been evolved the majesty of law, the
benevolence of pity, the mutual help of
co-operation, the restraints of conscience.
So will go on being evolved still nobler
theories and more perfect states. It is the
Law of Progress—the law under which all
creation lives until it changes into that dis-
persion of forces we call death and disinte-
gration, to be followed by a nobler reconstruction. We have no explanation to
give. Agnosticism has no pillar of cloud
by day nor flame of fire to lead by night,
marking the way and illumining each step
as we go. It has only the guidance of
experience and scientific truth as its way-
lines. But the Wherefore and the Whither
are as obscure as the Whence and the How
—as the future destinies of the race or the
undetected relations of the spheres.

I see no more difficulty in educating men up to the highest possible moral point, without the incentive of religious hope or dread, than there has been in educating them to be honourable, chivalrous, refined gentlemen, independent of the religious idea. A man does not forbear to peep through the keyhole, read an open letter, pocket a forgotten sum of money, or do any other purely dishonourable action, for fear of God or the devil, but because of that self-respect which is the root-work of all honourable thought. This sentiment carried farther comes to Altruism ; and altruism is the basis of all the higher morality, and is cultivable without reference to personal gain. We must all confess that religion, minus moral and intellectual education, does but little for the world. The Neapolitan lazzarone is intensely religious ;—that is, believing in the personal and ever-present as well as omnipotent power of unseen deities. This does not make him other than a thief or a murderer when occasion offers itself. It is the fear of the law and the certainty of the material policeman which debâr men from crime. The hidden deities are to be propitiated; and the sword which is not seen may never strike.

Personally, the religious sentiment embodied in a creed and an actual God has immense private influence. It gives a man a force beyond himself, and helps him to bear misfortune because it leaves him always hope. Still, even here, we find that resignation and self-control are matters of temperament rather than of intellectual assent; for some who believe devoutly never reconcile themselves to their sorrow — never ' forgive God,' according to the saying of Talleyrand—and the willingness of the spirit never overcomes the weakness of the flesh.

On the other hand, we see both patience and self-control carried to the last point of perfection with some philosophers who have had recourse to no strength but their own.

I have taken all this from what I may call the itinerary of my thoughts. If the summary has the look of inconsequence to more trained dialecticians than I, to myself at least the attachments are distinct. It all seems to hang together—to pass step by step from the rejection of revelation to the confession of Agnosticism; from belief in Providence to the recognition of Law; from the crystallized definite to the nebulous un-known; from the happiness of the individual through eternity to the well-being of the whole human race in time; from Egotism to Altruism; and from personal rights to generalized duties.

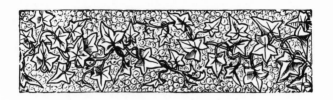

CHAPTER VI.

AFTER a few years' stay in America, where she lost some of her children, and others had married or made themselves an independent status, my wife came back to England. She was as sincerely persuaded that she was divinely inspired to return as that she had been divinely inspired to go. The field was wider there, she said, but the land was more stubborn here. Hence the need of workers was greater here than there, since moral cultivation has a tendency to spread itself when once begun; and it is better to make barren soil fit to receive the good seed than to devote one's energies to easy tilling and kindly harvests. Comparative weakness could do this; but it wants exceptional energies—or rather, in her vocabulary, exceptional gifts of inspiration and direction —to do the other. Anyhow, she made her duty quite clear to herself, dear soul! She would have made it just as clear had it been the contrary reading.

I confess I was glad to see her again, and I was much moved when we met. The agitation was only on my own side, She had attained a quasi-Buddhistic state of suppressed individuality wherein no personal circumstances stirred her. She lived only for her work — to spread the knowledge of the truth as she held it, and to bring feminine souls into the liberty she had found for herself. Her crusade was against luxury, fashion, dress, pleasure; her exhortation was for plain living and high thinking—agitation for the direct political action of women—and self-consecration of the choicer sort to celibacy and propagandism. Where she had been advanced before, she was extreme now, and sometimes out of sight altogether.

Since her residence in America she had grown stouter. Her thinned hair was grey; the low-toned creamy complexion of times past had become reddened and roughened. She was neither fresh nor well-busked; she was noticeably in want of strings and stays; and her dress gave one the impression of long service, hard usage, and crying need of repair and renovation. But she had lost none of that seraphic sweetness which had always made her beautiful, and which now shone out through all this personal deterioration as the soft glory of an opal comes up through the scratched surface. And she was the same kind of virginal matron she had ever been.

All my old affection for her, all my old respect for her sincerity, came back in a flood on my heart. The bitterness of the past was swept away; only its tenderness in the ideal remained. I forgot her high religious contempt for my lower moral nature, her doubt and disbelief, her reproach and opposition; and I saw her only in her own best form—faithful, enduring, real—one worthy of respect, and by her sex to be surrounded with that kind of protection which means honour and includes love. Perhaps on a second trial things would come more right than before. And life was lonely to me; and barren to her of all that made a woman's home.

I did not calculate, and I yielded to the impulse. But when I asked her to come back to me and try me once more as a companion and husband, she looked at me with her placid smile and serene far-away look, and refused me—not harshly, not unkindly, but without the faintest tremor in her level voice, the faintest note of hesitation or wavering.

' Live with you again, dear friend?' she said. 'If I did, I should be worse than Peter when he denied the Lord! Go back to the bondage of your worldliness? —to the religion of clean tablecloths and silk gowns?—to the soul-destroying materialism which makes time of more value than eternity, and punctuality in the hours of food of more importance than planting the good seed and saving souls alive? My poor Chris—never!'

' But, Esther,' I remonstrated; ' surely cleanliness and order and refinement are gains to humanity and helpers to better things!'

'I prefer the simplicity of goodness and the abnegation of all forms of sensuality,' she answered. ' Where so much is to be done, it is a sin to waste time on these minor matters. Souls are perishing for lack of spiritual sustenance, and you are occupied about dainty luxuries for your body; children are starving in the streets for want of bread, and you criticize the butter of which your cake is made. And you want me to go down into that pit of unrighteousness ? Impossible !'

'It is more impossible to go back to elemental conditions,' I said. 'In such a complex state of society as ours, all circumstances claim consideration. And these artificial wants, which you condemn, give the means of subsistence to thousands who else would not know where to turn for work.'

'Christ did not teach this,' she answered simply. 'And I would rather follow Christ than go into the heresies of political economy, or believe the materialism of that arch-heresy of all—that thing you call sociology.'

As I knew of old that argument on these points led to nothing but further dissension, I let the conversation drop, and, instead of taking her to my house, helped her to one of her own.

After some difficulty we found what she wanted—a gardener's cottage of four rooms, about half an hour's journey from London on the South-East line. Here she still lives, with a maid-servant of the not over-ripe age of sixteen, whom she instructs in godliness and woman's rights—God's law and the righteousness of celibacy—contempt for the individual, and respect for the abstract, man —in devotedness to works of charity and indifference to cleanliness, punctuality, the art of cooking, or methodical housekeeping. She takes these girls at fourteen and keeps them till they are twenty, when she has, as she says, made them efficient missionaries and fit to continue the work on their own account.

She comes to see me sometimes when she runs up to London; and she lets me help her with money, as in the old fraternal days when poor Joshua was alive. I go to her on the Sundays when she writes and tells me she is alone and wishes to have

me.   This is not often; for she has no
time to bestow on a castaway whom she
knows she cannot reclaim.   At first I
used to supplement her scanty larder with
external supplies.   But she was so sincerely distressed by the influx of unwelcome
luxuries, and lamented so pathetically the
moral harm I was doing her young servant
by thus pampering her sensual appetite,
that I have now given up the attempt.
So we 'share and share alike,' as she says
with her serene smile, when she conscienti-
ously divides into three equal parts a dish
which is about enough for one healthy appetite.

   After dinner she comes and sits beside
me, giving me the armchair, while she takes
one without a back and with a broken
seat.

   'Dear friend, how much nicer this is
than that hateful life in Cave Gardens!'
she often says, while she pats my hand and
sometimes strokes my coat-sleeve benignly.

'How much better you are as a friend outside my life than as a husband belonging to it! And what a mistake we made when we gave up the liberty of friendship for the bondage of marriage!'

'If you are pleased, I am also, my dear,' I answer. 'But I wish I saw you more comfortable.'

'More comfortable, dear friend? I am only too well cared for! Would that all my poor sisters were as well off as I!'

After a little preface of this kind, she generally reads me an address, a sermon, an essay—something which she thinks will be good for my soul and perhaps be the means of letting a little light into the dark places. When I assent to certain passages, or say something which seems to her less hopelessly unrighteous than usual, she looks at me tenderly, her soft eyes softer than ever, and her mild face illumined by that inner light which makes her always beautiful, in spite of the tarnished surface.

'How I wish I might be permitted to convert you, dear friend! How I wish God would grant me the grace to bring you to the light!' she says earnestly. Then she adds, with half a sigh and half a smile : ' In His own good time! He will not let you perish—the object of so many prayers as you are! For we all pray for you, Chris. May our voices be heard and our supplications receive a gracious answer !'

One day she was, for her, strangely sad-hearted. In general, her simple trust in the goodness and directness of Divine order-ing carried her over every trial with the quiescence of perfect confidence. But to-day she was overcome. She had just heard of the death of a friend whom she greatly valued—that very M. Boris who had been such a cause of contention be-tween us in times past. For the moment she was overwhelmed, feeling her loneli-ness with true womanly force, as well as grieving for the loss to the cause of one

who had been as uncompromising a partisan as herself. This young man had been
strangely dear to her. She had given him
more than ordinary love in its combination
of maternal fondness and spiritual comrade-
ship. On the one side, he had been like her
eldest and dearest son ; on the other, he was
her chosen companion, helper and even
leader.

She laid her head on my shoulder; and
when I put up my hand to her face, I found
it wet with silent tears.

For the second time impulse overcame
my better judgment, and the tenderness of
pity made me see in this grieving, lonely
woman one I might possibly comfort and
sustain.

'Come back to me, my poor Esther !'
I said. 'Let me take care of you, and
complete your life ; and do you help me with
mine.'

For a moment she did not speak, but she
drew my hand across her lips and kissed it

tenderly.   Then she roused herself, pushed back her hair, and cleared her eyes.

' No,' she said, a touch of regret in her face ; ' I should be denying God and betraying the cause of righteousness to live with you again.   You are unconverted and I am His servant ; and there can be no true union between us.   We cannot come together again.   It would be faithlessness and perjury while you are what you are !'

' My dear, what nonsense all this is !' I said.   ' What a sacrifice of reality for illusion and of things for words !   How far better for both of us it would be if you would see life in a more rational light, and make the best of the days which remain to us.   Have you no duty to me, Esther ? In all that world for which you sacrifice yourself, have I no place, no claim ?   Yet I would be your best friend and protector if you would let me !'

' No,' said Esther softly, but yielding no   more   for   all   her   softness   than yields a rock which is covered a foot deep with moss. ' I have no duty towards one who denies the truth. I have no part in your life and you have no claim on mine ; and to be your wife again would be a sin. So let us think of something else. I will read you this last poem by Victor Hugo—or shall it be one of Channing's sermons ?'

What could I do? Against such a strong principle of repugnance, it would have been useless to say more ; and I had too much self-respect to court my own wife in vain. From this day I finally accepted my position, without either the wish or the endeavour to change it. She lives in her way, I in mine ; and we meet on each side the ' gulf that separates heart from heart,' neither wishing it bridged over. She has even dropped my name. She calls herself now Mrs. Kirkland Lambert ; and when she speaks of her ' husband,' she means Joshua.

Some time ago a thing came into my life which caused me more pain than many other events of more importance. It was a thing which humiliated me on every side— as a man of the world who should have seen more clearly, and as a man who wished to do good and who did harm instead.

I had taken an unfurnished apartment in the house of a man who had been a butler in a family where the wife had been a lady's-maid. They were by no means coarse nor vulgar, having caught that superficial tone of refinement proper to well-conditioned upper servants ; and they seemed to be, and were, as honest and straightforward as most people who live on others. They also professed for me a great deal of kindly feeling outside their trade profit ; in which, as it was backed up by many uncovenanted attentions, and by uniform good-nature, I believed, according to the credulous sym-

pathy inseparable from an affectionate disposition. It is so easy to me to like and so
pleasant to be liked, that, when the gold of
kindness is paid over to me, I for the most
part neglect to ring it, but accept it as it
offers itself—as true metal, genuinely minted,
and capable of bearing the test of handling.

These people, the Penders, had an only
child ; a daughter at this time about nineteen ; for whom they had great expectations,
having done the best for her within their
power. She had been educated at a
boarding-school, whence she had returned
with a shallow knowledge of many things,
some literary aptitude, desires beyond her
means to gratify, and the wildest and
widest social ambition. She was clever,
quick to understand, with undoubted
imagination, though she failed in constructive faculty ; and the dream of her life was
to 'get on,' as she called it—that is, to leave
the house where at the best she was only the
landlady's daughter, and to have carriages

and fine dresses, money and amusements, like those others whom she had known at school. She was not beautiful—scarcely pretty ; but she had good colouring and vivacity. And, as a man, I was not very severe on a certain pertness of manner which amused me, though I can understand that it would have set the teeth of her own sex on edge.

When Mrs. Pender showed me the girl's productions, crude as they were, I saw the possibility of making something of them and her, and offered to give her lessons in composition and to help her with her studies. It satisfied my democratic instinct to put my hand to this work of levelling-up from the lower ranks, and lifting out of her inherited position one whose talent and ambition deserved better things than the continuance of her mother's business of keeping a lodging-house. I soon began to feel a really paternal interest in the girl. She was so quick and bright that it made teaching her both pleasant and easy. Moreover, she amused me. She was so naïve in her feminine affectations and impertinences; so frank in her girlish liking for sweetmeats and plum-cake; so audacious in her bold conclusions from slender premises, that she enlivened my lonely evenings not unpleasantly.

And I confess I like to hear the frou-frou of a woman's dress about me. I like to hear the softer tones of her voice, and to look at her shining hair and the smooth outlines of her flower-like face. The action of her small hands with their slender wrists, and the jingle of her trinkets, please me. The sense of her softness, sweetness, and dainty smallness compared to my own sinewy bulk, and the feeling that I can protect her if need be, soothe what I suppose is my masculine vanity. And I feel more at home with her now, in my old age, than I do with my own sex. Men often rasp me, while women never fatigue. Though I was not so old when this affair with Katie Pender took place as I am now, still I was old enough to feel at least the foreshadowings of all this quasi-degradation of age.

It was, then, a kind of consolation to have this girl come to my rooms in the evening, when I was tired with my own work and feeling solitary and out of gear. Her freshness and youth, and the diverting boldness with which she caught up and adopted as her own my hints and suggestions—and soon the, rather too forward perhaps, rather too pert and free, but, all the same, not unpleasant kind of familiarity she threw into her manner—made the hours go yet more smoothly. I did not want to be only a schoolmaster. I preferred that she should look on me as a half-paternal friend.

Interested as I was in her, however, I could not blind myself to the disastrous want of earnestness and thoroughness in my young pupil, which I did my best to combat. She did not care to be, nor to do ; she only desired to appear to be, and to seem to do. She would adopt a phrase, a fact, without knowing what it meant, content if it gave a false air of knowledge and a superficial brilliancy to her work. If asked to verify, she floundered, and tried to save herself by bold conjecture or random explanation—which at least had the merit of audacity. Thus, having read in a story she was writing the phrase: ' Going to Canossa,' I asked her : ' What is going to Canossa, Katie ?'

' Doing what you don't like,' said Katie, making a respectable shot in the air.

' But who went to Canossa ?' I persisted.

' Bismarck,' said Katie.

She had read the phrase in the paper, and had caught something of the meaning, which she had not attempted to really understand.

It was the same with words. She hated

looking out a word to get its real meaning;
and as for derivations and roots, she had
for these a kind of horror that was comical
in its excess.   But she liked to pick up
new phrases, new expressions, and to use
them liberally, if more than loosely; and
she was fond of the stock quotations, which
she always carefully guarded with inverted
commas.

'They make the page look furnished,'
she said in excuse, when I remonstrated.
'They are as pretty as curls on one's forehead.'

'But they are bad style,' I said.   'You
ought never to use a grand word when a
simple one will serve your turn, unless you
are writing scientifically, when you are
bound to the scientific vocabulary.   And if
you employ these old worn-out phrases and
quotations, at least leave them undistin-
guished by your favourite curls, as you
call them.   Who wants a sign-post for such
a phrase as better late than never, which

I see you have put between inverted commas ?'

' Bother !' said Katie laconically, as she scored out the offending scratches.

These efforts at literature were only a means to an end with Katie. If she could have made money in any other way, she would. She would have rather played at rouge-et-noir or ' little horses' than have written the finest book of the generation, if she could have made sure that her stakes would have turned up doubled. It would have been less trouble and more amusement. She took no kind of pleasure in her work for its own sake, but, as I have said, looked on it as simply a money-spinner to give her gold for her own uses.

In her plans for the future, her father and mother had no place. All was for herself alone. If she had had the trouble, was she not entitled to the reward? She thought so and meant to take it. Once when I gave her mother a small chamber in the golden palace of her dreams, she tossed her fair frizzly head and put on her pretty little pert air—an air that suited her Roxalana nose and bright, sharp, hazel eyes, as much as Esther's steadfast gaze and placid smile suited her Madonna-like face.

'Oh, mamma must take care of herself!' she said. 'She and papa get on better together than her and me.'

Only I am afraid she said 'pa' and 'ma.'

'Than she and I, Katie,' I ruled, in my quality of pedagogue.

'Of course I know that! I said "she and I," so what is the good of taking me up so short?' said Katie without blushing.

All this would doubtless have been very disheartening, had Katie Pender been a boy, or had I been a woman. But the mysterious influences of sex make us forgive in the opposite camp things which would be fatal in our own; and what man of my age could be extreme to mark amiss the follies of a young girl of Katie's?—whom moreover he is teaching and perhaps keeping from mischief. For there were certain loose points in my young friend's character which often made me tremble for her future. Her desire to have money was so intense—her love of pleasure, dress, display, delights, so unbridled.

'I would do anything to be rich!' she used to say, with a kind of passionate energy that seemed to open the door to really terrible possibilities. 'I do believe I would commit murder for it! I know I should, if I was sure not to be found out.'

'You will get money if you work steadily,' I said. 'You have it in you.'

'Work!' said Katie, making a little grimace. 'I hate work.'

'I am afraid, however, your scheme of murder will not quite answer,' I said lightly.

'Something else might,' she returned gravely.

I have no power on the press. Outsiders think I have, on account of my long literary life and early connection with journalism. But if it came to a pinch, I could get nothing done for myself through favour, still less shoulder up another. I explained this twenty times to Katie, as I have explained it more than twenty to others. On the twenty-first she went back to her old formula :

'You could if you would; but you won't.'

This meant that I could if I would get her story of about two and a half ordinary octavo volumes run through a magazine, of which I knew the editor and in which I myself often wrote. But to know a man well enough to dine with him once in the season is not to have his business judgment in one's pocket; and the strongest recommendation in the world goes for nothing, if made by one without power in favour of another who has not hit the mark. The very length of the story was in its disfavour. It was too long or too short, and an awkward quantity to handle for either a magazine or book issue. But this had been one of my recalcitrant little pupil's acts of wilfulness wherein she would not be advised. To compress into two or lengthen into three volumes, would have taken time and cost trouble; and she would not submit herself to my maturer judgment. In consequence of which her manuscript was returned; and she made me responsible for her failure.

I was very sorry for the poor child. She had been so confident of success that she had discounted her hopes and borne herself as if all her unhatched eggs had been stalwart feathered fowl. She had bought jewellery and dresses and feminine rubbish of all kinds, to the extent of thirty pounds; and this was a sum utterly beyond her power to meet or land, failing the acceptance of her manuscript. She dared not tell her parents. Fond as they were of her, they liked their money better; and Katie would have had a bad quarter of an hour had she confided her perplexities to them. Meantime, her debts pressed and her creditors refused to wait. The summing-up of it all was—an act of good-natured weakness on my part which led to all the rest. It was the initial loosening of the foundations which ended in the overthrow. I gave her the money to pay her debts, and in return she gave me a kiss; which I took as I should have taken it from my own daughter. But she startled me a little by saying very demurely, as she looked up at me from under her brows, her head bent down :

'I wonder what my mamma would say, if she knew that I had given you a kiss and you had given me thirty pounds ?'

'Say ?' I answered. 'Well, she would say it was dear at the price !'

'It might be dearer,' said Katie simply.

After this Katie adopted a curious manner to me—partly mysterious, partly familiar—as if we had some secret in common; —almost as if she had some hold over me. Here was my folly. I should have put my foot down now, and firmly, and I should have ended the whole affair. But I was weak in my good-nature and absurd in my quasi-parental indulgence, and so things drifted; and perhaps I deserved all that I received.

I am sorry to say that Katie got a good deal of money out of me. She was always going to pay me back, but when she did get a story published and paid for she had other claims more dangerous and pressing than mine; and the sums asked for as loans soon became confessed as gifts. Increasing with this facility for gratifying them, her demands became at last too onerous; and I found myself forced to make a stand. I was willing to help her to a moderate extent, but I could not carry her on my shoulders for life. Besides, I did not really care for her.

I had by now only a very feeble interest in herself, and none in her work; for I saw that she had no ambition of a noble kind, and only, as I say, desired success because of its result—money. So the end had to come, as the end of all false hopes and fancies must; and one evening, when she brought in the customary tale of her embarrassments, I put up my first stockade.

'I am sorry,' I said; 'but I cannot help you any more. Let me advise you again, as a man who has worked hard for his own hand—be less extravagant. Do not get into debt, and never buy what you cannot pay for at the time. Do not treat a possible gain as a certain possession. I am qualified to give you this advice, for I have kept myself free from debt from the first year of my working life up to now; and this has been done by self-denial and care.'

'What am I to do, if you do not help me?' said Katie, rather defiantly. 'You have accustomed me to look to you for help, and it is mean of you to throw me over now.'

'My good Katie, I told you last time that I was not able to go on with this,' I returned. ' Do you know how much you have had in six months ?—just a hundred pounds. And a hundred pounds to a girl in your position, spent in dress and jewellery and going down to Ascot, and all the rest of it, is too much.'

' In my position !' said Katie in a flame. ' What is my position so different from other girls' that I should never have any pleasure ?'

' Our position is determined by our means,' I answered. ' If we have not money for this or that, we cannot help it, and we must go without. And it is not every girl who spends a hundred pounds in six months, with only a few trinkets and silk gowns to show for it.'

' It was your fault,' said Katie, with a certain cruel justice. ' You ought not to

have begun it from the first.   And either
you should have got my stories taken or
you should not have encouraged me. You are
bound to help me now, seeing where you have
brought me.   It is you who have ruined
me.'

'I do not quite follow that argument,' I
said gravely, keeping down my temper with
just a conscious little effort.   'Because I
have done my best for you in teaching you,
and your work has not been accepted, I do
not see why I should have you on my
hands for life.   I have other claims; and
remember,.I am a poor man myself.'

Katie's face flamed, and her passion
with her face.   She burst out into a
torrent of invectives of which I remember
nothing but a few epithets, and a general
feeling of scalding water and fizzing fire-
works.   Then she flung herself out of the
room—her last words containing a vague
threat of some tremendous catastrophe to
happen before long, unless I would assist

her as I had taught her to expect I would.

The next day, however, she came and threw herself at my feet, clasping my knees and praying for forgiveness, weeping the while as if her heart would break, and sobbing hysterically.

It was a desperate pain to me to see the girl thus humiliate herself. All forms of abjectness, of grovelling, are worse to me than the wildest insolence; and I feel myself degraded in the degradation of another. I told Katie to get up, and I tried to lift her from the ground; but she clung to my knees with a grasp too tight and tenacious to be released, vowing all the time that she would not—she would not—unless I would say that I forgave her. She was broken-hearted—she was ill with sorrow and crying—she had cried all night—and she would never be happy again unless I said: 'Katie, I forgive you.'

And I—I committed my second act of

folly ;—and forgave her.   I believed in her sincerity, in the genuine source of her tears, in her sorrow and repentance. I was old and she was young.   It is for us who are old to show pity for the young—pity for their follies, their exaggerations, their faults, and above all, their sins against ourselves. It is for us to teach them the wise tenderness of magnanimity — to give them a practical lesson in benevolence, self-command, unselfishness.   If we are not pitiful, who will be ?   If we cannot forgive, who shall ?

Besides, I had already taught myself to forgive.   I had forgiven that young artist woman who had quietly stolen money out of my purse while I was out of the room— on an errand for her benefit.   I had forgiven more than one traducer; and I had said to myself: ' Strength can afford to pardon baseness.'

So I put my principles into practice once again;   and   this   time   I   pardoned   the outrage, believing that I was sowing good seed and doing the girl the service which comes from example.

For a few days all went well between Katie and myself, and I congratulated myself on the value of acted morality when I saw her modest mien, her renewed industry, her self-restrained air. But it was not for long. That pitchfork never does succeed in the end; and it did not now. Her former outbreak and my leniency were, in a manner, the spring-board whence she took her next leap into the arena of insolence; and we had another scene, even more violent than the first, when she asked me again for money and again I refused it.

Weak as I had been, and sorry as I was for her, I thought it best to let her finally understand that she must not depend on me, nor on anyone but herself, for what she wanted. I knew no better way to stem the tide of foolish extravagance which had set in than to make her feel her own responsibility. It cost me something to be firm. All that I have just said of the conduct of the old to the young plucked at my heart and troubled my conscience; for it is hard to persuade one's self that one is doing right when one gains by the process. Pleasure and self-interest somehow take the backbone out of virtue; and the most robust moralist may confess to qualms when his pocket is the fuller by just so much devotion to his principles.

Nevertheless, I held on; and Katie's flames, though they scorched me, did not consume.

Then suddenly, swift as a flash she calmed down, raised her eyes quite humbly, and said in a low voice : ' I am sorry I spoke as I did. You have been very good to me—far too good—and I have been an ungrateful beast.'

A few tears dropped quietly from her eyes as she spoke. There was no passionate bewailing, no hysterical tumult, as in the first scene. It was, on the contrary, a very womanly and dignified repentance which touched me profoundly; and I knew myself well enough to know that I would have yielded to a dead certainty had she not abruptly left the room. She did not hear me call to her to come back. Had she, I would have given her what she wanted.

The next morning Mrs. Pender came, as usual, to receive her orders. Her face wore a curious expression—doubtful, distressed, half-inquiring, half-suspicious—all underscored by a certain timid pleasure as if afraid to trust itself.

After we had said what we had to say about the weather, the gas, the water and the dinner, she put back a chair into its place, wiping the back with her apron and fingering it nervously. Then she cleared her throat and began, as if speech were a little difficult to her:

' You are very kind to my daughter, sir,

and I am sure both me and her father feel it much; but, if you will let me say so, I don't think you are quite judicious. My Katie is as good a girl as ever lived, but she is young yet and rather too fond of dress and all that. We didn't say anything to you before. A gold watch and chain, and a few brooches and bangles—well, they don't come amiss. And, of course, if she makes money, as she says, by her writing, she is right to spend it on her clothes as she likes. But when you come to diamond rings— then I think, sir, if you'll allow me, I must ask you not to. Diamond rings are not for the like of Katie, for all that she will not be a pauper when me and her father dies.'

All this was said with evident embarrassment, but with the verbal smoothness of one who has learned a lesson by heart and repeats it word for word without stumbling.

'Diamond rings!' I cried. 'What do you mean?'

Mrs. Pender looked at me with a little alarm. It struck me at the time that she looked at me as if I were mad.

'That beautiful diamond ring of yours that you gave Katie last night,' she answered. 'But I told her I would never let her wear it; and I want you to take it back, if you will, sir. Katie asked her father to change it into money, which would be more useful to her than them stones on her hand; but I stopped that. If, however, you like to give her a trifle, not to let her feel disappointed, I will not say nay; but that is as you like yourself, sir. You are not bound to do it if you don't choose.'

Now, what was I to do ?—tell Mrs. Pender the truth—that I had not given the girl that one costly gem I possessed — that diamond ring which Cordelia Gilchrist had given me, and which I did not wear, jewellery not being in my way ? Was I to tear the mother's heart and ruin the daughter's character by proclaiming her the

thief and liar she was ?—or was it the higher
duty to accept the situation, with all its
fraud and desecration, and save the mother's
pain while I shielded the girl's repute ?

I do not know how long I kept silent. I
was so overwhelmed by the discovery of
Katie's audacity and shamelessness, so per-
plexed between the conflicting duties of
truth and kindness, that I was, as it were,
struck dumb ; and what Mrs. Pender must
have thought of me was as much a mystery
as the rest.

'I hope you are not vexed with me, sir,'
said Mrs. Pender at last.

Her voice roused me.

'I would rather your daughter had
brought it back to me herself,' I answered,
speaking to the truth and not to the appearances of things.

She stared at me hard, and I could see
that some unpleasant suspicion was in her
mind ; but I was too much annoyed by
the whole affair to care what she thought.

I knew the truth ; and, knowing that, I was indifferent to the rest. That I should be suspected of heaven knows what iniquity would be only according to the irony of fate, which punishes our moral successes far more than our failures, and makes us suffer when we do right while it sets us in high places when we do wrong.

This little episode was really one of the most painful of the minor trials of my life. I, at my age and with my wide experience, to have been tricked and betrayed by a wretched little half-educated girl to whom I had done so many kindnesses, and to be bound by the law under which I strove to live to accept and not retaliate—to suffer and not betray—all the while knowing that this young creature was laughing in her sleeve at the very qualities on which she had planned the success of her crime—it was indeed a matter for anger and humiliation. I was disgusted with her and that mean phase of human nature represented in

her; but I was more disgusted with myself
—with my want of common-sense and firm-
ness in not refusing the girl at first—my
want of perspicacity in not seeing through
her shallow baseness of character—my mol-
luscous soft-heartedness which had allowed
me to be so played on. No one, I think,
ever belaboured himself more savagely than
I cudgelled myself at this time, nor was
less satisfied with any part of his moral
acreage.

Neither was I sure that I had done
right in not telling Mrs. Pender the truth.
Who was I, that I should ordain a fellow-
creature to live in a fool's paradise, because
I shrank from the pain of inflicting pain?
Would it not have been better to have
given the mother the power of rebuke, and
by so much therefore the stronger leverage
of reform? Who so fit as a mother to
know all about her child—even when to
know all would be to discover unsuspected
vices and even undreamt-of crime?

Yet, would she have believed it, had I told her the truth ? Between her daughter's word and mine, I think that mine would have been the weaker. Katie would have sworn to the gift, I to the theft; who would have judged between us ? For I could not have denied that I had given her such and such sums of money; and if the one, there was no valid reason why not the other. For all that, my tortured conscience accused me daily, and my life at this moment was by no means pleasant.

Of course this ugly little episode put an end to all my help in literary matters, and was the seal of Katie's banishment from my rooms. Soon also it was the cause of my leaving the house; for the whole thing was too painful to me, and I was in a false position throughout. I was conscious, moreover, that underneath in the hidden depths lurked other matters than those which came to the front. I saw this by Mrs. Pender's manner ; and I guessed what that little scaramouch had said; but I thought it best not to inquire too closely. So, when my quarter was out, I gave notice, and in due time left the house where I had made such a bad investment of hope and endeavour.

The sequel was a terribly sad one. Some years after this I was walking home one night when I heard a woman's step behind me, closing on me. Soon some one pulled me by the coat, and said softly:

' Mr. Kirkland! Mr. Kirkland!'

I turned round, and underneath her paint and haggard misery, her tattered finery and pitiful attempt at smartness, I recognised the wreck of poor, conscienceless, pleasure-loving Katie Pender. She had plunged headlong into the abyss for that cursed love of gew-gaws and dissipation by which many a better woman than she has been destroyed; and here was the end!—ruin, degradation, starvation; all for the sake of a few fine dresses and some days of false flourish!

She had begun by robbing me, she ended by robbing her parents. She had begun by giving me pain, she ended by breaking her mother's heart; while her father took to drink, as the best way he knew to meet his sorrow and conquer his despair. Now the end was near for her. The evil was too deep to cure, do what one would for her; and I did what I could. I at least managed that she should die decently, and so far in comfort.

I found her father and brought him to her bedside; and I made him forgive her at the last. It was a hard fight to get this done; but I reasoned him into a more generous frame of mind than he brought with him at the first. The ruin had been too terrible to be lightly passed over, even with the help of paternal love. For, as strong as had been that love, so strong and deep was the wrath following on the shame and sin and sorrow that the girl had caused. The hoarded savings of years gone; the house where they had lived so respectably given up after the bailiffs had been put in; the wife whom he had really loved dead of distress; the daughter, on whom both parents had lavished so much hope, so much pride, a mere castaway from whom good women drew back their skirts :—yes, it all made forgiveness hard! But he broke down at last into a flood of tears, and taking her in his arms, sobbed out :

' My girl! my girl! May God forgive you as freely do I, your father!'

So far the tragedy of the past was redeemed, and the sharpness of death's sting was blunted.

But the question always remains with me as a sore thought :—How far was I unconsciously answerable for this terrible destruction? If I had never tried to play Providence—if I had been as stern as Fate and Law are stern, and had suffered the natural consequences to follow unchecked on action—would it have happened at all? I think not. Sinless I might be, but I was Cain as well. I had slain my little sister in my well-meant efforts to help her ; and through her I had destroyed two worthy people who had never done aught but good and kindness to me. Wise after the event, I could reason it all out now and follow the crooked course step by step. At the time I seemed to be going quite the other way. It is not only in the material wilderness that we walk round in a circle, or lose our way altogether, when we believe that we are going straight as the crow flies and making a bee-line for a certain point. The moral path is just as unsatisfactory and as delusive. But to do evil where we seek to do good, to ruin a life we have done our best to improve, is the most painful of all these wanderings—these strayings. Sinless Cains—yes, there are many of these in the world, on whose brow Conscience has set the brand ! Homicides by misadventure ! The misadventure was unintentional, but the homicide is not the less a fact; and the death of that poor creature is no less due to our own hand. Yet, if we did not play Providence for our fellow-creatures, what would become of them? And is it not braver and better to dare the shame of failure, with its after-consequence of self-reproach, than to let the struggling wretch sweep by in the current, and not stir one's self to help, in fear lest one should be too weak to pull to shore and unable to set firmly on the dry land? Have we not to be brave to conscience and to dare self-reproach, as well as to withstand other dangers and support other pains without flinching?

CHAPTER VII.

VARIOUS legacies have been left me in my life—pictures, trinkets, ornaments and money. Only one has been paid over to me. This was the legacy left me by one who had been the very heart of kindness—the truest of all true friends to those who trusted him; and it came through the hands of her who is the soul of honour, as loyal as he had been faithful and with generosity and sympathy to match his. Now, however, I received a legacy which was duly paid over and delivered, no one disputing the claim. This was a young girl of eighteen, left to my charge by her father, my brother-in-law, who thought I would do well for my dead sister's only child, and that I would supply his place, at least so far as tenderness and paternal considera- tion went. Thus my niece, Claudia Hamil- ton, came to me to be my daughter, and the order of my life was changed to receive her.

I do not want to be hyperbolic, but I do not know the words which would be too highly coloured to express this sweet child's charm. Throughout my long life I have never seen anyone more thoroughly and essentially courteous in mind than she. I cannot express it differ- ently. Obedient, gentle, steadfast, un- selfish, Claudia was a typical woman of the best kind—thinking of others more than of herself, and in honour preferring one another to the letter. But she had nothing of the oppressiveness belonging to conscious unselfishness offering itself for admiration. She did not make you feel, as some do, that she was making this sacrifice for your sake, foregoing this personal pleasure, undertaking this burdensome office, all for your gain and delight ; but she did everything with that unconscious sincerity which gives additional value to an unselfish action—she radiated thought and consideration, love and attention, as the sun radiates heat or the earth sends up the dew. I do not know the moral faults she had. She must have had some ; but either they were so superficial they got brushed away in a passing breath, or so deeply buried underneath her virtues they never came to the surface at all.

Graceful and artistic, she was by no means markedly intellectual. She had excellent taste and as excellent judgment. But she had a certain slowness of thought which grew to be one of her charms to me. It was so pretty to see her soft face full of perplexity and doubt, and to hear her beg for a little time of delay, wherein she might think over a thing and make up her mind about matters which most people would have settled off-hand and decided on the instant—that I preferred this brooding, slow-paced reflectiveness to its antithetical sharpness. More especially as, when she had thought over a choice, a situation, and finally made up her mental packet, she almost always came to a just conclusion and showed a rather rare amount of reasonableness and balance. But she was undeniably slow in the process. Where Kate Pender had been like the sharpened point of a needle, Claudia Hamilton was as a smooth and rounded pearl. And after the needle-point, that smooth, fair pearl was decidedly a relief.

She was pretty too ; and that went for something. She had hair and eyes which would have been a fair stock-in-trade for a professional beauty. The sun had entangled itself in the one ; the others were soft as velvet—like great brown moths, sleepy, tender, almost pathetic in their patient quietness. Her hands and arms were absolutely perfect; and her figure was slight and singularly graceful in its lines. So pretty, so well-bred, so charming in her character, so sweet in her temper—she was a prize; and when I had fully learned the true nature of my latest legacy, I was well content with the bequest.

This child gave me back my home. I took a pleasant house, and engaged as her chaperon a well-mannered, well-educated lady, as frigid as an iceberg so far as men were concerned, but sympathetic and maternal enough to girls. As I was married, she could not have any designs on me; and even if I had been a bachelor, she would have had none. So we made a delightful home of it—we three units coming together in this casual way and soon welding into a compact and harmonious whole. And for four years all went merry as a wedding-bell. There was not a hitch anywhere; not a cross no heavier than a shred of pith; not a stumbling-block no bigger than a straw. We got on together in the perfect accord proper to people whose intimacy never degenerated into familiarity, and who respected themselves too much not to respect one another.

Those four years were the happiest of my life—the only perfect years when I was free from clouds or storms. I had as my daily companion this dear child whom I loved like my daughter; and her chaperon, Mrs. Olly, was all that she should have been —quiet, unobtrusive, well-bred, high-principled, and of good influence in things purely feminine over Claudia. Our joint moneys—for my niece had her own fortune —made a home of sufficient luxury for all moderate wishes; and I was both happy and proud when I introduced my pretty girl to my friends as some one claiming all men's admiration. For her sake I once more took up the lapsed habits of society, and went out into the world I had so long abandoned. I liked to see how much she was admired, and how prettily she bore herself among the youths and men who fluttered round her, and singed their wings to no purpose save their own pain. She was fond of admiration to a certain extent, just as she was coquettish in her dress to a certain extent; and I was content that it should be so. I would not have wished her other than she was—of her age, and perfect in that; but not unnatural either in self-abnegation or asceticism. We went a great deal abroad, where she was besieged with offers of marriage from men who were in love with her beauty truly, but to whom her fortune—magnified by report—had also something to say in the matter. But no one would do —no one exactly fitted; and she kept her heart whole and her fancy free and did not wish for a change. She was so happy as she was, she used to say with her sweet half-tremulous smile, she did not wish to turn down the present page. And sometimes she added that she did not think any one would care for her so much as I did. She was about right there. For, my love had idealized her, and I saw in her only her angel—her highest, best and flawless self; and even affectionate husbands do not often do this with their wives. It takes the distance which lies between a parent and a child to give this power; standing close, shoulder to shoulder and on an equal height, makes it almost impossible. And so far the old saying holds true: ' It is better to be an old man's darling than a young man's slave.'

In an evil hour—wretch that I am to say so !—there was brought to our house a young barrister, Launcelot Haseltine, already beginning to be favourably known in his profession. And with his advent the web of peace which my sweet Lady of Shalott had been hitherto content to weave floated wide—the mirror through which she had seen the world of love at second-hand cracked—and she found her fate and sealed my sorrow.

I had nothing to say against the marriage. It was all lucent and lustrous; and if Claudia wished it, what was I that I should object? The end of all things dear and pleasant to me had to come. The enchanted castle of my content had to fall; and I had once more before me the loneliness which this quasi-daughterhood had dispelled.

Mr. Haseltine received a good appointment in India, and I looked into my Claudia's pale face for the last time on board the steamer which in her bore away all my joy.

I tried hard to be grateful for what had been, and not to sour the past by lamentations in the present; to be cheerful and to take an active interest in things and

people as I had done when my heart
was at rest and I was happy in my home.
But human nature was too strong for me ;
and I had again the old conflict to go
through—again to fight with my wild-
beasts of sorrow and disappointment and
loss, till I had conquered them—unless I
would be conquered by them.

The time was very dreary, very sad.   I
thought that all love had died out for the
rest of the years I had to live.   I promised
myself I would have no more enthusiasms,
make no more close friendships, open my
inner heart to no ideal for the future;—never
again—never again ! Love had ever brought
me pain in excess of joy; and henceforward I would live on the broad common-
land of friendships that were kindly, refreshing, sustaining, but not exclusive to me ;
friendships where I was one among others,
and where I made numbers stand in stead
of specialities.   I would have no more
private gardens cultivated with my heart's

blood, to see them laid waste by disappointment, separation, death.

What supreme folly it was to put one's happiness into the power of others—to hang one's peace like a jewel round another's neck! The wise man keeps his own possessions sure. It is only lunatics who scatter their treasures far and wide among those who, by the law of their own life, cannot guard them. And what was I but a lunatic, with this insatiable need of loving —this inexhaustible power of giving? Why had I ever let this dear child creep so far into my heart, so that when the appointed end of a girl such as she came, as come it must, I should suffer as I did? For indeed her loss was quite as severe a trial to me as the break-up of my married life had been, when I had had to begin again the struggle proper to youth, without the hope, the energy, the unworn nerves of youth, and further handicapped by the sense of disappointment and illusion. Truly I was

an unlucky investor of affection !—but the
strange law of loss—the strange ruling of
fate that I should not root—had never
pressed so hardly on me as now. For long
months I was spiritually sick, so that
sometimes I despaired of my own re-
covery.

By degrees, however, the old recuperative
force made itself felt, and my vigorous
vitality reasserted itself. I recovered my
moral tone. My power of hope and love came
back to me; and life was not over for me.
Struck down again and again as I had been,
I was not conquered; and I should continue
the fight till yet later in the evening. The
sun was westering rapidly, but daylight still
remained. The present had its flowers, the
future might bear its fruits; and neither I
nor nature was exhausted. My wounds
healed as they had healed before, and I
seemed to wake as from sleep and to bestir
myself after. It was impossible for me to
live this self-centred kind of existence—

this retracted, mutilated moral life, and not
put out my feelers for that touch of my kind
which is to my soul what breath is to my
body.

The first person who roused me out of
the emotional lethargy into which I had
fallen was a mere boy—the youngest of all
who had ever interested me. When I first
saw him, he was only seventeen. When I
came to know him well, and love him, he
was just two years older.

I suppose my love for my step-children
had roused into full activity that parental
instinct which most men have in a greater
or less degree. For since the break-up of
my home, all my lovers—if the word may
be allowed me—had been young creatures
who had been to me like my sons or
my daughters. My interest in them had
been of a more tender, less exacting and
less reciprocal kind than for men and women
of my own standing. That is, it had been
purely a paternal interest, such as is proper

to a man of my age when selfhood has con-
tracted to a mere speck in one's horizon,
and the future of the son has taken all the
space which one's own possibilities and
desires once filled.

It did not need an abnormal amount of
the paternal instinct to be interested in
Arthur Ronalds.   The difficulty would have
been to have passed him by as one just of
the ordinary kind—no more beautiful and
no less faulty than the rest of the world.
Far from being thus just of the ordinary kind,
the boy stood out as something unapproachable.   His intellect was of the finest quality.
His head and face were curiously like the bust
of the young Augustus.   His character combined the strength of a man with the purity
of a woman.   He was essentially a measure
of the highest standard to which humanity
can attain under its present conditions.
Quick to learn ; accurate in memory ; with
a critical faculty not often found in an intelligence even more mature than his, nor with

an experience far wider; full of poetic fancies and at the same time philosophic and constructive to a remarkable degree; innocent of evil in his own person, but already a rationalist in the calm way in which he could look on human life as it is—analyze passions and accept results — examine motives, detect error, and assign beliefs and practices to their causes;—his youth, full of charm as it was, seemed to promise a manhood of surpassing brilliancy and power. In him I saw one of the world's future leaders of thought and epoch-makers in the history of mental evolution. His name would be immortal, for his work would be eternal; and in the long vista of ages yet to come I saw the light of his mind as an illuminating power equal to that of Aristotle and Plato, of Shakespeare and Newton, of Galileo and Darwin.

We soon became great friends; and I had but one regret, that I had not been his father—but one fear, the delicacy

of his health. His brain had developed at
the expense of his physique; and the consequence was a certain constitutional delicacy
which gave those who loved him cause to
doubt and dread. At nineteen, to possess
the learning and the critical acumen of a
man of twice that age means corresponding loss somewhere. The law of compensation is inexorable, like all the other
laws of nature, and a weighted balance neces-
sitates a kicked beam. Meanwhile, Arthur
enjoyed life in his own way, though that
way was not according to the robust athleti-
cism dear to the average youth. And he,
too, had his romances, his dreams, his un-
acted poems, like any other.

His great dream of all was the kind of
life that he would make for himself, and the
good that he would do, when he should
come of age and be in all things his own
master. He was heir to ten thousand a
year; and ten thousand a year seems like
ten millions to the young—more especially

when they spend nine thousand five hundred
in projects, and content themselves with the
remainder for their own modest share.
Arthur did not often speak of his future
wealth. When he did, it was for the foundation of Chairs and Professorships, for the
advancement of science and philosophy, for
the endowment of research, which he sketched
out as his intended contribution to the great
sum of the general good. To this he added
the maintenance of those families of scientific men which had been left in poverty by
the premature death of the breadwinner.

He was a nineteenth-century St. Paul,
substituting philosophy for theology, and the
love of humanity for faith in Christ. A
grand and noble life lay like a pathway of
light before him. In him I saw that ideal
self which lives in each of us—a man
purged of all my special faults, superior to
all my weaknesses, and strong enough to
consolidate the hopes and aspirations which
had helped me to live but which I had

done so little to realize. An epitome of all humanity as is each individual, potentialities for good are as real as those for evil; and the master in our own special line of thought or being is our translated self, perfected and endowed.

This is especially true of the young when judged by the old. We have reached our limit and fallen short of our aim. But they are as yet unexhausted. Who knows what hidden wealth lies within the years ? Who can measure the possibilities of the future? Torch-bearers as they are, we see them seize the light which we have done our best to carry so far—but they will bear it farther. They will go beyond our halting-place— and here again we shall be the dead selves from which they will rise to higher things. This, after all, is the great link and continuity of human society—the essential meaning of paternity, which in its turn is self-renovation—personal resuscitation.

There was no point of speculative opinion

on which Arthur and I differed, save that he
was perhaps more a necessitarian than I,
and less tender to the faith which he had
not been taught to accept. He had none
of the old memories, the sympathetic sentiment of childhood, to blunt the keen edge of
criticism. And, never having believed, for
his own part, either in the divinity of Christ
or the inspiration of the Bible, he was unable
to put himself in the position of those who
had believed, or did yet believe. Save for
such portions of the philosophy as seemed to
him more beautiful, more true, the whole
scheme of Christianity ranked no higher
with him than that of Hindùism or the
Greek Pantheon; and it fell below the
dignity of Buddhism and the strength of
Mohammedanism.

The one wonder of his intercourse with
me was that there should have ever been
the time when I had believed in the
creation of the world in six days, in the
Incarnation, the Atonement, the miracles,

and the devil ; or that I should have hesi-
tated as to my choice when I came to the
age of reason. How could anyone with a
robust intellect, he used to say, consent to
be bound by these cobwebs which one
vigorous effort of the reasoning faculty
could brush away for ever ? How could
such a man as I have believed that once
upon a time, just as in the fairy-tales,
humanity was different from what it is now,
save as a matter of relative development ?
or that things took place eighteen hundred
years ago which would be absolutely impossible to-day ? Of all follies, this belief in
the solution of continuity seemed to him
the most foolish ; and he did not understand
how, at seventeen—his own age when I
first knew him—I had ever troubled myself
twice about it.

If this absolute negation ab initio so far
narrowed his intellectual sympathies, it
cleared the groundwork of his thoughts,
and saved him from that exhaustion which

both accompanies and follows our struggles to break loose from educational trammels. I could appreciate by my own mental history the value of this stored and conserved energy, and by my own loss, judge of the greater length of the stride it allowed and the time it saved. And if I sometimes wished that Arthur had at one time realized the wonderful feeling of pity for the human sufferings of the man Christ Jesus, reverence for His teaching, adoration of Him as God eternal, and trust in Him as the Saviour of mankind, which makes the poetry of Christianity and is a perpetual possession of memory, I balanced the gain against the loss, and felt that it was better as it was for him and for the world he was to influence.

After I had known Arthur Ronalds for some time, I became acquainted with his aunt, Mrs. Barry. She was the elder sister of his mother, and worthy to have in her veins some of the same blood as ran in his.

At that time I could say nothing more honourable of her. Before I knew her as she was—before she became absolute in my own life—she was relatively of interest and importance because of her relationship with Arthur. And I carried to her both praise and glory as the reflection of my love for him. She was very fond of her marvellous young nephew—considerably fonder indeed, than was his own mother, who would have been better content with a more ordinary son. Having no children of her own and being essentially maternal in her nature— being besides, broad in her philosophy and of an intellectual development capable of understanding his—this boy had taken with Mrs. Barry the place of an adopted son; and she was really more to him of a mother than was anyone else. She had been abroad when I had first known Arthur; which was the reason why I had not seen her until I had become the lad's nearest male friend. But I had heard of her from him, and I was prepared to find her the more than admirable—the more than lovable—person she was.

I did not much care for his mother, Mrs. Ronalds. She was a slight and flimsy kind of fashionable butterfly who put her salvation in material things, and cared for brains only when they gave artistic results which made her appear more profound than she was. To her way of thinking, Arthur was a ' sport ' more curious than beautiful, and she used often to wonder how she had borne a child so unlike herself in all things. His father had been dead for many years; and what the boy was, was due partly to himself and partly to his tutor, a man of greater breadth of thought and deeper scientific attainments than Mrs. Ronalds knew, or could have understood had she known. However, here he was—in his mother's eyes a strange production of nature, an ugly duckling of no special value in the farm-yard nor drawing-room. That he was a wild and noble swan, who would one day soar up to the skies, she did not believe. He was only 'odd' and 'unlike other boys' to her; and she knew no better commentary than : 'It is a pity he is so extraordinary !'

She was, however, both good-natured and indifferent, so that she did not worry herself nor others. As Arthur was too delicate to go to school, he must be kept at home. Wherefore she gave him this tutor who had been recommended by his guardian; and when she had done this, and furnished and arranged his special set of rooms according to her own ideas, she troubled herself no more about things she could neither alter nor control. For how could she, a mere woman, dive into the mysteries of Latin or Greek, mathematics, logic, philosophy, history, to verify what she did not understand, and make sure that Mr. Satterthwaite was teaching what she would approve ? It was either trust or intelligent interference; and as she could not give the latter, she had sense enough to accord the former, and to abandon the appearance of command with the reality of responsibility. In this way, then, it came about that young Arthur had been moulded into such a widely different form from that which he had inherited. His exceptional powers had received exceptional treatment; and the result was, a lad who, it was no exaggeration to say, promised to be one of the kings of men in the world of thought, when his adolescence should be passed and his maturity fairly reached.

CHAPTER VIII.

MY friendship with Mrs. Barry was still only in this stage of what I may call incidental light, when one day I received from Arthur Ronalds a pencilled note, asking me to go and see him. He was not quite well, he said, and the doctor forbade him to leave the house; would I therefore go to him? He wanted to see me for no special purpose, he added; only for the simple pleasure of a talk. So that, if I were engaged elsewhere, I was not to think twice of his request.

He was always this unselfish creature!—always ready to give up his own desire for the sake of another; as indeed belongs to the highest class of mind.

I went at once, and found him indisposed but not in actual suffering. He had a slight pain about his heart, was a little feverish and flushed, and certainly too actively brilliant in mind.

'I feel to-day,' he said, 'as if my thoughts ran through my brain in lines of light. And how nimble-footed they are !'

The doctor, whom I met in his room, said there was a certain disturbance of the circulation which would soon pass. He recommended rest and a reclining position; and allowed me, he said, smiling, to say and talk with the patient, provided I did not argue nor let him become excited.

Arthur himself made light of his indisposition. He was always averse from confessing either his transitory ailments or his constitutional delicacy; and he did his best to forget that he was below the average in physical power. He was not foolhardy in action, but he was both sensitive and reticent in acknowledgment.

We had a long but perfectly quiet talk that day, skimming over many subjects of interest to each and of grave importance to the world at large. It was a synoptical talk—the heads of that Confession of Faith to which we subscribed. But it was Arthur more than I who both took the initiative and gave the affirmative.

Suggested by the fearful sufferings of a certain man we knew, dying by inches of a cancerous affection of the pylorus, we discussed the benefits as well as the dangers attending that euthanasia which has been too noisily advocated and too coarsely ventilated. And we agreed on its advisability, as an act of mercy as well as reasonableness, given the consent of the tortured dying and the strictest safeguards against abuse.

We also went over the whole question of suicide, and the right of a man to cast off his individual existence, when this has become intolerable. Arthur maintained this right—always with the limitation of those more imperative duties to others which would be abandoned by the act. As, in the case of the bread-winner of the family, who was bound to remain at his post so long as those who depended on him required his support; or with the mother, whose love and care and moral influence were needed by the children—no matter what her own sorrows and weariness might be, she too was bound to remain at her post till no longer needed; or where the happiness of another life was bound up in the continuance of this.

'Then,' he said, 'the martyrdom of life must be bravely borne to the end; and a man may no more take premature rest than he may shirk the battle and slink to the rear before the bugle sounds a retreat. But,' he added, 'outside these conditions of absolute usefulness to others,

I hold that a man is justified in dealing with his life as he would with his money or his books. It is his property; and he is the master of his own possessions.'

He then told me a touching story of a Scottish peasant, by his father's death left the head of the house and caretaker of the family. He was a thoughtful, well-educated, high-principled man; and he accepted the charge laid on him by fate as such a man would. He wrought for, supported, educated and set out for themselves all his younger brothers and sisters; and then there remained to him only his aged mother. For her sake, and to carry his burden loyally to the end, he consented to live; but he made no secret of his intention to kill himself so soon as she should die. He was weary of life, he said. With his mother the last of his duties would be fulfilled; then he might think of himself.

So it all came about. His old mother died and he saw her decently buried. When he

got home from the funeral he said ' Good-
night ' to his friends, shut the cottage door,
and cut his throat.

We met on the matter of cremation, and
confessed its superiority to the system of
earth interment—especially in view of the
increase of the race in civilized centres,
and the greater perils therefore run by the
living by the greater chances of disease
sown with death in the soil.

' I like to think that when I am dead I shall
be resolved at once into my original elements
—not by the slow and hurtful process of decay, but by the quick purification of fire,' said
Arthur, tossing back his hair with a broad
sweep of his hand, familiar to him. ' If
we can do no more good, it is pleasant
to know beforehand that we can do no
harm. A negative virtue is better than a
positive wrong. And I have my mother's
promise.'

' We will add that codicil to your will
when the time comes,' I said lightly.

And yet I confess to a certain superstitious creeping of my skin as I spoke. I did not like to hear him talk of his death and burial to-day. And we had wandered among the graves too much as it was.

'Dies datus? Who knows when?' he answered.

'Not yet for you, at all events, my boy. You have your work to do before you can be allowed to sleep!'

I spoke with a rush of strange tenderness, like a flood about my heart. It reminded me of the old Biblical phrase used to express parental love. For indeed he was as my own—the Judah to whom had been given the crown and sceptre of sovereignty; the little Benjamin, born of love and cradled in tenderness from the beginning; the son of my soul and the heir of my spiritual estate—to be greater than I and all those who had gone before him. Had I not been an Englishman, and ashamed of my own emotion, I should have taken him in my arms and kissed him.

'Yes,' he returned rather slowly; 'I have my work to do. I often wonder if I shall be strong enough to hew down so much as one square yard of the jungle of superstition by which we are hemmed in on all sides—if I shall be able to add even one brick to the great Temple of Truth.'

'Your very existence answers that,' I said. 'What we are is as important as what we do. A noble personality is equivalent to a noble deed.'

'And the end of it all—the condition on which we hold the charter of life—death :—and each individual of no more account than one diatom in the whole mass—the bulk making an important stratum, but each separate unit, as a unit, valueless !'

He said this with a certain philosophic quietness—a realization of individual nothingness—singularly pathetic in view of the creature he himself was. His very individuality, so grandly beautiful and exalted, seemed of itself the warrant of immortality. And yet, was it in reality more than the individuality of a Swiss cretin, save in the accident of influence on others?

'We know nothing of ultimates,' I said. 'If the Christian heaven or the Mahommedan paradise fails to satisfy the philosopher, we have always the possibilities lying behind the unknown. If we cannot affirm we cannot deny.'

'There is no possibility of individual existence when the machine, the organism which made that individual, dissolves, or rather, I should say, resolves itself into its component parts,' he answered. 'It is the condition on which we live from the beginning. We came out of nothing, and we return to nothing. Willingly or unwillingly, we must accept the law!'

He smiled as he said this, then broke off abruptly into the woman question, on the

main points of which we were thoroughly
agreed—neither liking the situation, but
both seeing the futility of opposition. For
he too, as I, saw in this modern endeavour of
women to assimilate themselves to men and
to repudiate their own assigned functions,
an individually unconscious but practically
resultant check to population—inasmuch as
the self-sacrifice and quietness demanded of
mothers cannot exist with the personal
ambition of professional life, with feverish
absorption in social excitements, nor with the
physical enjoyment of a purely out-of-door life
devoted to sport and athletics, like a man's.
Thus, the movement, by centering in self
the energies needed for the continuance of
the race, is, by the very nature of things,
a movement in the direction of sterility.
It is the analogue of that well-known law,
so disastrous to stock-raisers, which makes
that, when the breed has been brought to
the highest possible point of perfection, it
stops—the female refusing to continue it.

Between the two, however, a milky mother of the herd is more valuable than the infertile heifer; and a brave, bright winsome mother does more for humanity in the noble men and women she brings into the world and makes fit to carry on the higher development, than does the sister who prefers individuality and a paying profession to the self-continuance, self-sacrifice and devotion of maternity.

We agreed on the lawfulness of vivisection—the future good of the greater number being of more importance than the sacrifice of the present few. And we saw in the agitation that had been carried on against it as much hostility to science as regard for humane principles—as much fear of what will be revealed, inimical to orthodox belief, as that generous philosophy which includes the whole of living nature in one ring-fence of affinity, and recognises for animals the rights we claim for ourselves. But, accepting as we did, this ring-fence, this affinity, we agreed that animals were therefore bound to contribute their quota of individual pain to the general good. Even the most humane objectors to vivisection are at one on this in the elemental matters of food and service. For these we may both sacrifice and pain our poor dumb brethren. It is only Knowledge—Science —that has to go bare rather than be nourished by the sorrows of these others.

'Food and service indeed, are primitive conditions, like flint implements or lake dwellings,' said Arthur. 'By increased intellectual needs we add confinement in cages for the purposes of observation—of itself infinitely more distressing to wild beasts and strong-winged birds than the short, sharp pain of a surgical operation, or even inoculation with a disease. Going a step further, and keeping pace with these ever-advancing intellectual needs, we add experimentalizing on the living body for the purposes of demonstration and the discovery

of such secrets of organization as could not
be got at in any other way. That benevolence which would create a sacred section
because of feebleness, and would forbear to
impose a tax necessary for the good of the
community because the creatures taxed are
unable to remonstrate or resist, is injustice
to the whole, however kindly to the part.
Here, as in all other things, the gain of the
greater number sanctions the sacrifice of the
few.'

'The reasonable verdict of scientific men
must be the final decision on a matter of
scientific need,' I said. 'All the same, the
law must be careful to ensure due protection against abuse, and these weakest
members of the community must be guarded
against needless cruelty.'

'Certainly,' he returned. 'But, I confess, it seems to me that what is called
sport stands in as much need of legislative
interference as does scientific experimental-
ization. I suppose this is because I am not

a sportsman myself, and therefore do not understand the pleasure bound up in hunting a hare or winging a pheasant. But I do see the enormous value of knowing how to stamp out cholera and consumption, and all other diseases which now more than decimate the human race. And I see also the quite as enormous value of finding out how the nerves act and are acted upon, and, if possible, of coming to the starting-point of even more important secrets still.'

'Just so,' I said. 'Knowledge is the distinctive possession and most urgent need of man. It must be had at all costs. And to acquire it, men suffer to the full as much as do those poor creatures more directly sacrificed.'

Then we touched on the possibility of educating the masses to think for themselves—to accept responsibilities, and to frame a workable theory of life without the authority of religion and on the platform

56—2

only of respect for humanity and doing
right for right's sake, according to the law
of moral evolution.   We spoke again of
immortality and the unprovable nature of
the whole subject.   Yet the strength of the
belief—its universality, not only with ignorance, but co-existing with bold thought and
scientific habits of mind—were claims to
consideration not to be satisfactorily dis-
posed of on the theory of illusion.   That
Something which lies behind matter is a
fact, call it what we will — that Force
which is given by intense religious conviction is also a fact.   We may not be able to
demonstrate the one nor catalogue the
other.   All the same, they are; and ignorance of the source does not destroy the
reality of the outflow.   Christ in Heaven,
the Saviour of mankind, may be a phantasm
of faith ; the houris of Islam may be the
projections only of a passionate imagination.   Nevertheless, for faith in that Christ
who will succour and can save—for hope of

that Paradise where houris are the believer's eternal delights—men have died by thousands, and in their death have seen the heavenly images of their hope advancing to receive them.

'But these mysteries of the spiritual life are also matters of comparative evolution,' said Arthur. 'When we come to primitive man—savages who live on raw flesh, and roots and worms ; who have no more sense of decency nor chastity than a herd of beasts in the jungle ; who cannot count, and whose language is little more than a bestial grunt sharpened to a cry—what spiritual life have we there ? And where does this soul, of which we are so sure, begin ? If at all, it is a result of evolution, like the rest—a potentiality to be realized by cultivation and endeavour. The grand mistake we have made is to suppose it universal— coincident with life, and as integral to man as are the lungs or the heart—and not something to be shaped and perfected according to the law which obtains throughout universal nature.'

'Even religionists feel the difficulty of the soulless man,' I said. 'The old phrase, "Ower gude for banning and ower bad for blessing," expresses what, if your theory be correct, would be the condition of a man whose soul had never come to the birth and was abortive and inert.'

'A large—by far the largest proportion,' said Arthur.

'Yes; our Buddhas are very few,' I answered.

'If any,' was the reply. 'But if one knew for certain that the immortality of the individual was in the power of the individual, what a tremendous leverage that would give to lift one into the higher life !'

'Religion, as it stands, gives this leverage,' I said. 'In our search after causes, we must not forget results. Whatever may be the cause of faith, the result is a power emphatically beyond our normal selves.'

'It would be more certain if we knew that we ourselves were the absolute arbiters of our own eternal destinies,' said Arthur. 'We are weighted rather than helped by the belief that we shall be saved, by faith alone —that grace and mercy will do what self-control has failed to accomplish—that an extraneous power will supplement the halting of resolve and the slackening of endeavour.'

'Spirituality governed by science?' I said.

'Yes,' he answered. 'Else has it no truth.'

We glanced off from this to the boy's own future, when he drew out in fuller detail than ever to me before, his noble schemes for the employment of his fortune when he should come of age—and how he would use, for the advancement of science and the good of the whole human race through the free-

dom of thought and the acquisition of knowledge, the resources which would then be
open to him. His belief in the glorious
future of mankind was very strong. He
looked forward to the time when the passions, which are now cherished as part of
the necessary furniture of self-respect, such
as jealousy, revenge, resentment—or as
lawful excesses of lawful emotions, such as
the sickness of love, the unjust partialities of
the family, exclusive clanship in any form of
association—would be regarded as belonging
to the Dark Ages, before the true light had
risen. He saw no limit ahead. From the
primal cosmic forces to Buddha, Plato, Christ
—where was the line drawn, and who
should dare to define the point marked No
Beyond?

I had never seen him so brilliant nor so
beautiful. Take him as the measure of his
own possibilities, and what a grand thing
indeed that future ideal humanity would
be! Arthur Ronalds as the type of the

masculine mind—just, far-seeing, self-con-
trolled, philosophic, altruistic ; Mrs. Barry,
whom I was getting to know for what she
was, as the type of the feminine character
—loving, sympathetic, devoted, strong to
suffer in her own person without complaint,
and, while smarting under her own wounds,
able to bear the burdens of others—who
could despair of the future ? who see in life
only a muddle, and in humanity only a
failure ?   Give us time and we will do all !
It has taken millions on millions of years to
evolve man out of protoplasm ; it will take
some thousands more for all the savage and
the beast to be educated out of him—for
knowledge to take the place of ignorance
—for reason, self-control, and altruism to
be the motive forces of society, rather than
passions, appetites and selfishness, whereof
the only check is external law.

As I looked at the boy whom I grudged
to the dead man who had been his
father—seeing in him a future leader of

thought, a future torch-bearer who would carry the light far and high—I noticed a sudden change in his face. He first flushed violently, then turned to a deathly pallor, more grey than white and livid rather than blanched. And then, with a deep sigh, he fell forward in a loose heap on the couch. I caught him in my arms. He was nerveless, powerless, speechless, paralyzed. The marvellous mechanism of the brain was stopped, and a travelling clot, entangled in the fine network of the veins, had been like a grain of dust entangled in the delicate works of a watch. The movement, not quite stopped, was rendered useless for work or indication. He was not dead ; but he was not alive as he had been a minute ago ; and once more matter asserted its supremacy, and arrested function forced the question : Where is now that independent entity you call the soul ? where that thing you call the mind ? Of this future leader of thought, this past culmination of intellect, what was left?—an inert mass of flesh, speechless and reasonless—a clogged mechanism, with all its forces sterilized and obscured.

All that evening, and through the night, and for some twenty-four hours more, the boy lay in this terrible state—breathing, but not conscious; dead to himself and to the world, but still existing as an organism—a mere combination of physical forces working irregularly—a mere automatic machine, no more conscious than a pendulum, and with no more constructive intellect than an amœba.

Then he died—one scarcely knew when. The breathing grew gradually slower and fainter, the action of the heart feebler, till at last even the sharpest sense could discern nothing. It was like the fading away of the twilight after the sun has set. You could not say at what precise moment the twilight became darkness. Till the night was fully in the sky, you did not know that the day was done. So with the moment when Arthur

Ronalds passed wholly out of life ; and the long lingering twilight, after the sharp sinking of the sun—that border-line where he had been neither alive nor dead—was unmistakably at an end.

Thus was quenched for ever one of the most glorious intellects which this generation would have had—thus was dissipated the force which, concentrated in that body and manifested through that brain, would have done so much for the world.   It passed away into space before it had made the faintest mark on the sands of time.   And what was left ?   A handful of milk-white ashes in a small alabaster urn—the incombustible residuum of that carbonized body, making a tangible memory to match the enduring thought ; but of him, as he was— nothing !

I have stood by the graves of those I have loved most and honoured most ; by the graves of my own people, whose lives seemed to be part of my own, so that when

they died it was as if some member of my
body had been detached and buried out of
sight ; by the graves of great men whose
work has changed the current of human
thought, enlarged the boundaries of knowledge, and whose influence will live so long
as the race endures : but I have never felt
that I was standing by more than that
which had been and now was not. Whether
they had lived to the last of their powers,
like Landor, or had done their life's work
nobly, like Darwin — whether they had
declined like Garibaldi, or had gone out in
the morning of their promise like Clifford,
like Balfour, like Buckle—or, still earlier,
in their mere dawn, like Arthur—they had
gone. Vixerunt :—they had lived. They
had written their verses in the great poem
of human history and had added their
volute to the carved capitals of the temple ;
and then, the great ocean of night and the
unknown had engulphed them ; and we,
standing on the shore—so soon to follow

them !—know no more of them than we know of the foam blown off from the crest of the wave by the wind.

Yet with this vague sense—mark ! I do not say conviction, for I know nothing—this dumb dread of the absolute annihilation of the whole personality in one moment of time, one supreme throe of dissolution, I preserve my loyalty to the dear dead as part of my religion.   They would not know if I were false to their love, treacherous to my trust. They are dead and done with.   No sorrowful eyes would look at me through the darkness of the grave to reproach me with my falseness.   The things of life and men are nought to them, and time and space are words which have no meaning for their closed ears.   But, for the loyalty and love which do not die, I could as little forget or betray them, dead, as I could were they living to meet my inconstancy with scorn and my treachery with reproach.

Is this faithfulness of love the original,

whereof belief in immortality is the enlarged transcript ? For those nameless, unknown units, those Gurths and Wambas and un-designated Roman slaves and Spartan helots, we do not formulate an individual immortality. But for the child, the father, the husband, the lover—for the mother who was our visible angel—for the woman we loved, who died before satiety had slain that love—for these, and for our friends, we create our place of departed souls, and house them there, still living though unseen —loving and beloved as when we last pressed their hands in ours, and last saw ourselves reflected in their eyes.

Oh for one to rise indeed from the dead, and tell us the Great Secret which ends all life ! Oh ! to be told the TRUTH, and to know if love be final here and hope a mere phantasy of love—no more solid than the Spectre of the Brocken—or if the instinct of that love has been truer than knowledge, and has revealed what science cannot touch !

The ghostly shapes of sorrow and despair crowd round us thick as summer corn. Were we veritably assured that this life is indeed only the time of trial and probation— transitory, preparatory, as they say—to how small a volume even its greatest miseries would shrink! But deeper and lower than all creed, all faith, lies the consciousness of loss, the sentiment of death; and the mother who does not think twice of her darling out of sight among the flowers in the garden, weeps night and day for the death which yet she believes has carried her up to God and His heaven, and landed her in the world of endless delight.

Would that we could know! For if following after a phantom be a delusion—and delusion is only madness; not seeing the light is blindness—and blindness is mutilation. Between dread of believing a sham, and turning into the darkness of the night when the day shines bright behind those closed shutters which we could open, if we would, the mind gets racked and riven. And the outside absolute to determine which is true, is yet to find—though we all so painfully seek, and some of us so firmly believe that we have taken secure and enduring hold!

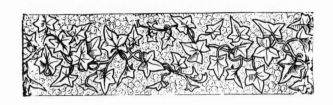

CHAPTER IX.

OO much pain had been crowded of late years into my life for even my robust physique to bear. My strength had been over-strained, and the penalty had to be paid sooner or later. After the death of this dearest child of my hope and love I fell dangerously ill; the cause being a chill; and Mrs. Barry came daily to look after me, as an uncertificated Sister of Mercy. My wife was away on a lecturing tour in the North; and as we did not correspond when she was absent, she did not know of my illness until it was over, else I am sure that she would have done her duty to me as

faithfully as to any other. Thus it was
that my dear dead boy's second mother
came about me as my caretaker; and it
was then that I got to know her as she was.

I scarcely know how to describe Felicia
Barry. She was one of those women who,
close on fifty as they are, all men wish
were under thirty and most forget that
they are not. She had never been supremely
handsome, but must have always been beautiful; and she was beautiful even now.
She had retained the luxuriance of her
glossy brown hair, the brightness of her
dark grey eyes, the graceful outlines of her
tall and generous figure, the delicacy of her
well-shaped hands and the sensitiveness of
her skin. She blushed as easily as if she
had been sixteen; and she was one of
those rare Englishwomen whose faces smile
from lip to brow, and whose eyes laugh
with their mouth. She had the charm of
two ages and seemed to be of neither.
With the fresh enthusiasm of a girl she

united the patience and knowledge, the tender sympathies and generous maternity, of a woman. Men loved her with passion, and little children went willingly into her arms, as if she had been a new mother, recognised before known. Young men and women made her their confidant and trusted to her sympathy, not in vain. Even when they had confided to her what was weak, or what was wrong, she helped them with her strength, her pity, her purity, her resolve. Tender and beneficent as the gentle rain which falls alike on the just and on the unjust, she knew no shrinking, no repulsion from those who failed the higher law—save for the two crimes of treachery and cruelty. With these she held no terms. For all the rest her pity overlapped repugnance.

Wherever she went she gave sympathy and garnered love — kinswoman of the whole human race as she was. Of all women ever known to me, she was the most many-sided and with the largest amount of emotional vitality. She always reminded me of the Venus of Milo; and her character harmonized with her form.

Her life had been sorrowful enough in its acted history; but her philosophy admitted of no closed tombs by the roadside where Love crouches in eternal mourning; of no slow marchings to the sound of a funeral hymn up the endless pathway of despair. While she lived, she used to say with me, she must conquer her sorrow or it would conquer her. She could not exist in that dull Nifleheim of melancholy where so many torpid souls find a weary kind of stagnant home; she must be out in the full sunshine, blessing others, and in thus blessing, blessed. She must love, if not in one form then in another—as wife or as mother, as sister or as friend, as equal or as protectress; and sometimes— but very rarely—as a willing and voluntary subordinate. Her life had been too independent, her character was too strongly individual, her affections were too opulent and her activities were too highly energized for this last phase to be either frequent or possible with her. Even where she loved, she held her own ; and, should her views chance to be at cross-corners with those of the man for whom, however, she would have died if need be, she kept true both to her principles and her love, and did not suffer the one to eat into nor undermine the other. Where she gave with most lavish prodigality, she always kept in reserve that inner citadel of conscience which no one can yield up without the loss of honour.

This is a doctrine unacceptable to men in general ; for almost all believe, if even they do not openly maintain, that a woman's love rightfully includes her mental subjection ; and that ' she to God through him ' is in very truth the norm of wholesome human life.

When I first knew Mrs. Barry, she was free, for the first time since she had been eighteen. She had been married at that age to a strange, unreal kind of man, who must have been more like a learned gnome than an average human being. He was an algebraic equation, not a man; a vitalized theorem, not a laughing, weeping, living creature, with passions, pleasures, weaknesses and virtues like the rest. He was not even personable, being tall, lean, dried up, even when he was young; and his temper was as perverse as his person was unlovely. But he was phenomenally learned; and his masterly intelligence won the girl's imagination.

Full of intellectual ardour and living in a home curiously arid and unsympathetic, she believed that in Josiah Barry she had found one who would be more than her guide, greater than her master—one who would be like some archangel carrying her through the upper air into the highest and purest regions possible to human thought. For she was inexperienced enough to imagine that the moral nature keeps even step with intellectual perception, and that the man who most clearly discerns an ethical law is sure to most faithfully translate it into daily action. She loved the ideal man projected on the screen of her fancy—she fashioned the crystal out of the earth; and she married Mr. Barry, believing that she was marrying the moral best of which humanity is capable. She found instead that she had married a magnificent intellectual synthesis; but something out of which all that is most lovable, most valuable in living human nature has been taken.

He married her for the strange pride which some have to be the public possessor of a beautiful woman. He did not love her; and he did not give himself the trouble of feigning what he did not feel. After he had married her, he did not care to continue to instruct her, as he had done in the beginning of things—by which indeed the whole affair had come about. He neither associated her with his studies nor directed her own; and the interest which he had taken in the girl's improvement fell off into worse than indifference for the wife's. It descended to contempt, set round with brutality. When she asked his opinion on any purely literary matter, his better judgment on a point of history say, or his help in a stiff bit of translation—he would tell her to play with her doll, if he were simply contemptuous, or to leave him alone and not talk of things she had not wit to understand, if he were more savage and discourteous than usual. At no time did he care to please nor to gratify her. And only when they were together in public did he treat her with courtesy or show her such attentions as western civilization has accustomed women to expect from the men with whom they are connected. And then his courtesy was so excessive, his attentions were so exaggerated, that all the natural truth and sincerity of the woman rebelled against the falsehood.

Thus she put herself in the wrong with others by her want of response to that which they looked on as the expression of faithful love, and which she felt to be an insult as well as a pretence.

They lived together for about six years; after which, by mutual consent, they separated—he living in London, she at Richmond. She had a small income of her own, just enough to keep her above actual want. What more she needed she worked for; and her work was of such quality as soon gave her more than mere comfort. When her father died she came in for her share of a fine property, by which her comfort was lifted into affluence. And just before I knew her, her husband had left the world he neither helped forward nor adorned, and the woman whom the law had made his prisoner on parole was free, when it was too late to make use of her liberty.

Mrs. Barry was to me the type of the Ideal Woman. She knew all the harmonies and all the discords of human life, and in her own person she had touched many of its deepest chords. She had suffered much, as must needs have been, but she had enjoyed more; and she remembered her pleasures while she let her sorrows fade away like ghosts in the dawn. Married as she had been at eighteen, and married to a phantasm, not a reality—at twenty-four thrown on herself for guidance, protection and support—young, beautiful, and what Americans would call alive and magnetic—greatly loved and greatly censured—in her own nature one to whom love was life and life was love—it can easily be imagined what she had suffered, what she had been made to endure and forced to renounce. But she was 'semper virent,' because she was strong, hopeful and unselfish. More than once she had lost the central treasure which had made her life desirable, but she had never owned herself defeated. Again and again beaten down like an Amazon to her knee, again and again she had risen up unconquered, to renew the fight with sorrow and disappointment—with personal pain and social peril.

Through all her hard and heavy trials she had kept her power of loving, of trusting, of sympathizing, of self-giving; and her great rich heart had never been drained. Like Hera, who renewed her youth when she bathed in the fountain of Canathus, Mrs. Barry renewed the springtime of her mind and heart when she bathed in the fountain of a new emotion—an unexhausted duty—a fresh study. She lived only for knowledge and humanity—to learn, to do good, to give happiness. While there was one unhappy person in the world to bring back to peace—one child to educate into a noble man or worthy woman—one sorrow to soothe—one desolate heart to cheer—she used often to say life would not have lost its charm for her. When she could no longer do good, then let her die, but not till then. And if ever that day should come, then she would indeed die, for then her work would be done. But she was far from that time yet—rich, unexhausted as she was.

It is impossible for me to say how much I admired this woman — this modern Demeter—this great Mother of Sorrows and Harvester of Love. If she renewed her own youth by loving, she renewed that of others by causing them to love. And especially did she renew mine. She seemed to knit up in herself all the poetry and vitality of my past life—to be a kind of microcosm, containing in her own person the qualities which had been divided among others, and repeating the experiences which had been scattered among those others. My physical sense could not refuse to see that, marvellously conserved as she was—beautiful as she still was—she yet was no longer absolutely young. Fifty, however good, is always fifty. But to my mind, to my heart, she was old no more than nature is old, than the sun is old to the fire-worshipper, than Ceres was old to the Roman who laid corn before her altar as his father and grandfather had done before him. What Ninon de l'Enclos was in a baser, Felicia Barry was in a nobler sense ; and the lines of their experience ran parallel—on different planes.

As my regret with Arthur was that he had not been my son, so my sorrow with Mrs. Barry was that she had not been my sister, seeing that she could never have been my wife. To have lived with her would have been to have lived in such intellectual and emotional opulence as would have compensated me for all I had lost. To have contributed to her happiness would have been the culmination of my own.

Her own history might be told in a phrase. ' He was impatient, and he would not wait.' Had he had self-control, it would certainly have been waiting for a whole life-time—but the reward at the end? Would not that have repaid him? He thought so now, when he sat by the hearth which gave him only the tie of a home with none of its deeper harmonies nor sweeter sentiments. Loving Felicia, but irritated and indignant at the obstacles between them, he suddenly flung off his wiser love, his better constancy, and married a woman who had nothing but her prettiness to recommend her. And marriage needs more than a pretty face to keep it fresh and wholesome! Besides, his past career had not been one to fit him for domestic life, save under exceptional conditions.

Handsome, clever, reckless and restless,

he had lived a stormy life, and had plunged up to the hilt in personal adventures and passionate emotions. He had been a great traveller and a famous sportsman; and, what with shipwrecks, savages, lion hunts and rogue elephants, dusky loves and crowned caprices, the note-book of his memory was pretty well filled, and not much was left for him to learn. But his charm for women was the wonderful strain of chivalrous tenderness and knightly loyalty which ran through a character where strength bordered on brutality, and where the violence of the darker passions made that gentler strain so much the more remarkable. He loved animals and children, was a good comrade with men and a devoted admirer of women. He never betrayed those who trusted him; and he had been trusted by more than the world either knew or suspected.

He had also had heavy losses and misfortunes; and this gave him the key to

woman's love by the way of her sympathy.
Perhaps this had been the strongest link of
all those which had bound him to Mrs.
Barry. Be that as it may, she had loved
him, and he her; but the patience which
would have carried her triumphantly
through a life-long trial failed him, and
he threw away the chance of that which
would have been his recompense for all
time, had he had but enough courage and
constancy of hope to have held on.

I knew what she suffered now, when the
final snapping of the shadowy link between
her and her husband gave her useless freedom. My own experience was the key
which unlocked all problems of love and
pain. If only he had waited! Fretting
under his self-imposed yoke; unable to
respect, but having no cause to repudiate,
the light-minded little feather-head, who
kept substantially straight because she had
not intensity enough to go wrong; offended
in his pride and dignity by the appearance

of things, his wife seeming to be ever on
the verge of toppling over into the abyss on
the dangerous edge of which she danced;
knowing what he had lost; loving Mrs.
Barry now as much as he had loved her in
the beginning—he too was to be pitied;
though naturally I had not so much sympathy for him as for her, arbiter of his own
destiny as he had been—' the careful pilot
of his proper woe.'   But she knew how to
bear with the dignity of self-control the
sorrow which no effort of the will, no energy
of action, could change into joy.   Strong as
she was to love, and sensitive to suffering,
she was yet stronger to resist the
demoralization of despair.   And that
light-minded, feeble-willed Helen has no
better friend than the woman whom her
husband . loves in sorrow and who loves
him in silence—keeping her faith to him
deep in that centre of the heart which no
time nor outward circumstance touches,
even with the lightest hand.

To me too she is a friend. And with this I am bound to be content. But sometimes, when I think of what might have been, I feel that smarting of the eyes which follows on the aching of the heart; and then I have to bestir myself and press back into the depths thoughts which only weaken and unman myself and do no good to anyone. Patience, hope, courage and the resolve never to be beaten and always to press forward—these are better than regrets. If we cannot have the noonday sun, is it wise to disdain the moonlight? Direct splendour the one, reflected glory the other; but is not that reflection better than the dead darkness of the sky where hang only clouds that drop down rain? For the noontide sun of love I am given only the pale beauty of the moon. So let it be. To my litany of thanksgiving I can add also this clause—gratitude for the simple friendship of the woman whose love would have given me new life.

CHAPTER X.

DOES the character make or attract the dominant circumstances of life? This is one of the problems I have never been able to answer. Yet it is specially interesting to myself, seeing that I have been in the wash of certain results, into which I was not conscious of plunging so much as of being overtaken by; as Orestes did not go to meet the Furies—they followed after him.

I have made, or attracted to myself, as the dominant circumstances of my life— Loneliness and Loss. Most of my moral investments have failed, and I have heaped up more fairy gold than substantial treasure.

This experience, so uniform in its working—must surely be due to some mental quality, as a man who takes all the epidemics afloat takes them because of some physical condition. Does constancy of circumstance spring from some personal fault, or is it the result of some uncatalogued law of attraction, which is to the moral life what facility for taking disease is to the physical? Is the silver spoon an airy fact, and luck more than the gambler's superstition? Yet how can one act differently from the law laid down by our moral condition? Let me go over those cross-lines which deface the smooth surface of a picture—give a list of various unfortunate investments whereby a man stands to lose all round.

With independence of judgment and inability to follow any leader, sheep-like, a man loses the support of every party, and may be attacked with most virulence by the very journals for which he himself has worked.

With a passionate temperament, yet by principle striving after the moralities of patience and forbearance, he suffers wrong up to a certain point, and suffers so quietly that he gets to be looked on as uninflammable as a block of ice and with no more resisting power than a flock of wool. When suddenly the whole thing blazes and breaks asunder, and long-suffering and patience go by the board, like hen-coops in a storm. In which case his reprisals are resented as aggressions.

In politics a democrat, by birth a Brahmin of the Brahmins, he suffers real pain when brought into contact with the jagged edges of his rough diamonds. Yet, being loyal, he sticks by his chosen friends of the third region ; and those of his inheritance despise him for his taste.

If a freethinker, all of whose early associations are in the camp of the orthodox, he has to submit to the condemnation of those he loves best—they believing that

faith is a matter of the will, and that unbelief is as much a voluntary crime as
murder or burglary.

Loving peace in private life, but a hard
hitter for conscience' sake, he offends those
whom personally he loves and privately
respects, because called on to denounce
their public work.

If largely vitalized, his moral atmosphere
has a certain quality of exaggeration which
makes that people read into him and his
words meanings other than his own, and
give his grip a power he neither intended
nor put out when he laid hold.

Having the courage of his convictions,
and ready if need be to stand in the pillory
for his flag, but as sensitive as a girl underneath his controversial armour, he suffers
acutely when the lash falls; and though he
makes no cry is tortured as severely as his
worst enemies would desire.

Cultivating trust in goodness as a counterpoise to that arid suspiciousness which

springs from knowledge of the world, he is for ever falling among thieves; and as he would rather suffer loss than protect himself by sharp practice, he has the satisfaction of keeping his integrity at the expense of his worldly substance.

By nature constant, by the circumstances of his life unanchored, and by temperament unable to live on memories and dreams, he is always hoping afresh, to be disappointed anew; and true love of a vital kind is the mirage ever before him and never attained.

Such a man is on all sides a kind of Mohammed's coffin, firmly attached to nothing.

And I ask again the question I have never been able to answer: Does character make or attract the dominant circumstances of the life? Is conduct indeed fate, in any other sense than that in which the form of a crystal is determined by its own law?

My own law of life has been, as I have said, that of loneliness and loss. This last is especially true of my deepest hopes and strongest affections. My friendships, on the other hand—friendships pure and simple—flourish when those others have withered and faded into nothingness. Without those friendships, I should be wrecked without redemption. With them, I can bear the intrinsic isolation of my life with the same feeling as I have when I warm my hands by another's fire. But friendship is not love ; and another's fire is not my own.

For all that, I have still a life to lead, and ulterior possibilities to attain.

Old, grey-headed, alone—my passions tamed, my energy subdued, my hope dead, my love futile—I sit in the darkening twilight and think over the problem of existence and what it has taught me. So far, all my sorrows and disappointments have been of this good to me : They have broken

down the masterful passion of my temperament and crushed out of me the egotistical
desire of personal happiness with which I
began my career. Life has shown me that
this personal happiness comes to us in
fullest quantity when we give most and ask
least; and that in the pain of renunciation
itself is the consolation which is born of
strength. It is only the weak who demand;
the strong give—and in that giving shape
for themselves the diadem which others
ask from a beneficent fate and a generous
fortune.

No age is too old for this outflowing of
love. When the day is spent and the sun
has gone down, the lustreless earth radiates
its stored energy of heat into the night.
And the old, who need care, can return
gratitude, and while they accept consideration can bestow sympathy. I, who say
this, say it with full knowledge of all that
my words imply. I, who advocate the
generous gift of love and the patient ten-

derness of altruism, speak from the door of
no full storehouse, but rather from among
the ruins of an empty and dismantled
home. I do not, like some wealthy man
married to the woman he loves and the
father of children he adores, preach content
with poverty and ascetic self-suppression to
the poor wretch shivering and starving in
the streets—to the heart-broken lover burning in the fever of despair on the other side
of that impassable gulf. The catalogue of
my possessions holds very little from which
to gather joy or on which to found content.
And yet I have both.

I stand absolutely alone, both spiritually
and personally; with only my belief in the
better future of humanity as a fixed point of
faith, and only my desire to help on that
better future as a stimulus to endeavour. I
have no fulfilled hope; no realized ambition;
no steadfast love to make life glad and the
grey days golden; and death brings with it
no certainty of amends, but only the vague

possibilities of the great Perhaps. Those whom I have most loved have most sorrowed me ; what sacrifices I have made for the good of others have been rendered barren and abortive ; my faith given to man has been again and again betrayed. The humanity, in the love of which I live, neither recognises my devotion nor knows of me as I am ; and my hold on the present is as unsubstantial as was my hope in the past. I have no resting-place on earth and no surety of a home in heaven ; and belief in the Divine Providence of God, which makes others resigned to their fate, has fallen from me, like the glorious dreams of my youth.

Nevertheless, I am neither broken nor unhappy. While there is a sunset to look at or a sunrise to watch for ; human sorrow to be soothed and human virtue to be loved ; knowledge to be gained ; a new fact in science to be learned ; a noble picture to see ; stately music to hear—while the great work of man's moral progress has to be continued and nature has still her secrets to be won —enough is left to make life worth living and energy worth preserving.

I repeat the words I have used once before, because the feeling repeats itself through the circumstance : Of what moment is individual happiness or misery, compared with the sum of the general content or loss ? The individual is nothing ; the Great Man is all. The present is the smallest of our possessions ; in the future lie the unmeasured potentialities. And I find in this altruistic philosophy, as well as in the confession of an absolute, immovable, and impersonal Law, as much help as the pious find in resignation to the Will of God. In each it is the annihilation of self. Thus, though the day is almost over for myself, and all personal fruitfulness of aspiration has become an impossibility—though my past has been a failure, my love a regret, my hope an illusion—I am young, because I live in the

race which renews its youth with every day
that dawns; and I am not disillusioned,
because I love the virtues which never fail
in the mass.

As I draw nearer and ever nearer to the
moment when I shall be resolved into the
Great Whole, and passion, which gives to
youth its sense of reality, loosens its grip
as vitality wanes in volume, I recognise
ever more clearly the shifting, phantasmagoric and subjective character of life—and
how that nothing is intrinsic nor essential,
but all is conditional and accidental. Yet
lying at the solid core within this changing
world of phantasms is one truth as strong
as a triple wall of brass—the great truth of
moral evolution whence springs the doctrine
of Duty.

Had I to write an ethical testament, it
would be to lay on the heirs of my thought
repudiation of the indolence of pessimism, of the sterility of egotism, of the
fossilization of theology 'that bastard

daughter of science and religion.' I would urge them to measure the distance already traversed between the highest thinker and the lowest savage, and I would ask them: Where, with that long stride from the past, are the limits of the future to be set? I would substitute the good of others for endeavours after individual salvation; and for belief in a special Providence, guarding some and abandoning the rest, the impartiality of Law, which knows nothing beyond itself. For the concentration of thought and energy on the elucidation of unprovable dogmas, I would urge the active amelioration of physical evils; for theological finality, that vitalizing faith in indefinite expansion which makes all things possible. For human insulation I would show the homogeneity of all nature, where man is the brain, truly, of the world, but not outside the ring-fence, nor differing, save in degree and orderly development, from the rest. For the confession of abject sinfulness I would teach a virile self-respect; for humility, magnanimity; for revelations, each differing from the other, the manly modesty of Agnosticism which knows nothing save the obligation of active well-doing; for imaginative hierarchies, the living truths of science; for the hope of Divine Blessing as the mainspring of endeavour, the practice of altruistic Duty as the absolute law of moral life; for the heaven that lies Beyond, doing the best we can with the things of time and space; and for an eternity passed in the companionship of saints and angels, cherubim and seraphim, the development of the living human being to the highest point of perfectibility of which he is capable.

THE END.

BILLING AND SONS, PRINTERS, GUILDFORD.

G., C. & Cc.